To thank our loyal readers for their continued support, Poolbeg want to offer YOU the chance to WIN €2,000 — simply by reading Mary O'Sullivan's powerful debut novel *Parting Company*. Your local bookshop could also WIN €1,000!

All you have to do is answer the question below, state the shop where you bought the book and it could be you!

What is the name of the company founded by Claire's father?

Answer: _____

Name: _____

Address: _____

Contact number: _____

Email: _____

Shop where book was bought: _____

Parting Company

Mary O'Sullivan

POOLBEG

Published 2006
by Poolbeg Press Ltd
123 Grange Hill, Baldoyle
Dublin 13, Ireland
E-mail: poolbeg@poolbeg.com

© Mary O'Sullivan 2006

Typesetting, layout, design © Poolbeg Press Ltd

1 3 5 7 9 10 8 6 4 2

A catalogue record for this book is available from the British Library.

ISBN 1-84223-255-X

Typeset by Type Design
Printed by Litografia Rosés S.A, Spain

www.poolbeg.com

Acknowledgements

Thanks is a very little word to express all the gratitude I feel. I have been lucky to have had so much help, support and encouragement in writing *Parting Company*.

Here goes with the list, and as the Oscar winners say, please forgive me if I forget someone. It's the excitement, you know!

To all the staff in Poolbeg, especially Paula Campbell, Kieran Devlin, Claire McVeigh, Aoife O'Kelly, Lynda Laffan, Emma Walsh – thank you for your faith in my work and your unfailing enthusiasm and patience.

To Gaye Shortland, gratitude for your editorial skills, encouragement, insight and guidance.

To my sons Paul and Owen, sister Annie, brother-in-law Emmett, Vera, Jessica, Karen, Siobhán, Jamie and Grace – my thanks for reading the fledgling manuscript and for your very helpful suggestions.

A special word of appreciation to Vincent McDonnell, whose creative writing class I found both inspirational and challenging. An extraordinary man of measured and beautiful words.

To the many friends who have patiently listened to me waffling on about *Parting Company* and have never once, in my hearing, told me to shut up!

Lastly I would like to express my gratitude to my husband Seán, for his unwavering patience, encouragement and help. Without his support, *Parting Company* would never have got beyond the idea stage.

Just one final word to all. Thanks.

About the Author

Mary O'Sullivan tries to be wife, mother, lab technician and writer. Sometimes she succeeds. Mostly she muddles along in a welter of multi-tasking, eating chocolate in times of crisis.

She lives in Carrigaline, County Cork, with her husband Seán.

For Peig and John

Slán go fóil

Chapter One

Brendan looked back. He knew Claire would be standing there, a small, dark oasis of gloom in the bustling airport. He waved to her and then continued on through passport control. As soon as he was seated on the plane he opened his briefcase and took out his reports. The pages lay unread. His mind lingered on his wife, on the clinging feel of her, on her draining intensity. He closed his eyes and took a deep breath. Three days. He was going to have three whole days without her. When he opened his eyes again, the Irish coastline was shrinking away. He smiled at the hostess as she offered him breakfast.

*　　*　　*

A wave of light and heat hit him as he stepped off the plane. Dusseldorf was warm and sunny. He shrugged off his coat as he crossed the tarmac. A few people glanced at him. Brendan Hearn, tall, dark-haired and broad-shouldered, was the type who attracted glances.

Checking his watch, he calculated that if the train connection to Bonn went smoothly he should have plenty of time to relax before his meeting. Thanks to German efficiency, he was soon collecting his case from the carousel. He stood for a moment in the Arrivals area to get his bearings.

"Excuse me. Mr Hearn of Dashern Chemical Company?"

Brendan looked in surprise at the man standing before him. He had not expected to be met.

The man offered his hand. "Klaus Haussmann. I am your driver."

"Oh!" Brendan said in surprise. "I didn't think the Conference package included transport."

"Nor does it," Klaus answered in his very correct English. "I have been sent to meet you by Mr Jacques Rondel of RTTI."

Brendan picked up his case. He should have guessed. RTTI was not a company to leave anything to chance. He followed Klaus to the waiting Mercedes.

For the first ten kilometres Brendan sat on the edge of his seat, conscious of hurtling along on what felt like the wrong side of the motorway. Eventually he relaxed into the luxury of the soft leather seats and let the Brahms from the stereo wash over him. He thought about Jacques Rondel. He felt he knew the man. They had spoken so often on the phone and had exchanged so many emails and faxes that their communications had developed an easy familiarity. But now that they want to be under any obligation to –"

"Don't be silly," Jacques interrupted. "RTTI just wants to ensure you enjoy your visit here. Now, let's arrange a meeting place. Would the bistro on the ground floor suit you? In fifteen minutes?" His tone was businesslike. The warm camaraderie of email and phone seemed subtly changed.

"Fine," Brendan agreed. "See you in fifteen."

Tie knotted and hair smoothed into place, Brendan stood in front of the full-length mirror. Pulling in his already flat stomach, he squared his shoulders. He smiled at the tall, well-muscled reflection, liking the way his pale blue shirt emphasised his tan.

He was ready to meet Jacques Rondel.

*   *   *

By the time Brendan reached the bistro, he had decided on a wait-and-see strategy with Rondel. A waiter met him at the door and led him through the crowded restaurant to a table in an alcove. Jacques Rondel was seated facing the entrance. Brendan knew that he had been under observation since he had walked in the door.

Jacques rose and offered his hand. As the men shook hands, they assessed each other. The Frenchman's handshake was strong, his silver hair perfectly groomed, the radar sweep of the blue eyes not missing a detail.

He waved Brendan to the seat opposite him.

"Is your suite to your satisfaction?" he asked as they both settled themselves into their seats.

Brendan hesitated for a moment. Was Jacques challenging him or was he just being polite? "Yes. It's very comfortable, thank you."

"*Bien*," Jacques said and the muttered word brushed over Brendan like a patronising pat on the head.

"I hadn't expected such a big crowd," Brendan remarked, looking around the packed restaurant. "Are all these people here for the herbal medicine conference?"

"Yes, certainly. We are not the only people who see a future in herbal medicine. Phytochemistry is 'hot', as you might say."

"And profitable, as *you* might say," Brendan shot back.

Jacques raised an eyebrow just a shade. He held up his hand and a waiter appeared at the table with a bottle of wine. "I have chosen the wine. I hope you approve. It is one of the best local wines from the Ahr Valley."

As the waiter poured some of the red Spätburgunder, Brendan noticed a third place set at the table. "Are we expecting company?" he asked.

Jacques smiled. "Our Public Relations Manager is joining us. I think you will both get on well. You have a lot in common."

"Is that so?"

"Judge for yourself." Jacques nodded his head in the direction of the entrance.

Brendan resisted the temptation to turn around and allowed himself one moment of gloating. The Public

Relations Manager! They *were* giving him the treatment!

"Ah! Yvette!" Jacques said as he stood and pulled out the third chair.

Brendan first became aware of a waft of perfume. Curious, he stood and turned around to look into the most beautiful eyes he had ever seen. They were amber, almond-shaped and fringed by long, dark lashes. He realised that other people were looking at this stunning woman, that he was staring like an awestruck adolescent, that Jacques was introducing her – but yet he could not look away from her warm, honey gaze.

She reached out her hand to him. "Yvette Previn. It is so nice to meet you, Brendan."

She had a really short haircut, emphasising the bone structure of her face. Her voice was husky, her fingers slender and her skin silky and warm. She was a warm woman. Warm eyes, warm skin. With a start Brendan realised that all these warm thoughts were generating heat in his crotch area. He released Yvette's hand and quickly sat before his gaucheness became too apparent.

The waiter arrived with the menus and Brendan was glad of the few minutes they spent poring over the extensive selection of dishes. By the time he had chosen melon for starter and veal for main course, he felt more in control.

"Is this your first visit to Germany, Brendan?" Yvette asked.

"It is indeed."

"Then you could not have chosen a nicer city to start with than Bonn. It is so historic and so very beautiful.

We must show him around, Jacques."

Jacques raised his glass. "Here's to new experiences, new friendships and new beginnings!"

"To the future!" Yvette said as the three glasses clinked together.

"To the future!" Brendan echoed and for the first time he allowed himself to really believe that RTTI International could be part of his future.

*   *   *

Brendan had been awake long before his morning call. As the dark of night gave way to the grey light of dawn he had lain in bed thinking over strategies. His plans for the future of Dashern Chemicals. He was more convinced now than ever that RTTI should be involved. Rest was not helped, either, by the knowledge that the stunningly beautiful RTTI Public Relations Manager was sleeping in the adjoining suite. His heart raced each time he recalled her amber eyes and honey-toned skin. She was, without doubt, the most fascinating woman he had ever met. He had learned with interest last night that she was to give a lecture this morning: "Herbal Medicine and the Media". She had spoken on the topic over dinner and he had been impressed by her knowledge of international legislation and regulations. He had been even more impressed by the outline of her breasts underneath her silk blouse.

He dressed carefully, choosing navy suit and white shirt, navy and blue tie. The tie had been a gift from

Claire. From his dark-eyed, solemn little wife. It reflected Claire's personality. He ripped it off and chose a red tie instead.

Checking his watch he saw that there were two hours to go before his meeting with Jacques. Two hours to study his proposition for RTTI. He opened his laptop and scrolled through the menu. Clicking on Projections, he checked and rechecked figures, tried to second-guess market trends. His conclusion was the same as it had been for the past year. Dashern Chemicals was heading for trouble. Evidence of the company's falling profits flicked across the monitor. Competition was eating up Dashern's share of the detergent market. Why could the old man not see it? Why wouldn't the bull-headed bastard listen? Brendan's knuckles whitened as he thought of his father-in-law. The great Frank Dawson. The man who had built up a thriving detergent manufacturing industry from nothing. The man who was wallowing in the shallows of past glories while the tide of progress was lapping against the foundations of his little empire. Closing off the projections, Brendan went straight to his proposal document and read through it point by point. He got up, poured some coffee and read it again. There was nothing more he could add.

He shut down his computer and checked the time. Still an hour to spare. He rode the panoramic elevator down to the lobby and headed for the Conference Centre.

The main hall was lined with display stands promoting different products and producers. Brendan

9

stood near the entrance, watching the crowds milling around the stands and listening to the vibrant buzz of conversations in so many different languages. There was so much to see, so many companies, so much research, so much to learn. A large banner caught his eye: *St John's Wort – Food Supplement or Drug?* As he started towards that stand, he noticed a signpost for the lecture theatre. An unbidden image of Yvette's nipples pushing against the silk of her blouse sent a shiver through him. St John's Wort suddenly lost its appeal.

Leaving the hall he followed the signpost until he came to the double doors leading into the lecture theatre. He stood outside and listened. The husky voice of the speaker could only belong to Yvette Previn.

He pushed open the doors and slipped quietly into a seat at the back. Yvette was speaking in French, the musical language enhanced by her rich intonation. He gave up trying to understand and just let the sound and the sight of her tease his senses. This morning she was wearing a beige-coloured suit, the jacket tailored so that it fitted snugly. It would have been an ordinary business suit on anyone else. Fitted as it was to the contours of Yvette's body, Brendan thought it a work of art. When she finished lecturing, she opened the floor to questions. He was impressed yet again as she slipped with ease from French to German to English in order to facilitate her audience. She seemed to effortlessly attract and hold attention.

He left reluctantly to keep his appointment with Jacques Rondel.

*   *   *

He had to fight the urge to pace the floor while Jacques read through his proposal. The Frenchman's face was inscrutable as he turned page after page. Eventually he put the pages down, sat back and turned the Rondel stare on full power.

Like a game of who blinks first, Brendan thought.

If it was a game, Brendan lost. He could not stand the silence any longer.

"Well, Jacques? Your reaction? Do we have a deal?"

Jacques laughed and the sound hit Brendan like a splash of cold water. The prick was laughing at him! Mocking him. Testing him? He took a deep breath.

"Do I take it you find my proposals amusing?"

Jacques leaned forward and the blue gaze knifed through Brendan. "Let me point out a few issues you do not seem to have properly grasped. Number one, RTTI is a global multibillion-dollar pharmaceutical company. We do not barter with low-tech detergent plants. Number two, if we do decide to have discussions with you, it will be on our terms. You will not presume to tell us how we should conduct our business. And –"

"What the bloody hell is all this about then?" Brendan cut in, sweeping his arm around to indicate the luxury suite. "Why the chauffeur-driven car? All the emails and phone calls? Don't fuck around with me, Jacques. You have spent time and effort communicating with me. You're interested in getting a foothold in

11

Ireland and your best way of doing that is by merging with Dashern."

"What makes you think Dashern is our only Irish option, Brendan? What makes you think we want to go to Ireland at all? Remember it was you who contacted me first. RTTI never went after you and we are not about to do so now."

Brendan was caught off guard. He needed to control his anger to think this out. He rose and walked towards the drink cabinet.

"Drink, Jacques?"

"Mineral water, please," Jacques answered calmly. "Still."

As he put ice and lemon into the two glasses, Brendan took stock. Rondel was bullshitting. He was almost certain of that. Almost. He took a steadying breath before handing the Frenchman his drink.

"OK," he said, placing his own glass of water on the table between them. "Let's stop trying to score points off each other. Yes. I made the initial contact after your article appeared in *New Scientist*. But why *did* you publish that article, Jacques?"

"Because I was asked to write a feature on the production and application of herbal extract, of course. Why else do you think I would do it?"

"Cut the crap. You published that article precisely because RTTI needed somebody like me to follow it up. Your company is a giant, a vast industrial and financial power, but your environmental reputation stinks. How could you seriously market a product that is supposed to be natural and clean? I read between the lines of your well-phrased article. You were offering profits in exchange for a clean image behind which to hide."

Jacques smiled. "Interesting interpretation. Now let us talk about Dashern Chemicals."

Brendan relaxed a little. It seemed liked talks were about to start. Jacques took a sip from his drink and opened a folder in front of him. He flicked through some pages and then fixed Brendan in his radar sights. His voice was as flat and cold as his stare.

"Dashern Chemicals is going to lose two major contracts during the coming year. You could struggle on with reduced staffing levels but you will not be able to compete with the increasingly competitive international market. You could diversify into another area but you can't afford the huge investment that would involve. You can't look for financing because –"

Brendan threw his hands up in the air, palms towards Jacques in surrender. "OK! OK! Enough! We've all obviously done our background research. But RTTI still needs a respectable front as badly as Dashern needs a wealthy backer. We have a supply and demand situation here. What's the problem?"

Jacques smiled at first and then he laughed. A deep, hearty laugh that seemed totally at odds with this sophisticated, controlled man. He held out his hand to Brendan.

"I admire your style. We have a lot of things to discuss yet but we *will* talk."

Brendan took the Frenchman's hand and solemnly

shook it. The moment was complete when Jacques told him they were to meet Yvette for lunch.

*   *   *

Interesting as the conference on herbal medicine had been, or phytochemistry as the industry preferred to call it, after two days Brendan felt saturated. He had lost count of the number of lectures, slide shows and presentations he had attended. Despite all the research he had done beforehand, he had underestimated the potential for this branch of medicine. An industry in its infancy, it was so full of untapped potential that even his stubborn father-in-law would have to be interested.

But best of all, each day had been touched by the unique magic of Yvette Previn. Like a moth to the flame, Brendan was drawn to the golden light of her beauty, snatching glimpses as she went from meeting to meeting, looking forward to the meals shared with her and the urbane Jacques Rondel.

When Jacques suggested that the three of them take an afternoon trip on the Rhine, Brendan had tried to accept the invitation casually. He was fairly certain his quickened breath and the slight tremor in his hand had gone unnoticed. Even by Jacques Rondel.

*   *   *

They sat on the top deck of a waterbus as it sliced through the blue-green waters of the Rhine. Yvette, seated opposite Brendan, had her eyes closed and her face turned up to the sun.

"And this is the famous Bridge at Remagen. Perhaps you have seen the film?"

Brendan became aware that Jacques was talking to him and that he expected a reply.

"George Segal, Robert Vaughan, Ben Gazarra," Yvette murmured without opening her eyes. "Directed by John Guillerman, 1969."

As the waterbus approached Remagen, the remains of the bombed-out Ludendorff bridge loomed dark and sinister on either side of the river, a monument to an era of powerful evil and evil power. Brendan shivered, chilled in the heat of the sun by the dark shadow of history. He turned his eyes away and looked downstream, towards the forested banks and sloping vineyards.

"Not long before we reach Linz now," Jacques said. "I promise you are going to love it, Brendan. It is a special place. Is it not, Yvette?"

She opened her eyes and sat up straight. The sun touched her short auburn hair with copper highlights. Brendan knew her hair would be soft to touch. Silky. Like her skin. He focused on the bare area between the top of her cropped blouse and the hip-band of her low-cut jeans. Her navel was small and neat. He needed to kiss it, to run his tongue over her honey-coloured belly.

"Claire would love Linz too. You must bring her here sometime," she said.

"Claire?" Brendan echoed in surprise.

"Your wife," laughed Yvette. "I know you have been very busy for a few days with the conference and with us but you cannot have forgotten your wife of three years already!"

"Yvette does her research thoroughly," Jacques remarked. "Just as your wife does. But while Claire's field is Biochemistry, Yvette's is personal history. She knows your deepest, darkest secrets by now."

Brendan laughed with them but he felt more puzzled than amused. He was surprised that Yvette knew his wife's name. But then Claire had a certain standing in the area of Biochemistry. She had published some well-received papers in the past. What shocked him was the realisation that for the past three days he *had* forgotten his wife, forgotten her depressing darkness and her accusing sadness. Forgotten to ring her! The old man would be furious if she complained to him. But Claire would not complain. She would just let him read the hurt in her tragic brown eyes. Shit! He took out his phone and tapped in a quick message: *C U 2morrow nite. Luv B.* He pressed *Send* and forgot her again.

People shuffled towards the lower deck as the ferry approached the dock. The gates of the walled town were a short walk from where they disembarked. Jacque's phone rang just as they reached the beautiful old stone walls. While he took his call, Brendan and Yvette read the high tide records carved into the stone. This town had been battered by floodwaters for many centuries. They were talking about global warming and rising tides when Jacques joined them, a very annoyed expression on his face.

"I'm sorry. I've got to return on the next ferry."

"Something wrong?" Yvette asked anxiously.

"Just some papers I need to sign for someone who is going home today. I must catch him before he leaves."

Yvette nodded.

She obviously knew what this was about. Brendan wished *he* did. Could RTTI double-cross him at this late stage? Rondel had been careful not to make any firm commitments. Nothing on paper. It would appear that RTTI was interested in a merger with Dashern but, under the polished exterior, Jacques Rondel was probably a ruthless bastard.

Brendan smiled at the Frenchman. "Never mind, Jacques. We can do this another time."

"No. No. No. Do not let me spoil your afternoon. This is the only time off you have had. I want you to see something of the scenery. You two young people enjoy Linz. I will see you back in the Konstantin tonight."

Before they could say anything he had turned and walked in the direction of the ferry. Yvette and Brendan looked at each other and laughed.

"Come on, youngster," she said, taking his hand and leading him through the stone arch onto the cobbled streets of Linz.

*   *   *

Brendan was tall. Six feet two inches. He felt at least

17

four feet taller as he strolled through Linz with this beautiful woman by his side. He noticed people noticing them as they sat at the fountain in the square eating ice cream, as they explored the little shops, as they admired the ornate facia on the buildings. By the time they had climbed the hill leading to the top of the town, they were hot and thirsty. Finding a café, they sat outside in the sun sipping their drinks. They were silent for a while, lulled by the heat of the sun and the quiet beauty of this secret little town behind the big stone walls.

"Wouldn't it be so easy to believe that life begins and ends here in Linz?" Yvette remarked.

Brendan knew what she meant. The calm and sense of timelessness had touched him too. It was as if they had always been here and they always would be.

She leaned towards him. "Talking about beginnings, Brendan, I want to know all about you. I want to know about your childhood, your family and your history. Talk!"

"Didn't Jacques say you knew everybody's secrets? *You* tell *me*."

She settled back in her chair and fixed her amber eyes on his face. "You were born in County Waterford, Ireland, in a seaside town called Tramore. You went to high school, or 'secondary school' as you call it, in Waterford City. Being a clever little fellow, you won a scholarship to University College Dublin, where you got a Masters Degree in Analytical Science. After working for three years with a pharmaceutical

18

company in England, you returned to Ireland as Chief Chemist with a meat-processing plant in Wexford. How am I doing so far?"

Jesus! Jacques had not been joking. Yvette Previn was either very inquisitive or else a damned good detective.

"Go on," he said, wondering what more of his history she had managed to dig up.

"You took a course in Production Management and applied for the position of Production Manager with Dawson Chemicals. You not only got the job, you landed a wife and a one-third share in Dawson Chemicals too. Soon after your marriage to Claire Dawson, the company was renamed Dashern Chemicals. And now, it seems you would like to change the name of the company again. How did I do?"

Brendan raised his glass to her. "You're good. *Salut!*"

"Public record," she said dismissively. "I want to know about *you*, Brendan, about what makes you tick."

"On condition you then tell me about Yvette Previn, about what makes *her* tick."

She offered him her hand and he held it as he began to talk. The sun slanted westward, shadows lengthened and still they talked. She told him about her nomadic childhood as her family followed her diplomat father from posting to posting. Beirut, Rome, London, Bahrain, Washington. The Previn family had moved from one diplomatic enclave to another, making new friends and learning new cultures and languages, only to leave them and start all over again somewhere else.

Brendan told her about his childhood, about the loneliness and isolation of being an only child. He had not thought about his dead parents for a long time. Now memories of the tight-lipped, ambitious woman who had been his mother came flooding back, shadowed as in her lifetime by the image of the gruff, silent man who had been his father.

"My father was a carpenter," he explained to Yvette. "He was a big, awkward man. Inarticulate. Insensitive. Until he held a piece of timber in his hands. Then he was a master craftsman. An artist."

"And your mother?"

"A typical Irish mother," Brendan laughed. "She pushed me out of nappies into school. Out of school into college. She planned my life and then made me think I planned it for myself."

Yvette leaned forward and stroked his cheek. "Do you miss them, Brendan?"

Brendan glanced around him. He lifted his eyes to the beautiful carvings adorning the top storeys of the buildings around them. His father would have admired them. And how his mother would have loved the flowers that trailed swathes of colour from window boxes and pots. Did he miss them? He looked back at Yvette.

"Yes," he said simply. "I miss them."

He was uncomfortable with the depth of feeling in his reply. He had not realised there was still a corner in his psyche that needed his father's silent approval and his mother's encouragement. In fact he had never known.

Bollocks to this amateur psychology! He stood up.

"We'd better think about getting back to the ferry."

"Are you afraid of being locked into the magic little town? With the Big Bad Witch?"

"You *are* a witch," he accused. "You've made me remember things I didn't really want to think about."

"Maybe you need to talk more," she said as she stood on tiptoe and kissed his cheek.

She turned quickly and started to walk down the hill, hips swaying. Brendan was startled when she broke into a run but then she turned back and laughed. He chased after her. They raced to the ferry and arrived together at the pier, laughing and out of breath.

They climbed to the top deck again and stood close together as Linz became smaller and smaller and finally disappeared from view.

*   *   *

Jacques announced at dinner that he would be leaving early in the morning.

"You'll be coming with me, Yvette. I'm afraid it's back to Zurich for us."

"Oh, well," Yvette answered, "this conference is practically over anyway. Tomorrow is just the wind-down. When are you leaving, Brendan?"

"Tomorrow afternoon."

Brendan swirled the wine in his glass. It was Spätburgunder again. He had developed a taste for this earthy red wine in the past few days. He had also developed a taste for dining with this beautiful woman, for talking to her, for laughing with her, for seeing her amber eyes sparkle, for touching her whenever he could. He did not want to think about tomorrow.

"So. What do you say, Brendan?"

Shit! He had missed that. He had not been listening. "Could you run that by me again, Jacques?"

"I knew you were miles away. I asked if you could organise things from your end for an RTTI visit to Dashern?"

Brendan's heart skipped a beat. They were going for it! The might and money of RTTI were going to be poured into Dashern!

"Of course. No problem. When?" he asked, hoping he didn't sound too eager.

Jacques stood up and offered his hand to Brendan. "I will let you know when we can fit Dashern into our schedule. I have a few people to see now, so I will excuse myself. I look forward to visiting your plant."

Brendan stood and shook Jacques' hand, resisting the urge to hug him.

Jacques went over to Yvette and kissed her on both cheeks. Then he turned back to Brendan.

"You will have your father-in-law and your wife on side, won't you? Make sure they understand our interest in Dashern includes your wife's department. Research and Development, after all, is our area of expertise. We would expect her to share her findings with us."

"Absolutely. No problem. You have my word on that."

Brendan stared at the Frenchman's retreating back. Claire's research? How could it possibly be of interest to RTTI? He had no idea what she spent her time on in that little lab but he doubted that it could be anything of significance. He and Claire never spoke about it. They rarely spoke. He turned back to Yvette.

"Would you like a walk?" he asked impulsively.

In reply she stood up and took his arm. They strolled side by side in the pine-scented air of nearby Rheinaue Park until the last vestiges of light left the sky. Yvette shivered in the cool darkness. Brendan put his arm around her shoulder and drew her close. He could feel her hip brushing against his, smell the rose-scented aroma that was uniquely hers. When they reached the grounds of the hotel, he stopped and turned her to face him. She looked up at him, her amber eyes glittering in the moonlight. There was so much he wanted to tell her. So much he wanted to know. So little time.

"Is there someone special in your life, Yvette?" he blurted out. He had not meant to sound so desperate, so blunt.

She nodded.

He knew he had no right to feel jealous but he could not help the wave of envy that swept through him. "Tell me about him. Is he French? Is he in RTTI? Does he deserve you?"

Yvette took a step closer. He could feel the heat from her body and the touch of her sweet breath on his face.

"My man is very special to me. I want him to be happy but I see sadness in his eyes and in the little lines at the corners of his mouth. I would like to kiss the sadness away. I would like to hold him and love him until the smile reaches his eyes. But there is a problem."

She reached her hand up to his face and her fingers traced the lines at the corners of his mouth. Brendan closed his eyes. She moved even closer to him and he could feel her breasts, soft and full, against his chest.

"What's the problem?" he whispered into the silkiness of her hair.

Yvette stepped back and took her hand away from his face. "The problem is that he is married. The decision must be his."

Reaching into her bag she handed him something and, turning, walked away towards the hotel. He stared after her, confused and frustrated. Then he looked at what she had given him. He held it up in the moonlight to make sure. *Yes! Yes!* He put the swipe card to Suite 133 into his pocket and ran after her.

Yvette was almost at the entrance to the hotel when he caught up with her. Together they walked through the busy lobby and rode the elevator upstairs. Brendan took the swipe card out of his pocket and opened the door to her suite. He followed her inside and watched as she flicked on the lamps. She waved him towards the couch and went to the drinks cabinet. Picking up a bottle of Scotch, she raised an eyebrow in enquiry. He nodded. She poured two glasses, handed him one and came to sit down beside him.

He began to feel awkward. What next? If he followed the demands of his body, he would rip her clothes off now, fill his mouth with her breasts and fill her with him. Wham! Bang! The bulge in his trousers strained uncomfortably against the fabric. He looked around the suite, trying to gain some control. It was the same design as his. Only the colour scheme was different. He counted the lamps. Six. He breathed deeply. Better now. More control.

"Are you sure, Brendan? I know you must think of Claire."

The "Claire" word hung in the air between them. It slowed his thumping heart, cooled his throbbing penis, focused his mind. She was right. What if Claire found out? What if his father-in-law found out? What if Jacques found out? There was so much to lose.

He looked at Yvette. She had removed her jacket to reveal a white top. He could see the dark outline of her nipples through the lacy material. Her breasts rose and fell in the same quickened rhythm as his breathing.

They had no choice. They reached for each other.

Their first coupling was there, on the couch. A desperate sating of tingling nerve-ends, a release for tensed-up muscles. It was over quickly. Then they started again. From lounge to bedroom, from head to toe, they kissed and licked, sucked and caressed. Dawn was lightening the night sky before they fell into an exhausted sleep.

Chapter Two

Claire stood still, scalpel in hand. She had cut a cross-section through the abdomen of a guinea pig. This animal was one of six which had died after treatment with Serum 6. She focused on the site where the large tumour had been. The growth had disappeared. But yet the animal had died. All the animals treated with her serum were now dead. The first live trial appeared to have been a complete failure. To make matters even worse, her new lab assistant, Kevin, was hovering over her, trying to be helpful. She lifted the ribcage and pointed out to him where the tumour had been.

"I'm going to prepare slides for microscopy," she explained as she sliced slivers of tissue.

"If the animals didn't die from cancer, then what killed them?" he asked.

Jesus Christ! Claire stood still, not trusting herself with the scalpel in her hand. What had Brendan been thinking of when he'd landed her with this assistant? She hadn't asked for anyone. She didn't need anyone. She took a deep breath and counted to five.

"We're dissecting them to find out exactly why they died. I'll tell you as soon as I know, Kevin."

They worked in silence then until everything was prepared to Claire's satisfaction. Straightening up, she put her hands around the small of her back to ease the stiff, tense muscles.

"Coffee?" Kevin suggested.

She turned to him in surprise, almost as if she had forgotten he was there. "Fine," she muttered and immediately he went to their canteen to put on the kettle. After storing the prepared slides she followed him through.

As they sat side by side, coffee mugs in hand, Claire could sense that Kevin was nervous. No wonder the poor kid felt uneasy. She was being unreasonable. She was unfairly taking her frustrations out on him. It was not Kevin's fault that Serum 6 was a failure. That was purely down to the quality of her own research. Nor was it his fault that he had been foisted on her without her permission. That inspired piece of meddling was down to her husband. Brendan seemed to have developed a new-found interest in her work recently. Too late. Over the years she had learned to accept his indifference and lack of support. She was not going to tell him anything about her research now. Not at this sensitive stage.

"Kevin," she began hesitantly, "I know this is not

easy for you."

He began to say something but she stopped him by putting her hand on his arm. She felt his muscles tense at the touch and she immediately withdrew her hand. He was terrified of her!

"Look," she said as gently as possible, "I have always worked alone. You are the first person with whom I have shared my lab. And we will both have to admit that I'm finding sharing difficult."

"Well, maybe I can train you into sharing while you train me into the work."

Claire looked at his shy smile and earnest expression and could not find the words to tell him to go. She would give him a month. That was fair.

"Deal!" she said and clinked her coffee mug against his. "The work is at a crucial stage. You do realise that, don't you? The serum has been one hundred per cent effective in cultures. You've seen that for yourself. Yet something went wrong when it was injected into these animals. Even on the lower dosage. I should not have expected the first live trial to be successful but I am very disappointed."

"Can I ask a question, Mrs Hearn?"

Claire frowned thoughtfully. Was she so taciturn that this youngster was afraid to ask her a question? She tried to smile reassuringly and nodded to him to ask his question.

"Does your serum cure all types of cancer, or is it just the type the guinea pigs have?"

"It's effective against all types, animal or human. It

has to be, because it works by manipulating the cancer cell into apoptosis. That means –"

"I think I remember learning about that," Kevin interrupted. "Apoptosis. It's cell suicide, isn't it? Something just tells the cell not to divide any more, so it just dies."

Claire laughed. "That's basically it. The cell says 'I've had enough' and it curls up and dies. It's a programmed cell death under genetic control. I did my PhD thesis on apoptosis and it fascinated me. It has exactly the opposite effect to cancer cells, which just keep dividing and dividing. I believed then, and I know now, that it is possible to manipulate the cancer cell to self-destruct. When I came to work here after university, my father built this Research and Development Unit for me so that I could continue with my research."

"So your serum can make the cancer kill itself! That's neat."

Claire stood up and brought her cup to the sink. "Not so neat if it kills the patient as well as the cancer. The treated animals fared no better than the control animals who died from their tumours."

Kevin judged from her tone that coffee break was over.

She turned back suddenly at the door of the canteen and stared at him. Kevin looked back at her, terrified that he had said too much or done something wrong.

"Did Mr Hearn speak to you about confidentiality, Kevin?"

He shook his head.

"Well, I am telling you now. You must never, *ever*, discuss the work here with anyone else. Not even your family. Do you understand?"

"Yes. I do realise it is very important research, Mrs Hearn."

She stared at him for what felt like an age and then she turned and walked back to the lab without another word.

Kevin stood stock-still. Bollocks! He had told Ria. He had to tell her. It was impossible not to answer his girlfriend's barrage of questions about his new job. Nothing he could do about that now.

Kevin shrugged and followed Claire into the lab.

* * *

Frank Dawson stood and surveyed his kingdom from his office window. His bulk would have blocked the light from a smaller window but standing in front of this expanse of plate glass he appeared regal rather than overweight. The view was his idea of beauty. He could see the whole spread of the plant, watch the busy container traffic loading Dashern products for distribution all over the world, see employees scuttling antlike between one plant and another, follow the plumes of steam rising from chimneystacks as they dissipated into the atmosphere. Research and Development was not visible from here but he knew his daughter was in her purpose-built lab, lost in her work.

Turning from the window, he stared thoughtfully at Claire's husband who was sitting on the opposite side of the large desk. Brendan seemed more impatient and driven than ever since he had come back from his trip to Bonn. As Deputy Director, Brendan Hearn was competent. As son-in-law, he appeared to be all that was required of him. And why not, Frank thought. It had been a lucky day for Brendan Hearn when he met Claire Dawson. But even after all this time, Frank didn't trust the smooth-talking upstart who had wormed his way into the company via his daughter's bed.

"Frank, you haven't been listening to a word I've been saying."

"No," Frank admitted. "I've been thinking about Claire. How is she?"

"You know she's fine. You see her every day."

An unspoken challenge hung in the air between them and a slight flush on Brendan's face betrayed anger.

"Why don't you ask straight out, Frank? You really want to know if she's pregnant yet. It must be three months since you last asked."

Frank sat down and busied himself shuffling papers around his already well-organised desk. Yes, he did want to know. Yes, he thought it was time the new heir to Dashern made an appearance. Jesus Christ! They'd been married three years! But he was damned if he was going to have this whippersnapper telling him to mind his own business.

"Right," he said, his tone putting their meeting back

on a businesslike track, "what did you want to talk to me about?"

"About that conference I was at a few weeks ago in Bonn. The conference on herbal medicines."

"Herbal medicines?" Frank narrowed his eyes and stared at his son-in-law. "You told me it was about detergent manufacture. That you were there to make contacts. What the fuck are you up to now? Why did you lie to me?"

"You make it sound as if I went to Bonn on a holiday," Brendan said peevishly. "I worked hard there. For Dashern and for you."

"Right. Right. Cut the crap. I should have known better than to let you off without checking. Now tell me what in the hell herbal medicines could have to do with Dashern. This had better be good."

Frank watched as the younger man's expression changed from anger, to defiance and finally to control. He was such a manipulative man, so cunning. It was these very qualities that made him an effective manager and a right pain in the arse.

Brendan leaned forward. The fanatical light in his eyes was familiar to Frank. It always glowed when Brendan had a new idea. The end result was very often increased profits.

Frank sat back and prepared to listen. He had to. He was desperate.

*　　*　　*

The first slide Claire examined under the microscope was tissue from the tumour site of one of the guinea pigs on high-dosage serum. When she refined the focus, the exquisite symmetry of the molecules came into view. She became totally entranced. This was the world she knew. This was her world, where every cell had a purpose, every atom a part to play in the grand scheme. Life, with all its chaotic, illogical permutations, did not impinge on Claire's micro-world under the lens.

She had no idea how much time had passed before she became aware of someone trying to catch her attention.

Kevin was apologetic. "Sorry to disturb you, Mrs Hearn, but I just want to let you know I'm going home now."

"Oh! Is it that time?"

Claire was looking directly at him but he was sure she didn't really see him.

"Respiratory tract infection," she muttered. "They died from respiratory tract infection. Of course their immune system was weak because of the induced tumours. Yet none of the control animals developed the infection –"

"I'll see you in the morning," Kevin said as he walked towards the door, unsure whether he should stay and listen to her mumbling or whether he should go. He had no choice. He must go. He was meeting Ria.

Claire gave a distracted half-wave as he closed the door.

*   *   *

Frank Dawson's anger rose with each page he turned in Brendan's report. It was slick. Convincing. It became more and more evident that his son-in-law had been researching this for months, had negotiated and bartered with RTTI on behalf of Dashern – and not one word, not one solitary hint, had he given Frank.

"The low-down prick," he muttered as he massaged the stiff muscles at the back of his neck. He took a deep breath and forced himself to analyse the situation as calmly as possible.

From a business point of view Brendan was on the mark. The projections for the sales of detergents were not healthy. The Asian economy, which up to now had been a huge export market for detergents manufactured in the West, was becoming increasingly more self-sufficient.

Frank lit a cigar and inhaled deeply on it before considering the next point.

The up-and-coming trend in detergents was tablets – washing-powder tablets and dishwasher tablets. Tableting would require new and expensive technology in Dashern. Unjustifiable for a reduced market. Anyway, bottom line, Dashern did not have and could not hope to raise, investment capital. Of course there were still the industrial cleaners and disinfectants. A profitable low-technology line, the cost to profit ratio pleasingly high. Yet there was no way the industrial products could compensate when profits now being generated by the domestic detergents dropped. But herbal medicines? With all the plethora of bureaucracy attached, regulatory requirements, a validated Quality System, FDA regulations? Funding and outside involvement in the day-to-day running of the company? No, no and no, was Frank's emotional response to all these questions but his business instinct told him he had to consider the idea.

He had heard the traffic outside and knew that the evening shift had gone home and the night shift were by now settling into their various roles but he was certain Claire would still be in her lab. He picked up the phone and dialled R&D. She answered immediately so he knew she was working at her desk.

"Do you ever go home?" he asked

"I notice this is an internal call. Like father, like daughter."

"I didn't get a chance to see you today. Your husband has been keeping me busy. How are you?"

"I'm fine but you sound tired, Dad. Why don't you go on home yourself?"

Frank hesitated for a moment, deciding whether to ask now or wait until they met. But he must know one way or the other. And Claire would tell him the truth. He took a deep breath.

"Claire, has Brendan mentioned any manufacturing changes to you? Has he said anything about, for instance, herbal medicines?"

Her response was immediate and unequivocal.

"Herbal medicines? No. He has not. Why? Should he have?"

"No. It doesn't matter," Frank reassured her. "Not to worry, Claire. I'll see you tomorrow. Goodnight."

Frank put down the phone and ground his cigar vengefully into the ashtray. Why had Brendan not told even Claire what he was up to? Why the secrecy? He squashed the remains of the cigar and watched the stub disintegrate under the force of his temper. Brendan had broken trust. He had underestimated his father-in-law. Bad mistake. Frank picked up the report and put it in his briefcase. He needed his wife to read it. Dorothy had a clear way of thinking, a way of seeing past the waffle. Maybe she could figure out just what their son-in-law was up to.

*   *   *

When Brendan pulled into the driveway, he was relieved to see that Claire was not yet home. He supposed that she was still playing in The Lab That Daddy Built. He went into his study, closed the door and poured a drink. Sitting in his comfortable leather chair, he took a mouthful of Scotch. Glancing at his watch, he noticed that it was almost seven thirty. He subconsciously straightened his tie and patted his hair before dialling Switzerland. The phone almost rang out before he heard the familiar voice.

"*Bonne nuit. Yvette Previn ici.*"

"*Bonne nuit, Mme Previn. Comment allez vous?*"

Yvette laughed her husky, throaty laugh and Brendan smiled his first smile of the day.

"It's done," he said. "I told him."

"*Bien.* How did he react?"

Brendan closed his eyes and reviewed his meeting with his father-in-law. How had Frank reacted? In his usual manner, of course. Cursing, swearing, bullying but eventually calming down and listening.

"I can't understand why you didn't want me to tell him earlier. It would have been easier after I came back from Bonn. Given him more time to think about it."

"That's the point, Brendan. The less time he has to object, the better."

Brendan flinched at the sharp tone. The enigma of Yvette Previn. Gentle, soft, alluring, yet cold and even domineering at times. As many peaks and hollows in her personality as in her beautiful body. He shook his head to clear it of her image.

"Anyway, he has taken the report to study now. I'm confident that he is interested in herbal medicines in principle but RTTI involvement is a different story. Getting him to give up an iota of authority is going to be hell."

"That's your problem to sort. Remember you guaranteed Jacques Rondel that you would have your father-in-law and your wife on side."

Brendan was silent. Yvette was right. He had promised. But he had thought RTTI would be here to give him support, to back up his arguments. Instead they seemed to have been quite happy to let things slide for the past few weeks. He had also promised that Claire would be willing to share her research with RTTI. That too was looking like an insurmountable problem at the moment.

"When are you coming here?" he asked for the umpteenth time, hating the plea he heard in his own voice.

"How soon can you have accommodation organised?"

"Why? When? You mean you are really coming to visit?"

Yvette laughed again and Brendan forgot the sharpness that had been in her tone earlier, he forgot about his stubborn father-in-law and his dour wife, he forgot about everything except the glorious thought that he would again see Yvette Previn.

"Is this weekend good for you? Friday to Sunday? There will be three of us."

Brendan didn't care if she brought the whole of RTTI with her. Just as long as she came herself.

Nothing else mattered now.

*   *   *

It was almost eight o'clock when Claire finally got home. Going to the study door, she saw that Brendan was on the phone so she waved to him and went to the kitchen. On top of her worry about the failed trial run, she felt hungry and tired. She opened the freezer to find something quick to cook. Pizza seemed like the best option. Better check with Brendan, she thought.

When she went back to the study he was still on the phone, talking animatedly. In French. French? Claire's grasp of the language was basic but Brendan seemed at ease with it. To her untrained ears at least, his accent and vocabulary sounded perfect.

While the pizza was heating, she filled the tub and stole ten luxurious minutes soaking in her favourite jasmine bubble bath. As she lay back in the soothing warm water, she wondered if she would ever really know her husband. Hearing him speak French so confidently had been unexpected. How many more surprises had he in store? Perhaps he spoke fluent Chinese and was an expert knitter. Brendan excelled at whatever he did. The aroma of freshly baked pizza wafting up the stairs brought her mind back to dinner. She quickly dried herself off, put on a dressing-gown and ran downstairs.

Brendan arrived into the kitchen just as she was ready to serve. He gave her a peck on the cheek before going to the wine-rack to choose a wine.

"Appropriate, isn't it?" she remarked, pointing to the French bread she was cutting into chunks.

"What do you mean?" he snapped and gave her one of those piercing looks which, even after all this time, made her feel uncomfortable, made her feel as if she had to explain herself.

"It's just that I heard you speaking French on the phone and I was surprised. I didn't know you were so fluent. I ..." She stopped, annoyed with herself for waffling on, annoyed with him for making her feel she had to.

He poured two glasses of wine and they sat down. "Tell me, Claire. How well do you speak French? It's not something we discussed before, is it?"

When he was in this mood she could never tell if he was being sarcastic or patronising. Or both.

"I have a vague recollection of my school French," she replied.

"Well, then, I'll have to teach you, won't I? Or better still I'll lend you my Linguaphone tape. Then you too can talk French. *Salut!*" He raised his glass.

Knowing that he was mocking her, playing some silly mind game, Claire raised her glass and touched it to his.

She was too tired and depressed now to deal with the complexities of her relationship with Brendan Hearn. Her problem with Serum 6 was all-consuming. She had abandoned the first five prototypes of her serum before the treatment stage, knowing that she had not yet unlocked the key. But with this, Serum 6, she had believed – she knew – she had answered all the questions.

Was Serum 6 the problem at all? Maybe the animals had been infected before they came into her lab. But then …

"Anything new in your research?" Brendan asked, as if he had known exactly where her mind had been. An easy guess.

"No."

"No need to be so abrupt. I'm only trying to show some interest. Be a supportive husband."

"Save yourself the effort. Too little, too late."

He carefully put down his fork and leaned across the table towards her. "You work too hard, Claire. I thought you might take it easier now that I got you an assistant."

"I didn't ask you to."

"I only did it out of concern. You look tired. Why don't you think about taking some time off? Let someone else bring your research forward. Someone who would have the expertise."

Claire stood and pushed back her chair. She was too tired for this recurring argument.

"I will never allow anybody else carry out my research. I started it and I will bring it to a conclusion. You can stop asking me. I won't change my mind. Now I'm tired. I'm going to bed."

Any other time Brendan would have been angry. Claire was guarding her bloody research like she had guarded her virginity before they married. He would have to rely on Kevin Trill to find out what was going on in the lab and hope that RTTI would somehow have more success in persuading her to share her little secrets with them. Tonight he just smiled. He was too happy at the thought of Yvette arriving in Ireland to let anything spoil his anticipation.

Claire was in bed before she remembered her father's phone call about herbal medicines. She would have to go downstairs again to ask Brendan about it. Deciding it wasn't worth the trouble, she pulled the duvet around herself and fell asleep.

Chapter Three

There was heat in the early morning sun. It was going to be a scorcher. A day to cool your sunburned body in the ocean and lick rivulets of melting ice cream off a cone. Kevin kicked little pebbles from the gravelled path ahead of him as he walked towards Dashern R&D. He didn't want to go into the lab. What mood would Claire Hearn be in today? Would she be withdrawn and silent, or confiding in him in that soft little voice, pinning him to the ground with the force of her sincerity? He quickened his step, trying to outpace his thoughts. He had no right to be thinking like this. He should be grateful to have a job. He was grateful. Better yet, Ria was pleased. And keeping Ria happy was what his life was about. He rounded the corner to R&D and almost collided with Brendan Hearn.

"Good morning, Kevin. How are you?"

"Well, thank you, Mr Hearn. Nice day."

Brendan Hearn was blocking the way on the narrow path. He seemed to have no intention of moving. Kevin shifted uncomfortably from one foot to the other, wondering what he was supposed to do. Brendan was looking intently at him, staring, as if he could see through skin and bone, right into the space where Kevin was thinking that both the Hearns were weird.

"Are you settling into the lab?"

Kevin was relieved. Of course. Brendan Hearn had recruited him for the job. It was natural that he would take an interest in his progress. It only seemed as if he'd been waiting here to pounce on him.

"Early days yet. I have a lot to learn but I'm enjoying it so far. And Mrs Hearn is pleased with me. I think."

Brendan moved a step closer and Kevin automatically took a step back. The tall man looked down on him and spoke quietly.

"You remember our little chat before you started? My wife is under a lot of stress with her work. I want you to take as much responsibility as you can off her shoulders. Give her as much support as possible."

Kevin nodded his head, wondering if this man had any idea how possessive his wife was about her work. "I'll try, Mr Hearn, but the bulk of the work is on Serum 6 and she prefers to handle that herself."

"Serum 6?"

"Yes. You know. Her cancer cure. The one she's using in the animal trials."

Brendan smiled at the nervous young man. This was going to be easy. So! Claire had named what she

43

believed to be her great discovery! Now all he had to do was convince her to share it with RTTI. Failing that, this quaking youngster would do that on her behalf. Simple!

"Keep me informed, Kevin. Just like we agreed before you started. I want to make sure Mrs Hearn has as much help as possible. We wouldn't want Serum 6 to fail because of lack of a proper development, would we?"

Brendan patted Kevin on the shoulder, sidestepped him and strode off in the direction of the main plant. Puzzled, Kevin quickly covered the short distance to R&D.

*   *   *

When he arrived at the lab Kevin wondered if Claire had gone home at all. She was seated in the same place he had left her the evening before. The mood was different though. She was all bright and breezy efficiency.

"Right, Kevin. Here is what we are going to do today. One, confirm exactly which respiratory infection this batch of animals died from. Two, contact the suppliers and order more guineas. Three, remind me to –"

The phone interrupted her. She cursed under her breath as she picked it up but when she heard her father's voice she relaxed.

"How are you?" she asked but then she gauged from his tone that he was not in good humour.

She was frowning when she put the receiver down. Her father had told her she was to come to the boardroom at once. He was calling an Extraordinary General Meeting of the shareholders. Now! This was indeed extraordinary and he sounded extraordinarily angry.

"Just keep preparing slides," she told Kevin as she slipped out of her lab coat.

She walked quickly to the Administration Building. She would not dare keep her father waiting when he was in this mood.

Brendan and Frank were already seated at either end of the long oval table when Claire entered the boardroom. The space between them shimmered with tension. She chose a chair equidistant from both of them, wishing she could also distance herself from whatever argument was obviously simmering between the two men.

"Go ahead, Frank. You called this meeting." Brendan's words were clipped, his voice controlled.

Claire sighed. These were two warning signs of Brendan's anger.

Frank looked directly across the table at his son-in-law when he spoke. "I have called this meeting because it appears to be necessary to remind some people that there are three shareholders in this company, three members of the board –"

"You disappoint me, Frank," Brendan interrupted. "Why not call a spade a spade, as you usually do?"

"All right, Brendan. I want to remind *you* that you

are only *one-third* of the decision-making body in Dashern. You do not have either the legal or moral authority to commit this company to any course of action, to any expenditure, to any policy change. And in any decision I, as MD, have the casting vote."

"So?" Brendan prompted.

"So why did you negotiate with RTTI without mentioning it? Why did you pledge manufacturing facilities we don't have? How long have you been talking to them?" Frank's voice had risen an octave with each question. He was shouting now. "What in the fuck have you been saying to them on our behalf? You had no right!"

Brendan leaned back in his chair and casually hooked his thumbs into the waistband of his pants. His demeanour was deliberately provocative, even insulting. "I gave you all the information yesterday," he told Frank calmly. "You've seen the research, the projections and the forecasts. Are you willing to bury your head in the sand and let Dashern just barely survive? Or worse yet, go under?"

"My company was operating very successfully for a long time before we even heard of Brendan Hearn. It could fucking well do so again!"

Claire drew in a sharp breath at the bitterness in her father's words. She was beginning to fit pieces of the puzzle together. RTTI was an international pharmaceutical giant. So that was why her father was questioning her last night. It would seem that Brendan had been talking to RTTI for some time. He had not seen fit to inform either of them. And now neither her father nor her husband saw fit to talk to her. They were like two stags clashing antlers, so involved with asserting their male supremacy that they were oblivious to all else. She had never seen her father so angry or her husband so defiant. Just what had Brendan done? And where did herbal medicines fit into the picture?

"Will somebody explain to me what all this is about?" she asked.

Her father pushed a folder towards her. "It's all in there. Your husband's secret plans for the future of Dashern Chem. Doubtless changing the name of the company to Hearn Pharmaceuticals is part of his agenda."

"Thank you, Frank. I hadn't thought of that. But now that you say it –"

Claire picked up the report and stood up abruptly before Brendan could say any more. She was angry with both of them. When had all this bitterness crept into their relationship? When had Brendan's attitude slipped from insolence to arrogance? Had she been so caught up in her work that she hadn't seen what was happening?

"I will read this and then talk to both of you," she said coolly.

Brendan turned towards her. There was a defiance about him, a certain air of recklessness that she had never seen in him before. Maybe she had never wanted to see it.

"You'd better make yourself familiar with that

47

report quickly," he said. "There will be an RTTI delegation here at the weekend."

"What the fuck do you mean?" Frank roared. "Who gave you permission to invite anybody into my factory!"

"Actually, it's my factory too. I'm perfectly entitled to invite whomever I choose!"

Claire had heard enough. She walked to the door and then turned towards them. Her father and her husband. One at either end of the long table. One young, ambitious and calculating, the other middle-aged, stubborn and very angry.

"Just a little reminder," she said. "You both seem to have overlooked something important. _I_ am a shareholder too. I have the same rights as each of you. Let me know when you two feel you can behave like adults. Then we will meet to discuss this matter with some degree of maturity."

The surprise on their faces as she closed the door gave her a great deal of satisfaction. She was probably the most surprised of the three.

Claire's calmness lasted until she had left the Administration Building. As she stepped outside, her mind began to whirr and hum in tune with the noise of the plant machinery. By the time she reached R&D, unanswered questions were chasing each other around her head in ever-decreasing circles. Compartmentalise, she ordered herself. Using her tried and tested Scarlett O'Hara technique, she put the folder Frank had given her into the top drawer of her desk and pushed the drawer closed. She would deal with it later.

* * *

When Claire looked up from her work again it was evening. She needed a reference book from the top shelf and was about to ask Kevin to get it for her when she realised he had already gone home. Standing on a stool, she hauled the book down. She flicked impatiently through the pages. It had to be here. It had been a long time since she last opened this book but she was almost certain this was where she had read about Guinea Pig Adenovirus.

Yes! Here it was. A chapter on Guinea Pig Adenovirus, a lethal virus commonly known as GPAdV. She skimmed through the information, nodding her head as she read symptoms, mortality rates and diagnostic techniques for Adenovirus. She had no doubt now that her guinea pigs had died from it. They had brought it with them from LabAn. Doomed, even before she had given them her trial serum. Bad, bad luck. GPAdV was rare. But they had not died from their malignancies. They had not been killed by Serum 6!

Claire felt a huge surge of relief. She felt like dancing, shouting, singing. She felt like reaching out to touch someone. Just as well Kevin was gone home. Her touchy-feely mood would scare him. Maybe she should tell Brendan. Apologise for being so cold towards him, for not appreciating his new concern with her work. For feeling mistrustful of his interest in R&D. Brendan. The report in her drawer. The fraught meeting in the boardroom.

Sobered, she flopped down on the stool and allowed the memory of today's battle between her husband and father to slip out of its hiding place. She opened the top drawer of her desk, took out the folder and opened it.

Proposal by RTTI for Amalgamation with Dashern Chem Ltd was typed in bold print on the cover page of the report. She closed the folder and put it into her briefcase. She could not cope with this now. She would read it at home.

After setting up her calendar for the next day with reminders to contact the suppliers of the guinea pigs and the veterinary college for confirmation of her diagnosis, she shut down her lab and went home.

*   *   *

The house was in darkness when Claire arrived home. For once she was glad. She needed the peace and quiet to calm her after the storm of today's argument. Besides, she wouldn't have to bother cooking now. A microwave dinner would be fine.

She had just finished eating when the doorbell rang. She was surprised to see her mother standing on the doorstep.

"You look great, Mum," she said, standing back to examine her mother.

A calmness always surrounded Dorothy, lending

her dark features and tall frame an air of serenity. Sometimes her stillness was so intense that she seemed like a reflection in a calm pond where not even a breeze rippled the surface.

"So, how are you, Claire?" she asked when they were seated at the kitchen table with two cups of coffee. "You look tired. I hope you're not working too hard. You're very like your father that way."

"I am tired," Claire admitted. "But I must keep going, Mum. Did Dad tell you I've been granted a licence to run animal trials with my serum?"

"He did mention it. Yes. But only in passing. He seems very preoccupied." She laughed and then corrected herself. "More preoccupied than usual, I should say."

"I know what you mean," Claire agreed. "I would even go so far as to say he's a bit depressed." Claire waited for her mother to take the bait, to give some indication that she knew about RTTI and Brendan's role in whatever was going on. Which reminded her – she yet had to read the report in her briefcase.

"And Brendan," Dorothy broke the silence, "how is he?"

"He's fine, Mum."

"Hmm."

The tone of the "hmm" conveyed Dorothy's disapproval. Her mother's disapproval of Brendan had always hurt Claire.

Dorothy stared at her folded hands on the table. They seemed to be fascinating her. When she looked up, her eyes were troubled. "I have something to tell you. Prepare yourself for some bad news. Your father is not well, Claire. His blood pressure is high. Off the scale, in fact."

After a moment in which she tried to absorb the shock, Claire said, "He hasn't mentioned it to me. Is he attending a doctor? Is he getting treatment?" She was attempting to mimic Dorothy's calmness but she could hear the panic in her own voice.

"He's on medication but the specialist has warned him. He's got to take things easy, relax, be calmer. Or else –"

"What specialist? Is it that serious? Why haven't you said something before now?"

Dorothy let the questions hang in the air unanswered. Typical. Claire had long since realised that Dorothy was gifted with an inbuilt filter. It allowed her to process only what she wanted to hear.

"What about retiring, or even working shorter hours?" Claire suggested.

"You know it would be difficult enough to persuade him to do that under ideal circumstances. But it would be impossible with the way things are now. There are so many potential changes in the air and so much disharmony."

So, her mother *did* know. She knew about RTTI and the tension between Frank and his son-in-law. Brendan must be told immediately about Frank's state of health.

"We must let Brendan know!" Claire said urgently. "If he thought for one minute that he was endangering my father's health, he would be very concerned."

"Brendan has known for some time."

The denial leapt into Claire's head, even before she allowed Dorothy's words to sink in fully. No! Brendan would never have behaved as he had today if he had known! Never. But it was even more certain that her mother would not lie to her. She trusted Dorothy. A cold feeling crept into the pit of Claire's stomach as she admitted to herself that she could not, and did not, trust her husband.

"He asked us not to say anything to you. We respected his concern for you," Dorothy said quietly. "But now . . . look, the last thing I want to do is interfere between husband and wife but I do believe you have a right to be informed. Who knows better than I how close you and Frank are?"

Tears welled up in Claire's eyes. Tears of fear at losing her father, tears of frustration with the animosity between the two men she loved. Angry, hurt, lonely tears for her troubled marriage. Maybe her relationship with Brendan had never been otherwise. Perhaps she had always been just an acquisition to him. A one-third share in a chemical company. It was a painful awakening to reality, an admission that she could no longer successfully ignore the pain of her one-sided relationship. She cried openly for her father and silently and secretly for her marriage. She needed her mother to walk over to her and hold her while the tears spilled over. Instead, with her usual detachment, Dorothy went about making fresh coffee for both of them. Claire knew then that the subject was closed and would not be discussed between them again unless absolutely necessary. She dried her eyes and took deep steadying breaths while her mother switched on the percolator.

"By the way," Dorothy said as she set the two steaming cups on the table, "the other reason I wanted to see you tonight was to ask you about Saturday. What are you going to wear?"

Claire's eyes widened and her hand flew to her mouth.

Her mother shook her head in disbelief and laughed. "You've forgotten, haven't you? The Annual Dinner Dance on Saturday night. The biggest social occasion of the Dashern year and one of the shareholders forgets!"

Claire mentally ran through the contents of her wardrobe as Dorothy kept talking on about the forthcoming dinner dance. She had the velvet trouser suit or the green silk dress or maybe her black skirt and cream blouse or maybe . . . Her attention was suddenly brought back to the kitchen. Had she heard Dorothy correctly? Had she said there would be an RTTI delegation at the dinner dance?

"RTTI people? At the dinner dance?"

"Yes," Dorothy confirmed. "As visitors, RTTI would have to be entertained anyway, so your father feels that since they will be here, though not at his invitation, they may as well attend the dinner. He has no intention of missing the dinner dance himself. Or, indeed, allowing Brendan to miss it. You know how the staff look forward to it."

That was true. Even though Dashern had grown so much over the years, the friendliness of the Annual Dinner always emphasised the family feel of the company. It would be a big break with tradition to have an outside group involved. Frank must feel the need to keep a close eye on them.

"I haven't read Brendan's report yet," Claire admitted. "I think I'd better study it and find out just why my husband wants RTTI here."

"They're sending a top-drawer delegation. The Technical Director and Financial Controller, who are part of their International Management team, and a PR Executive. Or so Brendan says and he should know." Dorothy pulled herself up to her impressive height and said proudly to Claire: "You go into town and buy a stunning gown, get your hair done, a manicure. The works. Let's put our best foot forward for the foreign visitors."

As Claire stood at the door of her home, waving her mother off, she felt like a spent force. Certainly no match for the high-powered visiting delegation.

After a quick shower Claire got into bed, propped herself up with pillows, put on her reading glasses and opened the file her father had given her. It was about time she knew exactly how Brendan had involved Dashern with RTTI. And why exactly he had been so secretive.

* * *

Brendan was feeling very relaxed as he enjoyed his after-dinner drink at the golf club bar. He had enjoyed a round of golf this evening. Dinner, in the plush surroundings of the club, had been delicious. Just the antidote he had needed to Frank's tantrums about the RTTI visit.

He frowned as he thought of his father-in-law. The old man had looked drawn and tired today. He would have to tell Claire soon about her father's illness. Not telling her in the beginning had been one of his nobler instincts. Well, almost noble. It was self-serving too. Claire could be so bloody depressing, so reproachful and silent. Far be it from him to add yet another tragedy-tipped arrow to her quiverful of sorrow.

If only the stubborn old bollocks would listen to his doctor's advice, to his wife, to his ailing heart, then he would retire and leave the running of the company to someone who could cope with it. To me, he thought, and knew that the grin on his face was silly but he was drunk enough not to care.

"You're in good form tonight," one of the group remarked.

Brendan narrowed his eyes and brought the face into focus. Yes. That was Clive Rigney, of the Rigney supermarket chain. A chain with four links: four shops straddling the local catchment area. A big fish in this small pond. A barracuda, Brendan thought, as he noticed Clive's mouthful of small, sharp teeth.

"Cultivate them," Yvette had said. "You've got to have the local business community onside."

Remembering her words, Brendan smiled at Rigney. He nodded and grinned and kept his thoughts to himself. They were all private thoughts anyway. All Yvette and Brendan thoughts. All thrusting, warm, wet, thoughts. He could not believe that in a few days he would see her, feel her smooth skin again. She would be here in Ireland. In his arms! Brendan got another drink and raised his glass in silent salute to Yvette.

*   *   *

Claire heard a car pull into the driveway just as she finished reading the last page of the report. The engine sound was unfamiliar and when she heard it turn around and drive away she guessed that Brendan had got a taxi home. The scraping of the key in the lock before it finally engaged confirmed her suspicion that her husband was drunk.

She slipped out of bed and went into the spare room. She had no intention of sharing a bed with a man who was drunk on both alcohol and power. Tomorrow, she thought as she settled her hot anger in between the cold sheets of the guest bed. I'll sort it all out tomorrow.

Chapter Four

Brendan was already up and gone when Claire woke the next morning. She rang his mobile to discover that he was in the office.

"This is a red-letter day, Claire," he said impatiently. "I assume you've read my report by now?" If he was suffering from a hangover, there was no trace of it in his voice.

"Yes. I've read it and –"

"Sorry," he interrupted, "I don't have time to talk now. RTTI are arriving at two o'clock. I've got to get finished up here and be at the airport to collect them. Talk to you later."

Claire put the phone down slowly. Yes, RTTI were arriving today on their fact-finding mission. They would be assessing the cost of adapting the existing plant from detergent manufacture to herbal extraction, reviewing safety and environmental systems and estimating the expenditure involved in converting the plant to comply with their procedures. Or so Brendan's report said. He had it all under control.

Or so you think, Mr Brendan Smart-ass Hearn, Claire fumed as she dressed carefully, choosing a black suit she had never worn before. She searched through her wardrobe looking for a chic blouse to complement the black. Everything she pulled out was wrong. But how could she have a selection of smart clothes when she never went shopping? Except of course for jeans and sweat tops. "You're dull and boring, Claire," she told her reflection in the mirror. She settled for a lilac-coloured blouse. She still looked dull. Uninteresting. After another search she came across a silk scarf her mother had brought her from Italy. It shimmered with many shades of purples and pinks. She draped it around her neck. Then she put on her black suede high heels. Twirling in front of the mirror, she was pleased with the effect. She felt more confident now.

* * *

Kevin raised an eyebrow when Claire arrived into the lab. She felt embarrassed.

"Visitors to the plant today," she said and was immediately furious with herself for explaining why she was wearing a suit. Claire the Apologetic!

Her first job was to phone LabAn, the supplier of the trial guinea pigs. She picked up their invoice from the desk. On it she had scribbled the name Ronan

Hennessey. He was her contact there, the man who certified the animals for clinical trials. She drummed her fingers on the desk as she was put on hold at the LabAn switchboard.

"I'm sorry," the receptionist told her after a three-minute wait, "Mr Hennessey is not here at the moment. Would you like me to take a message?"

Claire had really needed to talk to Ronan Hennessey. He had been very helpful when first she contacted him. He had given her invaluable advice on the number and type of animal to use, even sorting them into treatment and control groups for delivery. She needed to discuss the Adenovirus problem with him now. What if more of their animals were infected with the virus? But then, she couldn't be one hundred per cent sure that it was Adenovirus, could she? It was not GPAdV until the veterinary college said so. Better wait for official confirmation before causing a fuss.

"How soon do you expect him back?" she asked.

"Maybe later this evening."

Claire drummed her fingers again. More delays. Knickers to that! "Is there someone else I could talk to?"

"Well … Anne Moroney is Mr Hennessey's assistant, but she's at a meeting. She'll be tied up all morning."

Claire was getting more frustrated by the minute. It seemed like she was going to have to beg. "Could *you* arrange a delivery for me please, to R&D, Dashern Chemicals?"

"Go ahead," sighed the number-one contender for Receptionist of the Year.

"I want eighteen guinea pigs in total. Twelve for treatment and six controls. All active carcinomas, as with the last batch. And I also need them certified free of any viral infection before delivery. Have you got that?"

The receptionist read back the order and promised delivery by Monday. Just to be sure, Claire faxed the order, adding a note for Ronan Hennessey to contact her as soon as possible.

By the time she had arranged for samples from the autopsies to be sent to the veterinary college by courier, it was break time again and Kevin had made them two mugs of coffee.

"You'll be going to the dinner dance tomorrow night, Mrs Hearn?" he asked as they sat down.

"Yes, indeed, Kevin," she said emphatically. "I'll be there. And you?"

Kevin laughed. "I have to go. My girlfriend, Ria, is really looking forward to it. She would probably dump me if I didn't take her."

"I'll look forward to meeting her," Claire said.

Kevin smiled to himself. Not half as much as she is looking forward to meeting you, he thought. He was finding it difficult to keep his eyes focused on Claire's face. She had never worn a skirt into the lab before. His gaze kept drifting down to her legs, her delicate ankles and slim calves.

Glancing at her watch, Claire saw it was after twelve o'clock. Doing some quick calculations, she reckoned that Brendan must have left for the airport by now. It was thirty kilometres away and traffic would be heavy this time of day, so he would allow himself plenty of time.

"I've got to go to the main building, Kevin. Just continue on with media prep." She hurried to the door. "Sterilise the guinea quarters as well, please," she added as she left.

She crossed the plant as quickly as her high heels would allow. She had a lot to organise and not much time in which to do it.

* * *

Brendan's secretary, Hilary, had a reputation for being super-efficient and very competent at her work. Cheeky, Claire thought, as Hilary left her standing at the desk. The girl was on a personal call judging by the one side of the conversation Claire could hear.

Eventually she put down the phone. "What can I do for you, Mrs Hearn?"

"I'm afraid I've misplaced my schedule for today, Hilary. Could you remind me when our visitors will be arriving and give me a copy of the programme for their stay?"

Hilary stared back at Claire, her initial surprise being replaced by a superior, knowing smile. "I'd love to oblige you but that is confidential information. Mr Hearn would not be pleased if I gave it out."

The little minx! Claire took a deep breath and reminded herself that running back to the safety of her lab was not an option. "I would like to remind you that I happen to be one of the shareholders. I don't like pulling rank but the consequences for you could be serious if you don't do as I ask."

It was difficult to gauge which woman was most taken aback by Claire's cool, assertive tone. Hilary stared and Claire held her gaze as they both assessed the situation. Hilary was the first to lower her eyes. She went to her computer, printed out a page and handed it to Claire.

A quick glance told her that Brendan had booked the group into The Granary. She had guessed it would be there. It was the only five-star hotel in the district. He had reserved a lunch table for four.

"Thank you, Hilary," she said, in what she hoped was a gracious tone. Her new role was not coming easily to her. "By the way," she said as she opened the door, "would you please refrain from making personal calls during working hours?"

She closed the door and grinned. Maybe she could grow into this role. Maybe she would have to.

* * *

Anne Moroney was feeling pleased with herself by the time she got back to her office. The LabAn staff meeting had gone well. In fact everything seemed to go well for her when Ronan Hennessey was not around. She shivered now as she thought about him. He was a dour, ignorant man. A bully. And also a nephew of one of the directors. The only blessing was that he travelled a lot. Anne probably would have left LabAn a long time ago if she had to work with him on a full-time basis.

She frowned now as she picked up the memo from her desk. That company named Dashern had been on the phone. Reluctantly, she buzzed Sylvia in reception. After Ronan Hennessey, Sylvia was contender for Rudest Person.

"Dashern rang. Is there a problem with their order?"

"There was a Dr Claire Hearn on the phone. She's a real pain. She wanted to speak to Ronan."

Anne took a deep breath to control her temper. Sylvia would make her ask a thousand questions before giving her any information. "Anything I could help with? You know I'm Ronan's deputy when he's not here."

"Really? He never told me. Anyway, he's coming back tomorrow."

"Is there a message from Dr Hearn?"

"She wants twelve animals delivered. Carcinoma-induced. And she also wants them certified as virus free."

"Do you know if they are all for treatment or does she want controls as well?" Anne asked – she had been responsible for handling the control group for the previous order.

"She mentioned nothing about controls, so it has nothing to do with you."

Anne put down the phone and stood there wondering what to do. The Dashern order was very unusual. Ronan was taking a very personal interest in it. He had asked her to separate the last order into two batches: one for whatever treatment this Dr Hearn was going to give them and the other to act as controls. She was allowed to handle only the controls, those animals who would not receive any treatment with Dr Hearn's trial drug – yet another possible cancer cure according to her trial licence. Ronan himself prepared the group for treatment.

Anne glanced at the clock. It was almost coffee time. This would be her last relaxed break before Ronan came back. He would be in here tomorrow, even though it was Saturday. Sometimes Anne wondered what he did in LabAn on nights and weekends. Maybe he had no home. She shrugged. Writing a memo requesting twelve trial guineas for Dr Claire Hearn of Dashern, she propped it up on Ronan's desk. Just for back-up, she sent him an email to confirm. Then, satisfied that she had done all she could, she went to the canteen.

Sylvia sat at her desk in Reception and smiled in satisfaction. Anne Moroney, the silly bitch, had fallen for it. She had believed the Dashern order was for twelve trial animals. The snooty cow hadn't even thought to ask for the order sheet. Ronan would blow a fuse when he eventually found out that Claire Hearn had actually ordered eighteen animals. Sylvia, of course, had herself covered. She had written in the correct order and had the fax on file. She could just sit back and watch Anne Moroney get her comeuppance. The receptionist was almost drooling in anticipation.

*   *   *

Brendan drummed his fingers impatiently on the steering wheel. Just as well he had allowed himself plenty of time to get to the airport. The traffic was inching along in a single lane. Up ahead he could see the blue flashing lights of a police car. When he came abreast he could see two cars, superficially damaged, the drivers out on the road swapping names, addresses and insurance details. Assholes, Brendan thought, as he fought down the urge to raise two fingers in their direction. The policeman waved him on and he sighed in relief as he saw the Control Tower come into view. Luckily, he found a convenient space in the short-stay parking lot.

He went straight to the monitor and discovered that the flight from Zurich had just landed. Glancing at his reflection in a plate-glass window, he did a quick check. Satisfied, he went to the Arrivals area and joined the throng waiting for the latest influx of passengers. He pushed towards the front and then decided that he should not appear over-anxious. Not the image he wanted to convey. But in truth every nerve in his body, every fibre of his being was focused on that exit, waiting to catch a glimpse of Yvette. He forced himself to stand back, his height advantage allowing him to see the passengers who were beginning to trickle through.

The flow of disembarking passengers came fast and furious now and he began to worry that he had somehow missed them in the crowd. He should have had them paged of course. Annoyed with himself, he was just about to go to the flight desk when he saw two distinguished-looking men and a very beautiful woman walking towards him. Yvette! Vibrant, elegant, sexy Yvette! The air around her seemed to shimmer with colour and energy. She led the two men towards Brendan and held out her hand to him in greeting. How he wanted to kiss that hand, those lips, those breasts . . .

"Welcome to Ireland, Yvette," he said smoothly, shaking her hand briefly. He turned to Jacques Rondel. "Welcome, Jacques," he said and flinched when he was assaulted head-on with the Rondel stare.

"And meet the man who holds the purse strings," said Yvette, turning to the dark-haired man by her side. "Vincento McIntyre, Financial Controller RTTI. Brendan Hearn, Director and Deputy Manager of Dashern Chemicals."

Brendan could not help raising a quizzical eyebrow at Vincento McIntyre. If ever there was a swarthy Italian prototype it was Vincento. He was so Mediterranean in appearance that one look at him evoked scenes of vineyards and sun-drenched olive groves. McIntyre?

"Scottish ancestry," Yvette explained, reading his puzzlement. "Vincento's ancestors left the Scottish highlands for the Italian plains generations ago. He's a throwback."

Brendan joined in the laughter but he felt a twinge of jealousy at the easy camaraderie between Yvette and these two men. He asserted himself by taking charge and ushering them to the car. His schedule was back on track now. They should arrive at The Granary in perfect time for lunch.

* * *

"Hi, Dad," Claire said as she peeped around the door of her father's office.

He looked up from the computer monitor and waved her in. He was logged onto the Internet and not really giving her his full attention.

"Are you going to The Granary?" she asked.

He shook his head and pointed to the screen. "No. I'm staying here. I want to make sure I'm well prepared for them. Have a look at this."

She walked around the desk and looked at the screen. He was logged onto the archive page of CNN news. The picture showed the smouldering remains of a factory. The caption read, *Sixty-Two Die in Pharmaceutical Plant Inferno*. Scrolling through the text, she learned that a solvent storage facility on this factory site in Asia had exploded, killing sixty-two people and destroying the entire complex. The factory was situated in a densely populated area and the report said: "*There is a huge degree of concern amongst the local population about possible toxic effects from the fumes and smoke which covered the area within a five-mile radius of the fire.*"

The next paragraph made Claire slow down and take note of every word. It was a short statement from a spokesperson for the company, sympathising with the families of the deceased workers and reassuring the general population that there was no risk to the environment or to the health of those exposed. *"'RTTI deeply regrets this incident and in addition to co-operating with the investigative authorities, we are carrying out our own internal investigation,' said Yvette Previn, PR spokesperson for the company."*

"Yvette Previn," Claire muttered, repeating the name she had seen mentioned frequently in Brendan's report last night, the very same Yvette she would be meeting shortly at lunch.

"There's more," her father said. "A lot more."

Frank showed her reports from Chile, Argentina, Mexico and the Philippines. There was a horrible sameness about them all. One article after the other spoke of industrial accidents on RTTI sites. Explosions, emissions, allegations of water and air pollution. And always Yvette Previn, regretting the accident and promising a thorough investigation. A photograph of Mme Previn accompanied one article but the quality of the picture was too blurred to even discern her colouring.

"RTTI obviously solve their problems by moving them on," Frank pointed out.

"Cynic," Claire replied. But she had to admit the evidence was pointing in that direction. "Have they followed up on the promised investigations?"

"I'll tell you later. I have to make a few phone calls. Your old man is not without contacts, you know!" He

sat back in his chair and studied her. "You look nice. Are you going to lunch? Brendan didn't mention that you were."

"Brendan doesn't know," she said with a grin. "I've just rung The Granary and booked an extra place for lunch."

"That's my girl! I knew you had it in you!" He gave a loud hearty laugh and turned back to the computer.

Claire leaned over and kissed him on the cheek. He looked flushed and she was worried. She wanted to hug him and tell him how much she loved him but instead she played the pretend game, gave him a wave and went to lunch.

*   *   *

Brendan had spent some time this morning debating whether he should drive his visitors to The Granary via the scenic route, or by motorway to demonstrate the superb infrastructure so vital for access to ports and airports. He opted for the motorway. This was a business trip, he reminded himself, as he glanced yet again in the rear-view mirror to catch a glimpse of Yvette. She was settled in cosily beside Vincento, the smarmy Scot. Steady on, old man, Brendan warned himself as he almost missed the turn-off for the hotel. He was safely back in charming-host mode by the time they arrived at The Granary.

"I need to freshen up before lunch. Excuse me," Yvette said after they had booked in at reception. She asked for the keys to her room and followed the porter up the sweeping staircase. Brendan could not help staring after her. His eyes were drawn to the swivelling hips and the defined muscles of her long legs as she climbed the steps.

Guiltily he dragged his attention back to the two men, just in time to catch Jacques staring at him. They ordered drinks and settled down to wait in the lounge. Like Jacques, Vincento spoke excellent English. The conversation seemed to drift aimlessly from one general topic to the next but Brendan knew that, contrary to appearances, neither would waste time or thought on trivia. They would always have an agenda. As they had now. In the short time it took Yvette to change her clothes and retouch her make-up, Jacques and Vincento had gleaned a lot of useful local information by asking seemingly innocuous questions.

The headwaiter arrived on cue to usher them to their table.

The dining-room overlooked magnificent gardens. They were led to a round table set into a bay window. Brendan frowned when he noticed that there were five places laid out for lunch. Nothing less than perfection would do for the exorbitant price the Granary was charging. He would have a few words to say to the manager later.

Yvette was seated directly across from him. He paid as much attention as he possibly could to Jacques and Vince, as Vincento preferred to be called, but his thoughts were drawn to Yvette like iron filings to a magnet. As he kept track of the general conversation with one part of his mind, the other part was frantically trying to plan time alone with Yvette. A few hours. An hour. He had imagined so many scenarios. He could bring her to Tramore, to Blarney, to Donegal. To bed. Anywhere they could be alone. Anywhere they could relive the magic of Suite 133 in the Konstantin.

The headwaiter came to the table and spoke discreetly to Brendan. "Your other guest has arrived, Mr Hearn. Shall I bring the menu now?"

Brendan felt surprise, shock, annoyance and anger in quick succession as he watched his "other guest" cross the dining-room. What in the fuck was she doing here?

He stood up as Claire approached the table and recovered sufficiently to say suavely, "Glad you could make it."

"You know I wouldn't miss welcoming our guests," Claire replied, hoping that she was matching his smoothness.

Brendan could detect the nervous tremor in her voice. What in the hell was all this about? And why was she wearing that suit and ridiculous scarf? Had the old man put her up to it or did she have suspicions? A hot dart of fear seared his gut. Jesus! No! He immediately quenched the fear with a douse of cold logic. Nobody, but nobody, knew about himself and Yvette. He relaxed a little. Claire must be here because of the proposed merger. That he could handle.

"My wife, Claire," he said to the company at large and then proceeded to introduce her to each one individually, leaving the introduction to Yvette until last. "Yvette Previn. RTTI Public Relations Manager."

The two women exchanged looks. Claire's dark brown eyes seemed to be absorbing every detail of Yvette's features, while the French girl's slanted amber eyes glinted as they scanned Claire from her straight dark hair to her unvarnished nails.

"Very nice to meet you, Claire. Brendan has told me so much about you."

Brendan felt a moment of panic, fearing that Yvette was going to amuse herself by playing games. He shot her a warning glance. It would be foolish to underestimate his wife's intelligence. Claire's IQ far outweighed her dress sense.

"And I am pleased to meet you, Yvette," Claire replied. "Your press reports have told me so much about *you*."

Brendan took in a sharp breath. No need now for his warning glances. Claire had shown them all how very sharp and bitter she could be. Without missing a beat, Claire turned to Vince and asked the question he had come to expect.

"McIntyre? Do please tell me the story, Vincento."

They all laughed and there was a visible easing of tension as Vince explained his origins. Yet again.

The food was excellent. There were no more awkward moments as conversation flowed from one non-contentious topic to another. Well-practised corporate lunch conversation, Claire thought, as she listened. And learned. She excused herself immediately after the main course.

"I'm sorry, I must leave now," she apologised. "I have a heavy schedule this afternoon."

"Busy in your research lab?" Yvette asked.

Claire nodded and wondered just how much this woman knew about her. "I'll see you all at the plant later. Enjoy the rest of your meal."

She steeled herself for the walk across the dining-room knowing there were four pairs of eyes boring into her back. The silk scarf was slipping and she prayed for it to stay in place until she was out of sight. It fell to the ground just as she was opening the door to her car. She picked it up and stuffed it into the glove compartment. She had more important things to think about.

Chapter Five

"It must be the miserable weather," Trish remarked as she finished the paperwork for her last booking.

There had been a steady stream of customers into Travelbug travel agency all day. Friday was normally busy but this Friday had been unusually so. Both she and Ria had taken deposits for a record number of sun holidays.

When she leaned back in her chair to take a rest she noticed that Ria was still fiddling with her hair. "Not again, Ria. Not the up or down saga. Would you ever make up your mind!"

Ria looked across at her friend and boss. It was obvious that Trish was annoyed. "I promise you – just once more! You give me your honest opinion and then that will be that. OK?"

"Why don't you wear a hat?" Trish suggested with a sigh.

Ria caught her long blonde hair in a ponytail and

deftly twisted it on top of her head. She twirled it around, holding the topknot in place with one hand. "Now, Trish. What do you think? Sophisticated? Too old-fashioned? Maybe if I loosened a few strands it wouldn't look so severe ..." She turned back to the mirror propped up on her desk and began to tease tendrils into place on the nape of her neck, on her cheeks, on her forehead. The topknot collapsed and Ria's long mane of hair tumbled around her shoulders. "Oh, bugger it!" she said crossly.

Trish walked over to her and put a hand on her shoulder. "Look, Ria, you are getting yourself into a state about nothing. You'll look terrific tomorrow night."

Ria patted Trish's hand and smiled at her. "I know you think I'm being a pain about this and I'm sorry for annoying you with it but it is important."

"Yes. I do know how important it is."

How could she not know when Ria had been prattling on endlessly about the Dashern Dinner Dance for days. She was determined to make an impression on the Dashern management. Then, in her scheme of things, her boyfriend Kevin would bask in her reflected glory and be promoted from lab assistant to some prestigious post and they would all live happily ever after. Poor Ria, Trish thought, and then straightaway switched her sympathy to Kevin. Ever-patient, calm and tolerant Kevin Trill. Poor Kevin! And why not poor Trish? She was the one who had been foolish enough to employ Ria. Guilt at that thought made her want to do something nice for her assistant.

"By the way, Ria, Paul is doing the pics for the dinner dance. I will tell him to look out for you."

Ria's eyes lit up at this piece of news. Paul was Trish's boyfriend. He was a photographer with *Newstrack*, a locally based newspaper that was slowly but surely building up a national reputation. Ria went into daydream mode. She could see the photograph in *Newstrack* now . . .

Before she could discern whether her hair was upswept or loose in the photograph she was brought back to reality by a customer. She would have to ring Kevin later and ask his advice on her hair.

*   *   *

Claire had stopped off at home en route from lunch at The Granary. She needed to change her clothes before going back to the lab. She felt more comfortable and in charge now that the suit was back in the wardrobe and she was wearing her jeans again. She made a deliberate effort to shove the impressions and half-formed opinions, the sheer dread of lunchtime to the back of her mind.

Standing at the entrance to the lab, she closed her eyes and breathed in the calmness, the gentle hum of instruments and the ventilation system, the familiar slightly acidic atmosphere. This was her kingdom. Hers alone.

"Hello, Mrs Hearn."

Claire felt a blush of embarrassment creep up her face as her eyes flew open. She had forgotten about Kevin. Again. Then she noticed that he was blushing too. Both pink, they laughed the awkwardness away.

She caught up with her work quickly. Kevin had been busy while she had been in The Granary. He had sterilised and freshly bedded the animal cages. A quick check assured her that he had done a very efficient job. He told her that LabAn had rung to confirm delivery of the new batch of guinea pigs for next Monday morning.

Her new batch of Serum 6 was at the last stage of preparation. As she put it in the centrifuge and set the timer, she wondered if it was time to start training Kevin in the initial stages of the serum preparation. Could she trust him enough? She would have to ask some questions first.

Claire felt drained and badly in need of the coffee she had not waited for in The Granary. The coffee she could not wait for – her store of courage had been used up by the time the main course was over. She put on the kettle, got the two mugs ready and called Kevin.

They sat on their high stools in silence. Kevin seemed to have an unerring sense of when to talk and when to stay out of her quiet space.

How to get the information she needed without appearing to be foolish and inept? She decided there was only one way.

"Kevin. How were you recruited for this job? Did you answer an advertisement or was it through an agency?"

"Neither," he answered, looking both puzzled and worried.

"How then?" Claire prompted.

Kevin hesitated, sensing that there was something very wrong here. She *did* seem out of touch with reality at times but could she have forgotten she asked Brendan Hearn to find her a research assistant? Was she not happy with her husband's choice? Was his work not up to standard? He had been working hard, thought they were building up a good relationship.

The phone rang. Claire picked it up impatiently and then handed it to Kevin.

"For you," she said.

It was Ria, breathless and excited.

"Hi, Kevin. Paul Gregan is going to cover Dashern Dinner for *Newstrack*. Trish told him to look out for us so we will definitely have our photo in the paper. Now, tell me. Will I wear my hair up or down? What do you think?"

Kevin sighed. "Ria, I think your hair suits you either way. I'm busy now. We'll talk later. I'll see you in Mellow Drama at seven."

He put down the phone before she could say any more. He'd deal with her inevitable tantrum later. He obviously had a much bigger problem here.

"Have I done something wrong?" he asked quietly

"No, Kevin. Absolutely not. It's just that I need to straighten out a few things. Lay down some ground rules before we go any further."

"I assumed you were aware of how I got this job.

79

You know obviously that Dr Walker, my Chemistry lecturer in college, is a personal friend of your husband's?"

"Yes. They were students together."

"Mr Hearn told Dr Walker you were looking for a Research Assistant in your R&D lab. Dr Walker recommended me. Mr Hearn interviewed me and gave me the job. That's how I arrived in your lab. "

"Did Brendan outline a job description to you? Did he mention any special conditions?"

"He told me you were researching cancer treatments. He said the workload was demanding and that you needed someone to do routine analysis in order to leave you free to develop your research."

"I see," Claire nodded, even though she did not.

Why Brendan's sudden interest in her welfare? He had never shown any interest in her research before. In fact, he had treated her work as if it were occupational therapy to keep her amused while he went about the important business of being Deputy Director of Dashern. He had had no right to land this young man into her lab without even a consultation. She could have refused to allow Kevin into her lab. R&D was hers. But the thought of the gossip an open argument like that would have generated had been enough to kill off that idea. So now she was stuck with an assistant she had not recruited and was not sure she could trust.

"Mr Hearn also told me that one of my duties was to keep him informed of developments here. He said he likes to keep up to date with progress."

Claire frowned. "Do you discuss the work with him?"

In slow motion and full technicolour, his meeting yesterday morning with Brendan Hearn replayed in Kevin's mind. Jesus! What to say now? Admit that he had mentioned Serum 6 or say nothing. Lie. Tell a half-truth.

"Mr Hearn just feels responsible because he appointed me. He asked me yesterday how I was getting along. I told him fine because I thought I was."

Claire could see that Kevin was upset and worried and wondering just what was expected of him. Probably wondering exactly what was going on between the Hearns too. She looked at Kevin. Really looked at him for the first time. His eyes were dark blue and did not waver as they met hers. His face was broad, open and … yes. Honest. She made her decision.

"Kevin, I'm sorry to be questioning you like this. It's just company politics and no reflection on you."

His anxious expression eased and she could see the start of that open smile she was beginning to like.

"There are just one or two things to clear up," she added. "I will be contacting personnel to have a new employment contract drawn up for you. Your salary will be paid directly from the R&D budget in future. The confidentiality clause in this contract will require you never to discuss your work or my research with any person outside these four walls. What goes on in R&D is for R&D staff only. That means just you and me. Understand?"

Kevin nodded. He understood what was required of him. He must never tell anybody about the serum, especially, it would seem, Brendan Hearn. He did not understand why. But what did it matter to him as long as he still had his job? Some of his classmates were still looking for work. The jobs market was not very buoyant at the moment.

Claire held out her hand to him and they shook on the deal.

*   *   *

"Ah! Claire! You do like to surprise us."

Vincento smiled a welcome to Claire as she walked into the Conference Room. The welcome was very obviously not unanimous. A scowl darkened Brendan's face when he saw her making another uninvited entrance. He stood up to pull out a chair for her but she saw his disapproval in the narrowed eyes and the straight line of his mouth.

"No need for introductions. I believe you all lunched together today. So let's get straight down to business," said Frank, opening up the file in front of him.

Claire smothered a smile. This was the Frank of old, the man who had built up his business from scratch, her take-charge take-no-prisoners father.

"Before we consider anything in this file I would like to make one thing very clear," he continued. "Dashern is a family-owned company. There are three shareholders. Brendan, my son-in-law, you already know. Claire, my daughter, you met today. I am the founder member of this company. We three are equal shareholders. Any decisions about the future of Dashern will be made by the three of us. Not one acting alone. And certainly not by anyone outside our company. Is this clear to everyone?"

He looked slowly around the table and his eyes rested on Brendan. The tension between the two men was so intense that it seemed to cut through the air, crackling from one pair of angry eyes to the other. One silent second stretched into ten seconds of raging silence.

It was Yvette who spoke first, her slightly foreign accent making the husky voice sound even more attractive. "Yes. We all understand exactly what you mean. And now, if you are happy, Frank, we will continue." She smiled and the tension in the room eased as her perfectly shaped mouth lifted at the corners revealing perfectly shaped white teeth.

Everything about her is perfectly shaped, Claire thought as she saw Brendan cast a grateful glance in Yvette's direction. The French girl gave a barely perceptible nod, just the slightest inclination of her head to Brendan. So slight that only a wife would notice.

The play of power politics fascinated Claire during the following hour. The balance shifted constantly from Frank to Jacques to Brendan to Vince. Points were won and conceded. But it was game, set and match to Yvette,

Claire thought as she watched her manipulate the men. Yvette had such a subtle technique. A gentle hint here, a suggestion there. A smile, a gaze from those amazing slanted amber eyes.

Her technique was not nearly as subtle when it came to Dashern Research and Development. Despite the fact that Claire pointed out clearly that R&D would not be part of any amalgamation, Yvette persisted in mentioning it as an element of a possible merger.

Eventually Claire had stopped objecting and just listened and watched until Frank closed the file in front of him and leaned forward, elbows on the table.

"We have a basis for discussion now," he stated. "What do you say we call it a day and meet here in the morning at ten thirty for a tour of the plant?"

Heads nodded in agreement as notes and files were shoved into briefcases and stiff muscles were stretched. Claire discerned an instant swing in the mood from cut-throat to amiable.

Brendan shut down his laptop and stood up. "I've booked dinner at the Golf Club. Everyone ready?"

Yvette turned to Claire and her mouth smiled but her eyes raked over every inch of the smaller woman, from jeans to sweatshirt to hair tied back in a ponytail.

"Will you be joining us when you have changed or would you prefer to keep us in suspense?" Yvette asked, her tone sweet and convincingly friendly.

"Don't answer, Claire," Vince advised with a laugh. "That would ruin the surprise."

Claire joined in the group laughter as she worked

out how best to take her leave without appearing to run away. She had enough of them and their corporate games for now. "I have work to catch up on," she explained. "Do enjoy dinner and I'll see you tomorrow."

She need not have worried about having a convincing escape plan. Nobody noticed that she had slipped away. She needed the solitude to mull over the meeting and to figure out why Yvette Previn was so intent on including Dashern's R&D Department in negotiations.

* * *

Mellow Drama was an apt name for the pub on the outskirts of town. The mellowness came from the very subtle lighting, low timber beams and potted plants. The clientele supplied the drama. This bar was not one of Kevin's favourites but Ria liked it.

When Kevin got there, the Mellow Drama was already crowded with the usual mix of office workers, young executives on the ascendant and a few who had already arrived at the pinnacle and were holding court. But no Ria.

He ordered his pint and a glass of white wine for Ria and found a quiet corner seat. The hum of voices drifted around him and made him smile. It seemed that everyone was having the same conversation, using the same phrases, swapping the same buzzwords. What a shower of shits, he thought as he sat back to enjoy his pint.

Ria made an entrance. She was good at that. He

waved at her, indicating that he had her drink. She glided towards him, tall and blonde and very aware that she was centre stage. She settled herself opposite him, unloading the shopping bags she was carrying onto a spare seat.

"Hope you remembered to get your suit cleaned," she greeted him.

No, he had not, but he knew from his long association with Ria that he had better not admit that. "Yes, I did. And how has your day been? I see you managed to fit in some more shopping."

"I worked through lunch-time and finished early. I had to traipse from shop to shop but I eventually found the most perfect dress. It's blue with spaghetti straps. It's –"

"God almighty, Ria! How many dresses do you need? I thought you were wearing that black one."

"I look fat in that! You know I do. And you would have let me wear it!"

Kevin looked at her tall, slim frame, with not an ounce of spare flesh on the long delicate bones. She was frowning so he knew he was in for one of her, "you've got to take control and get ahead" lectures. He decided not to listen. His mind wandered back over the day's events, from this morning's encounter with Brendan Hearn to Claire Hearn's surprising announcement that she was going to draw up a new employment contract for him. It seemed that all was not well between Claire and Brendan Hearn and he was going to have to choose sides. Suddenly he became aware that Ria was talking about Dashern. He switched his attention back to her.

"You know what they say, don't you?" she was asking.

He shook his head.

"Brendan Hearn married her just to get his hands on the company. He had such a reputation with women. Love 'em and leave 'em type." She leaned forward and lowered her voice. "I heard there was a girl sharing his apartment up to the week he got engaged to Claire Dawson." She paused and looked quizzically at him. "What is Claire really like? You never say. Is she a bit loopy?"

He drained his glass and put it on the table with an impatient thud. Glancing at his watch he saw it was almost half past seven. He stood up and held Ria's coat for her.

"C'mon," he said. "I've booked a table at the Italian for eight o'clock. We'd better go."

As they walked to the restaurant, Ria kept bombarding him with questions about the Hearn/Dawson clan. By the time they reached the Dolce Vita she was in a tantrum.

"You're just hopeless, Kevin!" she hissed at him. "You tell me nothing."

"Never mind," he said calmly. "You can find out everything you so badly need to know tomorrow night."

Yes, she thought with satisfaction, instantly calming down. Now that she had the right dress, she was really looking forward to the Dashern Annual Dinner Dance.

*   *   *

Claire had decided to go home to make her phone calls. The company lines were monitored for security purposes and she did not want to risk sharing her conversation. After pouring a glass of wine she sat down at the kitchen table with the phone and the telephone directory. Opening the section on Security Consultants she highlighted several numbers. She picked up the phone and then put it down again. Was she being paranoid? Overreacting to real or imagined threats? Yet the facts had to be faced. Brendan had been in contact with RTTI long before he informed either Frank or herself. Why the secrecy? And what was RTTI's interest in Dashern? The phytochemistry route just did not seem to fit comfortably with the ethos of that company. And that, of course, would seem to be their motivation. They wanted to buy an image. Why then did Yvette Previn keep referring to Claire's research? She thought about the most puzzling problem of all. Kevin Trill. Why had Brendan recruited him? Had it been to spy on her? Why could he not have asked her directly whatever it was he wanted to know? And there was the nub of the problem. Having been indifferent to her work since she had met him, he had suddenly started asking her a lot of questions. Lately he had quizzed her repeatedly about her research. And she had not answered him. Something – her paranonia, her lack of trust in her husband – had stopped her telling him about Serum 6, about the hopes and expectations she had for her research.

Claire filled her wineglass again, still not sure that she should activate her plan. She had nothing more to go on except the gut instinct that told her Serum 6 was central to negotiations with RTTI. She picked up the phone and began to work her way through the list. On her third attempt she finally found a security man who would call to the plant in the morning. She arranged to meet him at the entrance to the site at eight o'clock, clear him with security and bring him to R&D.

She hesitated before making the next call. She could ask her father for the information she needed. But then he would want to know why and she was not ready yet to answer him.

Lowering her head onto her hands, she allowed the hard knot of sadness in her throat to unwind. For the first time in her life she felt lonely. What if she was just being stupid? Paranoid? What if Brendan really loved her and she was imagining RTTI interest in her research? Her elbow slipped on the table and the jolt made her sit up straight. The sadness and loneliness were shocked back into their hiding place.

"Oh! Stop snivelling and get on with it," she muttered in self-disgust as she reached to pick up the phone.

Jeremiah Audley had been the Dawson family solicitor for as long as Claire could remember. The Corporate sector of his firm handled Dashern company business but Jeremiah himself dealt with any personal matters. A friendship had developed over the years between the Audleys and the Dawsons so Claire felt comfortable with ringing Jeremiah at his home number. In fact, there had been a stage in the past when both sets of parents had nurtured the hope of romance between the Dawson daughter and Oliver, Jeremiah's son and heir. That, of course, was before Claire had met Brendan and Oliver had screwed every female within his reach.

Jeremiah answered on the first ring. After apologising for the lateness of the hour, she told him she had a query.

"Go ahead, Claire. I hope I can be of help."

"It's about our Research and Development facility," she explained. "I have always considered that my exclusive area but I need to know the legal framework. Is R&D part of the company proper or is it a subsidiary?"

"Well, well, well. What's going on in your R&D, Claire? There's a lot of interest in it lately."

"What do you mean?"

"You understand that it would be unethical to divulge details but you are the second person recently to ask that question."

"And the answer to the question?" Claire asked after a slight pause.

"As you are aware, your father set up a trust fund for you on your eighteenth birthday. R&D, which is registered under the name ClairCo, is an independent company, funded through the trust. ClairCo leases the premises from Dashern and pays a nominal fee for administration."

"Who then are the trustees?"

"I am one of the trustees and your mother is the other person involved. But, Claire, I'm not comfortable with discussing this in any more detail over the phone." He paused. "Why don't you make an appointment to see me in my office?"

"Just one more question. It's important that I know now." Claire hesitated, wondering how best to phrase this. "Just suppose R&D developed a commercially viable product. Could ClairCo develop this product independently of Dashern?"

She held her breath as she waited for Jeremiah's response. He was taking his time. When he answered he sounded cautious. "I would advise you to protect any development by taking out a patent. It's a competitive market out there. And do make an appointment. We could discuss this in more depth in the office. And Claire?"

"Yes?"

"I can't be specific on this but I would suggest to you that your husband is well versed in the legalities surrounding your R&D. Perhaps you would like to discuss it with him. Do you know what I mean?"

Claire did know. He was telling her that Brendan had already made the same enquiries she was making now. He was warning her.

Before going to bed she made out a detailed schedule for the following day. It read like a train timetable, rushing full steam ahead from one station to the other. From one battlefront to the next.

Chapter Six

The security consultant, John Gleeson, was waiting for Claire at eight o'clock the following morning as promised. She brought him to R&D and he worked on the locks and alarm while she did some media preparation. She had just finished sterilising when John tapped on the lab door.

"Job done, Mrs Hearn. I've fitted the panel box inside the front door and the new locks are in place. All you have to do now is pick your code and I can activate the system for you."

They went together into the hall and he explained in detail to Claire how the whole building would be protected from intruders by this sytem.

"Every window and the door are wired. There is no possible way to break in here now without setting off the alarm. Then it immediately rings through to our office. And the beauty of it is that it is a dual system."

"Yes. You explained that last night," Claire said quickly, hoping that he would not go into the whole spiel about the more sensitive laser option on the system that would pick up any movement inside the building. Her only concern was to stop people coming in.

"Is the intercom up and running now too?"

"Yes. Fitted outside the door. Any visitor to R&D will have to buzz and ask your permission to enter."

He handed her a shiny new key. She held it tightly and felt the beginning of relief. "You remembered to cut a spare set of keys? My assistant, Kevin Trill, is the other keyholder. You understand that nobody else is ever to be given a key?"

"Yes. Dr Hearn and Kevin Trill are the sole keyholders. I've got that."

Claire smiled, his sarcasm not lost on her. She could not blame him. She must have told him twenty times.

"Now for the code," he said. "Decide what combination you want and we will activate the system."

Claire thought for a moment before deciding on the most complex code the alarm panel would allow. After a few trial runs with the alarm they were both satisfied that R&D was well protected.

"I'll need your mobile number, Dr Hearn. We may need to contact you outside office or lab hours."

Claire hesitated. Only her parents and Brendan knew her cell-phone number. It was private. No. He could have her home number and of course her work number. But her cell phone? No. John was not too happy about that but he had no option but to agree. When he left, Claire smiled in satisfaction, secure in the knowledge that only she and Kevin would now have access to the R&D building. R&D had just been removed from the tour itinerary.

She rang her father to tell him she would not be at the meeting that morning.

"Don't you worry about it," he said. "I have everything under control."

"So have I, Dad," she replied quickly. "I want RTTI to understand that R&D is not up for grabs. It has nothing to do with any arrangement we may arrive at with them."

"Agreed. That is yours and –"

"And the research is mine."

"Who said otherwise?" he asked sharply.

"Nobody said anything specific. I am just being careful. That is why I have had the locks changed in R&D. There is a new coded alarm system in place. I'll get a set of keys cut for you, Dad, but for the moment I want only two sets in existence."

"Two?"

"One for me. One for my assistant, Kevin Trill. Keyholder status restricted to R&D staff only."

There was silence on the other end of the line for a moment before her father's hearty laugh almost split her eardrum.

"So, my little Machiavelli, will I convey your apologies to the visitors and let them know R&D is out of bounds?"

"Tell them I look forward to seeing them tonight. And, Dad ..."

"Yes?"

"No apologies on my behalf, please. R&D and my research is none of their business."

Frank was still laughing as she put down the phone.

She reached the city in good time to keep her next appointment.

*   *   *

Mellow Drama was usually quiet on Saturday evenings. The weekday patrons went clubbing at weekends. Paul noticed with relief that this Saturday evening was no exception. He eased himself down on the seat beside Trish and carefully unloaded his cameras onto the table in front of them.

"Tired?" Trish asked.

He took a long swallow of his pint before answering. "The road to photojournalistic success is paved with group photos of award ceremonies and posing politicians."

"Sounds like you had a great day," she laughed.

"Well, actually there *was* one bright spot. Ever hear of EnVirowatch?"

Trish nodded. "Yes. The group who are making all the fuss about the pylons."

"Pylons are just one of their issues. They had an AGM this afternoon and *Newstrack* was covering it. I went along to take the shots, intending to get out of there as quickly as possible. But it was so interesting I stayed to listen."

"From what I can see," Trish remarked, "EnVirowatch object to everything. Pylons, masts, new roads, industry, agriculture. They just object to progress. Welfare payments are about the only government policy they support."

"Oh, my, my! Who's a proper little conservative?"

Trish gave him a playful shove. He put his arm around her and pulled her closer to him. Every moment they shared was precious because they were both kept so busy with their respective careers. Sometimes it seemed that Travelbug and *Newstrack* were living together and Trish and Paul were just visitors to their apartment.

Even now, sitting here with her head on Paul's shoulder, Trish was thinking about her travel agency. It needed her full-time attention. Her selling point was personal service and she just had to be there to deliver. Travelbug was slowly building up a good reputation, despite the fact that she had been foolish enough to employ Ria as her assistant. To be fair, Ria, with her harebrained, bubbly personality was a factor in that success. But lately the young girl's behaviour was getting a bit over the top, even by Ria's standards. The sooner this Dashern Dinner was over the better.

"Bet you're thinking about work," Paul said.

"Guilty as charged. Why don't you tell me more about EnVirowatch? Keep my mind off work. Convince me they are not a bunch of pinkos."

"Tell you what – we'll make a deal. Come to the next EnVirowatch meeting. Listen to what they have to say and then decide."

"I think I have already decided, Paul. They're a bunch of cranks."

"C'mon now, Trish! You've never really listened to them. I didn't either until today. The chairman of the group is a guy called Peters. Ewan Peters. You should hear him speak. He has that gift of oratory. That JFK, Martin Luther King type of – of – charisma, I suppose you could call it. After listening to him –"

"Paul! Are you going to bat for the other side? Do you fancy this Ewan Peters?"

Paul took a quick glance around and, seeing that they had relative privacy, he let his hands slide over Trish's body before drawing her to him and kissing her.

"OK. I'm convinced! You don't fancy Ewan Peters," Trish laughed, her lips still tender from his kiss. "But I do believe you're going to turn into an eco-warrior. Will I have to knit you a woolly hat and live with you in a treehouse?"

"How bad! Me Tarzan, you Jane!" Paul looked at his watch and sighed. He would have to leave shortly for his next assignment. The Dashern Dinner Dance. More group photos and posers. He drained his pint and slung his cameras over his shoulder.

"See you later," he told Trish as he leaned over to kiss her.

"Paul," she said urgently, gripping his arm, "don't –"

"I know. I know. There's no need to remind me.

Don't forget to look out for Ria. Take ten photos of Ria! Take a Page 3 shot of Ria! Now there's an interesting idea."

"You can laugh but I'll have to work with her on Monday."

"Who's laughing?" Paul quipped as he left Mellow Drama to make his way to the Estuary Hotel on the other side of town.

* * *

Brendan rapped on the bathroom door. "Are you nearly ready? We should have left a quarter of an hour ago."

Claire had been dressed and her make-up finished for the past ten minutes. She had managed up to now to avoid coming face to face with her husband. The anger-driven confidence, the excitement, which had carried her through the day had fizzled out as soon as she had heard him come in the door. She had hidden in the bathroom since. She felt sick now as she looked at the unfamiliar image in the mirror. Why had she listened to the silly prattle? "Oh, Mrs Hearn, you have such a nice figure! You must show it off! You must bring out the highlights in your hair! You must emphasise your lovely eyes!" On and on it had gone from boutique to beauty centre to hairdresser. And this was the result. She picked up her evening bag, gave one last look in the mirror and told herself that she was at war and this was her warpaint. Taking a deep breath she opened the door.

Brendan was waiting for her at the bottom of the stairs, rattling the car keys impatiently in his hand.

"At last," he muttered and turned to glance at her.

He stood still and stared as she came down the stairs. His shocked expression took in her softly waved hair with the plum-coloured highlights, her silver strapless evening gown moulded to the shape of her body, a thigh-high slit revealing slim legs and the low-cut bodice revealing her small rounded breasts.

"You look ..." he started to say and stopped, struggling for a word.

Claire walked past him to the door, her hips swaying as she tried to find her balance on the three-inch-high sandals.

"Thought you were in a hurry," she said as casually as she could, holding her breath, waiting for him to find that word he was struggling for. Silly? Stunning?

"Different!" he announced. "You look different!"

You better believe I'm different, Claire thought as she settled herself into the passenger seat.

*   *   *

The Estuary Hotel had at one time been the ancestral home to the Boyd-Willis family. Those glory days of gracious living had ended in shabby gentility during the socialist sixties. By the time the FOR SALE sign had gone up, Estuary House had fallen into disrepair. It had been cold, draughty, leaking and damp. The syndicate, headed by Clive Rigney, which had bought the property had gutted it, tearing out rotting floorboards, crumbling plaster and the ghosts of a lifestyle dead and gone. They had installed plumbing, central heating and new life into the imposing granite stone mansion. It was now the centre for all important social events for the area, including the Dashern Annual Dinner Dance.

Tonight the house buzzed with the same excitement as it had in days past. Paul found himself a discreet corner in the lobby so that he could watch the arrivals. They were streaming in now, greeting each other, finding familiar faces in the crowd, the women glancing surreptitiously at the other women's clothes, the men glancing surreptitiously at the other women. The spacious lobby was getting crowded as more and more people arrived.

Ria saw Paul as soon as she came in the door. She made a beeline for him, dragging Kevin along in her slipstream. He stood to greet them.

"Hi, folks. Ria, you look lovely."

She did. Her long blonde hair fell softly around her shoulders and her face glowed with excitement.

"Would you like to do a photo now or later?" she asked.

"Better do it now, Paul," Kevin advised. "I don't think you'll get any peace until you do."

Paul was about to pose Ria beside one of the carved marble pillars when he noticed a hush in the buzz of conversation. He turned towards the door in time to see Frank Dawson make his royal entrance. His wife, Dorothy, tall and dignified, was on his left-hand side and on his other side was one of the most stunning-looking women Paul had ever seen. She had an aura about her that immediately drew all attention towards her. And it was not just because she was obviously foreign – French probably, judging by her flair and style. The overhead lights caught red highlights in her auburn hair, the short cut emphasising the exquisite high cheekbones and slanted eyes. Her dress, clinging to her body like a second skin, shimmered with reds and greens along the planes and curves of a figure honed to perfection. Whew! Paul thought and the look he exchanged with Kevin told him that they shared the same reaction.

"Who is she?" Ria whispered, catching Kevin's arm to bring his attention back to her.

Paul listened for the answer with interest. He had seen that face somewhere before. A news report? Magazine? Television?

Kevin shrugged. "Don't know really. She and those two men behind her are visiting the plant. They're French, I think. Or maybe Italian."

"Kevin, you're hopeless," Ria complained as she went to organise herself for her photograph.

*   *   *

Yvette feigned interest as Frank Dawson told her the history of the house. She stood beside him and gave him an occasional smile just to annoy Dorothy. Everybody was looking at their little group. It was apparent that the

101

workforce held the Dawsons in high respect. There was even a touch of awe in the shy salutes and timid smiles. Apparent also was the open curiosity about the three strangers accompanying them. The fact that Frank had introduced them, when he had to, only as business colleagues, never mentioning their company or their surnames, served to heighten that curiosity.

As Frank organised drinks for them Yvette noticed Dorothy glancing at her watch. So, she was also wondering where her little daughter and her son-in-law were. The hotel manager was hovering and it would soon be time to go to the dining-room for dinner. It was beginning to look like there might be two empty spaces at the top table.

Yvette frowned. Brendan was making a mistake if he underestimated the strength of his mousy little wife. It was obvious that she had inherited her father's stubbornness. Yvette had to admit that locking them out of R&D today had been a clever move. But Mrs Brendan Hearn had better realise she was out of her depth.

The flashbulb of a camera brought her thoughts back to tonight.

"Our local newspaper," Dorothy explained, as they watched a very pretty blonde girl happily pose for the photographer.

"Ah! The media," Jacques laughed. "Your forte, Yvette."

"*Newstrack* won't challenge your media skills, I'm sure," said Dorothy. "They're just here to fill their Social and Personal page."

Vince leaned towards Frank and spoke quietly to him. "Actually this is one area we have not covered in our talks, Frank. I can see there is a certain amount of curiosity about your foreign delegation. How many people know you are talking to us? "

"You are well aware I didn't know myself until two days ago," Frank shot back. "Besides, have you heard me mention RTTI outside the boardroom?"

Vince laughed. "I guess that answers my question. No unexpected public announcements tonight then?"

"We'll wait until we have something to announce. We don't have a deal yet. Remember?"

A gong sounded and groups began to drift towards the dining-room. Frank and Dorothy exchanged looks. They were both puzzled. Where were Claire and Brendan? Dorothy excused herself and went to a quiet corner to ring her daughter.

*   *   *

Claire wrapped herself in her silver shawl as they approached the hotel. Neither of them had spoken since they had left the house. Brendan swung into the only parking space available at the back of the lot. Claire picked up her evening bag and was just about to open the car door when Brendan caught her arm.

"We have to talk."

When she turned to look at him she felt the familiar need flash through her. She longed to reach out and touch that handsome face, to lose herself in the strength of his muscular body, to see approval in his eyes. Eyes that were now glittering with anger.

"You have embarrassed me in front of our visitors," he accused.

"*Your* visitors," she snapped back.

She started as he thumped the steering wheel in temper.

"You're a chip off the old block, aren't you? I *have* to work on my own. Your father is content to sit smugly on his fat arse and allow the company to crumble around him. And you live in your protected R&D world. Little details like the future of the company never impinge on your precious routine. If your father had any brain in his head he –"

"How dare you talk about my father like that! Remember you are where you are only because of him!"

"It's taken you a long time to throw that one in my face, hasn't it?"

His sneer hurt Claire more than a physical blow. Yes, it had taken her a long time to say it because she had not allowed herself to know it. She fought back tears as she searched his face for signs of an emotion other than disdain and anger. There were none. She sat in silence as he hurled accusations at her, the protective wall of cold politeness which they had built between them crumbling with each insult.

"Thought you were very clever locking us out of R&D, didn't you? And you didn't even have the guts to tell me yourself. You let the old man do it for you. How do you think it looked to RTTI? They must be very amused by our provincial family feud. You and your bumbling father live in cloud-cuckoo land. We need those people. We need their investment if we're to continue in profit in the future. Just think, Claire, you might have to face the real world if Dashern doesn't survive. And in the grown-up world, Claire, executive's wives don't dress like tarts for business functions – is this fancy dress Daddy's idea too?"

Her angry retort was silenced by an overriding need to escape this tirade. If she had built up hurt and rejection over the years, his built-up resentment and anger equally matched it. She opened the car door and got out, almost tripping as her high heels wobbled on the gravelled surface. What was happening to them? Wasn't the pretence and denial better than this?

He caught up with her as she approached the front door of the hotel. Taking her elbow, he gripped it tightly as she tried to free herself. He leaned down towards her.

"Claire, I'm so sorry," he said softly. "I didn't mean that. It's just that I'm so angry about the way you're behaving. As if you want to make me look foolish in front of RTTI. I can't understand it. And –"

Her mobile rang. He released his grip on her to allow her to answer it. The sound of Dorothy's calm voice was balm to Claire. She drew strength from it.

"My parents are waiting for us in the lobby," she told Brendan coldly as she walked ahead of him into the hotel, her head held high, her mouth curved in a determined smile.

*   *   *

The essence of Frank Dawson's after-dinner speech had been the same for thirty years. This year was no different. Having thanked all staff for their efforts during the year and reported continued progress, he urged everyone to enjoy the entertainment which would start shortly.

The only surprise, as far as Paul Gregan was concerned, was that Frank Dawson had not acknowledged the presence of the three strangers at the top table. According to the staff members he had spoken to, these same three people had been around the plant for the past few days. They had been given the grand tour. It was not unusual for groups to be shown around the plant but the staff were always told in advance. Not so with this group. There had been no word from the top as to who these people were or why they were visiting Dashern Chemicals. A new customer checking out the facilities? Why the silence? Interesting.

After the meal, the band took to the stage and the dancing began. Claire held herself stiffly in Brendan's arms as they circled the floor, aware that he was watching Yvette, as he had been all during the meal. To be fair, she had to admit that all male eyes were focused on the Frenchwoman and the teasingly see-through fabric of her dress. She was covered from head to toe but yet every inch of her body was subtly on display. A powerful weapon being used to full capacity.

As the band upped the tempo Claire decided to sit down. Despite compliments from her parents, Jacques and Vince, Brendan's "tart" remark still burned into her. She felt like a foil-wrapped whore in her silver gown. She sat at the table and tried to hide behind her drink.

Brendan took the opportunity, as she had known he would, to lead Yvette onto the dance floor. That did not surprise her. But what did shock her was the way they danced, their movements synchronised, their bodies swaying almost as one. Two halves of a whole. Familiarity. It was as if they knew each other intimately. Claire stood, unable to look away from the gyrating pair yet unable to stay watching.

"Care to dance?" Vince asked and she thought she read understanding in his eyes.

"Later, Vince, thank you. I must go powder my nose now. Excuse me."

A quick check assured Claire that the rest-room was empty. She sank into one of the upholstered chairs and closed her eyes. Images of Brendan and Yvette, their bodies intertwined, swam around in her head. She put her head in her hands. Jesus! She was going mad!

Three deep breaths later Claire opened her eyes and tried to reason more calmly. Yes, Brendan had been seeing RTTI without telling her. Yes, she now believed he had intended bargaining her research as part of a deal without telling her. Yes, he seemed to know Yvette well but then she had been involved from the beginning in the ongoing negotiations. And it was obvious that every man in the room outside wanted to get into the Frenchwoman's knickers so why should her husband be any different?

She stood before the full-length mirror. She liked the bodywave in her hair. Maybe she looked pretty in a fragile way, a pale shadow of the vibrant Yvette. She slipped off her shawl and examined her bare-shouldered reflection.

Music drifted into the room as the door opened. It was Kevin's lovely blonde girlfriend. Claire turned guiltily around, ashamed at being caught gazing at herself in the mirror.

"Ria Corkery. Kevin Trill's girlfriend," the girl said, walking towards Claire with her hand outstretched and a friendly smile on her face. "I am so glad to meet you at last, Mrs Hearn. Kevin talks a lot about you."

"Really?"

"Yes. He admires your work and he enjoys being your assistant."

"He is becoming indispensable to me," Claire replied and was surprised to realise how true that statement was. She had quickly gone from resenting having him imposed on her to relying on his input. Definitely not what Brendan had intended when he had recruited a lab assistant without her permission.

Ria began brushing her gleaming hair. Hairbrush in hand, she stood back and scrutinised herself. "Do you think I should have my hair up?" Without waiting for an answer she continued on, "I had a different idea about you. I was surprised when I actually saw you."

"What do you mean? "

A blush began to creep up Ria's neck and spread to her face. "Oh! There I go again! Kevin always says I talk first and think later. I only meant that you look so stylish and sophisticated and I suppose I thought you would have Coke-bottle glasses and a bun because you are always peering into microscopes. Kevin didn't say that. God! I'm waffling!"

Claire smiled at the confused girl. "It's OK, Ria. I know what you mean. And thank you for the compliment."

Claire carried her shawl in her hand as she walked confidently back to the function room in her strapless evening gown with the thigh-high slits.

* * *

Paul had photographed Frank Dawson on many social occasions so they were not strangers to each other. They chatted easily now as they waited on Frank's daughter to return from the rest-room to take her place in the management group photo.

Paul's eyes were continuously drawn to the beautiful stranger. Up close she was even more stunning, her skin creamy-smooth, an almost visible aura of energy surrounding her, drawing towards her. He still could not remember where he had seen that face before.

"The lady, Frank. A new member of staff?"

"No – no – just visiting," Frank said dismissively. He

turned away and looked towards the ladies' room. "Where has Claire got to?"

So, the staff members he had spoken to were telling the truth. Frank Dawson was being very secretive about the identity of the woman and her companions. Puzzling then that he put them on public display here tonight. Dashern clients? Maybe so. Brendan Hearn and the woman certainly seemed on familiar terms. So familiar, Paul noted, that Brendan availed of every opportunity to touch the glowing woman, brushing her fingers as he lit a cigarette for her, gently holding her arm as he spoke to her.

"Ah!" Frank said as he spotted Claire making her way towards them.

Paul hardly recognised the sophisticated woman approaching. Her new hairstyle and clothes emphasised her delicate prettiness. Claire Dawson had obviously had a makeover. The dark-haired, dowdy woman was gone. He looked from her to the mysterious foreign woman and knew instinctively that battle lines had been drawn.

It took ten minutes for Paul to organise the family group and photograph them. He had asked for, and been refused, permission to include the strangers in the picture. But before he left them he overheard one of the men address the woman as Yvette. He must remember where he had seen Yvette before. Frank Dawson's reluctance to reveal her identity made remembering a priority. Paul had trained as a journalist before going full-time into photography. His training now told him there was a story here. One that Frank Dawson was not willing to tell him. Yet.

*   *   *

After the photo session, Yvette called Claire and indicated the empty chair beside her. Claire squirmed inside. God! She was going to have to sit beside the Diva and try to chat to her while Brendan sat at the other side. Yvette smiled at her as she settled herself in. The smile seemed warm and welcoming. Bitch!

"Are you enjoying the evening, Claire?"

"Yes. And you?"

"Oh, wonderful! I do enjoy your Irish music. So wild and liberating."

"Is this your first visit?" Claire asked, knowing that it was a stupid question to ask when she already knew the answer but it was the only one she could think of.

"It is, for sure," Yvette replied in her low-key, husky voice. "But of course you know I hope to be a regular visitor in the future."

"I'll drink to that," Brendan said, raising his glass to her.

They touched glasses and the look between them was so intimate that Claire felt like a voyeur, a pervert out in the cold peering into the privacy of a special moment. She tried to think of something interesting to say, anything to remind them that she was there. "Your dress, Yvette. It's beautiful. So colourful. Paris?"

"Versace," Yvette replied matter of factly before

turning to Brendan. "Bren, would you be a darling and get me another drink please?"

Bren! How cosy! Claire glared at his back as he walked to the bar. The feeling of betrayal was so intense that she started when Yvette spoke.

"A handsome man, your husband. And such a nice sense of humour too."

"You know him well?" Claire shot back, realising that it was more of an accusation than a question.

"Yes. We have had quite a lot of contact during negotiations over the last months. I would say I know him a lot better than he knows me."

What a strange thing to say. Claire frowned and waited for an explanation.

"There is something he does not know about my life. In fact, very few people know. Not even Vince and Jacques. And not Brendan either. I want to tell you, Claire, because I sense some animosity from you. I want to, I think you say, set the record straight between us."

Claire nodded, not denying the animosity but willing to listen.

Yvette glanced around her first and then leaned towards Claire. She held her gaze with those slanted eyes, which were hypnotic at close range. "I must know first that this will be our secret. I opt to keep my private life strictly private. You must promise me never to discuss this with anyone else. Promise?"

Discuss what? How could she promise when she had no idea what Yvette was going to tell her? How would she ever know if she did not promise? Glancing over at the bar she noticed that Brendan was now being served. "Bren" would be back shortly.

"Yes. I promise."

"Well then, Mrs Hearn, I want you, and only you, to know that I am gay." Yvette smiled as Claire stared at her in disbelief. "I'm lesbian, Claire, and not in the least interested in men. Even the handsome, good-humoured ones. I have a partner and we have been together for two years. I am not ashamed of the fact but I'm sure you can understand why I prefer to keep my private life separate from my business."

Claire nodded her agreement, the revelation slowly seeping in. She felt a vicious tinge of satisfaction. How ironic that her husband was throwing away all the tenderness and longing she craved for on someone who could not and would not respond! What glorious justice! Let him have his secrets. She had hers now.

Brendan was on his way back, a tray of drinks balanced in his hands as he weaved his way through the dancers.

Claire turned to the Frenchwoman and grasped her hand. "I know why you told me, Yvette. It cannot have been easy for you." She hesitated before adding, "And I'm sorry if I've been unfriendly towards you."

Yvette squeezed her hand and whispered, "Secret!" just as Brendan approached. Claire returned the pressure of the fingers and their secrecy pact was sealed.

Frank came over and asked Claire to dance. As she twirled about the floor she realised that Yvette was right about the Irish music. It was wild and liberating and in tune with her mood. Yvette Previn did not fool her. She was a predatory woman, not to be trusted. But it was a relief to have the battle lines defined. She would not have to fight the beautiful French girl on an emotional level. Their differences would now be confined to business and the future of Dashern Chemicals. And of course R&D. Brendan was no longer an element in the war.

Claire had never before enjoyed a social function as she enjoyed this night. She danced with Vince and Jacques, with her father and Kevin. She danced with Brendan, enjoying his puzzled expression as she threw herself into the spirit of the music and the night. When Yvette pleaded tiredness and Brendan immediately volunteered to drive her back to her hotel, Claire happily gave her blessing to the plan.

"I'm enjoying myself too much to leave now. Will you drive me home later, Dad?" she asked a suspicious-looking Frank.

"If you're sure that's what you want," he replied, his eyes never leaving Brendan's face.

"I'm sure," Claire replied as she exchanged a glance with Yvette.

She could see that her father was worried. She would like to confide in him, realising now that he shared her suspicions about the Frenchwoman and Brendan. But a promise is a promise, she told herself, as she waved a casual goodbye to her husband and Yvette and then threw herself energetically into the intricate moves of the Siege of Ennis.

*   *   *

Brendan's efforts to concentrate on his driving were completely shattered as Yvette's long fingers crept along his thigh.

"You've been a naughty boy," she accused, increasing the pressure of her fingers.

"I am definitely going to be very naughty if you don't stop that now. Anyway, what are you talking about? I've behaved perfectly. Do you know how much I've wanted to take you in my arms. How I've wanted to —"

"I know, Brendan. So does your wife. And your father-in-law. You've made your feelings blatantly obvious to everyone."

The tyres screeched as Brendan pressed his foot hard on the brake. Without even remembering to indicate, he pulled in on the hard shoulder of the road. His face was pale as he turned to Yvette. "Claire knows? Frank knows? How? What did they say?"

Yvette raised an eyebrow as she stared at him. For one moment Brendan could see himself through her eyes. What a pathetic coward she must think him! But then she didn't know what was at stake, did she? Sweat prickled the skin between his shoulder-blades. And still she stared as if she was trying to read the terror in his soul. He leaned over and caught her two arms. "For God's sake tell me! What did they say? How do they know?"

"Why didn't you tell me about your prenuptial agreement?" she demanded, her voice cold.

He let go her arms and leaned his head on the steering wheel. So, Frank had told her. The twisted old fucker must feel very proud of himself. Not alone had he had the foresight three years ago to put that clause into the share contract but he had the satisfaction of proving himself right now.

"That agreement is private. Between Frank and me. The bastard should not have told you."

"He did not," Yvette said flatly.

Brendan lifted his head and stared at her. "So how do you know? Claire doesn't know. She would never have agreed to it. Only Frank, Dorothy and the solicitor who drew up the document know. Dorothy?"

"It doesn't matter how we know. We do. Wake up, Brendan! You signed a deal for your shares when you married Claire. And just in case you have forgotten, that means not giving her any reason to divorce you. If she goes, she takes your shares with her. While Dashern still wholly owns the company, you stick to that deal. You risked everything by sleeping with me."

"How much do they know?" he asked and held his breath waiting for the answer.

"They don't really know anything but they suspect a lot. You've been behaving like a lovesick boy."

Brendan was immediately hurt and angry at the cold insult. He wanted to hurt her back. "That's cool coming from you!" he said hotly. "You've been throwing yourself at me at every opportunity, flaunting yourself. What kind of game are you playing, Yvette? You lead me on and then blame me."

"Ah, poor Brendan!" she laughed. "The demanding little wife wants a faithful husband, the evil father-in-law wants to protect his property and the French mistress wants to lead you astray! And you, poor dear, want it all."

Slowly, painfully, the truth dawned on Brendan. Yvette wanted his Dashern shares. How ironic! An echo of Claire wanting Brendan and Brendan wanting Dawson shares. There was a certain natural justice in it. The lights of a passing car shone on them. Brendan jumped guiltily. Yvette laughed and he glared at her.

"Cheer up, Bren," she laughed. "I've covered your ass. This time."

"What do you mean?"

Yvette threw her head back and laughed, a deep, throaty, satisfied laugh. "I told your clever little wife that I am lesbian and not in the least interested in her husband."

"And she believed you?"

Yvette nodded. "We made a pact to keep my confession secret. Now we all have our secrets."

Brendan was silent, remembering how surprised he had been when Claire had encouraged him to drive Yvette home while she stayed on at The Estuary. It made sense now. "What about Frank? What did you say to him?"

"Don't you worry about him. I can handle Frank. All

you need concern yourself with is keeping your side of the bargain with RTTI. We want all three shareholders to sign the agreement for a merger."

"We're on track for that. You know the old man is coming around. He doesn't have a choice. Claire will follow on."

Yvette leaned forward and caught Brendan's hand in hers. She turned his palm up and gently traced the lines in the soft centre of his hand with her tongue. He closed his eyes as she licked his index finger and then sucked it into the warmth of her mouth. A spasm of need shivered through him. She released his finger from the erotic wetness, sat up straight and faced him.

"We want the shares. Yes. And we will get them. But we are keeping a close eye on Claire's research. You know, I assume, that she is carrying out animal trials. R&D must be part of the package."

"I know nothing about her research. It's her baby and she is very protective of it. That's why I put a co-operative assistant into her lab. Remember? I told you about Kevin Trill. Anyway, what could she have that the vast research teams of RTTI would need?"

"Maybe nothing but, on the other hand, maybe something very significant. Claire needs us a lot more than we need her. She just does not realise it. She has brought the work a certain distance but it will take all the resources of a multinational to bring it through clinical trials and FDA licensing. Your job is to persuade her."

"I hardly even know what she is *doing* in R&D.

Except that, according to Kevin Trill, she has come up with something she calls Serum 6, which she imagines is a cure for cancer. Anyway, you seemed cosy enough with her tonight. Why don't you just ask her?"

"Ask the woman who locked us out of her lab? Put her research out of bounds to RTTI? We don't want to upset her now, do we? It's up to you, Brendan, to persuade her. Or if you cannot manage that, get this Kevin Trill to deliver."

Brendan heard the unspoken "or else". Hand Claire's research to RTTI, or else no deal. There was no need to discuss it any more. He switched the engine on and indicated to pull back out onto the road. They drove in silence to The Granary, Yvette with her eyes closed, feigning sleep, Brendan with his eyes on the road, feigning indifference. As they approached the entrance to her hotel, Yvette put her hand on his arm and smiled at him.

He smiled back at her but it was a feeble smile. How in the fuck was he supposed to persuade Claire into anything when she was building a fortress around R&D? Even building a fortress around herself.

"*Bonne nuit, mon amour,*" Yvette said in her teasing, sexy voice as she opened the car door.

Brendan watched until she had disappeared into the reception area. Then he drove home and tried to figure out what the hell was going on. It all spun around in his head. RTTI wanted Claire's research. Claire wanted to keep her research secret. Brendan must keep his night with Yvette secret. Claire thought she must keep

Mary O'Sullivan

Yvette's sexual orientation secret. Secrets. Secrets. Secrets.

He was already in a deep, exhausted sleep by the time Claire came home.

Chapter Seven

Newstrack's newsroom was peaceful in the Sunday morning quiet. Sitting in front of his computer screen, Paul closed his eyes and allowed the almost forgotten feeling to ripple through him. For him, photography was a passion. But journalism was an instinct. Yes! Yes, his gut was tightening in that instinctive reaction, that hair-raising, skin-prickling phenomenon called a hunch. It coursed through his veins now as he thought about the woman named Yvette. He knew there was a story. A big story. And this Yvette, together with her smooth-looking sidekicks and Dashern, were all key players.

Paul mentally ticked off the information he had as he booted up his computer. Her name was Yvette. She was French and she was probably involved with the chemical industry. She was an exceptionally beautiful woman. Frank Dawson did not want to reveal her identity but yet he seemed happy to parade her in front of the staff at the dinner dance.

Where in the hell had he seen her before? It would have been about two or three years ago. She was not easily forgotten. He could remember so well what she looked like, the long legs, the sculpted features, the high, firm breasts. She was such an effective front woman that he had forgotten the story and remembered her. Front woman! A news reporter? Presenter? Nothing for it but to start searching the archives.

It took an hour. The picture in this article was not very clear but there was no mistaking the unique beauty of Yvette Previn, PR executive for RTTI. He remembered at last. He had seen her on a television news programme, ably defending RTTI after a chemical explosion in one of their subsidiaries. It was easy now to find more information. Half an hour later, he had printed out a comprehensive report on RTTI International, outlining a catalogue of accidents and environmental disasters. A smaller batch of reports detailed the outcome of various enquiries, inevitably exonerating RTTI of all blame, occasionally recommending minor manufacturing changes. There were several articles also on RTTI presentations to various communities. A scholarship here, a bursary there. A sop to the masses. He switched off the computer and gathered up the sheaves of paper. His film should be developed by now.

The photos were still wet. Paul handled them carefully as he searched for the one he needed. The one he had taken using the wide-angled lens. Yes! There it was. The Dashern management group smiling into the camera and, in the background, the beautiful Yvette Previn. He placed the photo on the scanner, zoomed in on the perfectly sculpted face and printed it out. Bingo!

Paul got a large envelope and placed the printouts and the photo into it. No wonder Frank Dawson had been reluctant to reveal the identity of his guests. Why was he wining and dining RTTI? Could he be selling out to them? Could he possibly be considering allowing them to operate their hit-and-run policy here?

He locked the envelope carefully into the glove compartment of his car. It would stay safely there until he handed it to Ewan Peters of EnVirowatch.

*   *   *

Claire had expected to feel tired and stiff this morning. Instead she felt a rush of energy as she opened her eyes to a bright sunny Sunday. She left Brendan to sleep on as she dressed, had coffee and planned her day.

She called him before leaving for the plant. "I'm going to do some work before the meeting. See you at the plant."

He grabbed her by the wrist as she turned away from him. "I hope we have seen an end to your childish behaviour. I want RTTI to see a united Dashern team today. Remember that we need them a lot more than they need us."

"Speak for yourself," Claire snapped as she jerked her wrist from his grasp and turned her back on him.

He was cursing as she slammed the bedroom door.

*   *   *

Claire had a few minutes of panic before she remembered the new alarm code for the R&D building. She smiled with relief when the combination finally clicked into place. She really would have looked very stupid if she had set off her own alarm system. How Brendan would have enjoyed that!

The lab had the usual soothing effect on her. She spent a few minutes just relaxing before opening her calendar and checking tomorrow's schedule. Monday would be a busy day. An exciting day. The new animals were due to arrive and the fresh batch of Serum 6 was ready and waiting.

As she pored over her notes, she tried to concentrate on the dosage programme for the new batch of animals but her mind kept skipping forward to the final meeting with RTTI before they flew out today. She would have to assert herself and leave no room for misunderstanding, leave Brendan no chance to outmanoeuvre her. It seemed that the unspoken battle between herself and her husband was being forced to find a voice. In public.

Claire blushed with humiliation and anger. How could she have been so naive? Why had she not allowed herself to see the sham her marriage had become? She smiled a bitter little smile as she thought what a lousy hand fate had dealt Brendan. How desperate he must be now to prevent Dashern shares plummeting! He could yet be left with a loveless marriage and worthless shares. Tough!

She went to her filing cabinet and unlocked it. Reaching into the back of the top drawer, she withdrew a manila folder with no nametag on it. It was a bulky file, the covers softened by years of handling. She brought it to her desk and carefully opened it up. This was it. Her life's work. Years of theorising, trying, failing and finally seeing the light. Serum 6. The cure for cancer!

Claire flipped the pages. Line after line of numbers flicked past. Not one letter. She smiled with satisfaction. Other than the brief outline she was required to submit for her animal trial licence, she had never written her formula for Serum 6 in anything but her number code. It was not on computer either. It snuggled safely here in this battered old file, buried in the intricacy of the number code. It was as if she had always known that RTTI and Yvette Previn would happen along and try to steal her work. Even if they got the file, it would be no good to them without the key to the code.

"And that is locked inside my head. Where it is going to stay," Claire said aloud as she closed the file and returned it to the cabinet.

Going back to her desk, she picked up a red marker and printed "PATENT" in large letters on a sheet of paper. She stared at the word for a minute, then locked up her lab, set the alarm and made her way to the conference room.

*   *   *

Her father was already seated at the head of the table when Claire went in.

"They're not here yet?" she enquired.

He shook his head. "They're on their way. Brendan has collected them. Anyway this gives us a chance to talk. I want to know exactly how you feel about the merger."

"Merger? Are we talking Dashern-RTTI or RTTI (Ire)?"

"The Dashern name will always be part of this company as long as I have a say. Then it's up to you. And your husband of course."

Claire sat down beside her father. She noted his high colour and the beads of sweat on his forehead. He obviously was not well. The stubborn man was going to kill himself with all this wheeling and dealing.

"Are you taking your medication?" she asked severely.

He laughed at her. "Do you realise you sound just like your mother? Yes, I'm taking my medication. And no, I'm not doing too much. Satisfied?"

"For now," Claire agreed. "But Mum told me what the specialist said. Are you sure you want to get involved with RTTI and all these negotiations? Do you –?"

Her father interrupted her, the high colour

heightened even more by anger. "Do I want to lie down and die now? Do I want to hand Dashern on a plate to Brendan? You bet your ass I don't! Frank Dawson isn't going anywhere before –"

Claire caught his hand in hers and squeezed it urgently. "OK, Dad. Calm down! I wasn't suggesting that you get out your pipe and slippers. I'm just saying that you should take things a bit easier. Delegate more."

"To whom?" he snapped "To you? You're so involved in your research that you have no time for anything else. I'm not criticising you for that. Just stating facts. To Brendan? Yvette would have him talked into any deal she wanted before you could say 'French knickers'!" He stopped and stared at her, a look of horror on his face. "I'm sorry, Claire. I shouldn't have said that. I didn't mean –"

"You didn't mean that he was having an affair with Yvette? I know he's not. But that doesn't mean he doesn't want to."

Frank looked into her face, wondering if she had somehow found out about the infidelity clause. He should have told her himself. "He knows which side his bread is buttered on," he said gruffly.

"He does," Claire agreed, more to finish the discussion on her husband than to acknowledge what her father had said. When the time was right, she would deal with it. No more hiding behind Daddy. She brought his attention back to the negotiations with RTTI. "My understanding of the proposals is that detergent production will be scaled down and the slack will be taken up by processing herbal products on contract for RTTI. That way, RTTI gets into the phytochemistry market here and Dashern keeps its head above water and its employees in work. Am I on the right track, Dad?"

"That's about the size of it," Frank agreed. "It's a compromise. It will give us a chance to see how we adapt, how we work together."

"But my research is off limits. If they don't accept that, I'm not voting for the merger."

Frank leaned forward and stared into his daughter's face. "Your research, Claire. Can you handle it on your own? I know you are carrying out animal trials now but can you bring it forward to –"

There was a knock on the door.

"I'm with you, Claire," Frank said quickly as they watched the four people enter the room.

Brendan stood aside at the door to allow Yvette precede him and devoured the Frenchwoman with his eyes. Yvette and Claire exchanged a glance and smiled at each other. Claire almost felt sorry for Brendan. Almost.

* * *

Ewan Peters put the phone down and stared at it as if the instrument was to blame for the disturbing phone call. He had briefly met Paul Gregan yesterday – he had known him before that only by his reputation as a prize-winning photographer.

Ewan was cautious by nature and suspicious through bitter experience. Why had Gregan developed this sudden passion for protecting the environment? He had never been active or shown any interest in EnVirowatch until now. And if RTTI were involved in negotiations with an Irish company, as seemed possible, how had they kept it so quiet?

He heard the door open. His wife came into the room and stood in front of him, hands on her hips. Even though she was only five foot one in height, Helen Peters could whip up a towering rage.

"Don't even think about it, Ewan."

"Don't think about what?" he asked, smiling at her.

"That smile doesn't fool me. I know you're off on one of your missions again. All it takes is a phone call and you're gone." She was warming to her subject now, a red flush spreading up from her neck, her breathing becoming more rapid, her green eyes beginning to glitter. "You promised the children. You have a son and a daughter in case you have forgotten. You promised them you would come to the Wildlife Park with us today. For once we were going to have a family outing. A Sunday treat. But no –"

"Helen, listen –"

"No! *You* listen. I'm sick and bloody tired of my hero husband. The Saviour of the Environment. Who are you saving it for? Your children? You don't even know them. You know every blasted effluent licence from here to Timbuktu but you don't know your son and daughter!"

Ewan sat down. "Helen," he said as calmly as he

could, "I have a job to do like any other working man or woman. Why do you always –"

"I'm sick to death of your tired old arguments!"

Ewan gave up as Helen raged on. He always did these days. And what use would it be to trot out his "tired old arguments" again? To point out that many a father had to spend long hours on the job and didn't have the luxury of regular Sunday outings or comfy evenings TV-watching with his kids – ask any surgeon, reporter, newspaper editor, security guard, taxi driver, fisherman! Why were all these people just doing their job in Helen's eyes but *he* was "obsessed", "selfish", "egotistic", "deluded", "a self-appointed hero"? No good to argue. The battle had been lost years ago.

He knew too well from experience that Helen would have her say no matter what. She would list the number of nights she sat watching television while he was away at meetings, the various landmarks in his children's lives that he had missed and the number of decisions she had to take alone because he was away. Her grand finale would be to say that she was, in effect, a single parent. When she calmed down, as she would, he would explain that he only had to meet Paul Gregan for ten minutes. Then it would be the Wildlife Park, as promised.

". . . and you always manage to be missing for parent-teacher meetings. They must think I'm a single parent!"

Ah! The storm was about to blow over. "Are you ready to listen now?" he asked patiently.

Helen glared at him but the glitter in her eyes was losing its angry edge. She nodded to him to go ahead and have his say.

"I have to drop into town to meet a photographer from *Newstrack*. I'll be an hour at most."

"Ha! If I had a pound for every time you said 'an hour tops' I'd be a millionaire. And you never mean it."

"I'll meet you in the park. OK?"

Helen looked at her husband and saw the lines which were beginning to map his heavy schedule on his face. She walked over to him and, reaching up, touched his cheek. "Poor Ewan," she whispered, "you have a world to save from destruction. You don't deserve a wife from hell. I'm sorry, darling."

Ewan held her tightly in his arms, resting his chin on her silky hair. "I love you, Helen. I really will try to spend more time with you and the children. When I —"

She silenced him. She had had enough of his promises. She just said a quick prayer that he would make it to the Wildlife Park before it closed.

*   *   *

The more Claire heard of the proposals the more they interested her. Herbal medicine was a fascinating, fast-growing area.

"All the big players are getting involved now," Jacques pointed out. "It's a multibillion-dollar market in the States."

"It's easier there," Frank grumbled. "They don't

have to worry too much about FDA regulations. American herbal extracts are still classified as food supplements. The European Law is tighter. Look what has happened here with St John's Wort. It can only be bought on prescription now since our Minister had his say."

Vince leaned forward and spoke earnestly to Frank. "We know the laws. Don't forget we manufacture globally. Let RTTI worry about compliance. We would ensure that all manufacturing procedures met quality requirements."

"And RTTI are good at meeting quality requirements? Especially safety?" Claire asked quietly.

Yvette looked sharply at her. "You have a specific point to make here, Claire?"

Before Claire could reply her father interrupted, an impatient edge to his voice. "Don't be coy, Yvette, and don't even think of patronising us. RTTI's safety record, particularly in Asia, is shit. We all know that and we have the evidence to prove it."

Yvette sat back in her chair and smiled at Frank. "Not a man to beat about the bush, are you?" she laughed.

"No," he agreed. "I'm not. And don't try to defend your record with the bullshit excuses you give the media. Dashern have a proud history of responsibility to our employees and the community here. We will not jeopardise that."

"Nobody's asking us to," Brendan snapped. "You surely can't be so stupid as to compare the high-tech operation proposed here with the basic chemical synthesis in underdeveloped countries. Those people are bound to have problems. They are lagging behind in technology, expertise, legislation –"

Frank could feel the blood pound in his head as his son-in-law called him stupid. If only Brendan could see himself, drooling over the Frenchwoman who was playing him like a violin. Frank looked away, knowing that he would lose control if he stayed focused on the handsome face he ached to punch.

Claire's voice was a welcome break in the tense silence. "Why here? Why now?" she asked, looking directly at Yvette as she spoke.

"We were over this ground yesterday, Claire. Such a pity you could not have managed to be with us."

Claire acknowledged the rebuke with a nod but added, "I still want to hear you explain why RTTI are interested in Ireland in general and Dashern in particular."

"Apart from the considerable tax benefits in Ireland?"

"I accept that one," Claire acknowledged. "Just surprised that it has taken RTTI so long to avail of our corporate-friendly tax system."

"Yes, well, hopefully we'll be availing of it in the future. It's also very important to us that you have a highly educated workforce. Good infrastructure, ready access to ports and airports."

"And why Dashern?" Claire prompted.

"Why not?" Yvette countered.

"You do realise, Claire, that the initial approach was made by Dashern," Vince interjected. "It's not as if we are trying to bully you into an arrangement. We do have other options we could explore."

Claire sensed Brendan's eyes boring into her, transmitting waves of anger and resentment. She could feel how much he wanted to reach out and clamp his hand over her mouth. "I would not expect you to make any decisions without exploring all avenues," she said looking directly at Vince. "I'm sure you respect our right to do the same."

"You do have the option of continuing to manufacture detergents and taking the downturn and the loss of profits on the chin," Jacques said.

"Not an option," Brendan said quickly.

Ignoring Brendan, Claire spoke to Jacques. "I have read all the reports, Jacques. I do believe that Dashern should be involved in developing the potential, both pharmaceutical and commercial, of herbal medicine. Provided of course that —"

"Why not leave all the nitty-gritty to our respective legal and technical teams?" Jacques interrupted. "We could be here forever arguing about details and conditions. In reality, all we need at this stage is an agreement in principal between our two companies."

"I'll second that," Yvette said quickly. She paused then, looking around the table, allowing the tawny gaze to rest on each one momentarily. "So, are we agreed that RTTI and Dashern amalgamate manufacturing, marketing and research resources?"

"Agreed," Brendan, Jacques and Vince chorused in unison.

"Claire?" Frank's voice was gentle as he called on her to cast her vote.

All eyes were focused on her. She felt hot, uncomfortable and shaky. Clasping her hands to steady them, she took a deep breath. "I want to make it clear that *my* research is not part of this deal," she said, relieved that her voice sounded strong and clear. "Does everyone accept that?"

Yvette sat forward and spoke slowly, as if Claire would not understand unless everything was explained clearly and simply. "What you are doing is not exclusive, Claire. Our R&D in Zurich is also working on apoptosis. In fact, there is a whole body of research worldwide aimed at curing cancer through manipulation of this process. Perhaps you could benefit from our experience. Especially with clinical trials, which will be the next step after your animal trials."

Claire had to grip the edge of the table to steady her hands. Just how much did these people know about her? True, her interest in apoptosis was no secret. She had published several theoretical papers, long before she had uncovered the real secret of apoptosis. Long before Serum 6. But how did they know about the animal trials? Brendan! The fool!

"My research has nothing to do with Dashern and what goes on in my lab is certainly no business of RTTI," she shot back angrily.

Yvette laughed and tutted. "No need to get upset,

Claire. We do realise that we are negotiating with Dashern and not ClairCo."

Frank and Claire exchanged glances. How did they know about ClairCo? Then they both instinctively turned towards Brendan.

Of course, thought Claire, RTTI would have known for some time. Ever since Brendan had made enquiries from Jeremiah Audley. She now felt seriously alarmed, as she admitted to herself that her husband's loyalty was not to her. Maybe not even to Dashern. Her research was protected by the company structure but was that enough?

Yvette smiled at them and her smile told Claire how easy it had been for the Frenchwoman to get any information she needed from Brendan. But then Brendan would never get what he needed from Yvette. What a satisfying thought! She smiled back at the amber-eyed woman. When she spoke, her tone was formal.

"I support the proposal that Dashern and RTTI join forces to process herbal medicines on the understanding, to be confirmed in writing, that ClairCo and my research are excluded from this deal."

Only Frank's vote remained to be cast. He stood up and walked towards the large window overlooking the plant. Looking out on the warehouses and production buildings, he wondered if any of the people in the room appreciated what this decision meant to him. This was his factory, his life's work, his legacy. What did they know of the struggles, the dreams, the plans, the compromises he had made to bring Dashern to what it was today? If he voted yes, they could work out the legalities, put controls in place, keep the Dashern name, but it would never be his again. On the other hand it would not be Brendan's either. The thought of keeping his son-in-law from having total control was almost reason enough for Frank to go with the vote.

A forklift drove towards the loading bay. Frank noticed that it was driven by Seán Farrell, one of the first employees he had recruited thirty years ago. Dashern owed Seán Farrell for his loyalty and there were many others like him. The way things were looking now with detergent projections, he might have to start laying off staff shortly. A contract with RTTI would ensure continuing and even increased employment for as long as there was money to be made. And herbal medicine was a good bet for the future. Something was going to have to replace increasingly ineffective antibiotics and serious research in phytochemistry was just in its infancy. Why shouldn't Dashern have a slice of that pie? And Claire's research, wherever it would lead, was safe from them.

Seán Farrell disappeared from view and Frank turned back towards the five expectant faces.

"We'll hang on your coat-tails," he announced.

"Does that mean yes?" Yvette asked.

Frank nodded. Yvette walked over to him and kissed him on both cheeks.

The tension in the room evaporated. There was a flurry of mutual backslapping and handshaking before

Frank went to the drinks cabinet and produced a bottle of champagne on ice. Claire got glasses while Vince made a ceremony of opening the bottle.

When the drinks were poured, Frank raised his glass. "To successful mergers!" he said.

They all raised their glasses in salute.

*   *   *

Ewan put the photograph carefully back into the envelope. Paul Gregan had been right. He had some very interesting information. These were top-flight RTTI people visiting with the Dawsons. But what Paul had not realised was that Yvette Previn had known she was being photographed. Ewan knew. He had watched her wield her magic in front of the camera for some time now. She was a huge asset to RTTI. God but she was good! Never missed an opportunity to justify the unjustifiable, to use her extraordinary sexuality to promote RTTI.

"Sure you won't have a drink, Ewan?" Paul asked.

Ewan shook his head. The Mellow Drama was quiet and peaceful on this Sunday afternoon. He was tempted to have a relaxing pint but he *must* make the Wildlife Park.

"Do you think there is a possibility Frank Dawson would sell out to RTTI?" Paul asked.

Ewan shook his head. "I can't understand any of this. If RTTI wanted to manufacture here they would build a factory. It's what they do. Buy a site, build, make money and run. I've watched them operate like this all over the world."

"So you don't think they are suddenly interested in detergents?"

"They would never be interested in anything that clean," Ewan laughed. "If they're interested in the Dashern factory, if, it will be for pharmaceuticals or else . . ."

Paul watched as Ewan seemed to work something through in his mind. Eventually he remembered that Paul was there.

"I have heard a rumour," he said, "that RTTI are interested in breaking into these natural medicines. Herbal cures, that kind of thing. It would make sense for them to hide behind someone else's name for that end of the market. They have already amalgamated with a small but high-profile English company to that end."

"In other words buy a clean image?" Paul asked.

Ewan nodded as he stood up. "I'm just thinking out loud at this stage, Paul. To be honest, I really don't know why they are here. What I do know is that they don't waste the time of top personnel like Jacques Rondel and Yvette Previn on provincial detergent companies. They are up to something and I appreciate your letting me know."

They walked together to the door. It was a lovely sunny afternoon. A great day for the Wildlife Park, Ewan thought as he checked his watch.

"I'll be in touch," Paul said as they reached the car park.

Ewan turned and shook hands with the younger man. Paul felt the same magnetism and power in the warm handshake that he had felt as he listened to Ewan address the EnVirowatch AGM. It was not surprising that this man had such a loyal following, always ready to man his picket lines, to join his protests. He smiled as he thought of Trish's words. Shit! Maybe he did fancy the EnVirowatch leader. All this hero worship was most un-Paul-like!

Paul was just walking away when Ewan called him back.

"There is something else puzzling me, Paul. I don't want you to take this wrongly. I appreciate your help. But your interest in things environmental is very recent, isn't it? May I ask you why?"

Paul hesitated. He would have to answer this question as much for himself as for Ewan. "I trained as a journalist. I chose to specialise in photography but I'm still a journalist at heart. I smell a story. A big one. I can't help feeling there is some sinister reason behind the RTTI presence here."

"I see," Ewan said, making it perfectly obvious that he was still puzzled by Paul's rapid conversion to environmental awareness. "I'd invite you to join EnVirowatch, but if you're going to cover the story there could be a question of conflict of interest."

Paul nodded. "I guess so. But I can keep in touch anyway. Let you know if I come across any more interesting details. Maybe you could do the same?"

"Sure," Ewan agreed as he got into his car.

* * *

As he drove towards the park, Ewan mulled over the implications of the photograph. Dashern had always been a responsible company, co-operating with local authorities on environmental issues. Why were they talking to RTTI? More to the point, why were RTTI talking to Dashern?

He pulled in to the side of the road and switched on his mobile phone. He punched in Liam McCarthy's number. If anyone knew, Liam would. The ringing sound went on and on. Ewan remembered guiltily that it was Sunday and that Liam was probably out with his family. Liam answered just as Ewan had decided that there was no one home.

"I'm sorry for disturbing you on a Sunday, Liam, but there's a little mystery you might help me to clear up."

Liam laughed. "You're all mysteries and intrigue, Ewan. What an interesting life you lead! Tell me about this latest one."

Ewan was thinking carefully about how to phrase his question. While Liam was very willing to share information which he considered rightly belonged in the public arena, he was too principled, and probably too shrewd, to compromise confidentiality. Nor would Ewan expect him to. Pensionable jobs in the Environmental Sector of the Council did not grow on trees.

"I have reason to believe that our local detergent

factory may be talking to a multinational pharmaceutical. A nasty multinational. Any comments?"

"Come on now," Liam laughed. "Are you talking about Dashern? They have expanded over the years but you know they're not in the multinational league. Unless, of course, they have suddenly discovered miraculous healing powers in their dishwasher powder."

"This is serious," Ewan said solemnly. "These people don't waste time unless there is big profit in it for them. I have been told that a high-powered delegation from this multinational has been at the plant for several days. They even attended the Dashern Dinner Dance. Obviously negotiations are far enough advanced for them to show their hand in public."

Liam was silent for a moment and Ewan knew he was mentally trawling through all the paperwork that crossed his desk.

"No," he said eventually. "There has been no application for a new licence, no notification of change of use. Whatever is going on, if indeed there is something going on, it's still at the idea stage."

"You bet your ass there is something going on," Ewan assured him. "And astute as Frank Dawson is, he's no match for these people. They'll chew him up and spit him out, along with a huge chunk of our clean air and water."

Liam sighed. "Ewan, it's Sunday afternoon. You should be out with your wife and family. Maybe if you took some time off from your witch hunt you might have a more balanced view of how the system works."

Ewan was furious with himself. It had not been very clever of him to ring Liam on Sunday. The last thing he wanted to do was to antagonise his Council contact. "I'm sorry for disturbing your time off, Liam. I should have left this call until tomorrow."

"That's not what I'm talking about," Liam said impatiently. "The call is no problem. It's just that, well, you're getting a bit fanatical. Not all multinationals are bad. In fact, the vast majority of them are very responsible. As you well know but don't like to admit."

"Yes. Yes. And they provide employment and boost our GNP. Philanthropists, the lot of them!"

"See what I mean! Calm down, man, and take some rest. How about a game of golf some time? It's been a long time since you gave me the opportunity of beating you on the golf course!"

"You're on," Ewan said.

They arranged to meet before saying goodbye.

Ewan switched off his phone and pulled out into the flow of traffic. He should just make the Wildlife Park before closing time.

*   *   *

Brendan knew his behaviour was juvenile but, try as he might, he could not keep the sulky look off his face as he chauffeured his guests to the airport. Yvette was seated beside him, Vince and Jacques ensconced in the back. They were all in good form, well pleased with their work.

And why not? They had got what they had come for.

"The real business starts now," Jacques said. "These legal people make mountains out of molehills. We'll have to push for early closure if we want to be up and running in any reasonable length of time. We have no deal until the contracts are drawn up and signed. How would you rate Audley as a lawyer, Brendan?"

"Slow but sure," Brendan replied dully. His mind was still on Yvette. What a fuck-up! If only he had met her years before. If, if, if ...

"Our technical team will be over to see you shortly," said Vince. "Then we will all have a clearer picture about the changeover."

"Always better to know exactly where you stand," Yvette said.

Brendan looked sharply at her but she had her head turned away from him, ostensibly to admire the scenery. She had shown him exactly where *he* stood, hadn't she? Even when they had been alone after the Dinner Dance, she had put distance between them. She turned now and smiled at him. His mood did another flip as hope returned.

There was no delay at the check-in. As soon as they had their boarding passes Jacques and Vince decided to go through Departures.

"You two go ahead. I'll follow on," Yvette said. "I just want to pick up a book in the shop here first – for English practice."

"Ten minutes," Jacques called to her as he checked his watch.

Yvette waved at them as she headed for the newsagent's in the Departure Lounge. Brendan shook hands with Jacques and Vince. He felt obliged to wait until they had finally gone through the checkpoint before going after Yvette. When he found her she was carrying a copy of John Grisham's *A Time to Kill.*

"See, Bren," she said laughing, "there is a time for everything." She caught his hand and moved close to him. "There will be a time for us too," she whispered. "But not yet."

Brendan took a deep breath and inhaled her perfume. "I don't want to wait, Yvette. I want to be with you now."

She leaned close to him and whispered in his ear. "We're getting there, Brendan. We're getting there. You just make sure Claire co-operates. You know what we want from her. And from you."

Brendan almost stamped his foot with frustration. "How in the hell can I do anything about her now? RTTI agreed to leave ClairCo out of the equation. And by the way, how did you know R&D was a separate company? I only found out recently myself."

"Ways and means," Yvette laughed and then her expression became serious. She put her hand around the back of his neck and drew his head down to her. Then with her face touching his, her body warming his, she told him to make his wife pregnant. He thought he had not heard properly.

"A baby?" he repeated.

"Yes," she agreed. "A baby. If Claire has something

else besides her work to think about, then she will be a lot more amenable. Think of it as an investment in *our* future." She kissed him on the lips and then, in one swift movement, she was walking away from him, smiling and waving as she went towards the checkpoint.

"Ring me!" he shouted after her.

She blew a kiss in his direction and disappeared from his view. He stood where he was, too confused, too frustrated, to move. It was not until he sensed somebody staring at him that he turned around to head for the exit. He came face to face with Clive Rigney, the supermarket tycoon. What was that little creep doing here and how long had he been watching?

"Just seeing my wife off on a trip. Sad business – this saying goodbye," Clive grinned and just in case Brendan was in any doubt about how much he had seen, he winked lewdly.

Brendan nodded to him and walked away with as much dignity as he could muster. He drove home by the scenic route. He needed time to think.

Chapter Eight

Kevin liked lunch-times in the main canteen. He was enjoying his work and was gradually gaining more confidence as his training progressed but there was an intensity about Claire which made escape to the noisy canteen a treat he looked forward to every day.

R&D had been particularly gloomy these past two weeks. Ever since the dinner dance. It had all started to go wrong when LabAn had failed to send the correct number of animals for the new trial. Mrs Hearn had gone into a quiet fury when only twelve of the eighteen animals ordered had arrived on time. The trial had to be kept on hold until the control animals arrived two days later. And to add to all the doom and gloom, the trials of the serum on the delayed batch had resulted in more animal deaths. Kevin empathised with Claire's disappointment but, even if he had wanted to, he could not share her black depression or get through the protective shell she had built around herself. The only time she had spoken to him in the past few days had been to tell him that his new employment contract was drawn up and that as soon as he signed it he would be employed solely by R&D.

When he had put his signature on the document today, she had shaken his hand and given him a wan smile that did not touch her eyes. He had wanted to ask her what would happen to his job if the serum proved to be a failure; he had wanted to tell her that her husband had been badgering him again for information about the serum. Instead, he respected her unspoken request to allow her suffer in peace and he made his way to the main canteen for lunch.

"Over here, Trill!"

Kevin waved to the gang at the window seat. It had become a habit now for him to join them for lunch. They all lived in the same neighbourhood and knew each other outside of work. He frowned when he noticed that Hilary Curran was with them again. He had never liked Hilary but she was definitely a person to avoid since she had become Brendan Hearn's secretary. Her self-importance knew no bounds. Still, she was one of the gang and Seán Farrell and the lads knew how to put her in her place.

As he queued at the counter Kevin noticed a crowd gathering at the notice board. Must be something serious, he thought, judging by the reactions. As he shuffled along the queue, he looked around the canteen. There were many quiet conversations going on, a lot of heads huddled together. Seán Farrell was leaning forward, an earnest expression on his face, patiently arguing some point with Hilary, while the others looked on solemnly. There *was* something different going on. The bang and clatter of ware was the same as usual but the buzz of conversation was subdued. Curiosity made Kevin walk to his table via the notice board.

MEETING IN THE CANTEEN TODAY THURSDAY 25TH

2PM SHARP

ALL STAFF REQUESTED TO ATTEND

Signed: FRANK DAWSON

"Well. What's that about?" he asked as he unloaded his tray onto the table.

"Hilary knows but she won't say," Seán Farrell replied.

"Not won't. I can't say."

"It's confidential!" they all chorused together and laughed.

Kevin glanced at Hilary's prissy face with the tight mouth and defiant expression in her eyes and he knew that she had as little information as the rest of them.

"I guarantee that it has something to do with that foreign crowd who were around here a few weeks ago," Seán said. "They were not run-of-the-mill customers."

"The woman wasn't run of the mill anyway," Jason, the youngest of the group, remarked. "She had a great pair of …" he glanced at Hilary before saying, "eyes!"

"Maybe we're getting a new order from them,"

Kevin suggested and then remembered that he was not part of the "we". He was now solely R&D and had nothing to do with production.

"Frank never called a meeting before to announce a new order," Seán said dismissively. "In fact, in thirty years this is the first time I can remember him calling a meeting like this."

"There was a meeting when the networked computer system came in," Hilary reminded them.

"That was different," Seán insisted. "And it wasn't called by Frank. That was Brendan Hearn's project."

"Maybe old Dawson is selling out. Or shutting down."

Jason's remark cast a pall of silence over the table. The unspoken redundancy word hovered over them like a vulture.

Kevin's gut twisted at the thought of Ria's reaction. She would be furious if her career plans for her boyfriend were disrupted. Jesus! He could hear her now. "This would never have happened, Kevin, if you were more assertive. How could you allow Dashern to close down? You're hopeless!"

Kevin had been wondering if he should wait for the meeting. But now he made up his mind to stay. Anyway Claire probably wouldn't notice if he were back on time or not. Hilary interrupted his train of thought.

"What have you been doing over in R&D?" she asked. "Brendan Hearn was asking about you this morning. He said I was to look up your employment contract."

"And did you?"

"They told me in Personnel that Mrs Hearn was dealing with it. Brendan was furious. Do you have a special arrangement with the Ice Lady? Just what are you up to over in R&D?"

"Let's make a deal, Hilary. You tell me what the meeting is about and I'll tell you about R&D. Deal?"

"You know I can't break a confidence," she said huffily.

"Snap!" Kevin laughed as they sat back to wait for the meeting to begin.

*   *   *

Claire went through the reports once again. Maybe this time she would see an explanation, a pattern. As she read she got more depressed.

There was no reason Serum 6 should cause respiratory tract infection in the guinea pigs, or no reason that she could fathom. And yet her findings on the autopsy, confirmed by the pathology lab in the veterinary college, was that they had died from just that – viral pneumonia, a particularly virulent strain. Adenovirus in the first batch had seemed like bad luck. But the latest mortalities were inexplicable. She had taken such care.

One by one she mentally ticked off possible causes. The animal housing had been sterilised after the first batch. The fact that this was a different virus reassured her on this point. The serum was sterile and was negative for the virus in cultures.

She went through the mechanism of Serum 6, step by step. It should not, in fact could not, compromise the immune system. By causing the breakdown of diseased cells and encouraging healthy cell reproduction it should have had the opposite effect. But there was no denying that only the animals treated with Serum 6 had developed infections. The control group had suffered only from their cancers.

LabAn had guaranteed the animals free of infectious disease. Claire frowned. Here was one area over which she did not have total control. LabAn was a very reputable firm and had branches all over the globe. In fact, as they had emphasised to her, they were a major supplier of experimental animals to international research facilities. They claimed that they had no other complaints about the quality of the animals they were supplying. And of course, as Ronan Hennessey had been at pains to point out, LabAn had also supplied the control animals and they had shown absolutely no trace of viral infection. But just suppose …

Claire walked over to the filing cabinet and flicked through folders until she found the invoices from LabAn. She brought them back to her desk and studied them. Her first delivery from them had been on time and correct but there had been a problem with the second one. Only twelve animals had been delivered though in fact she had ordered eighteen. When she had phoned LabAn, looking for the six animals missing from her order, they had said some problem with supply had prevented them from delivering all eighteen animals on the same day. She kept staring at the invoices but they told her nothing more than she already knew. All her trial animals treated with Serum 6 had developed viral infections, while the controls had not.

So, was it possible, despite LabAn's assurances, that the control animals were from a different source and that the trial animals had been infected even before they were given the serum? For that to be true it would have had to happen twice. Neither set of controls had died from infection.

Claire thumped the desk with frustration. She had spoken to LabAn several times about the possibility of the animals bringing the infection with them but they had been very emphatic in their denial and had the paperwork to back their claims. Maybe she was just looking for any excuse rather than admit that the serum was causing unexpected problems.

She returned the invoices to the cabinet. As she dropped them into the LabAn file she noticed the release certificates for the animals. She took them out to recheck. Yes. Each animal was certified free from infectious disease at the date of delivery. The signature on the forms was very distinctive. Ronan Hennessey had signed them with his boldly written, backslanted signature. He was proving to be very elusive since she started asking questions. They said he was away on holidays but Claire had her doubts. She flipped through the release certificates and then stopped and went through them more slowly. Not all the certificates bore the signature of Ronan Hennessey. Most did . . . except . . . yes! Except the control batches! The only experimental animals supplied by LabAn that had not died of respiratory infection! These certificates were signed by Anne T Moroney.

Claire sat down and mentally trawled through the data again. When she had finished the outcome was very clear. All the animals cleared by Ronan Hennessey had been for treatment with Serum 6. They had been separated from the control group and clearly marked as the treatment batch. He had told her he would do this for her convenience and she had been grateful. The animals marked and used as controls had been cleared by Anne Moroney. What if? What if Claire had swapped the groups around? What would the outcome have been?

Claire picked up the phone and then sat there with the receiver in her hand. Ringing LabAn again would be utterly pointless. They were making it clear that she was really beginning to annoy them. She could not get past Reception on the phone and it was Mr Ronan Hennessey she needed to talk to. Anyway, what could she say? "Hello, Mr Hennessey. I believe you sent me infected animals for my trial! And, yes, the animals Anne Moroney sent were satisfactory!"

Putting the receiver back on the cradle, she scribbled a quick note to Kevin: *Gone to LabAn. See you tomorrow.*

She propped the note against the phone, took off her lab coat, grabbed her car keys and locked up the lab before she could be stopped by the voice in her head telling her that she was just desperate for any excuse to justify her serum, that she was clutching at straws, that she was totally mad.

As she rushed to the car park, she was too preoccupied to notice the crowds heading for the canteen. LabAn was fifty kilometres away. She would have her head together by the time she reached there.

* * *

Frank waved Brendan to a seat while he continued his conversation on the phone. The old man's head was a deep shade of puce. Brendan felt a momentary sympathy for him. This was a big day for his father-in-law. Having been lord and master for thirty years, he was now going to have to tell his loyal and faithful followers that he was no longer the sovereign ruler. The sympathy evaporated quickly in a wave of resentment. Frank Dawson's reign would have ended a long time ago if it were not for Brendan's astute management and forward thinking. The man was a dinosaur.

A snippet of the conversation caught Brendan's attention.

"No, no. I know you are the PR expert and I appreciate your advice but –"

He must be talking to Yvette. Unless he was hiring a PR firm to handle the merger?

"I'll see you next week then. And thank you. *Au revoir.*"

Ah! That must be Yvette!

"Yvette Previn?" Brendan asked.

Frank nodded.

"I didn't know she was due to visit again. She hasn't mentioned it."

Frank stared at his son-in-law. "She's not. I'm meeting her in London. Not that it's any of your business."

"Of course it's my business. Unless, of course, your meeting with her is personal. How in the hell can we bring this merger forward if you are going to have secret meetings behind my back?"

Frank sat back and laughed. "That's rich coming from you! As a matter of fact she's visiting RTTI's British plant next week. There are parallels between that plant and ours and she's going to show me around. Let me see the phytochemistry operation up and running. Satisfied?"

Brendan took a deep breath and bit back his angry reply. The old fucker was teasing him. Hoping to push him into an admission. Brendan had to remind himself that his plans were long term. He and Yvette would eventually have it all. But why hadn't she told him about the London trip?

"That should be interesting. Maybe I should go along too. Pick up some pointers."

"Stay away from her," Frank snapped. "You might enjoy making a right prick of yourself but you are not going to mess around with my daughter's life. You do realise the Frenchwoman is playing you for a fool, don't you? She has no interest in you."

Brendan smiled and wondered if Claire had told her father of Yvette's "lesbian" confession. What an inspired idea!

"It's five minutes to two," he said. "Are you ready for this meeting, Frank?"

All the aggression seemed to seep out of the older man. His shoulders slumped and in an instant he seemed to change from being the aggressive bollocks he usually was into a tired, sick old man. He rubbed his hands over his eyes and looked up. Brendan stood and walked over to him. He put a hand on the stooped shoulders. The intensity of their love-hate relationship was reflected on both their faces.

They walked together to the canteen.

*   *   *

The silence in the canteen deepened as the hands of the clock swept towards two. Comments were whispered now and loud laughs had become quiet giggles.

"He's on the way," someone warned and all eyes focused on the door.

Frank walked straight to the notice board and stood in front of it, slowly looking around and taking in the sea of expectant faces. His eyes met Seán Farrell's. He tried to smile reassurance. Someone brought a chair for him but he waved it away.

"Are you OK? Do you want me to do the talking?"

Brendan asked quietly.

Frank shook his head and, pulling back his shoulders, took a deep breath.

"Thank you all for coming here. I won't delay you long but I have some important information to give you."

He paused and in the silence the room shimmered with tension.

"Dashern Chemicals is at a crossroads," he continued. "Thirty years ago I started manufacturing industrial detergent here with little more than one contract and a lot of hope. Seán Farrell can vouch for that," he added with a smile as he nodded in Seán's direction. "Over the years we have grown and diversified. Dawson Chemicals became Dashern. One contract became one hundred. Three employees have become one hundred and twenty. Our product range now covers domestic as well as industrial detergent."

Frank could see that they were hanging on his every word and wishing that he would cut the history lesson and get to the point.

"You'll all be aware that while our domestic market is steady, we depend mainly on exports. Unfortunately, in the present climate, the international market for detergents is getting more competitive and less profitable."

Frank thought he heard someone groan and he rushed ahead, anxious to get the bad-news part over and done with.

"Amlicon is one of our biggest customers. You all

know that. One-third of our production has been to fill their order. I have to tell you today that Amlicon will be downsizing their order with immediate effect. They will phase it out completely over six months."

The loudest gasp came from Brendan, who was standing on Frank's right-hand side. He was not surprised that the order was going. This was the point he had been trying to argue with Frank for so long. But he was shocked that it was going so soon and that the old bastard had chosen not to tell him in advance of the meeting. He was struggling now to keep a neutral expression on his face when every instinct was straining to thump the shit out of the old man. How long had he known about this? Was this why he had seemed to cave in and reluctantly accept the RTTI proposals?

Frank raised his hand to silence the murmurs.

"So, as I said at the outset," he continued, "we are at a crossroads. And Dashern is about to take a new direction. Our priority is continued and increased employment in Dashern. To this end we are negotiating a merger with RTTI, an international pharmaceutical company. I'm sure you have all heard of them. We will be processing herbal medicines on contract for RTTI."

The shuffling and coughing told Frank that he was not succeeding in reassuring anyone. Seán Farrell stared back at him, a look of disbelief on his face.

"Over a period of months we, under the guidance of an RTTI technical and engineering team, will be scaling down detergent production and adapting existing facilities, installing new machinery and training personnel. The target is to have Dashern-RTTI up and running and processing herbal medicines in six months' time."

"But how –" someone started to ask.

Frank interrupted straight away. "When I have finished, Mr Hearn will take your questions and answer them as best he can."

Brendan looked at the anxious faces, his smile hiding the murderous thoughts in his head. God! How he hated this devious man! Now he was going to leave him to face the frightened workforce, to give guarantees that were optimistic at best. It was obvious some of them would have to go under the new structure. The less educated, the older employees, would have no place in the new operation. Frank knew this too, didn't he? The – the . . . Brendan could not think of a term low enough to describe his father-in-law. Instead he continued to smile and seethe as he listened to Frank bring his speech to a conclusion.

"Herbal medicine is a huge growth area. Dashern are proud to announce our association with RTTI. There are a lot of legal issues regarding the merger yet to be agreed but the respective legal teams are working on them. I am confident that we will shortly be ready to begin our new phase as Dashern-RTTI. We can all look forward to increased prosperity and security as we embark on this journey with the company which once was known as Dawson Chemicals. Thank you for your patience and courtesy in listening to me. Mr Hearn will now take questions."

Frank smiled at Brendan, a challenge in his eyes. Then he turned and walked out of the canteen. He went straight to his office and opened the drinks cabinet. His hand was shaking as he poured a glass of brandy.

* * *

Under different circumstances Claire would have enjoyed this trip. As she drove through picturesque villages and busy little market towns she decided she would bring Dorothy this way for a spin some day. They could stop at one of the roadside cafés for tea and browse in the many craft shops dotted along the route. Even as she planned, Claire admitted to herself that the trip would never materialise. There was too much to do. Too little time.

Nearing the town where LabAn had their premises, she glanced again at the address she had scribbled on a piece of paper. She would have to find the Industrial Estate and then Unit 32. The town was neat and clean and all facilities well signposted. She found herself parked outside LabAn before she had decided exactly what she was going to say to them. She locked the car and headed for the reception area without any clear idea of which approach she was going to take.

"May I speak with Ronan Hennessey, please?"

The receptionist looked at her with disinterest. She sighed as she picked up the microphone for the intercom system.

"Your name, please?"

"Claire Hearn."

"Oh!" she said just as she was about to press the On button. "Dr Hearn. Mr Hennessey is on holidays. Is there anyone else you would like to speak to?"

"Anne Moroney then, please."

"Anne Moroney to Reception. Anne Moroney to Reception."

Claire took a seat in the waiting area and looked around her. LabAn gave a clinically clean and professional impression, despite the unenthusiastic receptionist. Framed quality standard certifications, awards and photographs hung on the walls, breaking the monotony of the plain white tiling. She stood up to inspect them, walking slowly from one to the other. There was a photograph of Ronan Hennessey. Claire thought Ronan looked like his signature. Big and bold.

The door marked *Authorised Personnel Only* opened and a small freckle-faced girl came towards Claire, hand outstretched.

"Dr Hearn. I'm Anne Moroney. I am Mr Hennessey's assistant. How may I help you?"

Claire smiled at her. "I'm using guinea pigs supplied by LabAn in trials I'm running."

Anne nodded her head and Claire thought she saw a flicker of fear cross the girl's face. She continued on quickly, anxious not to put the girl on the defensive. "I need to audit your premises in order to complete my reports. It would just mean showing me where the animals are housed and looking at their feeding and health records. I know this is short notice but would it be possible to do it now?"

Anne fiddled with nervous fingers at her gold neck-chain. Her eyes darted from the receptionist to Claire.

"I have a deadline to meet with my reports and I'm running late. It would be a great help if I could get this audit done today," Claire pushed on, in an attempt to make Anne's mind up for her.

"Well. Mr Hennessey is not here but I suppose . . ."

The receptionist had obviously been listening because she slid the visitor's book towards Claire.

"Sign here please and put on the protective clothing and goggles provided in the closet by the door before entering the authorised area."

Claire wondered how many times the receptionist had chanted these instructions in that bored tone.

But she was wrong. Sylvia was not bored. She was enjoying every minute of this. Anne Moroney's little deception was catching up with her now. Her scared white face was a treat. Sylvia felt so exhilarated that she even helped Claire to put on the protective clothing.

As she followed Anne through the Microbiology and Biochemistry labs, Claire began to panic. What in the name of Christ was she doing here? What did she hope to find? All she had seen so far was an efficient and well-run breeding facility. She tried to listen as Anne showed her around the animal food store and explained the dietary records in detail.

"And this is my office," Anne said as she led the way into a small room which contained a desk, computer, filing cabinet and two chairs. "Sit down, Mrs Hearn, please."

Claire looked at her in surprise. The girl's attitude had changed completely. The nervousness was still there but it was mixed with a strong undertone of determination.

"I know why you're here," said Anne.

Claire was so taken aback that she couldn't say anything. She took the seat the girl had offered and waited for her to continue.

"Mr Hennessey deals personally with your order for trial animals. My only responsibility is to select induced-carcinoma animals at random, mark them as controls and prepare them for transport. He told me you're carrying out some very important research on a cancer cure and that he wanted to ensure that the animals we supplied to you were top grade."

"That's reassuring," Claire said and then added, "Carry on," as Anne seemed to lapse into silence.

The girl took a deep breath before continuing. "Well, the truth is, I made a mistake with your last order. I never checked the order sheet. I understood you only needed twelve trial animals and that is what I told Mr Hennessey."

Now Claire understood why only part of her last order had arrived on time.

Anne was still talking, explaining nervously. "Mr Hennessey checked with me about controls and I assured him you hadn't ordered any. He went on a big rant about it being bad practice not to use controls. He was in foul humour anyway because he was due to go on holidays."

Claire nodded, remembering that would have been the Friday before the Dashern Dinner Dance. The day she had first met Yvette Previn and her two sidekicks from RTTI.

"He actually delayed going away because of your order, Mrs Hearn. He came in Saturday and Sunday to prep the animals for delivery on Monday. He said that he wanted to make sure everything was up to spec with this batch."

"What did he mean? Did he say there had been a problem with the previous one?"

Claire's question was so sharp that the young girl started. "No. Not directly anyway," she answered. "But I did get the impression there was something wrong."

Claire was silent as she thought back over the whole Adenovirus episode. She was almost sure – no, she was absolutely certain – that she had not told LabAn about the virus until the following week. Had she not decided to wait for confirmation from the veterinary college? Yes. She had. So why was Ronan Hennessey hinting at problems then? Or had this nervous girl just misunderstood?

"Well, your new batch of animals was delivered on Monday as you know," Anne continued, "and then you rang looking for the six that had not been delivered. That was when I discovered my mistake – when I realised that you had actually ordered eighteen animals, not twelve as I had told Mr Hennessey."

"By then Ronan Hennessey had gone on holiday so you decided to prepare and send six animals yourself.

Am I right?"

Anne nodded. She was so pale that the freckles stood out on her face like dark splotches on a blank canvas. The girl seemed terrified.

"The problem was, I had no idea how, or why, he prepared your animals. What special treatment he gave them. There were no instructions, either from him or from you. He was not contactable. I just didn't know what to do."

"Why didn't you ring me?"

"God! How I've wished since that I had! I suppose I didn't want to admit I had made a mistake."

"So what, Anne? We all make mistakes."

"You don't know Ronan Hennessey like –" Anne stopped abruptly and her eyes were huge as she looked at Claire.

"The six animals you sent me didn't cause any problems, Anne. They were used as controls and their pathology and mortality rates were exactly as I expected them to be. My query is with the other twelve animals. The ones I now know were prepared by Ronan Hennessey. My trial results on those twelve animals are puzzling. As they were on the previous batch. I am just trying to investigate every possible avenue to sort the problem. You have no idea why he quarantined my animals before he sent them to me? What special treatment he gave them?"

"On each occasion he separated your order before delivery and looked after them himself. He only allowed me to choose your random controls. Which is exactly what I did with your last order. They were just six randomly selected, carcinoma-induced, virus-free animals. I should have contacted you. I'm really sorry."

Claire smiled at the pale-faced girl and tried to reassure her. "No need to apologise, Anne. And as for Ronan Hennessey – well, he doesn't have to know about this, does he?"

"He knows about everything. And what he doesn't see himself, Sylvia tells him. She's the receptionist you met on your way in. Anyway, he'll come across the records."

They were both silent, each thinking about their own problems.

Anne suddenly sat up straight and smiled. "There's one good thing at least," she said brightly. "Mr Hennessey may not be here for some time. He was due to make a detour to Zurich on his way back from his holidays. His visits with RTTI often take longer than planned. I'm hoping . . ."

Claire did not take in another word Anne was saying. All she could hear echoing in her head was "RTTI, RTTI . . ." Could this be coincidence? The man who was supplying, and paying individual attention to, her trial animals was at this minute closeted in RTTI headquarters in Zurich! She rubbed her temples with her fingers. This was mad. Totally insane. Intrigue and deceit over guinea pigs! But yet . . .

"Anne, could I have eighteen more guineas now? Eighteen tumour-induced animals."

Anne looked doubtful.

"I'll take responsibility with Ronan Hennessey if he causes any trouble for you," Claire pressed on. "It's not reasonable to refuse a customer request, is it?"

Anne smiled and stood up. "This way," she said, leading Claire into the animal store where the familiar squeaks and squeals made Claire feel instantly more relaxed. She strolled around, admiring and even envying the marvellous organisation and state-of-the-art housing. As she passed by a corner cage a black, fluffy guinea pig caught her attention. He had his nose to the bars, sniffing and looking at her with curiosity. She laughed out loud – he was such a funny little fellow.

"He has a squint!" she remarked to Anne as she watched his antics.

"Yes. We call him Clarence. He's been with us for two months now. But his tumour is growing rapidly. See it on the side of his neck?"

"Oh! Poor Clarence!" Claire said and he twitched his nose as if in reply.

"Could you help him?"

"I'll try," Claire promised. "Just get me seventeen others with Clarence and we'll see how they go."

Anne boxed the animals for transport, ploughed through the paperwork and then helped Claire load them onto the back seat of the car.

"Remember, if Ronan Hennessey has any problem with this, refer him to me," she reminded a worried-looking Anne before she drove off.

Of course she would not hear from Ronan Hennessey. What could he say? "You can't use any animals unless

I've infected them?" Claire almost crossed over into oncoming traffic as she allowed the thought of sabotage to take form in her head. She banished the hideous notion. She could not cope with it now.

* * *

It was already dark by the time Claire got back to the plant. She unloaded the animals and prepared their bedding and water-bottles. When she opened the transport boxes Clarence squinted up at her, his head to one side, favouring the bulge of the huge tumour on his neck. She picked him up and his soft, warm body nestled against her. She rubbed his fluffy fur and laughed as he sniffed at her fingers.

"You poor, sick, little fellow," she crooned softly. "I promise you, Clarence, we'll cure you. We'll make you feel better."

On an impulse she prepared a separate cage for Clarence and gently placed him in it.

"You're special, Clarence," she told him.

Then, even though she knew she was alone, she looked guiltily around. Maybe she *was* going mad. She was imagining plots at every twist and turn and now she was talking to a guinea pig! Clarence stared back at her, his crossed eyes focusing in different directions. Two misfits: Clarence and Claire.

"To hell with them all, Clarence!" she said defiantly, loud and clear. "We'll show them!"

A laugh rang out behind her. She dropped

Clarence's water-bottle to the floor and whirled around in terror.

Brendan was leaning against the doorframe, his arms folded across his chest, a grin on his face.

"How did you get in? How long have you been here?" Claire snapped at him, her voice still trembling with shock.

His grin faded and anger flashed in his eyes. "If you really want to lock me out, Claire, you should remember to close the door after you. And in answer to your second question, I've been here long enough to hear you have more conversation with the guinea pig than you have had with me in a year."

Claire nodded, remembering that she had meant to go back to close the entrance door after she had unloaded the animals. Careless.

"What do you want?" she asked brusquely as she picked up shards of broken glass.

Brendan got the dustpan and brush and began to sweep up the splinters, which had scattered in a wide arc around the animal room.

"Where were you at two o' clock today?" he asked

"I was busy. Why?"

He dropped the brush and in one quick move he was standing in front of her, both her arms held in a vice-like grip. He was as angry as she had ever seen him.

"Because, you selfish little bitch, your father needed you today. He had to stand in the canteen and admit to his staff that he could not continue on here without the help of RTTI. Have you any idea how hard that was for him?"

Jesus Christ! She had forgotten all about the meeting! Oh, God! She should have been there, standing with her father. He had asked her and she had promised. A cold dread swept through her.

"Is he all right? Please tell me he's all right!"

Brendan dropped his hands in disgust. "Yes. He's all right. But do you care? Do you care about anything except your precious research?"

"That's not fair! Of course I care. You're one to talk anyway. Your only interest is in grabbing more and more power. Dashern is too small for your ego now, so you had to drag RTTI in to make it fit your inflated self-image!"

"At least I have a more realistic view of my abilities than you have," Brendan said angrily. "I'm not the one making claims about miracle cures. Where do you think you're going with this work, Claire? Are you going to stay buried in your gingerbread lab, fooling around with genes and proteins, or whatever, until you're an old woman?"

"How dare you!" Claire shouted so loudly that the animals squeaked in fright. "I am not fooling around, as you put it! I'm almost there, Brendan. My work is almost finished. If you had ever shown any interest in what I'm doing you would know that!"

Claire turned her back on him and swept up the remainder of the glass. After dumping it in the glass bin, she filled a new bottle for Clarence and clipped it onto his cage. He put his pink mouth on the dropper and drank thirstily. As she watched Clarence, her anger began to cool. She heard Brendan walk up behind her but she kept watching the guinea pig.

"I *am* interested in your work, Claire," he said. "I'm sorry I was sarcastic about it. We can talk about it now. Tell me about it. Tell me about your animal trials."

Claire turned around to face him. They stared at each other. The flint in his eyes did not match the softness of his voice.

"I'd love to tell you, Brendan. I'd like the two of us to sit down with a bottle of wine and talk and talk and talk. I'd tell you about my research, my findings, my animal trials, my ambitions, my hopes, my plans. Everything you want to know. But who else would I be telling?"

She watched the smile which had begun to lift the corners of his mouth disappear. "You're two years and a merger too late," she said coldly. "Not to mention the Mademoiselle Yvette."

She walked away from him and checked that everything in the lab was in order. At the door she reached for the light switch.

Brendan did not move, forcing her to speak to him. "Are you ready to go?"

She flicked the switch and the lab was plunged into gloom, lit only by the emergency lighting. As she walked along the corridor she heard his footsteps behind her. She quickened her step.

"Claire. I want you to have our baby."

Her legs refused to move. She stood stock-still and closed her eyes. She had wanted to hear him say those words for so long. He was standing close behind her now and she was aware of the heat from his body, the smell of his aftershave.

"A son," he whispered. "Young Brendan Hearn. With his mother's intelligence and his father's ambition, he could change the world. Make it a better place."

Claire opened her eyes and faced reality. Brendan wanted an heir, a little Brendan to grow in his shadow, a son to inherit the shares he had paid for so dearly. And then, when he could, he would take his son and his shares and leave her. She turned to her husband. They stood face to face in the dimly lit corridor.

"You don't love me, Brendan," she stated flatly.

He reached up and gently stroked her cheek with his strong fingers. Lifting her hair, he kissed her neck. Claire closed her eyes and savoured the warmth of his mouth. His hands moved over her back and her arms automatically slid around his neck. When his tongue gently opened her lips and slid into her mouth, the familiar hot burning sensation coursed through her. Her pelvis arched towards his and she felt the answering hardness in him press into her.

Suddenly he pulled away from her. "Not in front of Clarence!" he laughed.

Claire blushed, in self-disgust and embarrassment. Brendan knew the power he had over her and she, stupid, stupid bitch, allowed him to wield it.

As she was locking the door, she remembered her father.

"Where is my father now? At home?"

"No. He and Dorothy are at the Golf Club. I came here to collect you and take you back there."

She looked at him in surprise.

"I thought your father could use a little moral support so I booked dinner there for Frank and Dorothy, you and me. He needs his family around him tonight. Well?"

"Of course," she replied quickly. "That's very thoughtful of you. Give me half an hour to shower and change and I'll join you."

Brendan stood behind her as she keyed in the alarm code. He committed the sequence to memory. He also took note of the name of the security company. John Gleeson Alarm Systems Ltd. Then he stooped and kissed her softly on the lips.

Chapter Nine

Paul cursed when he looked at his watch. Time was getting on and he had promised Trish that he would finish early. She would be in a panic by now. The dinner party had seemed like a good idea a week ago. A good career move. Just a little get-together. A civilised way to build a relationship with an important contact. Someone Paul was convinced would one day have national, even international, importance. Four guests, good food and wine, some music, a lot of chat. Nice and relaxing. Like hell! he thought as he remembered Trish this morning, making shopping lists and checking cookery books, wavering between one recipe and the next. The tension must have reached a crescendo by now.

He decided to head for the office. He still had a flower show to cover but if he could arrange for a freelancer to do that he could go home. Shane Harvey, a local photographer, would probably be glad of the work.

The office was quiet. It usually was on Saturday. He phoned Shane Harvey who agreed to cover the rest of his assignments for the day. Just as he was about to leave for home, he noticed a light on in the Editor's office. He stood staring in the direction of Myles Flannery's lair. Was now the right time to approach the boss? If he waited any longer he could lose whatever slim chance he had of persuading the Editor. Someone else would get the job. Or more likely the Nationals would grab it. He walked quickly towards the light and knocked on Myles Flannery's door.

"Come in, Paul. How are you?"

Myles, peering over his bifocals, looked somewhat like a benign grandad, one who would indulge and spoil his grandchildren with great good humour. Everyone who worked under his regime knew that this was a completely false impression. Indulgence and good humour were not on Myles Flannery's agenda.

Paul took a deep breath and then plunged in. "I'd like to talk to you about an idea I have for a feature. A series of features in fact."

Myles continued to stare. Paul knew from experience that he should wait until given permission to continue.

"A journalistic feature?" Myles asked at last.

Paul nodded.

"Sit down then and shoot."

Paul told him about EnVirowatch, about Ewan

Peters, about RTTI and Dashern, about his own newfound awareness of environmental protection.

"I believe, Myles, that Ewan Peters is on the way to becoming a national figure. He has the commitment, the charisma and the support network in place. He is going to get increasingly more important on the local and national scene. And RTTI need to be carefully watched. There is no reason to believe that they play by any rules other than their own."

"And you propose that *Newstrack* set themselves up as environmental vigilantes?"

Paul bit back his immediate response and thought about his reply. He must prove to Myles that the feature would meet the most important *Newstrack* criteria. In other words that it would increase sales and prestige for the paper. "There is something big going on in Dashern and we are well placed to get inside information. I think *Newstrack* should be the paper to break the story and I want to be the one to write it."

"A big story about a small-time chemical outfit merging with a multinational to process herbal medicines? *This* is your big story? Jim Conrad covered Frank Dawson's announcement in his current affairs column during the week. I can't say there has been any huge public reaction to the announcement."

So! Myles was watching too, keeping abreast of developments in Dashern.

"I think there's more going on than meets the eye," Paul answered. "Why are RTTI interested in moving in here? They are global. What is their interest in this little corner of the world?"

"Tax incentives," Myles replied.

"Then they would have availed of them a long time ago. No. I have no doubt that profits are a big part of their motivation but why here and why now? I would like the chance to investigate."

The Saturday silence intensified in the office. Myles was weighing the pros and cons. Paul gauged that the time was right for some significant grovelling.

"I would really appreciate the opportunity, Myles. Perhaps if I wrote one feature article you could judge from there."

Myles cracked his knuckles in the silence and Paul had to grit his teeth.

"I could go with the story," said Myles at last, "if there is one, but get Jim Conrad to write it."

Easy now, Paul warned himself. Myles was taking the bait but needed some careful reeling in. "Of course. Jim is your senior writer. But I did qualify as a journalist, as you know."

"You chose photography as a career."

"Well, yes," Paul agreed, "but I haven't lost any of my journalistic instincts."

Myles pushed his glasses further down on his nose and Paul was hit with the full glare of the green eyes. "Right. Go ahead."

Paul was stunned. Had he heard correctly? After all the glares and silences, Myles had suddenly capitulated. He started to thank him but the Editor held up his hand.

"Just have the first article on my desk next Wednesday. We'll see where we go from there." He pushed his glasses back up on his nose and picked up the spreadsheet he had been reading when Paul had come in.

Paul walked slowly out of the office, through the newsroom and into the car park. Then, with a loud whoop, he ran towards his car.

*   *   *

Kevin always looked forward to the Saturday match from one end of the week to the next but today's game been a disaster for his team. Beaten 4-0 and one of the scores an own-goal. He was not in the best mood for Paul and Trish's dinner party. Ria's continuous prattling as they drove along was not helping either.

"Guess who I met today?" she asked.

"Who?" Kevin inquired disinterestedly, one part of his attention on the road and the other still thinking about the soccer match. That ref was a dickhead –

"Claire Hearn."

Kevin gripped the steering wheel tightly. Oh, no! Ria was a loose cannon at the best of times but she could be really lethal around a Hearn.

"Tell me," he muttered.

"You know I was in the town this morning before work. I had an early appointment in the beauty centre to have my eyebrows plucked. I got a facial too. Didn't you notice?"

"Yes. Lovely," Kevin agreed.

"Well, I wanted to look my best for tonight. Who do you think the mystery guests are? Bound to be someone very famous. Trish couldn't tell me who they are, in case word got out and her apartment would be mobbed with screaming fans."

"Trish couldn't tell you because you would have told half the town within five minutes."

"She didn't tell you either," Ria said sharply. "So are you a gossip too?"

Kevin looked across at her. Her face was flushed and her bottom lip was starting to quiver. Shit! He had really upset her now. She looked like a child whose toy had broken. He took one hand off the steering wheel and reached over to her.

"I didn't mean you're a gossip, Ria. I know you're not. Not in a nasty way. But you know what I always say?"

"Think before you speak!" they chorused together and then they both laughed. The threat of tears was gone.

"Anyway I was in my cubicle in the salon," Ria continued, "lying there with my face mask soaking in, when I heard Mrs Hearn being brought into the cubicle next door."

"You heard?"

"OK, I went out and peeped because I thought I recognised her voice. We get along very well, you know. And you should be glad we do because I can ask her questions you can't."

Jesus! What questions? Kevin held his breath in dread.

"People like her don't understand real life, Kevin. I explained to her that we were saving to get a deposit on a house but that with inflation house prices were rocketing. I asked her about your pay scale and if the annual increase would be index-linked. And I asked her were your promotion prospects affected because you were employed by her now and not by Dashern."

"You didn't ask her to fire me by any chance?"

"Don't be stupid! I explained to her that when we went to look for a mortgage, it would be very important to be able to say you had good employment prospects. These things impress bank managers. She understood and said the research you're doing is very important and that your pay will reflect that. And … wait for this …"

"I can hardly wait," Kevin muttered through clenched teeth.

"She said that when the basic research is finished she will probably need more staff for validation work, or something like that. Your training will be finished then and you'll be senior. She'll probably make you manager and she could retire and you would be totally in charge and you'd probably get a company car and –"

"Ria!"

"OK! OK! I'm getting carried away. But she did say that the R&D department would expand and that she was very pleased with your work. I invited her to come for a drink with us some night."

"I'm sure she agreed."

"Yes, she did. You're to let her know when."

Kevin laughed more with relief than amusement. It could have been worse. Considering.

*　　　*　　　*

When Paul walked into the kitchen, the atmosphere was one of controlled hysteria. He stood behind Trish as she furiously chopped parsley. He slipped his arms around her and she turned to face him, the knife still in her hand.

"Hey, drop the weapon!"

They both laughed and Trish had to admit that she was dangerously over the top. This was their first dinner party and she was so anxious to impress that she was uncharacteristically hysterical. As if that was not enough, she also had the worry of knowing that Ria had been in sole charge of Travelbug all day. Unsupervised.

"Any news from our special guests?" Paul asked.

"She rang this afternoon. He's back from Dublin. Both of them will definitely be here tonight. So it's six, as planned."

Paul smiled. Everything was beginning to fall into place very nicely.

"I'm sorry," she said, "I know I'm hyper but this is all new to me and I'm so nervous about meeting them. Especially him. I so want it to be a success."

"It will be," Paul reassured her. "Because it's going to be a celebration now. Flannery has given me the go-ahead to do the feature!"

Trish dropped her chopping knife and threw her arms around him. "Well done! Well done! I knew you could do it!"

Paul pushed her gently away and laughed. "Take it easy. It's a bit too soon for gloating. Myles may yet decide to go with the features I have suggested but ask Jim Conrad to cover them. I only got the go-ahead for one article."

She lowered her arms and a look of complete panic came over her face. "It's even more important now that dinner is a success. You'll need all the contacts you can get. What am I going to do?"

"Go and get yourself ready," Paul suggested. "Your Beef Bourguignonne smells delicious. The rice is bubbling away. Starters ready. Wine breathing. Dessert cooling. Candles flickering. What more do we need to do?"

"I need to calm down. I need to do casual but sophisticated, gracious but welcoming, as befits the partner of Ireland's leading journalist!"

"You go and have your shower," Paul laughed. "And Trish," he added as she was about to rush away, "not a word about the feature. Let it be our secret for tonight. Especially from Ria. Flannery may yet opt for Conrad so the fewer people that know the better."

She ran back and hugged him. "You'll do it, clever clogs!"

Glancing at her watch Trish saw that it was already a quarter to eight. Where had the time gone? She'd been a hive of activity since nine o'clock this morning, shopping, cleaning, peeling, chopping, stirring, but yet here she was rushing at the last minute.

"I'd better get ready. Ria is bound to be early. And gorgeous."

"Go on. Get going," he urged, giving her a tap on the bottom.

Trish had never showered and dressed so quickly. She was just finishing her make-up when the doorbell rang. She heard Paul greet Kevin and Ria. A touch of mascara and lipstick and she was ready. She closed her eyes for one second and said a quick prayer that nothing would burn or be too hot or too cold.

When she went to the lounge Paul had already poured drinks. She opted for a G&T. She had just taken one fortifying gulp when the doorbell rang again.

"Your mystery guests," Ria announced with excitement.

"No mystery," Trish explained as Paul went to the door. "It was just that we weren't sure they could make it tonight. They couldn't be certain until this evening. He's a very busy man."

"Oh! Important! Isn't this interesting?" Ria said. Leaning over she nudged Kevin in the ribs and whispered in his ear. "It's Prince Charles and Camilla! I know it! Or maybe Posh and Becks!"

Kevin turned to glare at her but then he saw the twinkle in her eyes. She was teasing him. *Touché!*

Paul ushered Ewan and Helen Peters into the lounge. It was a large airy room but Ewan seemed to dwarf it. His wife looked tiny by his side. As Trish walked forward, hand outstretched, to greet her guests,

Ria announced, "It's the Green Man! The one who hates pylons and factories and politicians!"

"The very same," Ewan agreed with an amused grin and they all laughed. They were at ease in each other's company by the time they sat down to eat.

*   *   *

Claire had meant to feed the animals on her way back from her trip to the beauty salon this morning and then go straight home. She had a vague plan for a lazy Saturday. A little housework. Maybe some television and reading. That plan had unravelled as she started filling out the patent application. These forms were so complex that the hours had flown past unnoticed. As she wrote the abstract, she was impressed yet again with the simplicity of the answer to the old question of the cancer cure. The secret had been embedded in the intricacies of human biochemistry all along, just sitting quietly, waiting to be released and unleashed on mutant malignant cells, the cure as natural as the disease was unnatural.

Sealing the envelope with the forms safely inside, she put it into her bag. This envelope would not leave her hand until she passed it over to Jeremiah Audley. He would deal with all the intricacies of filing for patent. One step nearer protecting her serum. Once the patent was through, RTTI and anybody else could copy the serum, could even independently develop the same formula, but only Claire could exploit it commercially.

When the envelope was in her bag she admitted to herself that she had run out of excuses. There was nowhere else to go but home. A fresh blush of shame flashed right from her toes to the top of her head. She had to think about it now, had to watch the images from last night scroll across her memory in slow motion. Claire, cooking Brendan's favourite Fish Ragoût, lighting scented candles, wearing her black silk camisole. Claire setting the scene. Claire in her submissive role, responsive to his every thought and touch.

It had, as always, been so easy for Brendan.

Dinner with Frank and Dorothy on Thursday night had been relaxed. She had called her father aside to explain why she had not been with him for the staff meeting. Well, a part explanation anyway. Just that LabAn were not satisfactory and needed a personal visit from her to sort out a few problems. She could not tell him of her suspicions about Ronan Hennessey. Apart from the fact that the whole idea seemed implausible, she did not want Frank upset any further. Not in his present state of health. "You did the right thing," he said and then allayed her guilt by giving her a big hug.

She had been both surprised and pleased to find him in such good humour. It seemed that now the decision to merge with RTTI had been made, he was going to accept it with good grace. They had all gelled as a family as they had not done for so long. Brendan had been kind and considerate towards her and her parents.

Charming, attentive Brendan. He had got his way with RTTI and now he was rewarding them. Claire had detached herself mentally from the cosy scene and watched him manipulate Frank and Dorothy, had clinically analysed the tricks she had come to know so well.

And yet, she had been the one to allow him the final victory, submitting to his lovemaking, inviting him to take her. She knew he was using her, deceiving her. She knew that, while he was making love to her, behind his closed eyelids he was conjuring images of Yvette Previn. But when Brendan held her, need outstripped pride. Her body responded to his touch, to the gentle stroke of his fingers. She had even agreed to try for a baby.

"I'm some hypocrite, Clarence," she informed the guinea pig.

He squeaked in reply, one eye focused directly on her as the other one rolled towards the ceiling. Clarence was sick. All the animals were sick but she could not start to treat them with Serum 6 until she was certain that they were not incubating any respiratory disease. This time she would make certain that Serum 6 and Serum 6 alone would determine their fate. The definitive test of her work. Where was she going to find all this strength she needed to see her trials through and sort out her marriage?

Then she took a deep breath and straightened up her shoulders. She might be physically vulnerable to Brendan but she still had control. The complete formula for the serum was known only by her. The abstract she had just written for the patent was theoretical. No specifics. Not even Kevin knew the formulation. Yes, she was safe. She stooped and stroked Clarence's soft fur.

"And Clarence, I have something else to tell you. No babies. I'm staying on the pill. That's our secret. OK?"

She turned off the lights. She was ready for her husband now, waxed and cleansed and moisturised by the beauty salon, her conscience squared by a chat with a guinea pig.

*　　*　　*

"Need a hand?" Paul asked, as he watched Trish put coffee on to percolate. She shook her head.

"Everything is under control. It's going OK, isn't it? Do you think dinner was all right?"

Paul touched her flushed cheek and pushed a stray strand of hair behind her ear. "Dinner was delicious and they seem to be getting along fine. You are good at this, Trish. You're good at lots of things," he said, nuzzling her neck.

Trish loaded the tray with coffee and after-dinner mints and handed it to Paul.

"Well?" he asked, an eyebrow raised. "What do you think of Ewan Peters now?"

"He's a lovely person, Paul. So self-assured and yet not arrogant. I like him but I'm still not sure about his politics. Helen is nice too. C'mon," she urged, "it's not safe to leave Ria for too long."

Paul was laughing as he followed Trish into the lounge. Their guests exuded that comfortable, satisfied afterglow of good food and wine. When coffee was served, Trish switched off the central light and turned on the soft standard lamps. Ewan was sprawled on the couch, his long legs stretched out comfortably in front of him.

"That was a lovely meal, Trish," he said. "It's so nice to relax for a change."

"Why are you so busy?" Ria asked. "Are you always organising protests and marches?"

"That's the easy part of my job," he explained. "Most of my work is done in the office. We have to co-ordinate with other environmental groups, keep up to date with legislation, meet delegations, liaise with local and international authorities. The list is endless."

"I can vouch for that!" Helen said and immediately laughed to counteract the underlying hint of annoyance.

"But I don't understand," Ria said and Kevin shifted uncomfortably in his chair. "Why do you always try to stand in the way of progress? Big factories mean employment. And they need power supplies so they have to be serviced by bigger power stations. They need motorways to transport goods. We would have huge unemployment if we listened to you eco-warriors and –"

"Ewan is hardly an eco-warrior," Kevin interrupted her. "Anyway I'm sure he wants to forget about his work tonight."

"He never forgets about work," Helen said in the same half-joking tone.

Ewan was leaning forward now, all the casual, almost sleepy, demeanour gone. "No. No. This is important. EnVirowatch, and indeed all the other environmental groups, have a public relations problem. Ria has expressed a very valid viewpoint. The powerful groups, including government bodies, have access to very professional PR facilities. They can afford them. So, they tell people that they care about the environment, that the laws protect our air and water and that people who protest or question their commitment are cranks. They are loud about the benefits of the employment they offer and quiet about the long-term cost to the communities where they make their profits."

They all sat back as Ewan warmed to his subject, his eyes glowing with fervour in the soft apricot lamplight. He led them through case histories and the implications of inadequately monitored industry. Paul and Trish exchanged glances as he spoke about global warming. Her look told him that she understood now why Paul said this man had a special gift.

"But people need jobs now," Ria protested. "They have families and mortgages to worry about. Polar ice caps have nothing to do with their day-to-day lives."

"But what about the quality of their children's lives, Ria? Their grandchildren's?" Paul asked.

"We won't have children or grandchildren if the big industries are hounded out of here. For instance if EnVirowatch start harassing RTTI, then Dashern would be in trouble. Then *our* future would be on the line.

Wouldn't it, Kevin?"

Kevin nodded, deciding agreeing with her was his best option.

"Ah! RTTI. Case in point," Ewan said and leaned back against the couch.

"Maybe it's different for us," Ria added, ignoring Kevin's warning glance. "Kevin is employed by Claire Hearn. The Research and Development section is independent of Dashern or RTTI. He's working on very important research. The cure for cancer actually."

"Really?" Helen asked.

"Yes. All top secret. And a lot of people want to know how they are curing the cancerous tumours in the guinea pigs but –"

"Ria!"

She ignored the note of warning from Kevin and continued on as if he had not spoken,

"Brendan Hearn is always snooping around, asking questions. Isn't he, Kevin? And he's all one with RTTI."

"Interesting," Ewan remarked, looking directly at Paul. "At least it would explain why RTTI are getting involved with Dashern. Yes. I think you have given us the answer, Ria."

Paul laughed at first. Ewan was humouring Ria. But then he noticed that the EnVirowatch man was not laughing. Surely he couldn't be taking Ria seriously? Nobody else did. Ever.

Ria glowed. "So glad I could be of help."

Trish noticed that Kevin looked very uncomfortable. He should know her better by now than to tell Ria anything he did not want repeated. Paul could glean some interesting information here and, after all, that had been the whole idea behind the dinner party. But poor Kevin was practically squirming in his seat. Time to do her hostess thing and rescue him.

"Anyone for a drink?" she asked in her most cheerful voice.

Three brandies later the conversation was flowing and non-threatening. Trish sat back and relaxed. Her first dinner party had been a success.

Chapter Ten

Paul clicked on *Edit*, *Select All*, *Delete* for the third time. He stared at the now blank monitor and cursed. It was Tuesday and he still had not come up with the groundbreaking article for his Wednesday deadline. He was too uptight, too anxious to impress Flannery. At the desk across from him, Jim Conrad's fingers were flying over the keyboard. Paul stood up to stretch his stiff muscles.

"Sorry you didn't stick to your pics?" Jim asked and Paul could not decide whether he was being concerned or sarcastic.

"No. I'm going to crack this, Jim. Even if it kills me. The story is in my head. I know what I want to say but it just isn't coming out right. It's dead on the page. Boring."

Jim stopped typing and leaned back in his chair. He smiled at Paul. "Human interest is the key, lad. Human interest."

"How do you mean?" Paul asked.

"Well now, I don't know if I should be telling you anything. You could end up stealing all my scoops."

Paul was about to reassure the older man that he was not after his job when he realised that Jim was teasing him. They both laughed but then Jim was serious again when he spoke.

"We have to entertain as well as inform. That's where newspaper reporting is at now. People haven't as much time or interest as they used to have. You've got to grab their attention."

"That's what I'm trying to do, Jim. This merger is so important to the future of our area that people must pay attention."

"Take a break. Go for a walk. Have a coffee. Think human interest. Then come back and write your article."

Jim turned back to his computer and immediately his fingers started flying over the keys again. Paul picked up his coat and walked out.

*   *   *

Syringe in hand, Claire walked to the guinea pig's cage. Clarence shoved his snout through the bars, twitched his nose and looked at her in his cross-eyed, curious fashion. Opening the cage, she picked him up and placed him on the bench. She hesitated. What if the serum really was weakening the immune system? What if this injection was a death sentence? She must make a decision now. The animals had already been five days in the lab.

"I'll inject him if you like," Kevin offered.

Placing her hand on Clarence she felt him quiver with fear. His eyes darted around, taking in the unfamiliar surroundings and open space of the lab bench. His tumour was huge, having grown one full centimetre in diameter since he had left LabAn.

"Just hold him steady, please," she told Kevin.

This time Claire was taking no chances. Not one animal of the batch cleared by Anne Moroney was showing any sign of respiratory infection. Her hand shook as she plunged the syringe into the animal's pink skin. If this batch died it would either be from their cancers or from Serum 6.

*   *   *

Paul got into his car when he left the office. Maybe a change of scene would start the creative juices flowing. He headed out of town with no real idea of where he was going. As he drove, he thought about what Jim Conrad had said. Human interest. Human interest was what he needed to bring his story to life.

He was not surprised when he found himself on the road leading to the Dashern plant. This place had been occupying his every waking thought for the past few days.

The approach road to Dashern Chemicals cut a swathe through a rural idyll. Green pastures gradually gave way to distant blue-hazed hills. A stand of evergreens, which almost but not quite disguised the holding tanks, signalled the entrance to the plant.

As he drove towards the car park Paul felt the stirrings of an idea. This sprawling, thriving chemical plant was testimony to one man's enterprise and business acumen. What an achievement! And what a bitter disappointment it must be now to have to merge with another company. Human interest! Frank Dawson, his history, his hopes, his fears. The Man behind the Merger! Yes! He could see the headline now!

Paul began to calm down as he reminded himself that Frank Dawson had not returned any of his phone calls in relation to the feature. "Mr Dawson is busy at the moment. May I take a message?" over and over until he had given up trying to contact the boss man. He looked towards the top of the car park now. Yes! There it was. Parked in the reserved space. Frank Dawson's silver Mercedes. He jumped out of his car and headed for the Administration Building.

Ten minutes later Paul was seated in Frank Dawson's office and suddenly he was panicking. How was he going to convince this red-faced, glowering man to give him his life's history?

"I was told you were trying to reach me," Frank Dawson said.

"*I* was told you were very busy. I thought you were trying to avoid me."

"I don't work that way," Frank said brusquely. "Now what can I do for you?"

Paul cursed himself. He should have thought this through, known what approach to take. The direct approach. That was it. He had always found Frank Dawson to be very direct.

"I'm writing an article on the Dashern-RTTI merger for *Newstrack* and –"

"I thought you were their photographer," Frank interrupted.

"I am," Paul agreed, "but I am also a qualified journalist."

"Jim Conrad has this covered already. He interviewed me on the merger. Surely you know that?"

"Yes. I read his article. But what I want to do is different. I believe this merger has huge implications, not alone for Dashern, but for this whole locality. It has the potential to change lives. For better or for worse. I want to run a series tracking progress from signing on the dotted line to up and running."

"So which do you think? Better or worse?"

"I have no preconceived ideas," Paul lied. "I just want to report it as I see it."

"What do you want from me?"

Paul took a deep breath. This was it! "I want your life story, Frank. I want to know how a farm labourer's son ended up owning a chemical factory. I want to know about the struggles you had to build up your business and how it felt when you succeeded. And then I want to know why in the hell you are handing it over to a multinational."

Frank opened the top drawer in his desk and took

197

out a box of cigars. He held it towards Paul who shook his head. The room was silent except for the little sounds of Frank preparing his cigar, clipping, tapping, sniffing, lighting. He eventually sat back and inhaled deeply. When he exhaled, the smoke spiralled around the office, the pungent aroma almost making Paul cough.

"So!" he said at last. "You want to do a word portrait of the demon of the piece?"

"No," Paul replied. "I want to write about *you*. I'll deal with RTTI later."

Frank laughed. "Just what I wanted to hear, son. A biased opinion."

"My personal opinion won't influence my writing."

"Bullshit! What kind of crap would you write if you weren't passionate about the issue?" Frank leaned forward and stared intently at Paul. "If you want to achieve the same standard in your journalism as you have in your photography, you will have to approach it with the same degree of honesty."

"Right, Frank. I'll be honest. Number one. The editor has given me until tomorrow to write an article on the merger. It has to be good. I have to prove myself to him. I think the way to do that is to write an in-depth article on you. People look up to you, respect you. But they really don't know much about you. They would be interested in reading about what makes you tick. "

"And number two?" Frank prompted.

Paul hesitated. How honest should he be? This man had decided, after all, to throw his lot in with RTTI. He obviously knew their history and had decided he could work with them anyway. He took a deep breath.

"I have been doing some research on RTTI. I'm concerned about their environmental record. I think people in this area have a right to know."

Paul stopped and sat back, wishing he could take all that back. He had said too much. Probably lost the interview. He bit his lip as Frank Dawson stared at him.

"Are you a member of EnVirowatch?" Frank asked.

"No, I'm not." Paul stared back at the older man and tried not to flinch from the intimidating fiery stare.

"Right then," Frank said finally. "Go ahead. Do your job. Ask what you like about me. I'll decide what questions I want to answer. But where RTTI are concerned, you are on your own. I am in negotiation with them, as you know, so I will not have anything to do with any article you may write about them. On the other hand, I respect the freedom of the press and the right of the public to be informed. Just don't ask *me* about them."

Paul nodded his head. This was as good a deal as he could have hoped for.

"I'll have to see the finished article before it goes to press and have the final veto on it," Frank added. "Agreed?"

"Agreed," Paul said quickly and got out his tape recorder before Frank Dawson could change his mind.

* * *

Ewan Peters shuffled his feet into a more

comfortable position and took a practice swing. He felt stiff and uncoordinated. He took another dummy swing and felt a little better this time. Conscious that other people were waiting behind him to tee off, he lined up his shot and went for it. His eyes followed the ball as it dropped, then dribbled towards the hole. Not bad! Not bad at all! Four more strokes. Maybe three with luck.

"Beat that, pal," he said to Liam McCarthy who was lining up his shot. Liam did. The rest of the game followed much the same pattern. Still, Ewan was pleased with his performance. He had ended up only six over par.

"If I had as much time to practise as you, I'd be challenging Tiger Woods," he said to Liam as they headed for the clubhouse.

"I've no doubt you would," Liam answered. "Can't resist a challenge, can you? Which reminds me, I have something to tell you. But let's get a pint first."

After he had knocked the edge off his thirst with the first few sips of stout, Ewan put his glass down and looked at Liam. "Shoot. What's the news?"

Liam looked around to make sure they could not be overheard. Not that he was breaking any confidence here. Just pre-empting publication. Just giving an old school-mate a hand.

"Dashern have issued notice of change of use. They've set the whole process in motion."

"From detergent manufacture to what? Would it have anything to do with herbal medicines?"

The look Liam gave Ewan was enough. The man from the Council could not, and would not, say any more. And that was fair, Ewan thought. So! RTTI had started the ball rolling. It was not yet Dashern-RTTI. The legal work would take some time but it was obvious that RTTI were already rushing things along.

"Where does it go from here?" he asked Liam.

"There's a long road ahead. We'll have to wait and see exactly what Dashern are proposing and how it would affect the present effluent and emission licence."

"And while we play wait and see, RTTI play hit and run. This isn't just Dashern you're dealing with any more, Liam. It's RTTI."

"Tell you what, Peters," Liam said, giving Ewan a light punch on the arm, "I'll buy the next round of drinks if you promise not to mention Dashern any more today. Better still, don't even think of RTTI. No wonder you're such a lousy golfer. You have your priorities wrong! Deal?"

"Deal," Ewan laughed but when Liam went to the bar for the drinks his thoughts returned to RTTI and the research Kevin Trill's mouthy girlfriend had been talking about. The cure for cancer? Whatever Claire Hearn's research was about, RTTI were certainly chasing it.

*   *   *

It was very late when Paul got home. He threw himself into a chair and closed his eyes.

"Tough at the top?" Trish asked as she started to

massage his knotted shoulder muscles.

"I'll let you know when I get there," he laughed.

"Well. C'mon. Tell me. You said on the phone you interviewed Frank Dawson for your article and that you were writing as fast as Jim Conrad. Have you finished?"

"Done and dusted. I took a shot of him too. Standing at his office window, looking out over his domain. Lord of the Manor," Paul said.

"And?"

"And it's good. As good as I can make it. Hopefully Flannery will think so too. Frank Dawson certainly wasn't born with a silver spoon in his mouth. He has worked hard to get where he is."

"Looks like he's fighting hard to stay there too."

"That's about the size of it. Maybe we'd all do the same if we were in his position."

Trish stopped massaging and went to stand in front of Paul. "I thought you were furious with Frank Dawson. Didn't I hear you say he was a traitor to sell out to RTTI? Are you changing sides now?"

Paul rubbed his eyes and stretched. He was exhausted. When he looked at Trish, she could see the confusion in his eyes. "That's the trouble, Trish. There are two sides to this story. Frank Dawson feels a huge commitment to his staff. It's genuine concern. I think he felt he had to go with RTTI in order to keep his people in employment. Looks like the only option open to him at the moment."

She leaned over and kissed him. "You're too nice,

Paul Gregan. You'll have to learn cynicism if you're to make it in journalism. Now would you like hot chocolate? It would help you sleep."

"I'm asleep now," he said as he stood up to go to bed. "By the way, how was your day?"

"Busy. And messy. Because of your Frank Dawson."

Paul sat down again. "Because of Frank Dawson? How do you mean?"

"Interview me!" Trish teased but then she answered him because she realised he was too tired for games. "He had booked to fly to London on Thursday. It seems there's a change of plan and he has to go tomorrow instead. He must fly into Stansted now and apparently that is not convenient to the RTTI plant. It was murder trying to get a seat for him at the last minute."

Paul felt his massaged shoulders begin to knot again. "He never mentioned the trip. I was talking to him for an hour and a half. I photographed him. I faxed him my copy for his approval before even Flannery had seen it. And he never told me he was going to meet with RTTI tomorrow."

"As I said. Learn cynicism. And how about this? Brendan Hearn had us plagued all day. He's on standby for a cancellation flight. The son-in-law wants to go on this trip as well but it would seem he is not invited. Thank God he was dealing with Ria. Do you know what he told her?"

Paul shook his head.

"That it is vitally important that nobody but she knows he is trying to book this flight."

"He swore Ria to secrecy?"

Trish nodded. They were both still laughing as they turned off the lights and went to bed.

*   *   *

Myles Flannery was smiling too. He loved the midnight peace and quiet of his Editorial Office. But even more than that he loved discovering new talent. Hidden talent. Like Paul Gregan, he thought, as he read through the article entitled, *The Man behind the Merger*.

Chapter Eleven

Claire had delayed coming in today until after lunch. She didn't like Wednesdays. A characterless weekday, sprawling as it did between a weekend past and one yet to come. That was her excuse. The real reason was that she had been afraid to see the guinea pigs. Afraid that they would be feverish and wheezing after their Serum 6 treatment. The day took on a much better aspect when she saw that the animals, Clarence in particular, were no worse than they had been yesterday. She was filling in chart entries when Kevin dropped some envelopes on her desk.

"I collected the post from Reception at lunch-time," he told her. "I noticed you hadn't been over today."

"Thanks, Kevin. I forgot about the post."

"I thought so." He wanted to reassure her. To tell her that he was sure the serum would work this time, but she had her invisible barrier up and he did not have the head for scaling such heights.

Claire flicked through the usual assortment of catalogues and invoices. She stopped when she came to a small blue envelope. The address was handwritten and vaguely familiar. Unusual.

When she opened the letter, she noticed there was no address at the top. Flicking over the first page she looked for the signature. The name she saw increased her curiosity. She raced through it once and then started again more slowly.

Dear Dr Hearn,

By the time you get this letter I will already have left LabAn. Ronan Hennessey was furious with me when he discovered I had supplied you with trial animals without his permission. He ranted and raved at me but for once I stood up for myself. I'm afraid I was very assertive in telling him exactly what I thought of his overbearing manner. The upshot of the whole episode was that he fired me. I suppose I could fight him on Unfair Dismissal but I am reluctant to take a case against so devious a person. I would probably end up with my professional reputation in shreds. At least this way he has agreed to give me a good reference.

I am writing to you now to tell you that I have tried, and failed, to find out why your trial animals had been treated differently to other customer orders. I searched through records to no avail. I asked Mr Hennessey but just succeeded in making him even more angry.

There is something I think you should know. I understand you sent tissue samples from your trial animals to the veterinary college. The man in charge there is a personal friend of Ronan Hennessey's. I overheard Ronan ask him to forward your samples to LabAn. He said something about wanting to do further study. I could not understand why he did not ask you directly for the samples. Then I saw him prepare slides of your samples, which he had sent by courier to RTTI in Cologne. To their Research and Development headquarters, I believe. His contact is somebody named Yvette Previn.

Perhaps you are liaising with RTTI in your research, in which case you will think I am at best an over-imaginative person and probably agree with Ronan Hennessey's decision to fire me. But if RTTI is analysing that tissue without your permission, at least now you have been warned.

I am going to join my sister in London for a few months and then I hope to get a twelve-month visa for Australia. I've always wanted to travel but never quite had the courage to get up and go. I have one reason to be grateful to Ronan Hennessey! I wish you the best of luck in your research.

> *Yours Sincerely,*
> *Anne Moroney.*

Claire let the letter drop slowly onto her desk. Her head sank onto her hands. Yvette Previn had been so right. She did not have the strength to cope with this on her own.

Tears welled in Claire's eyes as she sat there, the letter still on her desk. She picked up the blue pages and locked them into her filing cabinet. Glancing into the lab, she saw that Kevin was busy streaking plates. She needed to be alone for a while, to have space to think.

"Kevin, I'm going out for a couple of hours. I'll be back before you go. Just continue on with what you are doing."

Claire had driven out of the plant before realising she didn't know where she was going. The seaside was only twenty kilometres away. Maybe sea air would clear her jumbled thoughts. Her mobile phone rang just as she was indicating to pull out on the main road. It was her father.

"Red-letter day, Claire. I rang your lab to be told you had taken a few hours off! Getting sense at last?"

The tears sprang to her eyes again when she heard his voice. What a comfort it would be to run to him now and tell him about Anne Moroney's letter. He would know exactly how to handle it. He would blow a fuse and his blood pressure would soar. Telling him was not an option.

"Just decided on impulse to leave Kevin in charge and take time out. I'm heading for the beach. A breath of sea air."

"Good on you, girl! Enjoy. I'm heading off to London myself today. I'm just ringing to say goodbye."

Claire frowned. "I am very forgetful, Dad, but isn't today Wednesday? I was certain you weren't going until tomorrow."

"Change of plan. Yvette Previn runs on a very tight schedule so I had to move things around to suit her. I'm looking forward to this. She is bringing me to see a plant similar to ours. It should be interesting to see the distillation process in operation. Besides, I have a few other bits of business there I need to attend to myself."

Claire's stomach knotted with a sudden wave of anger. Yvette Previn! Yvette Previn! It seemed that this woman was creeping into every nook and cranny of her life.

"Be careful, Dad," she said and she could hear the panic in her own voice.

"You should know your old man well enough by now. RTTI are no match for me. They only think they hold the winning hand. The old dog for the hard road as they say."

"They don't play fair. Just be wary."

"Don't worry, Claire. I'll see you when I come back. I'm going home now to spend some time with your mother before I leave. I wanted her to come with me but she said she would be bored in London while I was busy. Truth is, she doesn't want to leave her garden!"

"I could pop over to see you both now. I can go to the seaside another time."

"Don't even think of it," Frank said. "You go and enjoy your break. You have little enough of it. See you on Friday evening."

"Take care, Dad! Bye!"

Thirty minutes later Claire was walking along the cliff path. The tide was full in and lashing against the rocks beneath her. A fine scatter of spray carried on the wind and sprinkled a salty mist on her face. Standing, she breathed deeply. Ozone-enriched air swirled around the lump of sadness in her throat. Not even the strength and beauty of the sea could lift her depression.

What was she going to do? She could, and had, put in hour after hour and year after year of intensive study and research. She had put her life on hold while she teased out the answer she had always known was locked in the cells. She was willing to continue on until Serum 6 was in every pharmacy in every country, until a diagnosis of cancer was no longer a death sentence. Yes, she was willing to work and work and work. But this! How could she fight them on her own? They would destroy her, just like they had Anne Moroney.

She must get some advice. Must talk to someone. Not her father. She could not risk upsetting him. Certainly not Brendan. Not Dorothy. Not Kevin. Maybe Jeremiah Audley?

Her spirits lifted a little as she thought about this idea. Maybe Jeremiah could prosecute RTTI for – for – for analysing her samples without her permission? But she would have to prove it first and she had no idea where to find Anne Moroney. Yet she had the letter from Anne. Would that be proof enough? Maybe Jeremiah could write to Ronan Hennessey, letting him know that she was aware of what he was doing. Then LabAn would deny it and prosecute her for libel. Say that Anne Moroney was just trying to get revenge for being fired. And how pathetic was it that Claire Hearn had nobody to talk to except the family lawyer?

Claire turned her back on the sea and sat into her car, the depression deeper now than when she had come here. Before starting the car, she looked in her bag. It was still there, her patent application. Careless, but she now had a legitimate excuse for calling to see Jermiah Audley.

At least she would have had. She was informed when she got to his office that he was away on holiday. His son was in charge in his absence. Claire looked at Oliver and wondered if she should keep her forms in her bag. She did not like Olly, as he liked to be called. He had all the charm and polish of his father but none of the warmth or sincerity. But if she did not start the process now she would forget it again for another month.

"This is a patent application I discussed with your father," she said, handing the papers to Jeremiah's son. "Would you see that he gets it please?"

He smiled at her as he took her application and assured her he would bring it to his father's attention as soon as he was back in the office.

Claire headed back for her lab. She had work to do.

Oliver waited until he was certain that Claire had left the premises. Then he faxed her patent application to the people he knew would most appreciate it.

*   *   *

Ewan Peters sat in the kitchen, reading the heating instructions on the packaging of a microwave dinner, trying to ignore the noise from the children's bedroom. He had just got as far as piercing holes in the plastic cover when there was a loud bang from upstairs. It sounded as if the children were bouncing each other off the walls. He dropped the frozen Spaghetti Bolognese and ran upstairs, his frustration and temper rising with each step he climbed.

"Stop it! Stop it at once or I'll give you both something to cry about!"

His son and his daughter stared at him in shock.

"Are you mad at us, Daddy?" His daughter's bottom lip was quivering and her eyes glittered with tears.

"When will Mam be back?" his son asked, sulky and defiant.

Ewan looked away from them. He was ashamed to meet their eyes. They were getting on his nerves and he had let them know it. So much for good parenting.

"No more fighting now. I'll have your dinner ready soon," he said quietly and then he turned and left the room.

Back in the kitchen, Ewan sat at the table and put his head in his hands. Determined to get control of himself and the situation, he put one dinner in the microwave, poured two glasses of milk and went out into the hall to call the children. The phone rang just as the microwave started beeping. He cursed as he took out the cooked dinner and put in the other frozen one. The phone kept ringing as the children trooped downstairs, both claiming the same chair and the one cooked dinner. He grabbed the phone.

"Hello. Ewan? Clive Rigney here."

Clive Rigney! What in the hell did he want?

"Hello, Clive."

"Interesting news today, isn't it? Not that it wasn't

expected. It's just the timing is surprising."

What in the fuck was he talking about? There was a crash as a glass of milk hit the floor. Jesus Christ!

"Don't move until I take away the glass splinters!" Ewan shouted at the children.

"Look, Ewan, this obviously is not a good time for you. When will you be free to talk? I'd like to discuss the latest developments with you."

"Are you going Green, Clive? Or do you want me to launch your 'Bag for Life' campaign?"

Clive laughed just as the microwave beeper sounded again. Ewan saw the resentful stare of his son and the smug smile on his daughter's face and knew another fight was brewing.

"OK, Clive. Not tomorrow. How about Friday night? Eight o'clock. Mellow Drama. We'll talk then."

It took ten minutes before all glass splinters were safely swept away. The dinners were cold by this stage. The phone rang. Ewan decided to ignore it. He had the dinners reheated and relative peace restored before it rang again.

"Ewan Peters."

"Would this be the environmentally friendly crèche centre?" Helen asked.

"Would you be the missing mother?" Ewan replied.

Helen laughed and Ewan suddenly realised how long it had been since he had heard that carefree sound.

"How was the big city?" he asked. "How did your shopping go?"

"I had a great day, Ewan. How are the children?"

"Fine. They're just after their dinner now. Bedtime soon, thank God. I'll be able to get some work done."

"Oh! Yes. Work. Important work."

Ewan closed his eyes and counted to ten. What in the fuck was wrong with this woman? Hormones? Or was it Julie? Her new best friend. Julie Rigney, the great organiser of shopping trips and girlie nights out.

"Are you on your way home?" he asked.

"Julie has booked us into a hotel tonight. I won't be home until the three o'clock train tomorrow afternoon. I want to talk to the children now."

"What? Why didn't you tell me that this morning? You said it was just a day trip!"

"Well, it's not now. I'm going out to dinner tonight with some friends of Julie's. Surely you can manage your son and daughter for a few more hours?"

Ewan gripped the phone tightly. He wanted to shout at this stranger on the other end of the line. He wanted to order her to come home, to allow him get on with his work, to look after the children, to end her friendship with that bitch Julie. What a perfect pair Julie and Clive Rigney made. A mating between the sleaziest and the silliest. He took a deep breath.

"I'll get the children for you. Take care."

When both children had spoken to their mother, Ewan took the phone off the hook. It was another hour before he had them settled down for the night. As he watched them sleep, he felt a wave of self-disgust at his earlier impatience. It was not their fault that their mother was being selfish and unreasonable. He stood still. He had to admit that their father wasn't blameless either. Poor kids! Two parents competing in the selfish-and-unreasonable stakes!

But Helen had changed so much. So quickly. She had always been a firebrand but now she was strident. She wanted respect. She wanted time off. She wanted a life. She wanted to be Julie Rigney. Fucking Julie!

He went to his desk but could not concentrate. There was a speech to work on and correspondence to deal with. The words blurred in front of his eyes. Helen, Helen, Helen. They had grown up together, had children together, had the same dreams. "*Your* dreams. *Your* ambitions, Ewan. What about me?" Her words pounded around in his head. He switched off the computer and wandered into the lounge. It was almost News time. He poured a drink and turned on the television.

"Tonight's main headline. The Taoiseach is now on his way to Áras an Uachtarán to speak to the President. It is expected that the Dáil will be dissolved . . ."

Ewan upped the volume and pulled in nearer to the screen. What a turn-up for the books! Gone after two years! This Government brought down by one allegation of corruption after another. So! Another election. More promises, more electioneering. A current affairs programme followed the News. All the political parties were represented, all trying to make party political points, all either defensive or triumphant, depending on their allegiances.

"Bastards," Ewan muttered as the scandal that had

toppled this government unfolded. It seemed that some European Infrastructure Funding had gone astray. It had somehow ended up in the personal bank account of the Taoiseach's brother-in-law. Ewan laughed as a government spokesperson denied that the Taioseach had known anything about the scam.

"The Taoiseach's brother-in-law runs an engineering firm. He submitted the most competitive tender so he won the contract. The Taoiseach had no knowledge –"

Ewan stood up and turned off the television. He felt the thrill of battle. EnVirowatch had gained a national profile since the last election. Membership and public support had doubled. EnVirowatch had grown to be more than just a pressure group. Maybe, just maybe, their time had come.

He put the phone back on the hook. There were a lot of messages, all about the election. As Ewan listened he remembered Clive Rigney's call. That unexpected call made sense now. Clive Rigney was an ardent government supporter. He must be campaigning early for EnVirowatch support.

"Slimeball," Ewan muttered as he turned off the lights and went to bed alone.

Chapter Twelve

Claire was already sitting at her desk when Kevin arrived into the lab on Thursday morning. She smiled at him.

"What do you hear?" she asked.

He listened. He could hear the hum of the air-conditioning, the whirr of instruments set on standby and … the chirp of guinea pigs.

"The animals?"

"Yes! The trial group are doing well. They're feeding. Temperatures normal. Eyes bright, coats smooth. Early days yet but so far, so good. Would you start on their bedding? I'll give you a hand when I have the write-up finished."

Kevin set happily about his work, glad that today was going to be a smiley day in the lab. The phone was ringing as he made his way into the animal room. He kept going. The call would be for Mrs Hearn anyway.

Much too early for Ria.

Claire was still smiling as she picked up the phone. The caller was John Gleeson, the security company engineer who three weeks ago had fitted the new alarm system to R&D. A few seconds later, the smile was frozen on her face.

"What do you mean? I told you. Only two keyholders. Kevin Trill and myself."

"I know that, Dr Hearn. How could I not?" John said with irritation. "That is why I'm contacting you now. I couldn't believe you had changed your mind so quickly but yet ..."

"You're absolutely sure, John? Tell me again."

John Gleeson repeated his story. Brendan Hearn had contacted Gleeson Alarms that morning claiming that his wife had authorised him as an additional keyholder for R&D and demanding that he be supplied with a key immediately.

"I specifically forbade you to give a key to anyone else, even my husband."

Claire could hear the panic in her own voice.

She must have shouted at John Gleeson because Kevin appeared at the door, a surprised look on his face.

"Are you all right, Mrs Hearn?"

She waved him away impatiently and turned her attention back to John Gleeson.

"I'm sorry, John. Go on."

"What was I supposed to think when he gave me the alarm code, letter and number perfect? Since only you,

Kevin Trill and I know that code, I had to assume you had given it to him."

"I did not."

"Well, that leaves your assistant. Did he?"

"Hang on, please." Claire put down the phone and strode into the animal room. She planted herself in front of a startled Kevin.

"Have you been talking to my husband? Did you give him the code to our alarm system?"

"No! No, I did not. I wouldn't let him have my key either."

Claire stood still and stared at the young man who had suddenly gone very pale. "He asked you for your key?"

"Yes. Several times. He said it was an insurance requirement that a spare key be kept in Administration. For access in case of emergency."

"And what did you say?"

A red flush began to suffuse the paleness of Kevin's face. His eyes, so blue, glittered with a flash of anger. "Mrs Hearn, I told him to talk to you about it. What did you expect me to do? Hand over my key to him? Why did you give me the key and code if you cannot trust me to keep my word?"

"Did he ask you for the alarm code?"

"No."

Head bowed, Claire stood still in front of her outraged assistant. Kevin was telling the truth. She could see that now. She could see it all. Brendan's treachery. He had somehow managed to get hold of the alarm code and now all he needed for access to her lab was a key. Had he tried to steal her key? To copy it? Probably. Just as well she kept it locked in the glove compartment of her car when she wasn't using it. There was some satisfaction but massive hurt in having her paranoia justified. Poor Kevin.

"I'm sorry," she said, raising her head and looking directly at the indignant boy.

"I'd never break my promise to you."

Claire nodded, knowing that he would not. Not deliberately anyway. She turned her back on him and went to the phone.

"John, it seems there has been a breach of security. I will need to change the alarm code. I want a system of revolving codes where the numbers change every day. Is that possible?"

By the time she put the phone down, they had evolved a code system so complex that even John Gleeson found it difficult to handle. Then she made two cups of coffee and called Kevin. She had fences to mend. He sat across from her, silent, confusion and worry etched on his face.

"I didn't doubt you, Kevin. It's just a complicated situation. We need to keep Serum 6 as confidential as possible until we are ready to make an announcement. The work we are doing here is of interest to a lot of people. We must keep them out."

"What about Calbitron? They come in here, don't they?" he asked.

Calbitron were the company Claire used to service

and calibrate her instruments.

"Well, yes, of course, Calbitron must have access –
but only under our supervision."

There was an echo of her own hurt in Kevin's
soulful gaze. He was too young, too trusting to be
caught up in a situation like this. It wasn't fair. Needing
to show him that she had confidence in him, she wrote
her mobile number on a piece of paper. Only she knew
what a huge gesture that was. She had given it to John
Gleeson this morning too. Feeling vulnerable, her
privacy invaded, she handed the paper to Kevin.

"Use this only in emergencies."

"And don't tell anybody," Kevin said solemnly.
"Need-to-know basis only."

"You've got it in one!" Claire laughed. The
atmosphere lightened a little as she set about explaining
the new alarm code system to Kevin.

*   *   *

Trish put down the latest edition of *Newstrack* and
allowed herself a glorious minute of gloating. Paul's
article was brilliant. It was at once incisive and
sensitive, informative and provocative. She felt she
knew Frank Dawson by the time she had finished
reading. His early history was one of poverty and
backbreaking labour on the fifty acres of scrubland his
parents called a farm. The childhood memories of
hunger, cold, life-quenching drudgery were to be the
fodder that fuelled his desire to succeed. This article

traced Frank's progress from the hillside farm to his first attempts at setting up a business.

"Isn't it just awful his parents died before they could see how successful he would become?" said Ria.

Trish looked across at her assistant and was surprised to see her reading the article. Ria usually preferred to read her stars and the social page.

"Yeah," Trish agreed. "Paul's next article will be about the setting up of Dawson Chemicals. I bet Frank's parents could never have dreamed that their son would end up owning a factory."

"Paul might want to interview Kevin, do you think? He has an important job at Dashern. Although he is employed by Mrs Hearn. Which reminds me. I got a cancellation for Brendan Hearn for tomorrow. Flying into Heathrow."

"Did you tell him?"

"I rang this morning. You'd think he was after winning the lottery. He's extremely anxious to get to London. What's on there, I wonder, that is so important to him?"

"Maybe he's keeping an eye on his father-in-law."

"Trish! I never thought of that. Does Paul know? That could be a big story. I'll try to find out more."

"Ria, just do your job," Trish said in exasperation. "And that does not include poking your nose into our clients' private business."

Ria waited until Trish was dealing with a customer before ringing Brendan Hearn.

"Travelbug here, Mr Hearn. Ria speaking."

"You're not going to tell me there is a problem with my flight, are you?"

"Oh, no, Mr Hearn! Your flight is confirmed. I was just wondering about accommodation. If you need us to book for you, we will be glad to do so. Perhaps you want to stay in the same hotel as your father-in-law?"

"What did you say your name was? Ria? If I had wanted your help with accommodation I would have asked. Since I did not, you can take it that it really has nothing to do with you."

"I'm terribly sorry, Mr Hearn. I was just trying to be helpful," Ria said as softly as possible.

She glanced at Trish as she put down the phone. Luckily her boss was still busy.

This was one call that Trish did not need to know about. But Brendan Hearn was behaving very oddly and Ria meant to find out why.

It was two hours later before she got the opportunity to ring the London hotel she had booked for Frank Dawson. It took all her ingenuity and tact to find the information she needed but when she did her curiosity was satisfied. Brendan Hearn, Frank Dawson and Yvette Previn, that beautiful woman who had worn a designer gown to the Dashern dinner dance, were all booked into the same hotel. And Brendan Hearn, the husband of Claire Dawson, had managed to get the room adjoining the RTTI beauty. Now she knew exactly why Brendan Hearn had wanted her to mind her own business.

*   *   *

Brendan was already up when Claire woke on Friday morning. He was sitting at the table writing when Claire came into the kitchen. She muttered good morning and went for the coffeepot.

"I was just writing a note to you," Brendan said.

"Writing a note? Why?"

"I thought I'd be gone before you got up. I didn't want to wake you. I'm going to London this morning. I'll be away for the weekend."

Claire slammed her cup so hard onto the counter that coffee splashed over the marble top. "I think I understand now why you didn't want to wake me."

"So you finally understand something about me." Brendan stood up, tore the note in shreds and threw the pieces on the floor. He was white-faced, every muscle in his body defined by tension.

His anger frightened Claire at first but then she felt a matching flood of rage. "How crass, Brendan. The 'my wife doesn't understand me' routine is low. Even for you. Am I supposed to think it is a coincidence that Yvette Previn also happens to be in London this weekend?"

"Think whatever you like. That is what you do anyway. The fact is that I have business with RTTI in London."

"My father didn't mention that you were going to join him."

"I'm not. He's flying back today."

Claire took a moment to enjoy the heat of anger in her heart and revenge in her gut: Brendan obviously didn't know that her father had changed his plans. Frank had rung her last evening to say he wasn't coming home today. The plant inspection had been postponed until Saturday and he had other business to see to as well. He would be staying in London until Sunday. Obviously, he had not seen fit to inform his son-in-law. How she would love to tell her cheating husband now but that would ruin his surprise in London. Poor Brendan! He had gone to all this trouble to arrange a dirty weekend, with a woman he didn't know was lesbian, only to have to share it with his father-in-law!

Brendan picked up his cup and drained the last of his coffee. Opening his briefcase, he threw the notepad and pen into it. His shirt was new. At least Claire had not seen it before. Pale blue with white collar and cuffs. It made him seem even paler and emphasised the angry white lines around his mouth. He looked vicious. A laugh almost escaped Claire as she suddenly realised why Brendan was so angry. The new alarm code. Of course! Brendan's anxiety about getting access to R&D made sense now. He had wanted to bring the key and code to Yvette in London. A gift for her. A love token. According to John Gleeson, Brendan had behaved obnoxiously yesterday, persistently ringing all afternoon, demanding a key, until John had eventually told him that the code had been changed. Now he would have to confess his failure to Yvette. Poor bastard!

"I changed the alarm code," she announced cheerfully.

He clicked his case shut, picked up his jacket and strode out of the kitchen. The triumph that Claire had felt went flat and cold.

*   *   *

"See you in the Mellow Drama later then," Paul said as he kissed Trish on the cheek and rushed out of Travelbug.

"Kevin and I will be there too," Ria said. "Maybe we could meet up and go for a meal."

Trish sighed. It was Friday and she just wanted to relax. Listening to Ria for the evening was not her idea of relaxation. "I don't know, Ria. I can't make any plans because Paul is very busy. The Editor was so pleased with the articles about Frank Dawson and Dashern that he has given Paul a weekly column to write as well."

"Oh, my God! His own column! That's brilliant, Trish. What is he going to write about? I have loads of ideas, you know."

Trish laughed. There was no disputing Ria had loads of ideas. It was just that they were all off the wall. "Well, the topic of the moment is the election."

"Boring," Ria said she logged onto her computer to start her day's work. She smiled as she thought of a plan to make the evening more interesting.

*   *   *

The sound and sight of the guinea pigs should have

had Claire singing and dancing for joy. Or at least feeling relatively happy. The trial animals continued to maintain normal temperatures, healthy coats, bright eyes, good appetites and best of all a measurable decrease in tumour size. She was working on yesterday's set of blood tests now. The results showed a very strong trend. A positive trend. Too early yet to give a definitive opinion, but Serum 6 was looking good. And yet she felt sad. Empty.

"You want me to get that, Mrs Hearn?"

Claire started as she realised Kevin was talking to her and that the phone was ringing.

"No. No thanks, Kevin. I'll get it. You can get on with the autoclaving."

Kevin shrugged and headed for the media prep room.

When Claire heard Ria's voice on the other end of the phone, she was just about to call him back but Ria said quickly, "It's you I want to talk to, Mrs Hearn. You know you said you'd come out for a drink with us some time? Well, I thought, now that Mr Hearn is in London for the weekend, you might like to come with us tonight."

"How do you know he's in London?"

"I'm working in Travelbug, Mrs Hearn. He booked his flight through us."

Of course. She should have guessed. Ria probably knew where he was staying and with whom he was staying as well. Probably the whole world knew. Then it dawned on her that if Ria did know, she would have blurted it out by now. Claire smiled. A few hours with this disarmingly guileless girl was exactly the antidote she needed to the blackness of the weekend stretching ahead.

"I'd love to, Ria. Thank you for asking me."

"I told Kevin you weren't a stick-in-the-mud."

"But I am!" Claire laughed

"Do you know Mellow Drama? We'll be there at about half past seven. Trish, my boss in the travel agency, and her boyfriend Paul will be there as well. He's the *Newstrack* journalist who's writing the feature on your father. Maybe he'll do an article on you too."

Claire laughed, infected by the girl's irrepressible optimism. "See you at around seven thirty then, Ria. Bye."

Still smiling, she put the phone down. She heard a noise and looked up to see Kevin standing at the door, the expression on his face a cross between shock and resignation.

"Looks like you're going to have to put up with my company this evening, Kevin. Ria has invited me along to the Mellow Drama."

"She's very ... enthusiastic. She means well."

"I'm looking forward to it," said Claire and was surprised to find that she meant what she said.

* * *

Ewan's hand went automatically to his pocket

before he remembered he had given up smoking. Ten years ago. He took a deep breath now, imagining how the back of his throat would burn if he inhaled a cigarette, how the chemical fumes would fill his lungs, his blood stream, his brain, how he would feel more in control, less a hostage to the unfathomable moods of his wife and the demands of his work. Less apprehensive as to the reason Clive Rigney wanted to meet with him.

The car park in Mellow Drama was full. He eventually found parking two streets away. As he walked back someone shouted his name from behind him. He turned to see Clive Rigney approaching, his usual dapper self in blue suit and white shirt.

"Good timing, Ewan. It's all about good timing, isn't it?"

"Are we talking groceries, politics or parking spaces?" Ewan asked, smiling at the little man with the big bank balance. What a smiley world this fucker lived in.

"We'll discuss all three as soon as we have a drink."

Ewan found a seat in a quiet corner in the pub while Clive got in the drinks. He watched as people stood aside to let the supermarket tycoon make his way to the bar. He was served immediately.

"Nice little place this," Clive remarked as he set the drinks down on the table. "Don't know why I haven't been to Mellow Drama before now."

Ewan nodded. "Well, Clive. Tell me. Why are we here? What is it you want to discuss with me?"

"What is everyone discussing? There is only one

topic these last few days."

"The election?"

"Of course," Clive agreed. "Bolt out of the blue. The Taoiseach will have to do a lot of fast talking to worm his way out of this one. He bloody knew his brother-in-law had his hand in the till. Not acceptable. "

Ewan put down his drink and stared at the man across from him. Clive Rigney was a paid-up right-wing party member. His anti attitude did not ring true. "What are you trying to say? That you have suddenly become disillusioned with the status quo? That you knew nothing of the cosy cartels? That you are shocked? C'mon, Clive! I'm not that naïve!"

Clive leaned forward, his small eyes narrowed to a slit, everything about him so angular and spare that he could have escaped from a Lowry sketch. "Right, Ewan. Here's the story. I think this government is finished. Banished to the opposition benches until the next crowd make a mess of things again. I don't back losers."

"Very loyal of you, I must say. I can't believe I'm listening to the same man who had every one of his supermarkets festooned with government posters for the last three elections."

Clive was not listening to him. He was staring towards the door. "Umm. Tasty!"

Ewan turned to see what had caught Clive's eye. A petite dark-haired woman had just come in. She was wearing jeans and a fluffy pink sweater. She stood uncertainly by the door. Vulnerable-looking and very, very pretty. The sort of woman you want to protect.

Then she obviously saw someone she recognised and walked to the other side of the lounge. She was out of their view now behind the masses of potted plants.

"Well, well," Clive muttered, "Claire Hearn has certainly come out of her shell."

So that was Claire Hearn. The great man's daughter and the Young Pretender's wife. Ewan remembered some weird stories he had heard of her living in her lab and never going anywhere but work.

"While the cat's away," Clive said and then explained that he had seen Brendan Hearn leave the airport today.

"You don't miss much," Ewan remarked sourly.

"Pays to keep your eyes open. By the way, my wife told me that she and Helen had a great time in Dublin. They really enjoyed the Club. The girls do enjoy their bit of freedom, don't they?"

Ewan picked up his glass and drained his pint. "Same again?" he asked and did not even wait for Clive to answer. He needed the few minutes at the bar in order to get his thoughts organised. Club! What Club? Helen said she had been out to dinner with Julie. That Rigney bitch had dragged his wife off clubbing. And what else?

"Ewan! Come and join us, Ewan!"

It was that girl, Ria, he had met at Paul Gregan's house party. The motor mouth. She was waving to him from the other side of the lounge. Ewan waved back. Paul and Trish and the henpecked boyfriend who worked in R&D were sitting with her. And the pretty woman with the pink sweater and big dark eyes. Claire Hearn. The woman whose research work was interesting, to say the least.

"Later!" he shouted back to Ria, pointing to the two drinks he was carrying back to his table.

Time to find out what Rigney wanted. "I've been trying to figure out why you want to talk to me, Clive. I thought you'd ask me to use whatever influence I might have to get the EnVirowatch vote behind the government. I wouldn't do it anyway but it's obvious now that's not why you're here. So why are you talking to me?"

"I have a suggestion to make. Don't dismiss it before you think it through. I believe you should go forward for election. You know who our representatives are in this area. They're not worth a shit. A pack of yes-men. We need a strong voice now."

Ewan laughed into Clive Rigney's weasly little face. "So I was right. You are going Green!"

It was amusing to watch Clive struggle with his temper. His features seemed to grow more pointed as he drew the anger inside himself. "We can score points off each other or we can be mature. You have a high profile and a significant support base. I have local concerns that I think you would best represent at government level. I am willing to support your nomination in any way I can."

"Say it, Clive. Say it. Money. You are willing to put money into my campaign. It's always about money, isn't it?"

"Don't be such a prig. Even principled environmentalists need money."

"You still haven't told me why," Ewan said. "Why is it that your own henchmen can't represent your point of view any more? What would you expect for your campaign contribution?"

Clive looked around the pub as if checking for eavesdroppers. He leaned forward, the features even more weasel-like up close. "RTTI," he whispered. "I don't want them here. I want to be sure they never operate in our constituency. We can agree on that, can't we?"

Ewan sat back. He needed to distance himself from the narrowed eyes. It was obvious now why Rigney wanted to be identified with EnVirowatch. What was not clear was why he wanted to oppose RTTI. Why should he? Would RTTI not bring increased employment to the area, increased custom to Rigney's supermarkets?

"You're not going to tell me you're worried about air and water pollution, are you? Because if you do I'll know you are bullshitting."

"Where do you and your crowd get off being so sanctimonious? You think you're the only people concerned with the quality of the environment. With the quality of life. Maybe you'd have a lot more support if you stopped being so patronising and elitist."

That would have been quite a convincing outburst if it had come from someone else, thought Ewan.

But EnVirowatch desperately needed funding. The

local committee would make the final decision this weekend but it seemed almost certain that Ewan would be putting his name forward as an election candidate. Endorsement by the national EnVirowatch committee would be just a matter of form. Now would probably be a stupid time to alienate Clive Rigney. Whatever his motivation.

"I'll talk to you next week, Clive. EnVirowatch will have decided on a course of action by then. But you may as well know, we are considering my candidature. Even before we knew about your new-found enthusiasm for all things clean and Green."

They both stood at the same instant. Their meeting was over. The crowd parted respectfully as Clive swept towards the door.

Rather than walk in his wake, Ewan went to the bar to buy another drink. One more before he faced home. Ria called out again. Ewan looked over and felt Claire Hearn's dark eyes on him. He was drawn towards her.

Once he was served his drink he walked over to the table.

"Was that Clive Rigney I saw you with?" Paul greeted him.

Ewan laughed. "You really are going for Investigative Reporter of the Year, aren't you?"

"Do the introductions, Paul," Trish said.

Paul introduced him to the woman in the pink sweater. The woman with the dark eyes and soft shiny hair. Claire. Claire Hearn. He sat beside her and breathed in her perfume. He half listened to conversation batting back and forth between Paul and Trish, Ria and Kevin. He found it hard to concentrate on the words while he was so aware of the woman beside him.

"I'm starving!" Ria announced. "How about Chinese?"

"Italian! I want Italian!" Trish insisted.

"We'll let Claire decide before you two start a fight," Paul said.

"Burger and chips," she said. "I'd like burger and chips."

"Cheeseburger with garlic and mayonnaise. Perfect!" Ewan said.

The night was mild and overcast. They walked through the darkness to the chip shop in the town. Ewan and Claire walked together behind the chattering group. They did not talk much. Their awareness of each other was robbing them of words. Silently, they exchanged mobile phone numbers. Claire felt none of her usual hesitation in revealing her number. She trusted this handsome, gentle man.

They shook hands when they said goodbye and they both knew they were just saying *au revoir*.

Chapter Thirteen

"We're almost here now," Yvette told them as they turned off the motorway and left the London traffic behind.

Frank sneaked a sideways glance at Brendan. His son-in-law was slumped in the corner of the car, white-faced and sullen. A file lay open on his knee but it was obvious that his attention was focused on Yvette. She was sitting beside the driver and chatting easily with him. She turned towards the backseat passengers and smiled.

"It is good that we will all carry out this inspection together. Then there can be no misinterpretations or misunderstandings."

"There are always misinterpretations and misunderstandings," Brendan snapped.

Yvette shrugged and turned her back to them again.

As they approached the plant, Frank noted that in

size and design it was almost a copy of Dashern. He leaned forward towards Yvette. "Am I to assume my counterpart here in London is waiting to tell us how happy he is with RTTI?"

"You know you have no counterpart, Frank. You are unique."

She had looked directly at him as she spoke and now she was smiling at him. "You're a unique bollocks," Brendan muttered just loud enough for Frank to hear.

As they got out of the car Frank whispered to his son-in-law. "Grow up for Christ's sake!"

Yvette pretended not to hear and pretended not to gloat. She turned her attention to the plant manager who was waiting to greet them. He offered his hand to Frank.

"Welcome, Mr Dawson. I hope you will find your visit here enjoyable."

"I'm looking forward to seeing your operation," Frank said as he shook hands. "And of course I'd like to hear the inside story on what it is like to be an RTTI partner."

Frank caught the quick look the manager threw in Yvette's direction before he led the party off on a tour of his plant.

*   *   *

The old man was totally absorbed. He seemed enthralled by the distillation units, the bottling plant, the quality control procedures and the labelling process. He walked ahead with the plant manager, asking questions, taking notes, poking and prodding at everything. Brendan nodded occasionally and pretended to show interest but all his attention was drawn to the woman by his side. He had to fight the urge to reach out and touch her.

"Well, Bren? What do you think?"

He stopped walking and looked at her. The amber eyes gazed back at him. "I think you're deliberately avoiding me. Why did you let the old man stay for the weekend?"

Her mouth smiled but her eyes glittered with anger. "You forget our agreement? We must get the merger through, get the phytoplant up and running. That is our priority now. When Dashern and RTTI are working happily together, then we will see where *we* go. Yes?"

Brendan stared back at her and for the first time he saw the steel in her eyes and in the set of her chin. "How did you get my father-in-law to change his plans? He should be at home with Dorothy now. What did you do?"

She turned her back on him and went to join Frank and the plant manager. Her hips swayed as she walked and heat surged through Brendan's body. Of course he knew the problem. It was the alarm code. He followed Yvette and stood beside her as the plant manager waffled on about licences.

"It's because Claire changed the alarm code for her lab, isn't it? RTTI desperately need her research, don't they?"

Yvette raised one beautifully shaped eyebrow. "If you cannot manage your wife, Brendan, how can you hope to manage a plant?"

Brendan felt a flush spread up his face. He shoved his hands into his pockets because they were shaking with anger. Claire, the bitch! Pretending to be so withdrawn, so academic, so naïve. And all the time she was really ruthless and calculating. She had her lab and her bloody research locked up like Fort Knox. His fingers curled as he imagined them tightening around Claire's throat.

"Someone steal your lollipop, boy? You haven't heard a word I've said."

They were all looking at him. His angry blush deepened into one of embarrassment.

"Just to bring you up to date," Frank said sharply, "we're going to see the holding tanks now. Would you care to join us?"

Brendan tagged onto the group as they made their way to the holding tanks at the back of the plant. Every step he took made him more determined to destroy the Dawsons, Frank and Claire. Father and daughter, wife and father-in-law. They had humiliated him for the last time.

*   *   *

Claire normally slept a little later on Saturdays but this morning she woke before the sun. She turned on her side and tried to snuggle under the duvet but each time she closed her eyes she imagined Brendan in London. The images got more and more vivid. Brendan chasing Yvette, leering at her, panting like a dog after a bitch on heat. She threw back the covers and got up.

By the time she had showered and dressed the sun had risen. It was going to be a beautiful day. A day to share. After putting the coffee on to percolate she opened the patio doors and walked out to the garden. The air was sweet. She walked towards the source of the perfume. It was a bed of carnations, pink and white and red. She looked around and saw smooth lawns, blooming shrubs, colourful flowerbeds and clematis trailing over a pergola. It was beautiful. A credit to the gardener. She walked about as if seeing it for the first time. Really seeing it. Standing by the water feature, she listened to the soothing sound of water trickling over the stones.

Back inside the house she wandered from room to room. The kitchen was state-of- the-art chrome and beech, the lounge tastefully minimalist without being cold, the dining-room classic, the study functional but stylish. Wooden floors gleamed and art pieces were discreetly displayed. A beautiful house. A house. A tastefully decorated space. She drank her coffee quickly and went to where she really lived. To her lab.

*   *   *

Claire had just arrived in the lab when the phone rang. It was her mother.

"Seems like the two of us are abandoned for the weekend, Claire. How about meeting for lunch?"

"That would be nice, Mum. Have you heard from Dad?"

"Yes. He's in good form. Seems to be enjoying his trip. They're at the London sister plant today."

"Sister plant?"

"Well, so to speak. It was in private ownership and now it is amalgamated with RTTI. Just like Dashern. Where will we go for lunch?"

Claire looked quickly around the lab and assessed the amount of work she had to do. She should have the animals monitored, records entered and preparations done in three hours.

"Mum, how about you come around to my place? I'll cook lunch. We can eat in the garden. It's a beautiful day."

"*You're* going to cook? I hope this isn't another one of your experiments. Are you using me as one of your guinea pigs?"

"Ha, ha! I'll cook you a beautiful meal. Two o'clock OK?"

"That is perfect," Dorothy said and then she paused before adding, "Claire, your father and I were going to discuss something important with you today. Since he has been delayed, I'll explain the situation to you. Then we can discuss it together when he comes back."

Claire frowned. Dorothy was not given to dramatics. This "something" for discussion must be very significant.

"See you at two then," Claire said and quickly checked the time before going back to her work.

* * *

The supermarket was busy. Claire strolled around the aisles, planning the menu as she went. This was so different to the dash-and-grab mission that usually represented her grocery shopping.

It was hard to concentrate. So many emotions vied for her attention. First, the elation, the sheer joy of success. The guinea pigs on Serum 6 were still fighting their cancers. They were recovering from the disease, their temperatures normal, their eyes bright and shining with health, their tumours shrinking. Clarence was chirping happily and greedy for his food. The animals in the control group were dying. Serum 6 was doing the job she had always believed it would. Alleluia!

The feelings of triumph were shot through with depression. The success of this trial was, to Claire, the definitive proof that Ronan Hennessey had interfered with the previous trials. Industrial sabotage. And Yvette Previn's fingerprints were all over the plot. And Brendan wished they were all over him too. Her marriage was dying. Dead. She stopped walking and allowed the thought find its place in her consciousness. She had known for so long.

"Choices, choices. Having problems deciding, Claire?"

She started guiltily and blushed as if Clive Rigney could read her thoughts. This was his flagship store and the great man seemed to be doing a tour of inspection with a retinue of suited lackeys in tow. Glancing around, she noticed that she had wandered into the fruit and veg section. "You've such a selection on display, it's difficult to make a choice," she said quickly, darting a look at the carrots and onions to add authenticity to her remark.

"We aim to please our customers. Keep them happy and healthy. I'm sure most companies are driven by the same policy. Wouldn't you agree?"

"That and making a profit – and you are obviously very good at both, Clive."

"At least my profits won't have to be repatriated. National pride and all that. Which reminds me. What do you think of Ewan Peters? I know you met him recently. He will be standing as a candidate in the General Election."

How did Clive Rigney know that she had met Ewan Peters? Then she remembered the Mellow Drama. She had not seen Clive but remembered that Paul mentioned him being there. What did she think of Ewan? That he was kind and sensitive and funny and very, very attractive. Clive's ferrety eyes bored into her and she blushed.

"He'll make a good candidate and representative, I'm sure. But isn't he with EnVirowatch? I thought your loyalties lay elsewhere."

"Changing times, young lady. As I'm sure your

father will explain to you when he gets back."

Claire opened her mouth to question him but he clicked his fingers and he and his retinue swept off before she could get a sentence together. She looked after him and wondered why he had mentioned her father.

A glance at her watch told her she had better get the lunch ingredients into her basket and head for home.

*   *   *

Brendan studied Yvette's technique over lunch. She was very subtle. No overt flirting. She was too clever and too accomplished for vulgarity. The slightest thrust of her breasts in the direction of her target, an amber-eyed gaze for a millisecond, a smile beamed directly at her unsuspecting quarry. These were her stock in trade and she was using them to good effect.

It was obvious that Frank was her man of the moment. She singled him out for thrusts and gazes, ignoring Brendan and the three people from the London plant. Frank must have been feeling the heat of her offensive because his face was red and little beads of sweat were gathering on his forehead.

"So you were impressed with the system, Frank?" she asked.

"I can see that herbal extraction and distillation is working well here. That doesn't mean I believe it to be the system for Dashern."

"Of course there will have to be adaptations and

modifications. Different plants, different parameters. Different countries, different requirements. But your overall opinion?"

"Well, I think . . ." Brendan began but his words died for lack of an audience. Everybody was waiting to hear Frank.

"Gut reaction? This plant is running very smoothly. The merger appears to be seamless. But I'd like a lot more time to reflect and study before agreeing that this is the ideal template for Dashern-RTTI."

Yvette lifted her glass in his direction. "That's good enough for now. We'll talk more later. OK?"

Brendan gritted his teeth as he watched his father-in-law and Yvette exchange a glance that could only be described as intimate.

*   *   *

The beautiful morning had developed into a beautiful day. Claire went into the garden, picked some of the fragrant carnations and placed them in the centre of the table. She stood back and admired her handiwork. Perfect! She was smiling as she went to answer the doorbell.

"Hi, Mum. Come through to the garden. I have the patio table set."

Dorothy followed her through and stopped in surprise when she saw the bottle of champagne in the ice bucket.

"What are we celebrating, Claire?"

"We'll think of something. The sunshine maybe?"

Dorothy gave her daughter a puzzled look. Then she sat down and smiled. How often had she wished that her solemn, workaholic daughter were more light-hearted, more in touch with the joys of life?

"To sunshine!" she said as she raised the glass Claire had filled for her.

The meal was delicious, the melon and orange appetising, the salmon succulent, the sorbet cleansing, the pavlova a perfect blend of crispy, fruity and creamy.

Dorothy sat back and loosened the band of her skirt. "Well, well! That was superb. Have you been taking cookery lessons?"

"I wish. Too busy in the lab. Too busy to do anything else. But it's all going to be worth it, Mum. I'm almost there. My work is almost done."

"Your research? It's going well? Frank said you are at animal trial stage. That is pretty advanced, isn't it?"

Claire absently cut another slice of pavlova and put it on her plate without really wanting to eat it. She pushed it around with her fork. She looked up at her mother.

"Look, Mum, I know I have never really discussed my research with you or Dad."

"It's on apoptosis, isn't it?"

Claire looked at her mother in surprise. Dorothy sniffed and raised her chin a fraction.

"Did you really think your father and I would invest all that money in your research facility without having an idea what you were up to in it?"

"No. I never thought you wouldn't understand. I –"

"You never thought about anything but your research, Claire. We understand that. We read the research other people have done in the same area. Both of us were confident that you would be the one to bring it to the final stage. That is why you got your lab and it is why your father set up the holding company to protect your work."

"ClairCo? And the trust fund that you and Jeremiah Audley manage?"

Dorothy nodded. She picked up her glass and took a sip of champagne. Everything about her said that she was bracing herself for an announcement. Claire held her breath.

"You know that I said I had something to discuss with you? Well, your father and I have decided to sell Grange House."

The shock was immense. A thousand images flooded Claire's mind as she thought of her childhood home. Grange House, with its sweeping driveway, gardens, grand entrance hall, cornices, the attic with the treasure trove of dusty chests, the stables. The history. It was home.

"But why? How can you? It's been in your family for generations. It's the Gore-Croft ancestral home. And where would you and Dad go? Who would buy it anyway?"

"Slow down, Claire! Too many questions together. I'll put the coffee on and then I'll give you the answers."

Claire sat in stunned silence while Dorothy went to the kitchen. The pictures kept racing through her head. Her room. A light-filled, odd-shaped bedroom, overlooking the lawns. The musty smell in the unused rooms. The secret places. Grange House had always been a place to feel safe.

"Coffee won't be long. Now for the answers to some of your questions."

Dorothy sat down beside Claire. "The why first. Your father is not well. You know that. The situation with the merger is not helping. He knows amalgamation is the way forward for Dashern. The only way. He is not as sure about RTTI. But Brendan seems to have taken the initiative there. So, taking everything into account, Frank decided that now is the right time for him to retire."

"Retire? Dad!"

"Amazing, isn't it? He is so looking forward to golf and swimming and sun."

"Sun?"

"Yes. We're going to live in Portugal. We're flying out next week to view some properties." She leaned down, picked up her bag from the ground, took out a bundle of brochures and put them on the table. "Look at these, Claire. Villas, apartments, all by the sea, all in the sun. We will probably go for a small villa. Near a golf course, naturally. And I want a garden. Maybe even a vineyard." She stopped when she saw the tears in Claire's eyes. "We'll visit each other," she said softly. "And Frank will retain his voting share in the company so we'll commute regularly."

Claire nodded and tried to smile. "When?"

"Soon. We have had a very good offer on Grange

House. Our client is willing to pay above market price. He is anxious for closure."

"Who is it??"

"Clive Rigney."

Her words hung like a black cloud over the sun-filled garden. Claire's stomach churned at the thought of that creepy man sitting in their drawing-room, his little feet walking their land, his bony hands touching their furniture, his vulgar wife playing Lady of the Manor. His changing-times comment in the supermarket today made sense now.

"Are you all right with this, Claire? You understand that it is not a *fait accompli*. We can discuss it. Rethink it if you want."

Claire stood up and walked around to her mother. She hugged Dorothy. "I'm happy for you and Dad. I hope you'll enjoy your place in the sun."

"But?"

"Yes, but. Your family built Grange House. Gore-Crofts have lived in it for two hundred years. Are you sure you really want to sell? And Dad? How long do you think he'll be satisfied with a few games of golf and a stroll in the garden?"

"How boring you make it sound! No, Frank and I have plans. Far more than golf and gardening. And of course it is going to be a wrench selling Grange House. But the upkeep is horrendously expensive. Not practical for a retired couple. Not even practical for a young couple today."

They sat in silence while the air cooled and petals

began to fold over the delicate centres of the flowers.

*   *   *

It was typical of the RTTI Public Relations department to have entertainment organised. It was typical of Yvette, as PR manager, that the entertainment should be elegant and exciting.

Brendan looked around him at the sophisticated audience. He felt gauche even though he looked the part now. He knew he did. His Louis Copeland suit, hand-made shirt, his grooming, his Rolex made him seem like one of them. Yet inside he was cowering, still the scholarship student, trying to compete with the upper-class fee-paying students. He straightened his silk tie and sat up taller. He was in the corporate section, seated beside the most beautiful woman in the theatre. To hell with insecurity.

"How did you swing this, Yvette?" Frank asked. "Tickets to an Andrea Bocelli concert are like gold."

"Just enjoy," she said, putting her hand on his arm and smiling at him.

The lights dimmed. The buzz of conversation faded. Brendan tried to tune into the air of anticipation that seemed to make even the stage curtains shiver with excitement but his senses were saturated with the sight, the smell, the sound of Yvette.

The orchestra burst into the silence and the curtains parted. Andrea Bocelli was distinguished, handsome. Beside him Sarah Brightman looked fragile and very beautiful in a floaty white gown. The theatre filled with their voices as they sang through all the raw emotions of parting in *"Con Te Partiro"*. Frank was leaning forward, his mouth slightly open, completely absorbed in the performance. Brendan glanced at Yvette and was surprised to see the same rapt expression on her face.

The audience clapped. And clapped. Sarah Brightman floated off stage and Bocelli sang alone, mesmerising his listeners with the range and passion of his voice.

By the end of the evening Brendan felt he had been dragged through every emotion from anger to ecstasy. He stood with the rest of the audience and applauded.

"I wish Dorothy was here," Frank said.

Yvette raised an eyebrow.

"She loves Andrea Bocelli. I always promised her we would go to a concert. Just never got around to it," he explained.

"Well, you will have the opportunity when –"

Brendan lost the rest of Yvette's reply in the applause as Bocelli returned to the stage for an encore. The unfinished sentence niggled at him during the encore, the drive back to the hotel, the late night drinks in the residents' bar. By the time they all got the elevator to their first-floor rooms, he was utterly convinced that Frank and Yvette were planning something and he was not part of their plan.

Brendan's knuckles were white as he gripped his swipe card for his room. All his work for this weekend had been a waste. It had not been easy to track down the hotel where she was staying and to find out her room number. It had cost over the odds to get the room next to hers. All that planning just to end up the gooseberry. He glared at the old man's back, at the fold of purple-tinged flesh that rolled over his shirt collar. Fuck him! Why hadn't he gone home as he was scheduled to do?

As if he sensed the anger directed at him, Frank turned to Brendan. "I want to talk to you. Come into my room."

Yvette leaned forward, kissed the old man on the cheek and said goodnight. Brendan tensed himself for his turn, for the closeness of her, for the chance to whisper in her ear, for a whisper from her. A promise. An invitation. She turned her back and walked away from him, hips swaying as she moved.

"Bonne nuit, Brendan. Sleep well."

That was it. That was what he got. A mocking goodnight wish.

* * *

Frank did not invite his son-in-law into his room. He ordered him in and then firmly shut the door, flopped onto one of the armchairs and loosened his tie. He nodded in the direction of the drinks cabinet.

"Get drinks. I must ring Dorothy before I talk to you. Maybe you should make a phone call too."

A shiver went down Brendan's spine at the thought of hearing Claire's voice, an accusation in every syllable. He could not subject himself to that. He got glasses and put ice in them. He could hear the old man babbling to Dorothy about the concert. As he poured the whiskey, the sparkling amber reminded him of Yvette's eyes. The way they glittered with anger, with laughter, with amusement. He stood still, a glass in each hand, remembering how those same amber eyes had looked on him with disdain this weekend. Amusement had glittered there too and even a shade of mockery. A blush of shame flushed his skin.

"What are you doing with those drinks? Bring them here."

He walked over and handed Frank his whiskey without looking at him. How that old prick must be enjoying this! Brendan turned on the television and muted the sound. A news presenter looked solemn as she read the latest headlines. Brendan did not see her as he sat in front of the screen with head bowed. He was watching the scenes of the past few days as they replayed in his mind, frame by humiliating frame. The subterfuge as he organised his trip here. The disappointment as Yvette made it obvious that she did not want to see him, the embarrassment as she flirted with Frank and ignored him.

"Did you hear any of that phone conversation?"

Brendan was forced to look at his father-in-law. The big head was redder and sweatier than usual. The fucker looked as if he was about to burst with excitement. "I don't eavesdrop."

"Maybe you should. It might do you good to listen

to something other than the sound of your own voice for a change. Anyway Dorothy and Claire – Claire is your wife, by the way, in case you had forgotten –"

Brendan jumped to his feet. A lecture from the old man heaped upon self-disgust and humiliation was more than he could sit for.

The old man shouted at him. "Sit down, you oaf! I have something important to tell you. And I'm not going to talk to you while you're looming over me like a thundercloud."

Brendan's instinct was to walk away. Tell the old man to screw himself. Not true. His instinct was to punch the fucker in the angry, red face, to out-bully the bully. They stared at each other. Pragmatism won. Brendan sat.

Satisfied, Frank spoke. "I am going to retire. Dorothy and I are selling Grange House and moving to Portugal. And before you wet yourself with excitement, you should know I am retaining my voting share in Dashern. Or Dashern-RTTI."

Here it was at last. The day Brendan had waited so long for. Frank Dawson gone from the factory. No more reporting to the self-styled God, asking permission, waiting for answers, backing down, giving in. No more regular inquisitions into his marriage.

"Dorothy told Claire about our plans today. Claire is very happy for us. How do you feel about it, Brendan? Apart from being glad about having me out of your way."

His first thought was to deny being glad but the

denial would have been a waste of breath. He closed his eyes for a moment and saw himself in Frank's office, sitting in that big chair, the throne as he had come to think of it. Respect! Yes. They would all have to respect him now.

"Is it relief or disbelief has stunned you into silence?"

"Maybe both."

They were silent while they each came to terms with their reactions. Frank stared at the bowed head of his son-in-law.

"We're alike in a lot of ways, you know."

The softness of the tone made Brendan look up in surprise. "In what way?"

"We are both ambitious men. Both started with next to nothing and clawed our way up. Both married to further our careers."

Brendan smiled. Of course he would have to mention Claire, to have a go at him about their marriage. But confession time? Not Frank's style. Not his either.

"I married Claire because I love her. Are you saying now you don't love Dorothy? What was it? Why did you marry her? The big house, the bank balance, the Gore-Croft land?"

Frank filled up his glass again and sat opposite Brendan. He relaxed back into his chair and took a cigar out of his inside pocket. He went through the ritual of lighting up in silence. A haze of blue-white smoke engulfed them.

"Yes. I married Dorothy for all those reasons. Especially the land. Dashern is built on Grange Estate. She sold off land to fund me and keep me going in the early days. That is why I married her."

Brendan stared at his father-in-law. Everybody knew why Frank Dawson had married Dorothy Gore-Croft. But he had never admitted it before. And he never did or said anything without a payback. What was he after now?

"That is where we're the same, Brendan. You married Claire to get your hands on your share of Dashern. I married her mother in order to set it up. But the similarity ends there. I grew to love Dorothy. More than anything else. I have never cheated on her. And never would."

Brendan's laugh was loud and mocking. "What kind of a fucking hypocrite are you? All this sentimental tripe about loving Dorothy when you have spent this whole weekend trying to worm your way into Yvette Previn's bed! Have you any idea how pathetic you look? A middle-aged relic drooling over a young woman! Why didn't you go back home like you were supposed to? Do you really believe that Yvette feels anything more than disgust when she looks at you?"

It was Frank's turn to laugh now. White ash tumbled from the tip of his cigar as his bulky body shook with amusement. "If you used your brain for one minute you would realise that Yvette has been doing all the chasing. And yes. I'm sure I physically disgust her but that would not stop her getting into bed with me to get what she wants. She wants Claire's research. She desperately needs to deliver that formula to RTTI. They believe Claire has found the cure for cancer and they want to control it."

"What could Claire have found? She's been messing around with her pet apoptosis theory for years. So have a lot of other people. Any of the big research teams would be more likely to advance the research than your dilly-daydream daughter. Don't try to fuck me around with lies, Frank."

Frank dumped his cigar onto the ashtray and stood up. Beads of sweat dotted his forehead as he walked to the door. Hand on the doorknob he turned to Brendan. "Get out of here. You make me sick. You used my family and my daughter. You cheated on her with that French whore. And don't try to deny it because Jacques Rondel told me all about your trip to Bonn. I've known for some time now. The only reason I haven't told my daughter is that I don't want to hurt her. Yvette is leading you around by the balls, you imbecile! Did you really believe that Dashern was in any way important to RTTI? It was *always* Claire's work they were after. Just as well I have it legally protected. Claire's research is safe from RTTI. And Dashern will be safe from you because you will be well monitored by the new manager."

Brendan had no time to assimilate and rationalise. His emotions engaged away ahead of his brain. The blood surged to his head on a wave of rage. He lunged towards Frank and grabbed him by the collar. He shook the older man.

"What do you mean? New manager? Who? What have you done, you bastard!"

Anger gave strength to Frank's untoned muscles. He pushed his son-in-law away from him and stared into the ugliness of a face distorted with hate. He was sure then about the decision he had made.

"I stayed on here this weekend to interview my successor. If you had taken your eyes off Yvette's tits you would have realised what was going on. He was on the plant tour with us today and at the concert with us tonight. Trevor Langley is Deputy Manager at the London plant here and he is going to be Acting Manager of Dashern when I go to Portugal. You will be his deputy, just as you are mine. You are not fit to fill my shoes."

The punch was clean and strong and came from Brendan's heart. It connected with all the might of suppressed anger suddenly released in a flash of bone-crushing temper. Frank reeled back as the fist slammed onto his cheekbone. As if in slow motion, Brendan saw the contact spot on the cheekbone go white, then flood a vivid red as blood seeped from where the skin had broken. The red stream welled at the edge of the wound and began to trickle through the folds and creases of the puffy face. Brendan lifted his hands instinctively to protect himself from reprisal. Then his hands dropped to his sides.

Frank was standing still. Stunned. His eyes staring in shock. Slowly he turned the knob and opened the door back. He spoke very quietly.

"Get out of my room. Get out of my company. Get out of my daughter's life. You're fired."

Fired! Fired! The softly spoken word roared in Brendan's head. His knuckles stung and there was a hot, salty stinging behind his eyelids that could only be tears. Jesus! How had this happened? Fuck!

He took a step back and saw the steel that had been momentarily knocked out of Frank creep back in. He could not, would not, beg the hard-faced bastard. He turned his back and walked into the corridor. He heard the door click shut behind him.

His legs felt weak now, as if he had been the one to take the blow. He passed Yvette's room. Light seeped out from under her door. He turned back, knocked gently and called her name. The door opened and he knew then she had been waiting for him. The lacy white negligee, the soft lighting, the warm glow in her eyes told him that Yvette wanted him as much as he wanted her. She opened her arms and he went to her. He held her tightly as he tumbled out the story of his row with Frank, his anger at being sidelined, his loss of control when he hit the old man. He did not tell her that his father-in-law had fired him. He could not and would not accept that he had been fired. Yvette held him and stroked and caressed him.

"Is Frank all right now?" she asked.

"Of course. It is only a small cut," Brendan said, annoyed that she should show any concern. "The bastard had it coming to him."

Yvette smiled. It was a satisfied smile. She had all

she needed. Then she allowed her negligee to drop to the floor and she gave Brendan what he needed.

* * *

Frank stood with his back to the door for several minutes after Brendan left. His face hurt but not much. The fact that his son-in-law hit him was the real agony. He had always hoped, dreamed, that Brendan would mature into the son-in-law he wanted him to be. He had it in him. But there was no going back now. The fact that Yvette had turned his head so easily spoke volumes about his lack of character and loyalty. Claire deserved better. He would have to have a serious talk to her when he got home. Explain to her why he had fired his son-in-law. Tell her what a prick her husband was, tell her about Yvette Previn, confess to the pre-nuptial agreement. The rest would be up to her then but Frank knew his daughter would do the right thing. She was a Dawson.

He walked towards the bathroom. There must be a first aid kit. He reached his hand towards the cabinet over the sink. The pain shot down his left arm. A weight wrapped around his chest and crushed his lungs. Fuck! His medication was in the lounge. In his jacket. His head felt as if it was about to burst. A heart attack! He was getting a fucking heart attack! He tried to shout for help but his breath was locked in his lungs. If he could get his spray. If he could get to the phone. He turned to go out the door but the room began to waver and darken. He focused on the light from the bedroom and tried to walk towards it. A massive pain seared through his chest. He felt his knees weaken, felt his face hit the corner of the vanity unit. Then Frank felt no more.

Chapter Fourteen

The figures were not registering. Claire's eyes slid over graphs and columns but her mind stayed with the ugliness of death. The coldness of it. The stillness.

"At least the guinea pigs seem to be doing well."

She jumped and turned around. Kevin was standing behind her. He had obviously adopted what he considered to be the appropriate pose. It was a cross between the professional solemnity of an undertaker and the anxiety of a puppy to please. He thrust his hand towards her with a jerky movement.

"I'm really sorry about Mr Dawson. About your father."

Claire took his hand and smiled at him. She was still in shock, even though it was four days since she had got the awful call from Brendan telling her Frank had died. Four days of hiding from people and daylight, from life without her father. The shock made it easy to smile now, to accept the condolences gracefully, to be dignified. "Thank you, Kevin. And thank you for looking after the animals for the past few days. I really appreciate it."

He blushed and she squeezed her eyes shut as an image of her father's face flashed into her mind. Not now. Later. Much later.

"I don't know what to do about Serum 6, Mrs Hearn. The stocks are running low. If you left instructions for me maybe I could make some up. I have already done the preparatory work."

"No need, Kevin, thanks. I have it under control. The new batch is in the cold room, ready for use."

Kevin's surprise was apparent. He was probably trying to figure out how she could possibly concentrate on work when her father had just died or just when she had done it. The work had been the easy part. The difficulty was in trying to find a permanent place in her head for the death part. At times she knew, recognised that Frank Dawson was no more, that her father was gone. When the pain became too intense she let the knowing go.

Claire had come here to the lab at six o'clock this morning. Straight from the airport. Making up the serum, weighing, measuring, centrifuging, had been comforting after the cold vigil she and Dorothy had endured. Two hours they had waited in the airport for the chartered flight to touch down. That was the worst part. Seeing Brendan walk off the plane while her father had been wheeled across the tarmac like a piece of baggage. The undertakers had taken Frank's body away to ply their mortician's trade. He would be suited, made up, combed and powdered by the time she and Dorothy would see him, all traces of his dying disguised. No open, staring eyes, no signs of terror, no traces of struggle. Frank would have struggled. He would have fought death like a lion. Dying had not been part of his plan.

"He was about to retire, you know," Claire said to her bemused assistant. "He and my mother were going to live in Portugal."

Kevin made the only reply he could think of. "Coffee?"

She dipped her head slightly so Kevin took that as a yes. He put on the kettle and spooned coffee into the mugs. His head was buzzing with questions and not just because Ria had him pestered. He needed to know how Frank Dawson's death was going to affect Dashern. If it meant the end of the research lab. The factory was rife with rumour. Everyone had a different take on the future. Brendan Hearn would take over, RTTI would buy the entire plant and there was a school of opinion that said the whole operation was going to close down.

Claire walked into the canteen and sat down at the table. He put her mug of coffee in front of her. She was so pale that her eyes looked black rather than brown.

"How is your mother bearing up?" asked Kevin.

"Mum is strong. She is coping as well as she possibly could in this situation."

"Do you know yet what happened? How he . . . how he died?"

"Yes. There was an autopsy in England. He had a heart attack. A massive heart attack."

She was silent again. Kevin finished his coffee but she did not touch hers. The animals were due their morning feed so he stood.

"I'd better get on with work, Mrs Hearn."

She nodded. He washed his cup and went back into the lab. It was thirty minutes before she joined him.

"I'm going home to get some rest, Kevin. I've left a list of instructions. You know the dosages of serum and where to find the new batch. You're doing fine. I really appreciate all your work. Thank you."

"When will the ... the ...?"

Poor Kevin. He just could not say funeral. Claire put him out of his discomfort. "The removal will be tonight and the burial tomorrow. I'm going to put a notice in the plant now."

She was just by the door, notice in hand, when Kevin remembered LabAn. "Someone named Hennessey from LabAn has rung for you several times. Ronan Hennessey. I told him you had a family bereavement but he is very insistent. He wants to come here to check something about the last batch of animals they delivered."

She swung around at the door. Sparks of anger exploded in the dark numbness of her mind. Ronan Hennessey and Anne Moroney. Ronan Hennessey and Yvette Previn. Yvette Previn and Brendan. Had Frank known? Why, oh why, hadn't she talked to him, why hadn't she told him about – about everything?

Claire realised she had been holding her breath. She exhaled and a sob escaped on the shuddering breath. She ran back to Kevin and stood in front of him, small and dark, shaking with shock and grief and anger.

"Don't let him in here, Kevin! Don't ever let anybody other than you and me in here! Do you understand? Nobody else sets foot in this lab. Not Ronan Hennessey, not Brendan, not RTTI. Nobody!"

Her intensity stunned him. He wanted to remind her that Calbitron were authorised to come into R&D too but instead he just nodded, afraid that any word might break the fragile hold she seemed to have on her emotions.

"They know!" she went on. "They're aware that our research here is ready for development. Do you realise that the animals on treatment are no longer dying from cancer? They want it, those ruthless people. They want our serum. They want to patent it, produce it and sell it to the highest bidder. They don't want to cure. They want to profit. You must never, *ever*, let them get hold of any information. Understood?"

Her eyes, which had been so dark and listless, were blazing now. They riveted him, defying him to disagree. And why should he? This was only confirming what he already knew. Claire Hearn had found the cure for cancer. The secret was in her serum mixture. The secret was in her head. What a big secret for such a little woman! Should he tell her that Ronan

Hennessey had offered him a job, claiming that one of his LabAn staff had left to go to Australia and that he had a position vacant? When Kevin had heard the exorbitant salary on offer, it was obvious to him that Ronan Hennessey had been trying to bribe him. He had been foolish enough to tell Ria. What a mistake that had been! Her nagging had been relentless since. He was not going to repeat that mistake. No. Shut mouth. Anyway, this outburst was reassuring. He was satisfied that Claire Hearn was not about to give up or sell out.

"Don't worry, Mrs Hearn. I will look after your lab."

She sagged as if an invisible puppeteer had relaxed her strings. Lifting her hand, she patted him on the arm. "I know you will, Kevin."

Claire turned and walked away towards the plant, the notice detailing arrangements for her father's removal and funeral flapping in the breeze as she went.

*   *   *

Paul opened the note again. The page was getting tattered from all the folding and unfolding. He read it through, knowing the words by heart but yet needing to see them. He drummed the desk with his fingers. What to do?

He glanced towards the Editor's office. Myles Flannery was standing behind his desk, picking up papers and putting them into his briefcase. That meant he was on his way out. Enough thinking! Note in hand, Paul crossed the newsroom and tapped on the Editor's door.

"Is this important, Paul? I'm due in town in ten minutes."

In reply Paul pushed the note across the desk.

It was short. Myles had it read in seconds. "Where did you get this?"

"A courier dropped it off here last week. Said it was given to him at the airport."

Myles sat down and waved at Paul to follow suit. "Are you sure this is actually from Frank Dawson?"

"The handwriting matches. So does the timing. Frank Dawson was catching his flight to London at the time the courier said he collected the note from the airport."

"Hmm." Myles fell silent, rereading the note. "What do you think he's referring to in *'very important developments of global significance. A scoop in your parlance, Paul'*?"

"Read the postscript."

Myles looked down at the end of the page and read aloud. "*'PS. You asked me what I thought was my greatest achievement. It will become very clear that my daughter is. Talk soon. Frank.'*"

Myles stood and began to pace. It was a well-known fact in the newsroom that the faster Myles paced, the more important he rated the story. He was walking, and talking, fast now.

"So. Obviously Frank was telling you that these 'important developments' are connected to his daughter. What does she do in that factory anyway?"

"Research."

"On detergents? Hardly earth-shattering. We've been through this before. Is there something else going on in Dashern? Is that why a multinational like RTTI is suddenly buying into Dawsons?"

Paul knew it was decision time. Myles was interested, curious but not yet fully convinced. Hazy facts and speculation never impressed Flannery.

"Claire Hearn is researching a cancer treatment," he announced, carefully watching Myles for any reaction. "Her work is so far advanced that she has been granted a licence to run animal trials. As soon as her licence was approved, RTTI appeared magically on the scene, supposedly interested in setting up a herbal medicine facility in Dashern."

"Hmm."

"I have contacts, Myles. Inside Dashern. Inside Claire Hearn's lab."

"Go on."

"All I need is a little more time. I guarantee you this will be big."

Myles stopped his pacing and sat at his desk. He stared at Paul for what seemed like a long time before finally speaking.

"Take all the time you need. Do you want someone to cover your column while you work on this?"

"I can manage, Myles. Thank you."

Paul hid his smile of satisfaction until he was back sitting at his own desk. He was already on the phone arranging to meet Ria before Myles had left the office.

* * *

It had seemed to be a dark, dreamless sleep. Claire could not remember any images, any sounds, yet her face was wet with tears when she woke. The room was dim, the heavy curtains shutting out the daylight. How long had she slept?

A huge weight of sadness pressed on her chest, making it difficult to breathe. Somebody was touching her face, brushing her hair back from her forehead, whispering to her. She focused on the person leaning over her. It was Brendan, his face drawn and haggard in the half-light.

"I'm sorry, I'm sorry," he whispered over and over.

The weight inside her chest began to move, to grow hot. It pushed up into her throat, burning and aching. She opened her mouth and all the despair and fear compressed in the hot weight was released in a long, agonising wail. It mingled with Brendan's whispers. She heard herself call for her father, saw his face smile lovingly at her, saw him holding her hand as she skipped along beside him, Daddy's girl, a child safe and secure in her father's love. The wailing turned to sobbing. She clung to Brendan and cried until the space in her chest where the hot weight had been was cold and empty.

* * *

Ria had reacted just as Paul had supposed she would. He could sense her hysterical excitement on the other end of the phone line.

"Of course I'd love to be interviewed! Is it for your column? Where will I meet you? When will –?"

Paul sighed. This was not going to be comfortable. "Whoa! Hang on there. It's just background research on an article I'm doing and I think you may be able to help me. I'll pop around to the shop now and we can do the interview."

"No photo?"

He could hear the disappointment in her voice. "I'll do that later. Give you a chance to get your hair done or whatever. Could you put me on to Trish now, please, and I will see you in about twenty minutes."

It was a relief to hear Trish's calm voice on the other end of the line.

"What's going on, Paul? You've just sent my assistant into a tailspin."

"I'll explain later. I need some information from Ria. I don't want her to contact Kevin Trill until I have spoken to her."

"I don't like the sound of this. What are you up to?"

Paul's reply was sharp but he had to be sure that Kevin would not have the opportunity to warn Ria. "Just do as I ask. Keep her away from the phones. I'll see you soon."

Traffic was unusually heavy for the time of day and it was half an hour before he was parking outside Travelbug.

Ria was at the door. She grabbed his arm. "I thought you had changed your mind. Where are we going to do the interview?"

He looked into the shop. Trish was busy with customers. "An hour? OK?" he called.

Trish waved a hand at him. He turned to Ria. "Mellow Drama. C'mon."

The pub was quiet. Just a few seasoned drinkers staring into their pints. Paul seated Ria in an alcove at the back of the lounge and then went to the bar for two coffees. She was sitting on the edge of her seat when he came back. He smiled at her.

"Don't look so nervous, Ria. This is not an exam."

"What is it then? What is this about?"

Paul took a mouthful of coffee to give himself time. He hadn't thought about how much he was going to tell Ria. Or how little. He put his cup down.

"I'm writing Frank Dawson's obituary for *Newstrack*. I'm trying to get a broad picture of his life. I know you didn't know the man himself but you're acquainted with his daughter, aren't you?"

"Yes, I've met Claire Dawson. So have you. So has Trish. Try again, Paul."

He blushed. Silly mistake. Ria was a bit dizzy and indiscreet. She was not stupid. "OK. I'm sorry. That was a bit clumsy. The truth is that I wanted to ask you about something you said at the dinner party Trish and I had."

"Oh! That was the time I met Ewan Peters and his wife. Isn't it great he's going up for election? Maybe he'll become Taoiseach. Did you hear that he and his wife are having a few problems? Can't say I'm surprised. He is always busy with one cause or another. It'll be worse now that he will be out canvassing, morning, noon and night. I might –"

"Ria!"

It was her turn to blush. She folded her hands together, put them on top of the table and looked steadily at Paul. "Right. Sorry. I do waffle on. Let's agree that I'll stick to just answering your questions. So shoot."

Paul decided to go straight to the heart of the matter. "You said Claire Dawson was researching a cure for cancer."

Ria narrowed her eyes. She did not appear nearly as naïve without the wide-eyed blue gaze. The silence seemed to go on for an age before she finally stood up and buttoned her jacket, her long fingers moving swiftly. She was angry. Shit! He had handled this all wrong.

He stood to face her. "I'm sorry, Ria. I should have been honest with you. Please sit down and I'll tell you why I really need your help."

She stared at him, forcing him to stand there and explain himself. He told her about his research on RTTI, about their appalling environmental record, about his need to discover just why they had bought into Dashern. He told her about everything except Frank's note. He saw the anger fade from her eyes to be replaced by a sharpness he had never guessed at.

"If you remember me talking about cancer research

at the dinner party, you should also remember that I am in favour of RTTI taking over Dashern. I don't agree with you or Ewan Peters. Anyway, you're fighting a losing battle. Do you really think that a local news sheet and a Looney Left politician can stop a multinational? And did you believe that I was going to sit here and blab my guts out to you? Just what do you think I could know anyway?"

Paul sat down and waved at Ria to do the same. He had totally underestimated her. So had Trish. There was more to Ria than a good figure and blonde hair. There was a well-concealed astuteness and ambition underneath the harebrained image. Ewan Peters had taken her seriously. Had he guessed that she had some significant information? She was holding out. For what?

"What do you want?"

"It's simple, Paul. I want press coverage. I want my photo in your paper, in magazines, in the national press. I want a portfolio to send to model agencies. I want the catwalk, the excitement, the celebrity."

"You just called my paper 'a local news sheet' and now you want to use it to launch a modelling career!"

"You do a photo-shoot for me. Give me plenty of exposure on *Newstrack*. Call in your contacts in magazines. I know you have them. You give me a guarantee and I'll tell you what I know."

It was a long shot. Kevin would probably not have told her much anyway. It was even possible that Kevin himself didn't know much about Claire Hearn's work. Yet Paul's gut instinct was telling him to take what was on offer. A photo-shoot wouldn't hurt.

He reached across the table. "Deal."

She took his hand and smiled. The old Ria was back, all guileless smiles and innocent blue eyes. "Deal. But Kevin must never know."

"Or Trish."

They shook on their deal and then Ria told him about Serum 6, about the disappearing malignant tumours in the guinea pigs, about the new alarm system, about the distrust between Brendan Hearn and his wife Claire, about Brendan booking a room beside Yvette Previn's in London, about Ronan Hennessey of LabAn offering Kevin a job at an exorbitant salary.

And Kevin had refused the offer. Now Ria's co-operation made more sense to Paul. She was furious with Kevin and was determined to get her revenge. What better way could there be than to break all his confidences and then break his heart? There were certainly many hidden layers in Ria's character.

After Paul had dropped her back at Travelbug, he went straight to the office and took out Frank Dawson's note again. Then he opened the directory and looked up the number for LabAn.

*　　*　　*

Claire walked beside her mother. Dorothy held herself tall and straight and proud. She did not hesitate as they approached the funeral home, continuing her calm march towards her husband's coffin. Claire followed on, trying to emulate her mother but feeling so lost and shocked that her legs were shaking. She hated these funeral parlours, this commercialising of loss and grief, this sanitising of death.

The funeral director led Dorothy into the main area. He was speaking softly to her, anxiously checking that everything was to her satisfaction. The air was thick with the scent of varnish and candle-wax and decay. Claire felt nauseous. Brendan caught her by the elbow and held tight as they walked. The thick carpeting and abundance of dusky pink drapes lent a dreamlike quality to their trek. Every step brought them closer to the coffin at the top of the room. Claire stood and squeezed her eyes shut. If she did not see, did not look ... Against her will, her eyes opened and looked at the ornately carved coffin, at the silk lining, at Frank's dark grey suit, at the blue and grey tie Dorothy had chosen, at his hands joined together as if in prayer. At his face. His lips were blue. His eyes closed. There was a mark on his cheekbone. It was very faint. She had to lean close to see it.

"He fell when he ... when he got the heart attack. Hit his face against the vanity unit in the bathroom."

She looked up at Brendan and realised that up to now she had not asked for details. Had not wanted to hear the minutiae of her father's passing. Brendan had been the one, hadn't he? The last to talk to Frank and the first to see the body.

"I need to know," she whispered. "We must talk."

He nodded. They stood beside Frank Dawson's

corpse, wife, daughter and son-in-law, each silently and separately suffering their grief. They kept their vigil until people began to arrive for the removal.

*   *   *

Paul slammed down the phone. He was furious with himself. He had not been able to get past the receptionist at LabAn and it had been his own fault. He had told them he was researching an article on live animal use in scientific trials. How could he have been so fucking stupid? Now he had put them on alert. Any ruse he would try now to get to Ronan Hennessey or inside LabAn would be a waste of time. They must be used to fielding journalists. An article on animal experimentation was a useful little seller for most hacks. Which brought him to protesters and by association to Ewan Peters. Ewan must know this company. He must have had some confrontation with them at some stage in his career.

Helen Peters answered the phone and she obviously was not very happy. "I assume he is somewhere on the campaign trail. I have not seen him for the past twenty-four hours."

She did, however, give him Ewan's mobile number. When Paul rang, Ewan said he had been canvassing in the west of the constituency but that he was heading back for Frank Dawson's funeral tomorrow. They arranged to meet after the ceremony.

Paul did some more research on Ronan Hennessey

and discovered that he had graduated from University College Dublin with a degree in Zoology. An interesting piece of information he turned up was that LabAn was a privately owned company with three directors, one of whom was named John Hennessey. Paul smiled. No wonder Ronan had done Zoology. There had been a cosy job waiting for him at the end of his degree.

The other two were a Mr David Molloy and a Mr V McIntyre. McIntyre? Northern Irish? Scottish? He trawled through Irish Business Directory pages for any other reference to V McIntyre. There was none. It was in the International Business Directory that he discovered Vincento McIntyre. And his association with RTTI.

* * *

Claire stooped and kissed Frank's forehead. The coldness of that touch spread from her lips and seeped through her body. It stayed with her long after the lid had been closed on the coffin, after the procession had wound its way to the church. It was still there when the ceremony was over and they had left Frank to rest in the church overnight.

Chapter Fifteen

It did not seem right that the funeral day was warm and bright. Claire stood by the kitchen window, watching the sun mock the solemnity of her father's burial day. A good day to be buried. Friday. The end of a working week. The end of a life.

"Will you have toast?"

She turned to look at Brendan. While her grief wrenched her insides, his seemed to have ravaged his face. He was haggard, white-skinned and dark-stubbled. She shook her head.

"Just coffee, please."

They sat at the table, forgetting the meagre breakfast in front of them. There was so much to do today. Burial things.

"Is everything organised?"

"Dorothy didn't leave the undertakers much to do. She knows exactly what she wants." Claire smiled. She was proud of her mother. Dorothy seemed so in control. So dignified.

"Of course she's still marching to Frank's tune. He would have had all this well planned."

Was that a note of bitterness in Brendan's voice? Claire examined his face but saw nothing there except devastation. She reached over and touched his hand. "We never did talk about what happened to my father in London. Will you tell me now?"

He put his hand in his pocket and took out a pack of cigarettes. It had been two years since she had last seen him smoke. His fingers trembled as he raised the lighter to the cigarette. He inhaled deeply and blew out the smoke.

"I think he knew it was coming. Had a premonition or a feeling or whatever. You know we had been at the Bocelli concert?"

Claire nodded.

"Well, he called me into his room as we were saying goodnight. Said he wanted to have a chat. Then he told me about his retirement plans."

"Doesn't sound much like a premonition of death so far."

Brendan took an impatient drag of the cigarette and blew out the smoke on his next sentence. "Wait until you hear the full story. He told me he and Dorothy were planning on moving to Portugal. He said that he was under pressure from RTTI to appoint a person of their choosing as managing director when he retired. They mentioned the Deputy Manager of the London plant as their choice. Someone named Langley. Frank was very agitated. He said it would be a huge mistake for Dashern to have a stranger at the helm. He asked *me* to succeed him as manager. Said I was to look after the family interests. Look after you and Dorothy if he was not around to do it. He made me promise that I would follow his wishes. No matter what happened."

"And did you promise him?"

He looked at her for a moment before answering. "I did eventually to calm him down. But I really wasn't looking for a battle with RTTI. Anyway, we shook hands on it and I went to my own room."

"And in the morning?"

He had puffed halfway through the cigarette. He stubbed it out viciously on his saucer. "I thought he had overslept when he missed breakfast. I rang his room. No reply. I knocked on his door several times. Still nothing. Eventually I called the manager to open his door with the master key. You know the rest."

"No, I don't. Tell me where –"

The phone rang. Claire got up to answer. It was Dorothy, still organising, still ensuring that Frank's last wishes were carried out.

Brendan had left the kitchen by the time she put the phone down.

*   *   *

The old graveyard was perched on a hill overlooking the sea. The ruins of an eighteenth-century church stood in the grounds of the cemetery, guarding the remains of so many people, the relics of so many lives.

Two hundred people trod on graves, climbed over kerbstones, nudged and elbowed each other as they followed Frank Dawson's coffin. The cortège stopped at the edge of the freshly dug grave in the Gore-Croft family plot. The chatter of the crowd faded to a murmur. The coffin was placed on a bier and Dorothy stood beside her husband for the last time. The only sound now was the grating of pebbles as feet shuffled on the gravel paths.

The priest began the religious rite of burial. He spoke the age-old words and the crowd muttered their responses. The sounds dipped and rose. Claire lifted her eyes from the deep rectangular hole prepared for her father's coffin. She looked out towards the sea. It was busily ebbing and flowing, curling onto the rocks, then gathering itself together in a grey-green mass and swelling back towards the horizon. Gulls wheeled and dived in the wake of a harbour-bound trawler. She noticed a red tractor driving across a field way off to her left. She was noticing things. Dorothy's perfume, the streak of freshly dug earth on Brendan's black shoes, Clive Rigney perched on a kerbstone in order to get a better view, Ria all decked out in black as if she were chief mourner.

The priest sprinkled the coffin with holy water. Someone sniffled. It was Seán Farrell, Frank's old friend, all the pain of loss apparent on his woebegone face. He was standing beside Kevin, who could not decide whether to smile or not when she looked at him. She saw Ewan Peters, head and shoulders above the group around him, solemn and dignified.

The pallbearers moved forward and took their positions. The undertaker lifted Dorothy's bouquet of white roses off the coffin. Claire heard Brendan's intake of breath and the shuddering exhalation. Still she went on noticing and not feeling. The Gore-Croft headstone was one of the most imposing in the cemetery. Frank Dawson would be in prestigious company. *Lieutenant Cyril Gore-Croft 1798-1838. His wife, Lydia 1800-1856.* Claire read on, blocking out the sounds of the coffin bumping into the grave, scraping off the sides as it was lowered. Not much space left on the stone for inscriptions now. Dorothy's father had been the last name inscribed. The old Commander himself. He had not lived peacefully with Frank. Claire believed that Dorothy's last act of defiance against her father and act of love for her husband was to lay the two men to rest side by side. Frank's final acceptance into the bosom of the Gore-Croft family. A carved granite archangel capped the headstone. The features on the face were eroded, a finger on one hand was missing but yet the lichen-covered angel seemed to offer protection to its Gore-Croft charges.

Brendan caught her elbow. "It's over now. He's at rest."

A green mat of artificial grass covered the space into which the coffin had been lowered. The undertaker was placing the bouquets and wreaths on top of it. Claire saw the gravedigger in the ruins of the old church, shovel in hand, leaning against the wall, waiting for the crowd to go so that he could get on with the job of filling in Frank Dawson's grave.

Brendan cleared his throat and stood in front of the angel with the broken finger.

"The family wish to thank you all for attending Frank's funeral and would like to invite you to The Granary Hotel for a drink in his memory."

People began to shake Claire's hand, to sympathise. Brendan led her out to the car and brought her to the hotel. She kept on noticing and not feeling. Yvette Previn was there. She had changed her hair colour. It was redder. Her embrace was warm.

"I'm so sorry, Claire. Your father was a great man. Such a loss."

Yvette's embrace for Brendan was warm too, her consoling words whispered into his ear.

The noise level in the hotel was beginning to rise. People were in groups talking about Frank. Everybody seemed to have an anecdote, a special memory. Dorothy walked calmly from one group to the other, chatting, thanking people, smiling. Brendan and Yvette were the centre of attention at a corner table. Paul Gregan worked his way around the room, trailing after Dorothy, discreetly eavesdropping. Not discreetly enough for Claire. She noticed. She also saw that Ria was heading towards her. Enough. She went to see her mother.

"Mum, I'd like to go now. Do you want to come with me or will you wait for Brendan?"

"Duty calls," Dorothy said. "I must thank people for honouring your father. You go on. I will ring you later."

Dorothy put her arms around her daughter. A hot, hard ball of grief filled Claire's throat. She almost choked. It was hard to talk.

"Tell Brendan that I'll see him later," she managed to whisper before walking quickly to the door.

The driver of the funeral car was very professional. He did not raise an eyebrow when she asked him to drive her to the plant. She went into her lab and stopped noticing. She was just feeling now. Terror at a future without Frank, anger at the powerlessness of life in the face of powerful death, guilt at not having spent more time with her father, not telling him how much she loved him, and loneliness – aching, destroying loneliness.

She went into the animal room and stood in front of the cages. Clarence scurried to the front of his cage and chirped at her. He looked up at her in his cross-eyed, funny way. She opened his door and picked him up. There was no trace of his tumour now. He was healthy.

"Why in the fuck didn't you get cancer, Dad? I could have cured you."

She did not realise she had shouted until Clarence jumped in her arms. She rubbed him to soothe him. Then she cried. And cried. Claire and the guinea pig mourned in the privacy of the research laboratory Frank Dawson had custom built for his adored daughter.

Chapter Sixteen

The space was little more than a cupboard but to Ewan it meant the difference between raving madness and a sad sort of sanity. He closed the door to block out the noise of the outer office. To shut out the people. In three strides he was behind his desk. He swept a stack of paperwork aside and, putting his elbows on the desk, dropped his head onto his hands. Was this not what he had always dreamed of, what he had worked towards? A chance to bring his policies before the nation, an opportunity to inform the uninformed.

His phone rang. He took it off the hook. He could not listen to another frantic call about promotion posters or photo opportunities. Just two weeks into his election campaign and he felt burned out. Had he been so naïve that he had not realised what a political campaign was all about? Had he not known that he would have to knock on doors, traipse from one village hall to another, shake hands that he would prefer not to touch, bend the knee to gobshites in order to secure their support? He had certainly anticipated all that. It was the all-consuming intensity of it that had caught him off guard.

Even as this thought settled into place, Ewan had to admit he was not being honest. His stressed-out, angry bewilderment had little to do with the campaign. It had a lot more to do with Clive and Julie fucking Rigney! They must be laughing at how easily their Peters Plan had worked. First get the silly Peters wife in your debt and then put the Peters husband under a compliment by backing his election campaign. What in the fuck did Rigney want? Why was he going to this trouble? What was his payoff? How could Helen have been so gullible and so, so deceitful? He thumped the desk with his fist. The file tray rattled for a second before falling to the floor. As he stooped to pick up papers there was a tap on the door. Jesus! Ten minutes he had asked for! Ten lousy minutes to get his head together. He dropped the papers again when he saw his wife open the door.

"Can I talk to you, Ewan? Give me a chance to explain. Please!" Helen asked in a pleading little-girl voice.

The noise and clatter of the outer office rushed in and filled his cupboard space. He nodded to her and she closed the door behind her. They were entombed in silence. It took her five cautious steps to reach the desk. She stood before him, like a pupil called before the headmaster. He stared at her. At her green eyes and red hair, her pale skin, her petite frame. The woman he had thought he had known so well. A stranger to him now.

"What are you doing here?" he asked coldly. "Have you come to make more confessions? Maybe you forgot to tell me that you signed our home over to the Rigneys, to add to the other damage you've done?"

Helen pulled a folding stool out from underneath the desk and sat opposite him. She joined her hands together. He noticed that her fingers were shaking. When she spoke her voice was shaking too.

"Do you remember when we first met? When you and I spearheaded the anti-nuclear movement in the college?"

"Of course I do," Ewan answered impatiently. "What has that got to do with this mess you've got us into?"

Helen stood, put her hands on the desk and leaned towards him, her eyes flashing, the little-girl attitude forgotten. "It's got everything to do with it, you selfish pig! We were in that *together*. We plotted and planned, campaigned and marched *together*. *Together!* It all went wrong when you became the sainted Ewan Peters, Saviour of the Environment. That was when I was relegated to the role of the Mother of the Great Man's Children. Not your equal, not your partner. Not even your friend. Just the mother of two children you don't even know!" She sat again. Her whole body was trembling now.

Ewan shook his head. What twist of fate had brought them to this tiny space where Helen could play the bullied so that he could fit into the role of bully? Even now, at this late stage, she was trying to shirk responsibility for her greed and stupidity.

"Is this your explanation for what you've done? You've behaved like a moron, like a selfish, grabbing half-wit. And now you're trying to blame me for it. You did it on your own. You borrowed those huge sums of money from Julie Rigney. You put us in this awful fucking position. You think the state of our marriage is an excuse? Come on, Helen!"

"Yes! Yes! Yes! I had to make a life for myself. I am no longer part of yours. And how do you think it's going to be if you get elected? You'll be in Dublin or Brussels or wherever and I'll be left here with the kids. A single parent!"

"*Shut up!*"

Helen shrank back in fright. He had never shouted at her like that before.

He had never had such rage before.

"You can play the martyr all you want but it won't impress me. I admit I left the day-to-day rearing of the children to you. But that was our agreement. Or don't you want to remember that? There was a time when you believed in what I was doing. That was before your clubbing and shopping trips. Before your so-called friendship with Julie Rigney. And so much! How could you have let the debts get so out of control? Why didn't you tell me earlier? Helen, we need to communicate!"

Her head was bowed and she was still but he knew she was crying because a tear splashed onto the desk.

There had been a time when the sight of Helen's tears would have had him holding her in his arms, kissing the tears away. Not now.

"My only mistake was in trusting Julie Rigney," Helen whispered between sobs. "She reeled me in very cleverly. It was just one sweater first. It was a Lainie Keogh. You know the cream one. You admired it on me. She gave me the money for that. Then there was the gym and massage. Beauty treatments. More designer clothes. She said I could pay her back in my own time. That you didn't have to know anything about it."

"Jesus Christ! How could you have been so stupid? Didn't it ever dawn on you that it was his money you were spending? Did you ever wonder why she was suddenly slumming it with you?"

"You bastard! You're glad to take Clive Rigney's contribution for your campaign. Why is it different when it's me?"

Ewan frowned. No, he was not glad to take Clive Rigney's money. EnVirowatch were glad of it, yes. He hated taking anything from him. He shivered at the thought of the small-featured, small-minded, small man.

"His contribution was to EnVirowatch. Not to me. It was political. When you took money from his wife, that was personal. Couldn't you see that she was cultivating you for a reason? Did you really believe she just enjoyed your company? Didn't you realise for one minute that it was me they were trying to manipulate?"

Helen's bowed head snapped up and her tear-filled

eyes glistened. "It would have to be about you, wouldn't it? You think the whole world revolves around you. Why –"

"Look, stop, Helen. Enough! There is nothing to be gained by us trying to score points off each other. We will have to sort this out together. What we have to think of now is how we're going to pay this money back."

"She wants it by next week. She said he would find out if it wasn't back in her account by then."

Ewan laughed but there was no amusement in the sound. "Don't compound your naïveté with stupidity. He already knows. He set the whole thing up in order to have a hold over me. You fell for it hook, line and sinker. You made it easy for them."

There was so much more Ewan wanted to say. About how cheaply Helen had sold herself, how shallow her aims and ambitions, how far removed from the girl he married she had become. If she had continued to argue with him he might have told her. Instead she seemed to shrivel up and become even smaller.

"I'm sorry," she whispered. "Really, really sorry."

And she was. Truly sorry. It was evident in the droop of her shoulders, the bowed head, the tiny hands clasped together as if in a prayer for forgiveness. Ewan wasn't sure at that moment if he could ever forgive her but he knew he could no longer blame her. She was too fragile, too innocent for blame. The blame fell firmly on the Rigneys.

Standing up, he led her to the door. He caught her shaking hands and gave them a reassuring squeeze. "Go home," he said gently. "I'll think of something. It'll be all right."

When she had gone Ewan kicked the leg of his desk in frustration. Then he picked up the phone, rang his bank manager and made an appointment to see him. The house was already remortgaged anyway. He could say he wanted to build on an office. That should do it. An office to facilitate his constituency work. Now all he had to do to back up his lie was to win himself a constituency seat. It would have been difficult for him at any time to break the stronghold of the established parties, but since this campaign was to be so short he was facing the impossible. Pushing that negative thought to the back of his mind, he opened the door of his cupboard office and threw himself back into the hysteria of his election campaign.

*　　*　　*

Dorothy seemed to walk with a shadow beside her. It was ten days since her father had been buried but Claire could not yet look at her mother without seeing Frank peering through that shadow.

"You're really sure about this, Mum?"

They were sitting in one of Claire's favourite rooms in Grange House. It had always been known as the breakfast room but it was where the family normally dined. They had used the formal dining-room only on special occasions or when entertaining. This was a south-facing, sunshine room, the light enhanced by a huge bay window. Dorothy and her shadow were sitting opposite Claire at the glass-topped table.

"I'm sure. After your father's will is read and his affairs sorted out, I won't have anything else to hold me here." She immediately reached across the table to touch Claire's hand. "I'm sorry. That sounded as if you don't even count. Of course I have taken you into consideration. But you don't need your widowed mother on your doorstep. You need to get on with your own life."

Claire squeezed her mother's hand. "You would never be a burden, Mum. You must believe that. I know you and Dad had decided to go before – before . . ."

"Frank died."

"Yes. Before he died. Won't it be very lonely for you on your own in a strange country? No family. No friends."

"The rest of my life is going to be lonely. No matter where I am. At least this way I feel I am doing what Frank wanted. He was so looking forward to the move." Dorothy's voice wavered and, for the first time since Frank's death, Claire saw a chink in her mother's armour. For one second Dorothy's face crumpled and her shoulders sagged. When she straightened up, the mask was back in place. "Anyway, that's it, Claire. Jeremiah Audley's office tomorrow for the reading of your father's will. Then I won't delay with the sale of the house. I will accept Clive Rigney's offer and

293

exchange the contracts as soon as possible."

When Claire drove away, she stopped at the bend on the driveway and looked back at Grange House. Home. The big, grey, old building sat comfortably in the middle of the gardens, basking in the sun, reflecting light off the windows, soaking in the heat, untouched and unmoved by the lives and deaths of past, present or future tenants. The warm, comfortable feeling of Grange House stayed with her as she drove to her lab.

*   *   *

Claire tried to ignore Frank's parking space as she drove past the car park in the plant. Sooner or later she would have to look at the space marked *"Reserved for Managing Director"* and see someone else's car parked there. Brendan's car. Or maybe even that person named Trevor Langley who, according to what Kevin told her, was making his presence felt in Dashern. The only thing Claire knew about him was that he had some connection to RTTI. Definitely time for her to turn her attention back to the here and now.

When she reached her own parking space, she switched off her engine and sat for a few minutes. The cooling engine clicked in the silence. And still she sat. She was trying to piece all the bits of her life together. She rested her arms on the steering wheel and lowered her head onto her hands. All her troubles seemed to weigh down on her bowed head. Feelings. That was it. Feelings. Horrible, swirling emotions.

She thumped the steering wheel with her fist. What a drama queen! How her father would laugh at her if he could read her mind now. Immediately one of the muddier thoughts floated to the surface. It was his fault. All his fault. He had always protected her from, from . . . life. He had protected her from everything and now she could not cope with his death. She did not have the tools, the weapons, the inner strength to cope without him. Another muddy thought rushed at her. Dorothy. Dignified, strong. Self-possessed. Cold. Unfeeling. She jumped out of the car and slammed the door. She took a deep breath and headed for the lab.

Claire smiled at Kevin and put on her lab coat. A few hours in the uncomplicated, logical word of biochemistry was what she needed.

* * *

My God! Could Ria play to the camera! She pretended to offer her face to the lens, open-eyed, smiling, but all the while she was merchandising her body with a slight thrust of a hip, a glimpse of cleavage.

"Just what type of modelling are you hoping to break into, Ria?"

"Depends," she answered as she flicked her long hair over her shoulder and turned her profile to the lens.

"Highest bidder?"

She turned to face him and narrowed her eyes, adding about twenty years' worth of cunning and cynicism to her appearance. "What are you trying to say, Paul? Calling me some kind of slapper, are you? Remember it was you who approached me in the first place."

"Yeah, yeah," Paul muttered as he continued clicking and Ria continued posing.

An hour later they were both satisfied that they had done enough work to put together a decent portfolio. Paul flicked through the stored images. They were impressive. Ria projected all her best qualities so well. Innocence, energy, enthusiasm, touching trust leapt out at him from the screen.

"Ever think of acting?" he asked.

"Who owns this studio?" Ria asked without answering his question.

"A friend of mine. Just a family photographer. No use to you in your quest for fame."

In two long strides Ria had crossed the room and was standing in front of him. She was very angry. "Don't patronise me with your superior attitude! Mr Investigative Journalist! How genuine is your interest in protecting our already polluted environment? How come you have hidden behind your camera all these years while incinerators and chimneystacks rained dioxins down on top of us? You are glad of the business Trish gets from the factories. A nice little earner she has there. No wonder you can afford such a stylish apartment!"

Paul opened his mouth to defend himself but Ria held up her hand.

"No. Don't say anything. I don't want to hear. I will

tell you. You got bored with your photography and intimidated by Trish's success. You needed to change your image. And guess what? Along came Ewan Peters and his Green campaign at the same time Frank Dawson sold out to a multinational. Bingo! You rediscovered your oh-so-principled journalistic instincts. So you see, we are both posing, Paul. Just different sides of the camera."

She grabbed her bag and headed for the door before Paul could say anything. Hand on the door handle, she turned towards him.

"By the way, Hilary Curran, who is Brendan Hearn's secretary, told me the reading of Frank Dawson's will is tomorrow in Audley's offices. It seems that Mr Brendan Hearn is very concerned about the contents of the will. That is your back scratched. I expect my portfolio to be distributed shortly and out there working for me."

Paul had cooled down by the time he had all his gear packed up. Maybe Ria was right. Maybe that was why he was so angry with her. Was he just using the RTTI takeover of Dashern as a platform to launch himself as a journalist? Maybe. He looked at his watch. He was already late for his meeting with Ewan Peters. Ewan would not wait. His time was worth votes now. Paul drove without delay to EnVirowatch election campaign headquarters.

*   *   *

When Paul came into the EnVirowatch office the

campaign staff were clapping and cheering. He made his way Ewan's desk and sat down, puzzled by all the excitement.

"Have the opposition thrown in the towel? Appointed you Taoiseach, have they?"

"I've just been asked to sit on the panel of *Questions and Answers* next week. Prime time televison no less!"

"Well done!"

"Could be the turning point for EnVirowatch. Give us the national profile we need, exposure across the board. Anyway, Paul, I'm sorry, I must dash now. I should have been on the road thirty minutes ago. Walk to the car with me."

When they were out of earshot of the office, Ewan immediately stooped towards Paul and whispered, "Find out anything for me about Rigney?"

Paul shook his head. "No. Nobody seems to know why he's backing your campaign. How big was his donation anyway?"

"No worries there. I had that checked out before I accepted a penny from him. His donation is within the limits allowed. Just doesn't make sense though. I know he doesn't give a fuck about the environment. But for some reason he wants to be associated with the anti-RTTI campaign."

"That reminds me," Paul said. "Ria told me Frank Dawson's will is due to be read tomorrow. It should be interesting. Did you think about the other information I gave you? The possible cancer cure and the LabAn connection? It makes sense of RTTI's sudden interest in a little detergent company, doesn't it?"

Ewan was in the car now, fastening his seat belt. He had a distracted air about him. Almost of panic. He nodded at Paul. "Yeah, I thought about it."

"And?"

"And I think I had better have a chat with Mrs Brendan Hearn as soon as possible."

"Good luck with that. I've been trying to contact her and I can't get past the reception desk. Hope you have better luck."

"She gave me a contact number. Just keep a lid on everything for a little while. I'll let you know what she says."

"I can't afford to go to press with rumour, Ewan. That could end my career before it has even started. But there is obviously something big going on at Dashern and it has nothing to do with detergents or herbs. If the cure for cancer has been discovered and developed in this area, I want to be the one to break the story. It wouldn't do your career any harm to bask in the reflected glory either, would it?"

Ewan turned the key and the engine ticked over. He felt tired, drained by the intensity of the short campaign and the shock at so recently discovering that his wife was a spendthrift. With somebody else's money. He smiled at Paul and hoped it looked like a genuine smile. He revved up the engine and drove off to yet another venue where he would have to smile his hopefully genuine-looking smile. For the first time he questioned whether the prize of election was worth the fierceness of the battle.

*   *   *

Claire rechecked for the umpteenth time. Clarence was cured. No doubt about it. No excess tumour markers in his bloods, no malignant cells. No cancer. He had gained weight and was bright-eyed and lively. He was a healthy guinea pig. All the animals on Serum 6 had responded to the treatment. All the control animals had died of their disease. Their cancers.

She got up from her desk and stretched. She was stiff and tired. She had not realised it was getting so late. Kevin must have gone home hours ago. She walked into the animal room and immediately Clarence hopped to the door of his cage and squinted up at her. She laughed. Even now, with her heart, her mind, her soul suffocated with grief, Clarence could make her laugh.

"What now, Clarence?" she asked him and then realised that it was a measure of her mental state that she almost expected an answer from him. She switched off the lights and went back to her office. She opened a foolscap pad and started to write.

Serum 6 trials successful on guinea pigs.

More runs of animal trials required for statistical verification.

Patent. Check with Jeremiah Audley.

Human Trials???

She dropped her pen and sat staring at the page. Human Trials. The theory was perfect. It must work.

There would be no rejection issues, no possibility of failure. If it worked on the guineas, which it had beautifully, it would work on people. So. Human Clinical Trials next. She became aware of her heartbeat and her breath came in short, shallow gasps. She was having a panic attack! Her father would have taken care of this. He would have dealt with all the bureaucracy. He would have known what to do. Why hadn't he talked to her about it? Why hadn't she talked to him about it? Why did he die? Why? Why? Who could she talk to now?

The phone rang. Claire looked at the console and her heart stopped beating. Number one was flashing. Frank's internal line. She stared at the flashing green light and illogical thoughts of a voice from beyond the grave darted around the shocked space in her head. She whispered the word "Dad . . ." The madness, the pathetic stupidity of the trembling whisper, brought her back to reality. She took a deep breath and picked up the receiver.

Brendan skipped the greetings. "I assume you haven't eaten. Want to join us for dinner?"

"Us?"

He sighed impatiently. "Claire! I told you this morning that Yvette Previn arrived in the plant today. There's a lot to sort out. We can't afford to lose any more time. Now do you want to join us or not?"

"No, thank you. I have things to finish up here. I'll just get something at home."

"See you later then."

She was just about to ask what in the hell he and Yvette Previn were doing in her father's office when he cut the connection.

*   *   *

Brendan watched Yvette eat, watched the pinkness of her tongue, the whiteness of her teeth, the way her lips closed around the fork.

"You not hungry?" she asked, pointing at his almost untouched food.

He shook his head and pushed his plate away.

"You must eat, Bren. You have a lot of work ahead of you. You must be strong."

"I wish tomorrow was over."

Yvette ate the last morsel of her monkfish and put her knife and fork together on her plate. She sat back in her chair and stared across the table at Brendan.

He tried to interpret the look. Critical? Loving? Accusing?

"You look very tired, Brendan. In fact, you look sick."

He glanced carefully around to ensure that he could not be overheard. He leaned towards her. "You know the situation, Yvette. Suppose Frank had already changed his will. Suppose he had mentioned appointing a stranger as managing director. If –"

"You know he intended to. But fate intervened. With a helping hand from you, of course."

Brendan got even paler. Right on cue, the knuckles on his right hand began to sting. He rubbed them with his left hand but the stingy feeling stayed. It would always be there, the memory of that vicious contact with Frank's face burned into the skin-cells of his right hand.

"You know I didn't mean it. He provoked me. I never wanted this to happen."

Yvette just raised one of her arched eyebrows and stared at him. Whatever composure he had managed to maintain began to melt under the amber gaze. Something deep inside in him, in that place where self-preservation is all that exists, told him that the most dangerous place in the world for his secret was with this woman. And for some twisted reason this made her even more attractive to him.

His hands began to shake. He was losing control of this conversation, losing control of himself. Every coherent thought was put off track by the image of Frank's damaged cheek. Waking or sleeping, that image had not left his mind since his fist had slammed into his father-in-law's face. What awful quirk of fate had allowed him to raise his hand at that moment and had then compounded the deed by allowing Frank's damaged heart to stop beating?

Yvette reached across the table and took his hands. He was gone beyond caring if someone noticed. The restaurant was half-empty at this time of night anyway. Her fingers were warm and soothing on his stinging knuckles.

"This is our secret, Brendan. No one else need ever know."

"Unless?"

303

"Bien!" she laughed. "We get to understand each other at last. You know what I want."

Brendan withdrew his hand and sat back. She was right. They did understand each other at last. He wanted her and she wanted Claire's research. Yvette was a heartless, conniving bitch and he loved every golden inch of her.

"You really believe that Claire's work is this valuable? Worth all the investment RTTI is putting in?"

"We don't waste time or resources on failures. We need her research. She can't bring it any further. Especially without her father. We must have it now. If she figured out the answer then it is possible that someone else is close too. RTTI want to be in there first. She holds the key."

The waiter came and took their dessert order. Yvette chose tiramisu, Brendan just coffee. Black. They did not talk while the waiter buzzed around the table. She nibbled around the edges of the chocolate confection, teasing her palate with little bites.

"Why can't you ask her?" said Brendan. "Why all this subterfuge? If you want what she has so much, just make her an offer. You're always saying everyone has a price."

Yvette banged down her dessert fork. It clanged on the plate. Several people looked in their direction. She smiled apologetically at them before turning her unsmiling eyes back on him. "Enough, Brendan! If it were that simple we would not be sitting here talking about it. We have already done too much talking. Your wife has built herself a fortress. Get in there and get what we want. And quickly! Or else …"

She did not have to say any more. Brendan understood. It seemed that the insipid little Claire, Daddy's girl, had stumbled on the cure for cancer. RTTI wanted to make their billions on its manufacture. They would have tried every trick, ethical and otherwise, in order to get Claire's work. They must have failed. Now they had found themselves a stooge to do their dirty work. Brendan the gullible. And he had given them the perfect weapon. It had taken him a long time to figure it out but now he knew.

"A question, Yvette. Have you got proof that I had a row with Frank? A tape? A video?"

She smiled at him. She did not have to say any more. Brendan bowed his head. Yvette must also know that one of Frank's last deeds had been to fire his son-in-law. What a valuable piece of information that was for RTTI and what excruciating shame it was for Brendan. It seemed like he had dug a grave for himself, deeper and darker than the one in which Frank Dawson had been laid to rest.

*   *   *

Claire closed her eyes and sniffed. The perfume was rich and sweet. Nightscented Stock. That was it. She smiled. How did she know? She must have inherited her mother's gardening genes. She shivered and pulled her robe more closely about her. It was getting chilly now, even on the sheltered patio. The garden was in darkness except for the blue glow from the solar lights. The gurgle of the water from the little fountain was so soothing that she pulled out a chair from under the table and sat down. The sounds and scents wafted over her and she felt safe. Safe enough to let her mind wander.

She thought about her father. The pain and grief were buried deeply. They stayed in a tight knot in her chest, too solid, too hidden to find the release of tears. If she squinted her eyes, she could see him, almost as if he was standing in front of her. Smiling. Telling her what to do. Doing it for her.

She opened her eyes wide and Frank disappeared. He was gone. Looking up into the night sky, she remembered Dorothy telling her long, long ago that the stars were the spirits of people who had passed on to the next life. A fairy tale for a child. Maybe there was a next life. Maybe Frank was organising a board meeting somewhere in the cosmos at this very minute. But he was not here. And what was she going to do without him?

She stood up and started to walk around. She was thirty-two. Heading for middle age. She felt like a twelve-year-old. A protected about-to-be teenager. One decision. One major decision she had made on her own in her lifetime. And that had turned out to be a mistake. Marrying Brendan had been her mistake. Now it was up to her to correct it.

Her phone rang. She stubbed her toe on the steps as she ran to answer. It might be Dorothy. It might be Brendan.

It was neither. The rich, deep voice was so distinctive he did not need to introduce himself. So! He had kept the number.

"Sorry for ringing you at this hour, Claire. Hope I'm not disturbing you."

"Not at all, Ewan. I was just sitting in the garden. Isn't it a beautiful night?"

"Yes, it is indeed."

He hesitated for a moment and Claire wondered if she should ask him why he rang. Would that be a bit churlish? She did not have to make the decision.

"Claire, there are some things I would like to discuss with you. I really apologise for intruding on you at a family time like this but it is vitally important that we speak. I wouldn't bother you otherwise."

"Sounds very intriguing. When and where?"

"As soon as possible. Tomorrow if you can fit it in."

The reading of the will was tomorrow morning. Claire had not thought beyond that. Now, as she stood in the darkened house, it seemed right that she should go to Frank's grave after his will was read. She needed to say her own goodbye to him. Privately, without several hundred pairs of eyes staring at her.

"I'm going to the cemetery tomorrow afternoon. I could meet you afterwards."

"Meet you there then?"

Claire hesitated. She wanted to visit the grave alone.

"Sorry," Ewan said. "Of course you'll need some privacy. How about we meet in the village at three thirty?"

The front door slammed. Brendan was home and

turning on all lights as he went through the house.

"See you tomorrow. The village. Three thirty," she said.

"Thank you so much, Claire. Sleep well."

She smiled as she put down the phone.

"Who was that?"

"My mother."

She was surprised at how easily the lie came to her lips and she didn't know why she had felt the need to pretend. Maybe it was Brendan's manic appearance. She stared at him, barely recognising the man she knew. He looked haunted. The paleness underneath his sun-bed tan gave him a jaundiced appearance. Everything about him, from his gaunt face to the frantic stare in his eyes spoke of somebody who was out of control. How had she not noticed that Frank's death was tearing Brendan apart? Had he been right in saying that she was selfish and obsessed? It was clear to her now that he was as affected by her father's death as she was. How could she not have shared the pain with him?

She moved towards Brendan and opened her arms to him. He leaned against her and put his head on her shoulder. She rubbed his back and was shocked to feel his ribs through his shirt. Waves of guilt flooded through her. She stroked his hair, his face and held him in her arms.

Later, in bed, Claire continued to hold her husband until he fell asleep.

Chapter Seventeen

It was business as usual. The whole world in general and Dashern in particular seemed to be getting on with life without Frank Dawson. Claire sighed and turned her attention back to her work. She would have to contact LabAn soon. If for no other reason than to stop Ronan Hennessey leaving messages. And Paul Gregan of *Newstrack* had left a raft of messages for her too. They must consider that she had now been given ample mourning time. So what should she say to Ronan? "Hi! Did you infect my trial animals with respiratory disease?" She would have to think about it. Stall him. She went online and sent him a *Talk soon* email. Paul Gregan's calls she ignored.

Kevin dropped a stock-take list on her desk. They were running low on some items so she busied herself ordering. The animals were fed, watered, weighed, measured and monitored. It was almost time to go.

She found Kevin sterilising cages in the animal room.

"Kevin, I'm going now. You're clear on your agenda for today, aren't you?"

Kevin looked up and nodded. "Everything is under control, Mrs Hearn. Don't worry. And, and … good luck."

Claire looked at him in surprise. So he knew where she was going this morning. Maybe she had told him herself in one of her hazier moments. He blushed. Claire walked towards him and gave him a pat on the arm. Even if his words were not appropriate, his good wishes were sincere.

She hesitated as she approached the plant. Brendan's car was in the car park. Should she ring him, ask him did he want to go with her? Show solidarity? Her lips tightened and she swallowed the hot lump in her throat. She put the car into neutral and sat staring at the plant. He should have rung her. He knew how traumatic this was for her. He should be here for her now. Like she had been there for him last night. Instead she had woken to an empty bed this morning. No note. No phone call. No support. No thanks.

The main door to reception opened and Yvette Previn emerged. The heels on her shoes must have been three inches high, yet she walked with an easy elegance. Brendan was following behind her. Trotting in her wake. Claire slammed the car into gear and drove quickly to Jeremiah Audley's office.

*   *   *

Claire hid a smile as she watched Jeremiah Audley fussing over her mother. He led Dorothy to a chair, held it out for her, practically picked her up and sat her on it. One of her mother's main strengths was that she knew how to appear to be weak.

"My son-in-law?" she asked.

"We've called him, Dorothy. He's on his way."

Sitting beside her mother, Claire tried to join in on the casual conversation between Jeremiah and Dorothy. They were chatting about the weather. About the sun and the high temperatures and how much warmer it was than this time last year. Calm and dignified. Respectful in a quiet way. Very Dorothy-like. Very well bred and tasteful.

Claire stood up and walked to the window. She had to turn her back to them, to take a huge intake of air, to swallow the knot of despair that threatened to well up. If only she could think of something else. Anything. Just not her father's will. Not her father's death. A car she recognised driving into the courtyard below caught her attention. Brendan was travelling too fast. He parked badly across two parking spaces and jumped out. She turned back towards the room.

"Brendan is here."

"Good. Good," Jeremiah muttered, going behind his desk. "We can get started now."

As Brendan stood in the doorway apologising for

being late, Claire noticed that he was even paler than he had been last night. He sat beside her and she could hear his fast breathing. She felt stronger.

Jeremiah cleared his throat. "First, deepest sympathy to you all on Frank's death. He is a great loss to his family, his friends and the community in general. Now we will proceed to read the last will and testament of Francis Joseph Dawson."

Claire raised an eyebrow in surprise. Had she forgotten that her father's second name was Joseph or was it that she had not ever known? How many other things about him did she not know, would never know now?

The old solicitor's voice was a gentle background to her thoughts as he reeled off a list of Frank's assets. He went through finances, stocks and shares portfolios, investment accounts and art works. Frank had willed them all to Dorothy.

Jeremiah now went on to dealing with the business interests. ClairCo would continue to be administered by the trust with the stipulation that Claire Hearn be the sole beneficiary should the company be dissolved.

Jeremiah looked up from the documents he had been reading. He eyed each of them in turn.

"Now we come to Frank's wishes for the future of Dashern Chemicals, the company he founded."

Claire heard Brendan's sharp intake of breath. That soft, panicky little hiss burst into her eardrums like a clap of thunder. Of course! The paleness, the gauntness, the panic, the sweating? It was fear! How had she been so stupid? How had she allowed herself to be duped yet again? Jesus! He wasn't mourning his father-in-law. He wasn't devastated by the loss of his mentor. The bastard was afraid of what was in the will. Terrified that Frank had wreaked his final vengeance and kicked the son-in-law he had never trusted out of his company. But Frank had told him he wanted him to take over, hadn't he? Had he?

Jeremiah cleared his throat. "Right then. I'll start reading now. *'To my wife Dorothy Gore-Croft-Dawson, I bequeath my share of Dashern Chemicals. Since my share, as per the agreement drawn up at formation, carries with it the position of Managing Director and also holds the casting vote, Dorothy Dawson will become MD of the company on my death and will have final say on any decisions to be made about the future of the company.'"*

Dorothy was staring ahead, shoulders straight, head unbowed. She seemed oblivious to the fact that Brendan was glaring at her in shock. She did not react even when Brendan suddenly leapt to his feet and strode towards the door.

"Sit down!" Jeremiah's voice was no longer gentle. It was full of authority. The old man removed his reading glasses and stood to face Brendan. Even though Brendan was the taller of the two, the solicitor seemed to be looking down on him. "It is a legal requirement that you be present for the reading of this will."

Brendan laughed. It was a petulant, infantile sound. Claire fully expected this boy-man who was her husband to stamp his foot next.

"Haven't you all had your pound of flesh? I got the message. What more do you want? I'm sure the new MD wouldn't want me sitting around here, wasting company time. Would you, Dorothy?"

"What I do want, Brendan, is respect for my husband's memory. I am disappointed that I should have to ask. Now sit down, please. You owe him that."

Brendan took a step backwards, as if the softly spoken words had hit him a body blow. Claire stared at him, willing him to sit down and not make the situation even more tense than it already was. Dorothy sat calmly, hands folded in her lap. Brendan put his hand on the door handle. He had a hunted, trapped expression on his face. Suddenly his hand dropped from the door; he walked forward and sat.

Jeremiah sighed, went behind his desk and picked up the documents again.

"Now for the final part of the will. This relates to you, Brendan. That is the reason why it is necessary that you be in attendance here."

Claire clasped her hands tightly together. The tension in the room was making it difficult to breathe. Only Dorothy seemed unaffected. Jeremiah put down the papers again.

"Look, Brendan, I'll explain this section in layman's terms first. We can read the legal document later. When writing this will Frank understood that you might not wish to continue on with Dashern Company. He believed that his decision to choose his wife to succeed him as MD and Chairman might not be what you had expected. So, with this in mind, he devised a severance package for you. It reflects the work you have done for the company. Its value is linked to the share value at the time you accept this offer. There are, of course, certain conditions attached."

"One of the conditions being that I hand my share back to the Dawson family? Am I right?"

Jeremiah nodded.

Claire's eyes were riveted on the dark vein that throbbed on Brendan's pale and sweaty temple.

There was a quiver in his voice when he spoke. "Will I go on? I am not to be told the value of the package until I sign on the dotted line. I must emigrate, disappear. Never breathe the same air as a Dawson again. He taught me well, the old man. But he always underestimated me." He stood again and this time nobody tried to stop him. "Just one question before I go? When did he make this will?"

Claire saw Jeremiah and Dorothy exchange glances.

"One month ago," Jeremiah answered. "It supersedes any previous testaments."

Brendan slammed the door and left without saying another word.

*　　*　　*

Ewan felt uncomfortably exposed as he sat on the plush upholstered chair in the waiting area of the bank. He could he see people as they queued up for service at the cashier's counter but they could also see him as he sat waiting for the summons into the inner office. He tried to shrug off the humiliating idea that everyone in the shuffling, silent queue knew that he was here to beg for money to cover his wife's debts. He took out his newspaper and was pretending to read it when he was called.

"Mr Lomasney will see you now. Follow me, please, Mr Peters."

Ewan folded his paper and followed obediently. The chair in the bank manager's office was even more plush than the chair in the waiting area. Ewan sank into it while Richard Lomasney scrolled through the screen in front of him. The vaguely smiling expression on the manager's face never changed as his eyes flickered over the data. Ewan began to feel a little confidence.

Richard Lomasney took his hand off the mouse and looked directly at Ewan. He was smiling. A big, broad smile that seemed to encompass the whole room. Ewan was feeling better by the minute. Remortgaging seemed a distinct possibility from where he was sitting now. He had prepared what he wanted to say. His pitch. He quickly organised his thoughts and took a deep breath.

Richard Lomasney spoke before Ewan had even exhaled his deep breath. "Glad you came in, Ewan. Always the best policy. Catch these things on time. Better to reach agreement now than have one forced on you later. You agree?"

Ewan nodded, not sure exactly what he was agreeing to. He took in another deep breath, readying himself for his speech.

Lomasney got there first again. "You understand why we cancelled your credit card? Helen was quite upset, I know, but as I explained to her, it is to your benefit, as well as ours, to limit the debt to manageable levels. Especially since you will most probably be one of our public representatives shortly. You can't afford any question marks over your personal finances now, can you? How do you feel about the repayment schedule we outlined?"

Ewan's bemusement must have shown on his face.

"In the letter we sent?"

A smile, Ewan's professional one, appeared from somewhere. "Yes. Yes, of course. You know, there is so much on at the moment, I just can't remember the details. Would you mind going over it again please?"

What letter? What repayment schedule? Helen! Spendthrift Helen! Why hadn't he realised about the credit card? Of course she must have had it in shit when she started borrowing from Mrs Bloody Rigney. How in the name of Christ could an intelligent woman get into such a stupid mess? Why hadn't she told him? Had she thought it would all go away if she ignored it?

Richard Lomasney did not mind going over the details at all. Nor did he mind getting Ewan's signature on an agreement committing him to paying an extra ransom per month until the credit-card debt was cleared. A crippling debt on his EnVirowatch salary but at least that would keep the bank happy.

As he left the smiling bank manager, Ewan felt physically sick with worry. How in the fuck was he going to repay Rigney? Obviously borrowing from the bank was not an option now. There seemed little choice but to crawl to the twisted little man for – for what? Mercy? Time? Pride instantly stiffened Ewan's spine. He had just been humiliated by Richard Lomasney. His ego could survive that. But he would never, never crawl to Clive Rigney. He could not stoop that low.

*   *   *

Claire's mind went into autopilot as she drove to her father's grave. She probably noticed the tranquil and beautiful scenery of the coastline. She must have noticed because she always did. But today she did not remember.

She parked at the gates of the cemetery and walked to Frank's grave. The scar of recently dug earth was an affront to the dignity of the Gore-Croft burial place. Claire stooped and picked up a fistful of the clay. She held it in the palms of her hands as if touching the earth that covered her father's remains could bring her close to him.

The angel with the broken finger looked down on her. She stared back at the figure. Her eyes blurred as the stone features of the angel seemed to become her mother's face. Dorothy's stone-cold features looking down at Brendan as he left Audley's office, a broken and defeated man. Dorothy's face as she calmly wound up business with Jeremiah Audley.

Claire stood in the graveyard now, lump of clay in

hand, and trembled as the mantle of protection that had surrounded her all her life fell away. She cried. She cried for her father, for his strength and support that she was never going to have again. She cried for the husband she thought she had loved. She cried for the child that she had been for thirty-two years and cried for the woman that she had yet to become.

*   *   *

"Hey, slow down! You're like a man possessed today!"

Ewan turned around and noticed that his team were red-faced and sweating from trying to keep up with him. He stood and waited for them. It was easy for him. He was supercharged by anger and desperation. He knew he would have to calm down. His doorstep manner today was a little manic, even to his own ears. It was one thing to convince people to vote for him, quite another to bully them into it.

"Sorry, guys. Just trying to finish the door to doors today. And I have an appointment in the village at three thirty. Pressure is on."

They stood around him in a protective ring. His team. People who had faith in him. People who were giving up their time to help him even though they knew he had only an outside chance of success. They owed him nothing but gave him everything. Helen had betrayed them too.

"How about we canvas the village now," said Eva, a

young Economics student. "That should place you nicely there in time for your appointment. We can leave you to your meeting while we go back to headquarters and collect leaflets and posters for tonight's rally."

Ewan smiled at her. In her own quiet way, she seemed to be assuming leadership of the group. "Good thinking. Thanks, Eva. We did well today, didn't we? The doorstep reaction is fairly positive. What do you think?"

They all spoke at once. They always did. The group moved towards the pier end of the village. As they neared the trawlers berthed at the pier it began to drizzle. Ewan tried to push the thoughts of debt and Helen out of his head as he braced himself for the inevitable discussion with the fishermen on the Fisheries Limits. The group moved from the pier to the shops and pubs until the whole circus arrived at the other end of the village. It was lashing rain by now and a fresh breeze was tugging at the yachts anchored in the marina. Ewan looked at his watch. It was almost a quarter to four and he had seen no sign of Claire Hearn anywhere in the village.

"We'll head off now, Ewan," Eva said.

His little group looked frozen and very wet. He felt a moment of panic as they stood around him. So many people were depending on him, trusting him to represent them, believing in his ability to win. Standing here, surrounded by his followers, with the kind words of voters ringing in his ears, he felt like a fraud. What would they say if they knew he could not communicate with his wife, that he could not control her and she could not control her spending? He dug deep and found his smile.

"We'll meet up at seven in headquarters and collect the gear. OK?"

They left with waves and smiles. Ewan drove out of the village towards the cemetery, where he knew he would find Claire Hearn.

*   *   *

Looking down her nose at them was not a deliberate tactic. It was physical necessity. They were very little people. Even seated, it was difficult to view them eye to eye. Dorothy had to admit to herself that she was enjoying their discomfiture. He was squirming in his seat as if he could fill the large chair by wriggling himself around. His wife was having difficulty striking a pose. She had already tried legs crossed at the ankle, knees crossed, legs straight and glued together. She was fast running out of options. Dorothy's innate good manners came to the fore. These people were guests in her home and it was her duty to make them feel comfortable. While it was still her home. She smiled at them.

"Mr and Mrs Rigney, I think we have –"

"Clive and Julie, please."

"Very well. Clive and Julie. We have reached agreement in principle. I want to sell Grange House. You want to buy. Can we agree on the price we have already discussed?"

"Buying is just the start of our outlay. We will have to make a huge investment to modernise."

Dorothy shivered. When Julie Rigney said "modernise", it most probably meant that she intended destroying the two hundred years of history of Grange House with an onslaught of interior design. The Gore-Croft ghosts would be seared back to the netherworlds by chrome, plaster cornices and saunas. She looked around the room and tried to see it through Julie Rigney's eyes. It was sombre, dominated by the huge family portraits. The Commander, depicted in ceremonial uniform, glared down at them. How her father would disapprove of her decision to sell Grange House! But he had disapproved of everything she had done, including her choice of husband. She drew back her shoulders and sat even taller. The Rigneys could afford Grange House. Let them have it. She touched her wedding ring and felt strength from the contact with the gold band.

"I don't have a right to ask, I know, but what are your plans for Grange House? Do you intend to make a lot of changes?"

Julie's eyes lit up and she sat forward, uncrossing her carefully arranged legs. "Oh, we have such plans! We'll change not alone Grange House but the whole –"

Clive Rigney almost jumped out of his chair in an attempt to stop his wife talking. "No. No. Nothing definite yet," he spluttered. "Just some ideas we're tossing around. No concrete plans."

Dorothy raised an eyebrow and wondered if Frank had known that Clive Rigney had big plans for Grange House. For the whole estate by the frantic look in his eyes.

"It is a big property. It takes a lot of planning to keep on top of it. Frank and I are getting too old to keep up with it. Or we were …"

She sat staring at her hands while the Rigneys stared at each other. The only sound was the whirr of the carriage clock as it busily marked the minutes of silence. Dorothy suddenly looked up at them and smiled.

"Four million. That's my price. Agreed?"

Clive stood and walked across to Dorothy. He held out his bony little hand to her. "Deal."

For one moment Dorothy thought he was going to spit on the deal. She shook hands with him very quickly. "Agreed. I hope you will be very happy here. Audleys are our solicitors. If you would have your law firm contact them we could get our business sorted quickly. All the title deeds are in order and as I am sole owner there should be little delay."

As she walked them through the hall towards the door, Dorothy noticed that Julie Rigney was like a dog straining on the leash. Every time she passed a doorway the invisible leash seemed to draw her towards it. She was anxious to poke and pry and impose her bought-and-paid-for taste on every object in every room of the house. Dorothy knew she should put the silly woman out of her misery and offer them a tour again but she did not want to. She just wanted to be rid of them.

"What about the furniture?" Julie asked.

"Our solicitors will sort that."

"But I don't want it because it won't fit in with –"

"Julie!"

His one word was followed by glorious silence. Julie did not speak again until they were standing outside the door.

"I never asked you where you are going to live," she said then.

"No, you didn't," Dorothy agreed and turned towards Clive. Now was the strategic moment to bring it up. "There is one other thing, Clive. The factory. Dashern Chemicals."

He was instantly alert. "Yes. What about it?"

"It is built on the northern end of this estate. Frank and I had a little arrangement. He leased the factory site from me for a nominal fee. The lease is due for renewal at the end of this month. The sale would be conditional on that arrangement continuing."

His beady eyes bored into her. He pursed his lips and a white line appeared around his mouth. An angry glint flashed in his eyes and quickly faded as he remembered his solicitor's advice. Snap up Grange House. It was a bargain at the price. The question of the lease could be dealt with at the renewal date. He was confident that his legal team would find a loophole through which the lease could fall. That's what he paid them for. He held out his hand again.

"Well, like you said, Mrs Dawson, our solicitors can sort out the details."

"Indeed," Dorothy replied, touching his hand as lightly as possible.

She waited until their Mercedes had disappeared down the driveway before closing the door. She walked slowly back to the drawing-room and went to the drinks cabinet. She poured herself a glass of sherry and stood in front of the newest portrait in the room. Painted only last year. Her gift to Frank for their wedding anniversary. How he had laughed at the idea of his portrait hanging next to that of the Commander! She stared at the painting. At the big, open face, aesthetically paled by the artist, eyes glinting, lips parted in his wide and generous smile. Not generous enough to live. Not generous enough to be here for her now.

She drew her arm back and threw the full glass with all her strength. It smashed against Frank's smiling face. Streams of sherry dribbled down the canvas and shards of broken crystal sprayed onto the Persian rug.

She turned her back on the mess and went to the gardener's shed. There she donned her gardening gloves, wellington boots and a jacket, collected the hoe and wheelbarrow and headed for the shrubbery, her favourite part of the gardens. It was raining and the wind was getting up. She pulled up the hood on her rain-jacket and busied herself with the care of growing, living things. The dead could take care of themselves.

*   *   *

Ewan had to turn the windscreen wipers to full power. The rain was lashing down and the narrow road was awash with overflow from the ditches. The grey of the ruined church at the top of the hill merged with the greyness of the sky. The only splash of colour visible was Claire Hearn's metallic blue BMW parked at the entrance to the graveyard. He parked beside the BMW and went into the cemetery.

He could not see her. He looked out towards the harbour at the sheet of rain sweeping in and wondered where in the hell she could be. He called her name. His voice was whipped away on the wind. He walked towards the big stone angel, remembering that was where Frank Dawson had been buried. The funeral flowers were withered clumps of compost by now, the bright ribbons that had adorned them faded and flapping in the gale. He called again and a faint sound carried back to him. He turned towards the old chapel ruin. Claire was standing in the doorless doorway, her hair and clothes so heavy with rain that they clung to her skin. She looked like a waif. He hurried towards her.

"Claire! Are you all right? You're drenched. What are you doing out here in this weather?"

Her face crumpled. Tears joined the rain dribbling down her cheeks. Ewan gathered her in his arms and held her close to his chest while her body shook with sobs. He tightened his arms around her, needing to protect her, wanting to save her from the terrible pain he heard in her muffled cries. He pulled his raincoat around her and rocked her gently until at last the crying stopped.

She moved back a pace and looked up at him. "I'm so sorry, Ewan. What must you think of me?"

He smiled at her and lifted his hand to brush her hair back from her face. His fingers touched her soft skin as he brushed the rain-slick strands. She was shivering with the cold and her eyes were huge in her pale face. She lowered her eyelids and he noticed that her lashes were very long and dark. He wanted to kiss her eyelids. The urge was so strong that to control it he had to drop his hand from her face and look away from her. He turned towards the harbour. The water was heaving, waves jostling each other in their race towards the shore. The deep, eerie sound of the foghorn vied with the whine of the storm.

"Where did all this come from?" Claire asked. "It was beautiful this morning."

Ewan listened to the thumping of his own heart and felt the blood surging through his veins and asked himself the same question. Where had all this come from? He took a deep breath and hoped his voice was steady.

"First things first, Claire. You must go home and get changed before you get pneumonia. Then maybe we could meet to talk. I really need to discuss some things with you."

She put her hand on his arm and smiled up at him. "I'm really sorry about not meeting you in the village. I know how precious your time must be. I just didn't notice how late it was getting. Why don't you follow me home and we can talk there? Have a drink to warm us up maybe. You are drenched too."

He tried to concentrate but his senses were filled with her. Standing in the storm-lashed graveyard under the gaze of the Gore-Croft angel, Ewan thought he would follow Claire anywhere for the chance to hold her in his arms again. His head told him he had more than enough problems to cope with now without inviting this new and totally unexpected barrage of feelings for Claire Hearn.

He tried to sound casual and in control. "Fine, Claire. You lead the way. I'll follow."

*　　*　　*

The plant was hissing and clanging and producing detergent as busily as if Frank Dawson was still seated on his throne overseeing operations. Brendan parked in Frank's space and jumped out of the car. The anger that had kept him driving around at top speeds all afternoon had not burned out. He strode towards the Admin Building and past the reception desk without acknowledging any salutes. He felt eyes boring into his back as he ran up the stairs to the first floor. He threw open the door to Frank's office. The impetus of his anger had carried him forward before he realised there were two people in the room. He looked from one to the other, from Yvette's striking features to the bland face of the man sitting behind Frank's desk.

He walked up to the desk and glared.

"What in the fuck are you doing in here? This is the manager's office."

"I could ask you the same question," the man replied.

Brendan felt his hands balling into fists. He wanted so badly to hit this bastard, to watch blood stream out of his nose, see his mouth puff up and his eyes go black and blue. "Look here, whatever your name is –"

"You know well it's Trevor. Trevor Langley."

"Well. Trevor Langley, you can –"

"Shut up, Brendan," said Yvette coldly. "Sit down."

Brendan swung around to face Yvette. The steely expression in her eyes matched the coldness of her voice. She nodded to Trevor. He stood and left the room, closing the door quietly after him.

Yvette pointed to a chair. The anger drained out of Brendan to be replaced by a profound exhaustion. He sat because his legs were incapable of supporting him any longer.

"That's better. Your tantrums are most undignified, Brendan. Silly."

He looked at her as she settled herself across the desk from him. In Frank's chair. He needed her so much now. He needed to bury his face in her breasts and hide from the world, to have her hands soothe away the feelings of pain and betrayal. There was neither pity nor passion in her eyes. He looked away from her and down at his haunted hands with the stinging, itching knuckles.

"So. Frank had the last laugh at his son-in-law. He outsmarted you."

"How long have you known?"

"Dorothy told me this morning. Before she went to the solicitor's."

"Jesus!" Brendan felt tears in his eyes. The final indignity. He had been totally screwed by a group of vultures and now he was going to blubber. He took a deep, shuddering breath and swallowed the hot lump of sadness and self-pity.

"So Dorothy's first act as MD was to appoint Langley as her deputy. Am I right?"

"In a way. What she did was to ratify Frank's decision. The old man had no intention of leaving you in charge when he went to Portugal. He was tying it all up neatly before he retired to the sun. You can hardly have forgotten that he told you about this. Just before you hit him and caused him to get a heart attack."

Brendan jumped up out of his chair and Yvette put her hand on the phone.

"You sit down and listen," she said, "or I'll call security and have you removed from the building. For good."

This time the tears did spill over. Tears of regret for opportunities lost, tears of hurt at Yvette's cruel words, tears of rage at Dorothy's gloating triumph. Most of all, tears of self-pity. He was ruined.

"You are in big trouble, Bren. In the shit, like you say. Crying is not going to help you now."

"What if I told you Jacques Rondel was the one who told Frank about us? Would you feel as smart then?"

"Grow up, Brendan. Of course he told him. It was part of the plan. The old divide-and-conquer principle."

Humiliated, Brendan wiped the tears from his eyes with the back of his hand. He sniffled and straightened up, trying to retrieve a little dignity. Yvette handed him a tissue but made no attempt to comfort him. She sat back in her chair and seemed to grow in stature while Brendan felt himself shrink until he was an insignificant, powerless blob, impaled on the chair in front of this Amazon.

"If you take control of yourself," she said, "you will see that you have several options."

He meant to laugh but the sound came out as a snort. Options? Like what?

"You can take Frank's offer and accept the severance package. Just take the money and run, so to speak. Of course that would mean the end of your marriage too but —"

The anger that had drained from him began to well up again. Jesus! "How in the fuck do you know all this? You were not at the reading of the will. Does everyone know? Am I the only one kept in the dark about my future?"

"What future? You threw that away when you slept with me. It was just a matter of time before Frank found out. Whether Frank Dawson had lived or died, you were out of his company. Lucky for you he died and you can benefit from the terms of his will."

Yvette stood up and walked around the desk.

Brendan's heart began to thud. He closed his eyes and anticipated her gentle touch at long last. When he opened his eyes he was looking into Yvette's beautiful but cruel face. There would be no gentle touch. But she was not finished with him yet. He knew that. She had a plan. She always had a plan. And of course she had that tape or video. Her proof. Her leverage. His despair.

"What do you want me to do?"

"What you should have done in the beginning. Get Claire's research for us."

He banged his fist on the desk in frustration. Everything came back to Claire and her fucking little experiments. What made them all think it was so important? The cure for cancer! As if! Daddy probably fixed it for his little girl so that she thought she had made this earth-shattering discovery. Anyway, her secrets were buried inside her head and nobody, but nobody, could get in there.

"What do you suggest I do? Open up her head and take out the information? If it was on computer you would have got it. I know you must have tried. I gave you the code number for the R&D alarm. It's not my fault that Claire decided to change it."

Yvette laughed. A mocking laugh. "Poor Brendan! She is ten steps ahead of you."

"And you!"

Yvette's mouth tightened and her amber eyes

flashed with anger. "All right. Here's the deal. Your secretary, Hilary Curran, is best friends with a girl named Ria. This Ria is Kevin Trill's girlfriend. She has a truly amazing big mouth. As you know, you have failed dismally in getting information directly from Kevin. Your job now is to cultivate Ria and find out exactly what her boyfriend has told her about Claire's research. They must have some very interesting pillow-talk. This shouldn't be too difficult for you. Ria is very attractive."

Brendan did not have to ask what would happen if he disagreed. Dorothy and the police would be told that he had assaulted Frank shortly before his death.

"I don't have a choice, do I?"

Yvette shook her head.

"Will you hand over whatever compromising evidence you have against me if I get Ria to talk?"

Yvette did her full coquette drill. A glance from underneath those curling eyelashes, a slight thrust of breasts, a flash of gleaming white smile. "Don't worry, Bren. I'll keep it safe for you."

He flinched at the mockery in her tone. He was not going to compound his humiliation by begging. Fuck them all. He looked at Yvette as steadily as he could.

"And what am I supposed to do? Hang around here until I get some information? You know Dorothy wants me out."

"Leave that to me. I'll talk to her. Tell her we need you here until after the takeover."

She had thought of everything. And left him with nothing. Not even self-respect. He got up and walked out before he cried again.

*   *   *

Ewan sank back into the soft couch and closed his eyes. He could hear the shower running. He pictured Claire standing underneath the water jets, face turned up, her dark hair with the red highlights streaming down her back, lather clinging to her arms and breasts. He opened his eyes and took a mouthful of the coffee she had made for him. For fuck's sake! What was wrong with him? His marriage was in tatters, he was in debt, he was in the middle of an election campaign, yet here he was fantasising about a married woman. And not just any woman. Claire Hearn.

The water stopped running. She must have opened the bathroom door because a hot flowery aroma drifted into the room. He tried to concentrate on the points he wanted to discuss with her.

"Sorry for delaying you, Ewan. Can I get you another coffee?"

She was wrapped in a large white, fluffy bathrobe and had her hair wrapped in a towel. She smelled as clean and fresh as a summer garden after a shower of rain.

"No. I'm fine, thank you. I have a big rally tonight so I must be moving on soon."

"How is your campaign going?"

"Surprisingly well. People are ready for a change from the big parties. We're hopeful."

She unwound her head towel and shook her hair loose. Her sensuality was all the more potent because she seemed entirely unaware of it. She sat on the chair opposite him and tucked her feet underneath her.

"You had something to discuss with me?"

"Yes, I have. Where to start is the question. Maybe your research."

"My research?"

"Is it true that you are conducting animal trials?"

She sat up straight and was immediately alert. So that was it. She should have guessed that EnVirowatch would be against animals being used in clinical trials. These Green people were all the same.

"Yes. I am. Under licence. So there is nothing your protesters can do about it. My animals are humanely treated and they are only used so that people can benefit . If you –"

"Stop there, Claire. I appreciate all that. This is not an animal rights issue. I just wondered if you would confirm that LabAn is your supplier?"

She nodded confirmation, a puzzled expression on her face.

"Did you know that Vincento McIntyre is one of their directors?"

"The same Vincento of RTTI?"

"The very same."

She was silent as she absorbed this piece of information. She thought of Anne Moroney's letter. Warning her. Telling her about Ronan Hennessey's contact with Yvette Previn. And now Vincento. RTTI definitely had their fingers in the LabAn pie.

"I believe you are carrying out some very important research. That you may have made a significant discovery."

Claire pulled her bathrobe more closely around her as if she felt threatened. "And what is your interest in my work? Why should I tell you anything?"

"EnVirowatch oppose the RTTI takeover of your father's plant. As far as we are concerned, RTTI are criminal polluters of the environment and we don't want them here. We've done our research. Sure, they are trying to create a clean image for themselves with this herbal medicine business. But mostly they don't care about image. Just profits."

"It's my mother you should be talking to then. She has the casting vote now. She will decide whether to complete the amalgamation with RTTI or not. And it is amalgamation. Not takeover."

Ewan stood up and went to sit on the couch beside her. His negotiating skills were letting him down. Claire was very defensive. He must get her to understand.

"Look, I'll put my cards on the table. The rumour is that you have developed a cure for animal cancer. That your trials have been successful. So obviously the next stage is human clinical trial. Then manufacture. Then massive, multibillions of profit when all the cancer patients worldwide start buying the new cure. Which is where RTTI come in. They obviously believe your human trials are going to be successful. That is why they are here, Claire. Your animal supply company kept them informed of your progress and then they pounced. Now tell me. Am I close to the truth?"

Claire put her head in her hands. Legs curled underneath her, head bowed, she felt small again. And safe. Protected. She could still trust her parents. Had not yet met Brendan. Had not unlocked the key to apoptosis. She began to rock gently. Strong arms slipped around her and held her. She looked up into Ewan's face. Her eyes were sparkling with unshed tears.

"I don't know if I can trust you. I don't know how you got hold of this information or what you are going to do with it. I don't know who to trust any more. Everybody seems to want my research for their own reasons. Curing cancer patients appears to be last on the list of anyone's priorities."

"That's not true. Of course there are people you can trust."

"I don't know, Ewan. Even my mother has let me down. My rock-solid mother. She is taking off for Portugal and selling my childhood home to Clive Rigney, of all people."

He caught Claire by the arms. "What did you say about Clive Rigney? He's going to buy Grange House?"

"Lock, stock and barrel. The house, the grounds, the woods, the whole estate."

Ewan looked at his watch. It was gone six thirty and he had to be at headquarters by seven. He needed to shower and change. He needed to talk to Helen about the bank. He needed to think about Clive Rigney and his new role as Lord of the Manor and supporter of EnVirowatch. He needed to remove himself from Claire Hearn so that he could think. He stood and handed her a folder.

"I have to go but I'd appreciate if you would read through this. It's an alternative route for you to take with your research. Think about it, Claire, please. We'll have to talk again soon."

She stood to walk him to the door. They suddenly seemed more conscious of each other and kept space between them as they walked.

"How did you find out about my research? Was it Kevin?"

"No. It wasn't. Politicians have sources."

"The media? Specifically our local paper? Maybe Paul Gregan in *Newstrack*?"

Ewan stopped walking and looked down at her. His mouth was half-open as if he was just about to say something but considered better of it. When he spoke each word was carefully measured. "Paul is a responsible journalist. He will not jeopardise any plans you might be making. He's on the right side of the fence, if you know what I mean."

"If you mean that he is against RTTI setting up here, then I suppose I know what you mean. Maybe I owe him a story after the wonderful series of articles he wrote about my father." She opened the door for him. "Thank you for telling me about LabAn. I had suspicions of them but this confirms it. My research is safe from them. It is safe from everyone. But I just don't know what to do with it next. I wish . . . I wish my father . . ." Her voice trailed off.

Ewan could not bear the sadness in her eyes. He stooped and kissed her on the cheek.

Brendan almost forgot to stop the car. His eyes were riveted on the doorway. On Claire in her bathrobe and Ewan Peters leaning over her. Kissing her. The knuckles that had been itching all day began to throb. The anger, the hurt, the hatred, the humiliation that had been churning in his stomach exploded in a gut-wrenching loss of all control.

He jumped out of the car, raced up the steps and punched Ewan in the nose. Blood spurted out and stained Claire's white robe.

His anger spent, Brendan jumped into his car again and drove away from his wife and the man he assumed to be her lover.

Chapter Eighteen

Claire rarely watched television. It just happened that on Monday night she needed the sound and colour to fill the bleak space in her head. She flicked through the channels and seeing nothing to hold her interest she started over again. *Questions and Answers* was just beginning on RTÉ 1. She sat back. This should be interesting because of the election fever which seemed to have gripped the whole country.

She leaned forward. Was that Ewan Peters on the panel? Yes, it was. He looked handsome. And unblemished. Of course they would have used make-up to cover any trace of swelling or bruising. It was just good luck that the blow from Brendan had not broken his nose.

She sat back and watched the *Questions and Answers* debate. Ewan was a natural in front of the camera. He seemed relaxed and in control and very *au fait* with all

the topics discussed. Some of the other politicians on
the panel were blatantly waffling, trotting out the party
line and talking over the other speakers. Ewan listened.
That is what made him different. He cared. He was also
better-looking than any of the others.

"Lover Boy on telly? Think I should ring and tell the
nation about his doorstep technique?"

Brendan was standing just inside the door, drink in
hand.

Walking unsteadily over to the television he raised
his glass. "To the best fucking politician on *Questions
and Answers*! Cheers! Tell me, Claire, is he? Is he the best
fuck? Was it all politically correct and environmentally
friendly?"

She snapped off the television and went over to him.
He looked dishevelled and dirty. She caught him by the
arm. "Bed. We'll talk in the morning. C'mon."

"Is that an invitation? Want to put in a bit of practice,
do you?"

He started to laugh. The noise rose in strength and
pitch until the room was filled with the mocking sound.
She tugged at his arm and managed to get him as far as
the stairs. He seemed to lose all motor control then and
just flopped onto the first step. She left him sitting there
and went upstairs to get the bed in the guestroom ready
for him. When she got back he was asleep. Or
unconscious. She shook him and called him to no avail.
There was no way she could get him upstairs now. The
idiot!

It took her ten minutes to get him back into the

lounge. Even though he seemed to have lost a lot of weight recently, he was still a very heavy man. His feet dragged on the floor as she caught him underneath the arms and hauled him along. She got him as far as the couch and let go her hold on him. They both flopped onto the floor, she in exhaustion, he in a drunken stupor. She looked down on him and tried to pity him, tried to remember her years of obsession with this man. She felt nothing but disgust at the pale, sweating, stinking creature lying beside her. He was sick. Out of control. Dangerous.

There was a gurgling sound. Claire jumped up and rolled him onto his side. He was going to vomit. She ran to the kitchen and grabbed a roll of paper towels and her rubber gloves. The sharp, acrid smell in the hall told her she was too late. He had already thrown up. She felt her own stomach tighten with nausea as she went into the lounge. She took a deep breath, swallowed the saliva welling up in her mouth, put her head down and dashed through the door. She almost collided with her mother.

"What are you doing here, Mum? When did you come in? Why didn't you ring?"

Dorothy looked from her son-in-law lying on the floor in a pool of his own vomit to her daughter's ashen face. She took the paper towels and gloves from Claire and began to mop up. The smell got more intense as Dorothy scooped up the vomit.

"Don't just stand there, Claire. Get water, disinfectant and a bin bag, please."

Claire was incapable of doing anything else but standing, watching in horror as her mother tended to her drunken husband.

"*Move!*"

There was no disobeying the command in Dorothy's tone. Claire felt like a six-year-old again as she did what Dorothy ordered. They managed to lift Brendan onto the couch. He was snoring and a stream of saliva drooled from his open mouth. Dorothy folded a towel and placed it strategically to soak the drool, then propped his head up on a pillow and covered him with a duvet Claire had brought down. She peeled off her rubber gloves.

"Right, lady. Coffee and talk. Now!"

Head bowed, Claire trailed out to the kitchen in her mother's wake.

"Do you want something to eat?" Dorothy asked.

Claire shook her head. She did not trust herself to say anything. She watched as her mother buzzed about making coffeee, getting mugs and milk and sugar, opening the cutlery drawer for a spoon, behaving as if it were her kitchen. She had looked after Brendan as if he were her husband. She had barged in here as if it was were house.

"How did you get in here, Mum?"

"I used my key, of course. I rang on the doorbell several times. When I got no reply I knew there was something wrong. So I let myself in. Just as well."

Of course. Claire had forgotten that her mother had a key to this house. Mother and daughter sat opposite

343

each other now. The silence dragged on as Dorothy waited for her daughter to speak and Claire waited for her mother to go away and leave her alone.

"I'm not going until we talk," Dorothy said as if she had read Claire's mind.

Claire fiddled with her mug of coffee. Talk! What could she say? Brendan saw another man kissing me? I am angry with Frank for protecting me so much that he has left me defenceless. I am angry with you for being so in control. I am angry with myself for, for . . . just for being me.

"I can't cope."

Claire's words were out before she had given them permission to leave the safety of her mind. They opened a floodgate. She had always considered anger to be a very hot emotion. She felt very, very angry now but cold. Unacknowledged resentments surged out from their hiding place. She wanted to hurt her mother and the expression on Dorothy's face told her she was succeeding. Birthday parties! For Christ's sake, she found herself ranting about birthday parties! How she had never had anyone but her mother and father to blow out the candles on her birthday cake. How everyone at school had been given cindy dolls and *Girls' Annual* while she had got chemistry sets and Dickens. How Dorothy had always bought clothes for her in an upmarket store while the other girls bought their own clothes in boutiques.

"You made me different when all I wanted was to be the same. I wanted to belong to the gang. Be one of the girls. Wear short skirts and glittery make-up. I wanted to try smoking and drinking and fumbling with the boys."

"No need to be coarse, dear."

"For God's sake! That is what I mean. Life is coarse, Mum. It is rough and common and vulgar. And I can't cope with it. My chemistry set and Dickens have not given me the skills I need to deal with a husband who doesn't love me, a vile corporation who are trying to steal my work, a father who has just gone and died on me. I am thirty-two and I haven't had a childhood yet!"

"I see."

"Do you? You've always had your gardening and your dignity. Not much space left for a child."

The sharp intake of breath told Claire that she had really hurt Dorothy now. The handsome, aristocratic features were as composed as ever but there was a darkness in her eyes. This was coming out all wrong. Yes, her mother had always been somewhat remote and preoccupied but never, ever unkind. She had no right to accuse her like this.

"I'm sorry, Mum. I know I'm not being fair. But –"

Dorothy raised her hand and would not allow Claire to finish the sentence. "You must say what is on your mind. And yes, you have every right to be angry. We overprotected you. I thought it would change when you went to college. That you would change it for yourself."

"College!" Claire spat out the word. "That was just more of the same. I was always on the outside looking in. There were parties, clubs, societies, rallies. I was never invited to anything and I was afraid to invite myself. I didn't know how to approach people and they obviously did not want to approach me. So I studied."

"But look what you have achieved, Claire. So young when you got your PhD and now your research."

"What have I achieved? A farce of a marriage and some research that I don't know how to handle? Brilliant!" She stood up and walked over to the door. "I'm going to check on Brendan."

He was snoring. He was disgusting. The towel had slipped from underneath his chin. When she tucked it back he muttered and threw his hands around. She closed the door on him.

Dorothy had not moved. She was still sitting, straight-backed, at the table. Since she seemed to have no intention of moving, Claire sat down again.

"How long has he been like this?" Dorothy asked.

"He has been behaving oddly ever since Dad died. He was there. It was very hard on him. Ironic, isn't it? Brendan was the last one of us to speak to Dad."

"Hmm . . ."

Claire felt another wave of anger wash over her. She had suffered Dorothy's "hmm" all her life. "Look at my drawing, Mum. Look how high I can jump. This is my school report. Here is the man I am going to marry." Every milestone was marked by a judgmental "hmm". No more!

"I know you never approved of Brendan and I admit in some respects you were right. But not about his relationship with Dad. He truly loved Frank. And if you say 'hmm' again I will scream!"

There! She had said it. She felt lightheaded now, like a helium balloon floating higher and higher, looking down on the storms below. She gripped onto the edge of the table for support.

Dorothy reacted by holding her head even higher and sitting even taller in her chair.

"Scream at me if you want to, Claire. If it makes you feel better. But don't deceive yourself. Brendan acted with total disregard for Frank's state of health. He dragged all this RTTI business on us at a time when Frank needed calm. And their last conversation cannot have been too pleasant. Maybe Brendan feels guilty."

"Their last conversation was very 'pleasant', as you put it. Dad told Brendan that he was going to retire and asked him to take over the running of Dashern. Obviously he didn't have time to alter his will again but his last wish was that Brendan would fill his shoes. So Dad had more regard for my husband than you do. And what have you to complain about? You have control of it all now. You are good at control, Mum."

Dorothy stood up and looked down on Claire. Claire watched fascinated as a red blush began to creep up her mother's neck. It skipped her chin and appeared on her cheeks as two red blotches. Her eyes were glittering. She was awesome in her rage.

"Right, Madam. You've had your say. It's my turn to talk. Brendan lied to you. Yet again. Frank was in London interviewing Trevor Langley for the position of

Acting Manager. The interview went well and a contract was drawn up. Frank signed it the day before he died. So Frank never told Brendan he wanted him to 'fill his shoes'. He was allowing Brendan to keep his present position as Deputy Manager until you had made a decision about your marriage. He could have kicked him out when he found out about Yvette Previn but –"

"There is nothing between Brendan and the Frenchwoman."

"Maybe not. But they did sleep together."

"They couldn't have! Yvette told me she –"

"Of course he would have lied about that too. He was always very careful because of the pre-nuptial agreement."

Stunned, Claire asked, "What pre-nuptial? I never signed one."

Dorothy's rage calmed. She stared at her daughter for a moment and then sat. She reached across the table and caught Claire's hand. Her eyes were glittering with tears now, not anger. "Your father was a very obsessive man. And you were one of his obsessions. Work was the other one. Over the years I lost the will to fight him. You are right. I took the easy option. I lived my own life and allowed him to control yours."

"The pre-nup. Tell me."

"When you decided that Brendan was the man you wanted to marry, Frank put legal safeguards in place. He was always suspicious of Brendan's commitment to the marriage. Brendan got his one-third share in the company on condition that he remained married to you. In the event of marriage break-up, his shares revert back to the family."

"So you all played silly beggars with my life and tied it up in a contract without ever consulting me? And Dad compounded it in his will by offering Brendan a bribe to leave!"

A tear trickled out of Dorothy's eye and tracked down the side of her nose. It dribbled over the top of her lip and splashed onto the table. Claire stared at the vulnerable woman sitting opposite her and felt she was looking at a stranger.

"I'm so sorry, Claire. What have we done? I should have stood up to Frank. Forced him to let you live your own life. I just gave up fighting him. I opted for the easy way out."

"I always thought you and Dad were happy."

"We were. On his terms."

"But you were going to Portugal together. He was leaving Dashern."

"I gave him a choice. I was going anyway. He could come with me or stay here and work himself to death."

Claire was shocked. Dorothy would have left Frank! They had always seemed such a self-contained system, Frank the storm and Dorothy the calm at the centre.

"But he decided to go, Mum."

Dorothy smiled. "Yes. The time was right. Your father was an old-fashioned man with old-fashioned principals. This amalgamation upset him but it was the only way he could see to keep continued employment

349

for the staff who had been so loyal to him. But he did not like having to deal with RTTI. Leaving you was his hardest decision. He had ClairCo set up a long time ago to protect the discovery he always knew you would make. When he learned that you were curing cancers in your trial animals his resolve nearly wavered. He felt he should be here to guide you through all the bureaucracy. To protect you from people like Yvette Previn and Jacques Rondel."

"And my husband."

Dorothy nodded.

Claire got up and put on the kettle again. They both needed fresh coffee. Dawson women did not handle emotion easily. Her mother's back was turned towards her. It was ramrod straight. The elegant, dignified Gore-Croft deportment. But Claire knew that if she walked in front of her and looked into her face, she would see a woman who was suffering, a woman of feeling and sensitivity, a woman she had never been allowed to know before. For the first time ever Claire felt she could talk to Dorothy and that her mother would listen and not judge. She needed Dorothy to understand.

She walked around to face her mother, to look into her eyes.

"Mum, I know Brendan married me to get his hands on Dashern shares. I think I always knew at some level. Deep down. I must have inherited Frank's obsessive genes. Brendan was my obsession. From the moment I set eyes on him, I wanted him and I didn't really care if the price was one-third of my father's company."

"That would have been a small price. Mr Brendan Hearn has cost this family much more. He divided us. Let us down. Let himself down."

"I must take some of the blame too. I wasn't really a wife to him. We didn't have a grown-up relationship. We couldn't because I haven't yet grown up. Don't you see? He was a toy I wanted and Daddy bought him for me. You of all people must understand, Mum. Dad's work came first. So does mine. We obsessed Dawsons do not make good marriage partners. So Brendan is not entirely to blame for the breakdown of our relationship."

"But this …" Dorothy said, waving her hand in the direction of Brendan's loud snores coming from the lounge. "There is no excuse for this. Nobody but himself to blame."

Claire went to the press and took out some bread to toast. She put it in the toaster before she turned and said to her mother's ramrod back: "Brendan lost control when he saw Ewan Peters kissing me. He's been out of control since."

Dorothy had turned to stare at her daughter, her mouth agape. "Ewan Peters, the environmental man? The one who is going up for election? I should have guessed there was something when you got so concerned with your appearance. You never were before."

Claire busied herself making the coffee, waiting for the inevitable question.

"Are you having an affair?"

Smiling, Claire turned again to her mother. "No. I am not having an affair. I was upset and he gave me a kiss on the cheek. A brotherly kiss. We share a common distrust of RTTI. I think he may be able to help me place my research in the direction I want it to go. He has given me a set of proposals, an alternative plan of action. I am assessing it at the moment."

The toast popped and Claire quickly buttered it, then carried it to the table with the fresh coffees.

Dorothy was looking very thoughtful. Claire sat and waited for the next question, cradling her mug in her hands, taking comfort from the heat.

"Do you trust this Ewan?" asked Dorothy at last.

Did she trust him? It was hard to believe she had met him such a short time ago. Yet when they were together it was as if they had known each other forever. Maybe crying on someone's shoulder and seeing your husband punch him in the face made you feel that way. Their relationship was intense.

"Yes, Mum. I trust Ewan Peters. He is a good man. And by the way, my interest in my appearance started as a pathetic attempt to compete with Yvette Previn. I do it now because I have found I enjoy taking care of myself. It's fun."

"Short skirts and glittery make-up twenty years later?"

Claire nodded. "Something like that." She sipped her coffee, then put the mug down rather unsteadily. "Mum . . . did Brendan really sleep with Yvette? She told me she wasn't interested in him. Actually, she said she was lesbian."

"Maybe she is but that didn't stop her sleeping with your husband. In Bonn at some conference. At least that is what Jacques Rondel told your father."

They ate their toast in a silence broken only by the distant sounds of Brendan's snores. They both had a lot to think about.

*　　*　　*

Ronan Hennessey was slightly green about the gills.

"Seasick? Surely not! We are only on the Seine!" Yvette laughed.

Ronan swallowed hard and tried to smile. They were in *Le Galion* Bistro on Allée Du Bord De L'Eau, one of Yvette's favourite haunts in Paris. The gentle swaying of the fifteenth-century galleon was not upsetting him. The company was. He looked around the table and his stomach lurched. Jacques Rondel was an intimidating man, even when everything was going his way. He was terrifying when he was displeased, as he was now. He never lost his temper, never raised his voice. He did not have to. The icy-blue look was enough and Ronan felt it was being directed at him. Even the normally talkative Vincento McIntyre was quiet. Yvette was the only one in a sociable mood. Good food always did that for her.

The waiter cleared off after their main course and brought the dessert menu. Yvette ordered crème brulée, while everyone else opted for coffee. Ronan looked around him, at the other diners, at the timber decks and beamed ceilings, at the lights of Paris reflected on the water. At anything except the three people at his table. They were conversing in French now. Speaking quickly. Way too quickly for him to understand. Maybe they were talking about him. About how stupid and inefficient he was.

When Yvette had finished her dessert, Jacques lit up a cigar and sat back in his chair. He stared at each of them individually through a haze of smoke. The people at the table beside them stood up to leave. Ronan wondered if Jacques had organised that too.

"Right. Time for work," Jacques said as the diners walked past, leaving only the RTTI group seated at the tables. "I want to know why we still do not have Claire Hearn's research to hand. Ronan?"

Ronan had rehearsed his speech. He had muttered and mumbled to himself all during the flight from Ireland. He had been word perfect. Now he knew he could not say what he had planned. It would sound like a string of excuses. It *was* a string of excuses.

"Claire Hearn has her lab secured like Area 51. I can't get in there."

"How hard have you tried?"

Ronan leaned towards Jacques, as if being closer would lend credibility to what he was saying. "I have arranged for samples from her trial animals to be analysed. I've slowed down her progress by introducing infections into her animals. I've contacted her personally. I've even spoken to her lab assistant but she has him brainwashed too."

"And?"

"And nothing. She is a very clever, very secretive woman. The analysis of the slides from her animals proves that she has cured their cancers. You know that. You have your research teams working on them. No one knows how she is doing it though."

"Well done, Ronan! Now you are beginning to understand the situation. Are you always this slow getting to grips with things?"

There was silence as Ronan absorbed the insult.

"Vince? Your take?"

Vincento looked steadily back at Jacques. He seemed to have respect but no fear.

"Unfortunately much the same as Ronan. We just don't know how she is manipulating the apoptosis process to work so effectively against the cancers. Bloody clever!"

Yvette sighed in disgust. "Next you'll want to nominate her for a Nobel Prize, Vincento!"

"And she may deserve one. For security! We've hacked into her computer system. Nothing. We have spoken to her lab assistant. We got nothing from him. We have examined the plant in detail and it is strictly detergent manufacture, so nothing there either. Brendan Hearn has not managed to get any information for us. Our scientific team cannot glean anything from the slides of the animals she treated. So there you have it. Nothing on computer, nothing on paper other than the outline for licence and patent application. And no way into the research lab. Short of breaking and entering into her lab at the considerable risk of getting caught, I don't see what else we can do now."

Jacques drummed the table impatiently with his fingers. He stopped suddenly and stared at Yvette. "This is getting messy. Yvette. What has gone wrong?"

"Frank Dawson. He has her and her research too well protected."

"What about our contact in the law firm that represents Dashern. Oliver Audley. Can he do anything about ClairCo?"

Yvette shook her head. "No. Frank has it all legally watertight. Everything in Research and Development is Claire's, independent of Dashern. Besides, Oliver has to be very circumspect. His father takes a very personal interest in Dashern affairs. He would not appreciate his son's lack of loyalty to the Dawson clan. On the positive side, Claire has made no further enquiries about patent. At least Frank's death has distracted her from that."

For the first time that evening, Jacques smiled. "Just what I like to hear, Yvette. A positive note. Anything else?"

The Frenchwoman flashed a smile at Jacques. She even thrust her breasts towards him. Just the slightest provocative movement. Ronan watched as she played the game. She did not seem to be able to help herself.

"Well, Brendan Hearn is well under control. Dorothy is all set for fleeing to Portugal and we have Trevor Langley in place. Our contacts in Audleys and LabAn are keeping us informed. Claire is getting more isolated."

Jacques joined his hands together and placed them on the table. He bowed his head over his folded hands. Vince and Yvette stayed still, their eyes focused on the perfectly groomed silver hair of RTTI's top man. It almost seemed as if he was in prayer.

Ronan knew instinctively that this silence was to be respected so he listened to the background noises. Ware clattered in the kitchen, water lapped against the galleon, timbers creaked, a police siren sounded in the distance. A trickle of sweat ran down his back as he thought of Anne Moroney. Had she warned Claire Hearn or had he managed to fire the bitch before she could do damage? He shivered. If this crowd found out . . .

"How has she done it? We invest billions in recruiting the best brains and providing state-of-the-art equipment. She is working in a very basic research facility and she –"

Ronan stopped listening to Jacques. The hair prickled at the back of his neck. Why hadn't he thought of it before? Why hadn't any of them thought of it? His heart began to beat quickly. If he was right, and he knew he was, then RTTI investment in LabAn would be safe. And when they made megaprofits from the manufacture of Claire Hearn's cancer cure they would owe him a debt of gratitude. A place on the board, maybe. He took a deep breath and halted the flight of his imagination. He must tell them now.

"I think there is a way to get into Dashern R&D."

They all stared at him. He had done the unforgivable and interrupted Jacques Rondel. Yvette smiled but it was not one of her sexy smiles. It was a sneer. "Are you going to disguise yourself as a guinea pig? Sneak yourself in with the new batch tomorrow?"

Ronan felt strong enough now to ignore her. "Equipment." As he said the word he could see that all three realised at the same instant that they had missed something obvious.

"Equipment needs to be calibrated. She must have incubators, fridges, freezers, balances, waterbaths, centrifuge etc. etc. that need servicing and calibrating. And there are only three companies in Ireland involved in that work. LabAn uses all three on contract. I can find out who Claire Hearn uses."

"Maybe she uses someone from the plant?" Vince suggested.

Ronan shook his head. "No. She must have her equipment calibrated by an accredited agency. Otherwise her results would not be accepted."

Jacques banged his fisted right hand into the open palm of his left hand. The sharp slap brought them all to attention. "We should have thought of it long ago! Well done, Ronan! Just let us know the name of the company she deals with and we will take it from there."

"Surveillance?" Vince asked.

"The works," Jacques replied. "Cameras, mikes, the lot. Yvette, you'll organise that as soon as we have the name of the calibration company?"

Yvette nodded. Her lips were parted and her amber eyes glowed. It was not just good food that excited Yvette. Espionage and revenge were her ultimate aphrodisiac. Vince exchanged glances with her. Jacques pretended not to notice. He had been pretending not to notice for a long time. But he did enjoy the videos. Seeing the Technical Director bound up with silken ropes and having his bottom whipped by the leather-clad PR executive was entertaining. And might prove to be a very useful lever at some future stage.

He stood. "Good meeting. Contact us as soon as possible, Ronan."

They all left *Le Galion* feeling happier than when they had boarded.

*   *   *

Ewan splashed water onto his face. His skin still felt sticky from the make-up. He was buzzing with the excitement of his television appearance. Staring at his reflection in the bathroom mirror, he tried not to be too smug. It was so easy to believe all the compliments. He had been told he was a natural in front of the camera, that he put EnVirowatch policies across in a very professional way, that he left the opposition looking inept and amateur. "Nice one, Peters," he said and smiled at his reflection. He leaned closer and examined the bruising under his eyes, extending from his injured nose. Lucky it hadn't been broken. Even though the yellow and blue marks were fading they were obvious again without the make-up. Most people probably believed that he had tripped getting out of the car and fallen against the door. That is what they believed because that is what he told them. And they trusted him. He looked away, unable to meet his eyes in the mirror. He turned off the light and went into the bedroom.

Helen was sitting up in bed reading. He had expected her to be asleep at this hour.

"Congratulations, Ewan. You did very well. The children were very proud of Daddy."

He gave her a half nod, half smile. She was trying so hard. He knew she was.

"The phone was ringing all night," she told him. "People just wanting to congratulate you."

"I hope they turn that into votes."

"Paul Gregan rang. He said to tell you that you're running very well on the latest *Newstrack* opinion poll."

He stopped halfway through unbuttoning his shirt. "Really?"

This was a four-seat constituency. Could it possibly happen? Opinion polls, especially at this stage, were unreliable. There was a week to go yet to Election Day. The big boys fought dirty. No way would they sit still and allow an outsider steal one of their comfortable seats. And EnVirowatch funds were running low. Money, money, fucking money!

"It was nice seeing you on telly tonight. At least I knew where you were."

"Don't start, Helen! I just couldn't take it now. I'm too tired."

She sat up straight in bed and arranged the pillows behind her back. Ewan turned off the light and got into bed beside her.

"Lie down, Helen, please. I must sleep. I've an early start and I'm exhausted."

"Do you imagine I will have a lie-in? The children will have me up at cockcrow. Stop feeling sorry for yourself and tell me all about *Questions and Answers*. Tell me about the studio. And what were the others like? Was it terrifying?"

"I'll tell you all about it tomorrow . . ." Ewan pulled the duvet up around his ears and turned his back to his wife. He muttered goodnight and closed his eyes.

Helen reached out and turned on her bedside light.

"Ewan! You are the one who said we have problems because we don't communicate. I'm trying. But you're shutting me out!"

He threw the duvet back and sat up. He turned to glare at her. She seemed so tiny, propped up by her pillows, so helpless that he felt guilty. He took a deep breath and searched for the words that would convey the breadth of his annoyance but not the depth of his anger.

"Look, Helen," he said as gently as he could, "when I said we should communicate I didn't mean chatting in the early hours of the morning when we're both exhausted. And at the time I said it, I meant we should discuss any problems that arise – such as when you've spent our credit to the limit and you've borrowed money from someone else." He couldn't resist adding, with heavy irony: "And of course when warning letters arrive from the bank – that really is a time for sharing. "

She reached out a hand to touch his face. Her eyes were filled with tears. "I know I messed up, Ewan. I'm so sorry. I'm trying to make it right."

"What do you mean, Helen? What can you do? I'm clearing the card with the monthly payments but how are we going to pay the Rigneys back? How can you make that right?"

"TDs earn a lot of money. Much more than we have now."

Ewan shook his head in despair. "TDs don't earn a lot of money. It's just that I earn very little now. And what if I'm not elected, Helen? What then? Anyway, the Rigneys want their money immediately, don't they? I'll have to set up a meeting with Clive and see if we can reach some agreement. The little fucker will enjoy humiliating me."

Helen shrank even further back into her pillows, the duvet pulled up under her chin. She looked pale and drawn, the circles under her eyes almost as dark as the bruising under his.

He smiled at her tentatively. "Now let's get some sleep, OK?"

"I spoke to Julie Rigney today."

His eyes flashed with anger. "I told you to stay away from her! What has she talked you into now?"

"You always underestimate me, don't you? *I* talked her into giving us more time to pay her back. I told her we'd be in a better position when you are elected. And she agreed."

"Just like that? Didn't she previously tell you she

didn't want Clive to find out? That you would have to settle before he discovered the missing money? "

Helen sat up straight and the anger in her eyes matched his now. "No matter what I do, you're going to criticise me anyway. No, it wasn't 'just like that'! I had to beg her. And I hated doing it. But I had to. I signed her bloody document and –"

Ewan's heart lurched. "Document? What document? What did you sign?"

"Just an IOU."

Ewan put his head in his hands. This situation was getting out of control. The woman in the bed beside him was a liability. What had happened to her? What was happening to them?

"There's something else," she went on. "She said that you might be able to help Clive with some new scheme of his. Then maybe they might knock something off the debt."

"My God! How could you be so stupid, Helen! That's blackmail! Have you gone completely mad? Even if, and it's a big if, I am elected I can't promise Clive Rigney any favours. I won't offer him any favours."

Ewan threw back the duvet and sat at the edge of the bed. He was too angry and worried to sleep now. What in the fuck was Rigney up to and why did he need to have a hold over Ewan Peters? Could it have something to do with his latest purchase?

"Did Julie Rigney mention anything about Grange House?"

"That's a secret! How did you know?"

Jesus! So much for loyalty. Helen had known and had not told him. She was getting exceptionally good at keeping secrets from him. What else was she not saying?

"Did she say if they have plans for the Estate?" he asked.

Helen hesitated. She looked at her husband and seemed to be weighing up the pros and cons of answering him. "She's on and on about redecorating the house and putting in a swimming-pool and Jacuzzi and just about any other luxury you could think of. But I overheard him warning her not to talk about their plans. I think they are planning a lot more than decoration. You don't need an architect and a developer just to redecorate, do you? They warned me not to mention that either."

Ewan stood up and picked up his dressing-gown. He was not going to sleep now. Might as well get some work done. Anyway, he needed to go over the proposal for Claire Hearn's research before they met again. Make sure it was watertight.

Helen patted the bed beside her. "Don't go, Ewan. Come back to bed."

"I can't. You get some sleep. See you in the morning."

He could see that he had hurt her. He leaned over and kissed her on the cheek. He closed his eyes and for one second imagined Claire Hearn's soft cheek under his lips, her fragrance in his nostrils. He was so steeped in the memory that he did not catch what Helen whispered into his ear. She had to repeat it more loudly.

"We're going to have another baby, Ewan. I'm pregnant."

He stared at her, unable to control his thoughts. A baby? How in the fuck was he going to support another child?

Disgusted with his reaction, he leaned towards Helen and cradled her. He lay awake long after his pregnant wife had fallen asleep in his arms.

Chapter Nineteen

When Brendan woke, his neck was stiff, his mouth dry and fetid, his head throbbing with pain. And he was on the couch in the lounge. He sat up and tried to remember yesterday. He had been in a bar all afternoon. Mellow Drama, that was it.

He felt his stomach rumble. He threw back the duvet and made a dash for the downstairs bathroom. He got there just in time to be violently sick. He splashed water on his face and rinsed out his mouth. Standing in front of the mirror, he stared at the hobo in the reflection. He saw a dirty, down-and-out loser, with dark stubble on his face and greasy hair. How in the fuck had he sunk so low, so quickly? Tears welled up in the eyes in the mirror. He turned his back on the pathetic image and went to the kitchen.

Strong, black coffee had never been his drink of choice but he drank cup after cup now. Each mouthful brought more clarity to his thinking. He made toast and his stomach settled. He began to remember things. Flashes of shame. The shock in Frank's eyes when he had hit him, the blood oozing from the cut on his cheek, Yvette sneering, mocking, Dorothy's smug look as Frank's will was read, Ewan Peters bending over Claire, kissing her. The bastard! Standing on this doorstep, obviously thanking her for a fuck. The bitch! And then, for some peculiar reason, he thought of his mother. How proud she had been of him! She had died believing the name of Brendan Hearn would always be synonymous with achievement and success. He put his head in his hands and wept for shame.

Going upstairs to the bathroom he turned the shower to full power and stood underneath it. For ten minutes he thought of nothing but the stinging needles of water spray that were washing away the filth of his drinking binge.

He felt cleaner and stronger as he dried and dressed. His memories of yesterday were still blurry at the edges but some events were quite clear. He had gone to Mellow Drama under Yvette's instructions. He was to befriend this girl Ria, the girlfriend of Kevin Trill. As usual, Yvette's information was accurate. At lunch-time, the very attractive blonde had come in, accompanied by a dark-haired girl. They ordered lunch from the carvery. Brendan managed to get a seat at their table. Talking to them was easy. He just let Ria take the lead.

"I know who you are. We've spoken on the phone.

I've booked flight tickets for you. London. Do you remember? I saw you at the Dashern Dinner Dance too."

"We're practically related then," Brendan had laughed.

"Almost. Hilary Curran is your secretary and my friend. And my boyfriend is your wife's assistant. Of course you know that. You interviewed him. Well, he's not just an assistant now. He's her deputy. He's been managing the lab single-handed while Mrs Hearn has been coping with her father's death. Terribly sad, his death, wasn't it? So sudden and so far from home."

Brendan remembered feeling relieved. Obviously this girl was going to blab out whatever she knew. He would have information to bring back to Yvette. It was the dark-haired girl who had been the problem. Trish, she said her name was. She owned the travel agency where Ria worked. She seemed to be a very reserved and cautious person, continuously warning Ria to be discreet. Trish's boyfriend came to join them. Paul Gregan, a photographer and journalist with the local paper. The one who had written the articles about Dashern and Frank Dawson.

Everything was a blur after that. He had been drinking wine with lunch. The girls had gone back to the travel agency but the photographer had stayed on for a while. Paul had bought him brandies. Said it was on his expense account.

He had stayed in Mellow Drama after Gregan had left. Had he gone to the golf club? Maybe. Was the memory of Dorothy leaning over him a nightmare, or did it really happen? Who had covered him with the duvet?

He examined his reflection in the full-length mirror in the bedroom. He looked more the executive and less the hobo now. He slapped on some after-shave and combed his hair. Then he went downstairs and tidied up the lounge before jumping into his car and going in search of Ewan Peters.

* * *

Dorothy pulled into the car park of the Granary Hotel. There were plenty of parking spaces available so early in the day. She found a space with plenty of room and manoeuvred in there. Parking was not her forte. She pulled down the mirrored sun visor and checked her hair and make-up. Satisfied that she looked every inch the Lady of the Manor, she locked the car and went to the reception area. He was waiting for her. He stood when he saw her coming in. She held out her hand to greet him

"Clive. Thank you for meeting me."

"Not at all, Mrs Dawson. I just hope you don't have bad news for me. You haven't changed your mind about selling Grange House, have you?"

"Let's get coffee first. Then we can talk."

"Of course. I'm sorry. This way," he said, leading her towards the lounge.

Clive was blushing and he hated himself for it. This

snotty old cow made him feel inadequate. He touched the collar of his silk shirt for reassurance.

They regarded each other in silence as they waited for coffee to be served. To the waitress serving them it was obvious that the tall, dignified woman had scant regard for the dandy little man sitting across from her. It was equally obvious that he was fighting a fear of the aristocratic lady.

"Well," he said, when the waitress was out of earshot, "is there a problem? Are you going through with the sale or not?"

She took a sip of her coffee and smiled. "Direct, aren't you? I suppose that is how you built your empire. My husband was the same."

Clive looked at her and thought about that. Yes, Frank Dawson had been direct, even blunt and verging on ignorant at times. Not the life partner one would imagine for Dorothy Gore-Croft. He had liked Frank. Felt comfortable with him. They had been kindred spirits. But only in the golf club. Frank had never invited him to his home. To her home.

"Why do you want Grange House? I got the impression from what little you allowed your wife to say that you have plans for it. She certainly has."

"Ah! Julie. Yes, my wife has plans. They all have to do with design and decoration and spending money. And I remember you saying yesterday that you had no right to ask about our intentions. That is still true today, Mrs Dawson."

Dorothy flicked her hand impatiently in his

direction. "My name is Dorothy. Call me Dorothy. And I am not trying to be awkward or to invade your privacy in any way. But there are some important decisions I have to make and I need to explore every option before I decide."

Clive sat back and examined Dorothy. She was a handsome woman. Not strikingly attractive but wholesome-looking. Good skin, good teeth, bright eyes. He smiled to himself as he realised he was sizing her up like he would a horse. Which immediately recalled his memories of seeing Dorothy ride out to the hounds, hair pinned up underneath her hat, riding jacket and jodhpurs cut to the shape of her slim figure, arrogant and proud astride her mount. She was just a child then but was already the perfect miniature of the Lady of the Manor she would become. She had never been aware of the snotty-nosed little village boy standing at the side of the road watching the hunt gallop by. Or of the other times he had peeped at her from the vantage-point of his father's Morris Minor van.

"Do you remember my parents, or my grandparents?" he asked.

"No, I don't. Should I?"

"Possibly not. They were just tradespeople who served the big house."

"Oh, dear! Are we going to have a class war here? I was born a Gore-Croft, my home was Grange House, my playground was the Estate. And yes, I had a privileged upbringing but that does not make me a snob. I don't judge people by what they own and neither should you. It's you who are the snob. I'll bet you have decided that I am a snooty old bag!"

Her assessment was so accurate that Clive blushed again.

"I thought so," Dorothy laughed. "Now tell me about your parents. Maybe I will recall something about them."

She was arrogant and dismissive. No denying that. But Clive sensed a warmth and understanding hidden underneath the reserve. He heard it in the tone of her voice and saw it in her eyes.

He smiled at her. "My grandparents started the village store. They supplied Grange House with groceries and shoe polish and yard brushes and whatever else was ordered by your housekeeper. In fact that little huckster shop stocked everything from the proverbial anchor to the needle. When my parents took over the business, they modernised and expanded the shop. We progressed to delivering goods by van. But Grange House was still our biggest and best customer. We depended on it to keep going."

"I do remember groceries being delivered. In a Morris Minor van, I think. A small man with a flat cap used to carry the boxes into the kitchen. If I was there, as I sometimes was with Cook, he used to give me some chocolate. He was a kind man."

"He was my father."

"I see."

"I doubt if you do, Dorothy. While my father was in the kitchen, giving you chocolate, I was sitting in the van, staring into the big house, hating the fact that we had to go to the back door. In our two generations of delivering to Grange House, we never once, not even once, were invited to set foot inside your front door."

"Well, you have now."

Clive straightened himself up in his chair and Dorothy was struck by the fierce pride apparent in his raised chin and squared shoulders. "Exactly. So I can answer your question. I have several reasons for wanting to buy Grange House. One reason is that I can. I have the money and I am happy to spend it. I do have a business plan for developing the property but I am not willing to discuss that with you. But my main reason is that I want to walk through that front door without getting a Gore-Croft boot in my backside."

Dorothy gave a big hearty laugh, which was totally at odds with her dignified image. "Oh! Come on, Clive! The Commander was gruff but my father was a civilised man. He would never have kicked anyone. At most, he would have got someone else to do it for him."

Clive looked down at his hands and seemed to get very interested in examining his nails. Dorothy noted his bowed head and realised that this man was far more complex than the money-grabbing little shyster she had taken him to be. She had hurt his feelings. He had been honest with her and she had laughed at him. She felt ashamed of her insensitivity.

"I'm very glad you are buying Grange House, Clive. I do hope you enjoy it."

He looked up from his examination of his hands.

She was sincere. He could see it. Knowing what people really meant, no matter what they said, was one of his greatest business assets.

"Thank you. Now that I've told you far more than I intended, are you going to tell me why you wanted to meet me today?"

"Well, it is about the sale of the house. I do want you to have it. I really do."

"But?"

"But I want to change one of the conditions of sale. And I need to know if this is agreeable to you. And to Mrs Rigney, of course."

"Better order more coffee, then. Sounds like we have a lot of talking to do."

By the time they had finished their second pot of coffee Dorothy Dawson and Clive Rigney had found a common goal to share and had reached a new understanding of each other.

*   *   *

Ronan Hennessey felt jet-lagged. He had flown this morning from Paris to Ireland and then driven from the airport to LabAn, all on four hours' sleep. Besides, sitting with Yvette Previn on the flight back from Paris had been draining. It was satisfying to watch other men watching her, knowing that they envied him his place by her side. He would have swapped with any one of them. She exhausted him, absorbed every ounce of energy from him. You always had to be on your guard with Yvette, always prepared to defend yourself against the stab of her sharp wit. Still, he had been the one to lead the way for RTTI, hadn't he? Not Mademoiselle Shove-Tits-in-Your-Face Previn. She was back in Dashern by now but she had warned him not to ring through the switchboard. He smiled in satisfaction as he dialled her cell-phone number.

"*Bon jour.*"

"Calbitron is the company."

"*Bien. Merci.*"

She clicked off her phone. Just like that. Ronan shrugged. Let RTTI get on with whatever it was they had to do to Claire Hearn's lab. He had a batch of animals to prepare for delivery to the very same Dr. Hearn.

Yvette immediately rang Jacques Rondel and their plan of action was put in motion.

*　　*　　*

Paul Gregan sat staring at the spreadsheet as if he was waiting for it to attack him. In a way that is what was happening. The figures of the latest *Newstrack* opinion poll were spread out before him. The post *Questions and Answers* poll. Ewan Peters was storming up the ratings. His television appearance had won him the housewives' vote. The time was right for a backlash against the Centre-Right government. The electorate was ready for a change, ready to drift to the Centre-Left. EnVirowatch and their charismatic representative were sitting pretty. Ewan Peters was well on his way to being elected. Unless …

Paul stood up and paced the space between his desk and Jim Conrad's. The older journalist stopped typing and watched.

"Seems like you have a hot story, Paul. Anything you want to share?"

Paul looked at Jim and wondered if he should ask his advice but he knew what the veteran reporter would say. Check and recheck your sources. What had he to go on now? The mumblings of a drunk. Yes. He would have to check his source.

"No, nothing at the moment, Jim. Working on it though."

Paul sat at his desk and rang Hilary Curran. She told him her boss had not been in his office for days and she refused to give him Brendan Hearn's mobile number. He wasn't answering the phone at his home either.

Next Paul rang Ewan Peters. He was at his campaign headquarters, the grand title EnVirowatch gave their second-storey office space over the hardware shop.

"I'm coming to see you," Paul said and put the phone down before Ewan could object.

Within ten minutes, Paul was puffing his way up the two flights of stairs. The higher he climbed, the mustier the air got. When he reached the second-floor landing, he stopped to get his breath. The door to the EnVirowatch office was open and the sounds of phones continuously ringing filled the landing space. He walked into a scene of chaos. Posters were stacked all over the place, tables that acted as makeshift desks were strewn with leaflets. Polystyrene cups, empty and full, littered the room. Ewan's band of faithful followers were answering the phones, taking messages, stuffing envelopes with EnVirowatch literature. There was a huge energy in the room. But no Ewan. Eva saw Paul and pointed.

"He's in his cupboard. He's expecting you."

Paul knocked at the door of the annexe the staff liked to call Ewan's cupboard. With justification. It was a tiny space. He closed the door behind him. A light bulb with no shade cast a harsh light over the desk and the man sitting behind it. Ewan looked haggard, the bruising underneath his eyes further darkened by puffy, tired circles. He waved to Paul to sit.

"When have you last slept?" Paul asked.

Ewan tried to smile but it was a pathetic effort. "Busy, busy, you know. Helen told me you rang last night. The polls are looking promising."

"Better than that. We commissioned another poll for after your TV appearance. You're coming out well ahead. Looks like Clive Rigney made a good investment."

Ewan looked sharply at Paul. He wasn't sure how far he should trust this man. He was a journalist, after all. "If you're hinting at a scandal about Clive Rigney's donation, you're way off the mark. Every cent he gave us is legal and above board and publicly declared. You've seen the paperwork anyway, so you know that."

Paul nodded. He had indeed seen all the information about Rigney's financial backing of EnVirowatch. It was kosher. What puzzled him was not how much but why. And why Ewan was being so defensive now.

"I didn't come here to talk about Rigney, although I'd love to know why he has suddenly strayed from his right-wing path. I'm here to talk about that bruise underneath your eyes. How did you get it, Ewan?"

"I told you. I slipped and –"

"Don't bullshit me!"

A flush spread up Ewan's face. Paul could not decide whether it was caused by rage or embarrassment.

Ewan fidgeted with a pen for a moment and then looked defiantly at Paul. "OK – you tell me, since you obviously don't believe what I said."

"Will I tell you what Brendan Hearn said?"

Ewan put his head in his hands and Paul had his answer. The ramblings of the drunkard had been true.

"Are you having an affair with Claire Hearn?"

"No, I am not! That idiot just jumped the gun. Made an assumption about what he saw."

"And what did he see, Ewan? He said he found you on his doorstep, kissing his half-naked wife."

Ewan sat back in his chair and sighed. What in the fuck else was going to go wrong? In debt to Rigney, Helen pregnant, Brendan Hearn spilling his guts to the press, the race against RTTI. How much should he tell Paul? How much would it take to keep him from asking more questions?

"I was comforting Claire at the time. She was upset about her father. They were close, you know."

"And she had to undress to be comforted?"

Ewan threw his pen down on the desk and this time there was no doubt but that the red flush on his face was caused by anger.

"For fuck's sake, Paul! Are you going to take the word of that snake in the grass over mine? Brendan Hearn is an RTTI lackey. He would do anything to damage his wife's reputation. He came on a perfectly innocent scene and put his own filthy interpretation on it. For Christ's sake! I'm married. So is Claire!"

"But you were in her house."

"I told you I was going to talk to her about her work. Jesus, Paul! It was you who told me about it."

"And?"

"And, yes. She has made some pretty amazing advances. And, yes, you were right. That is most probably why RTTI are here. They're trying everything to get hold of her research. With her husband's help. So, you see, you cannot trust anything he tells you, especially if it is damaging to his wife."

"Much more damaging to you, I would say. She's not going up for election."

Ewan took a deep breath. He was going to have to trust Paul. There was no other way.

"What she has done is far more important than just getting elected. It is the most important scientific and medical development of our time."

Paul smiled. So Ria had been right. Claire Hearn had

developed a cure for cancer. Maybe it had been worth shooting Ria's portfolio after all. Frank Dawson's cryptic note from the airport made sense now too.

"I know about her research. What I can't understand is where you come into it, Ewan. Is your relationship with Claire personal or is it related to the future of her cancer cure?"

"Off the record?"

Paul hesitated. He could have the story of his career here. Election candidate has affair with married woman and gets beaten up by woman's husband. And just to add a global dimension, the woman happens to have discovered the cure for cancer. His mouth watered at the thought of international headlines under his by-line. *Reuters, LA Times, Le Figaro*. But he did not have any concrete evidence yet. He could hardly build his international reputation on Ria Corkery's word. Then again, Ewan was confirming that Claire Dawson had developed the long-awaited cancer cure. He must get this story before someone else broke it first.

When Ewan spoke, it was almost as if he had read his mind. "It's too soon, Paul. Certain safeguards have to be put in place. But I guarantee, you will be the first to get the story when it is safe to speak."

"How do I know that? You've lied to me already about your bruises."

Ewan stood up and his head almost touched the ceiling in the slanted cupboard room. There was a desperate plea in his voice. "Claire and I are working together to ensure that her discovery will get to the people who need it. Everybody who needs it. Not just those who can afford it. You cannot endanger that, Paul. If you go public now, everything will just get out of control."

His plea made, Ewan sagged onto his chair again. They sat in silence, each trying to second-guess the other. The noise seeping in from the main office suddenly changed in tone. The phones still rang in the background but there were raised voices. Very angry voices. There was a knock on the door and Eva came in, looking flustered and annoyed.

"There's a man outside, a very rude man, insisting on seeing you, Ewan. Says you'll talk to him if you know what's good for you. I think he is one of those people who own the detergent factory."

"Brendan Hearn?"

"Yes. Hearn. That is what he said his name is. What will we do? He's quite aggressive."

Brendan made the decision for them. He pushed his way into the tiny space. Ewan nodded to Eva and she reluctantly left and closed the door behind her. Brendan looked from Ewan to Paul and sneered.

"I should have guessed! A cosy little cartel. The politician and the journalist in his pocket."

Paul got up from his chair and sat on the edge of the desk. He indicated the chair to Brendan. "Sit down and stop making a prick of yourself."

Brendan sat. He stared at Ewan, examining the bruises under his eyes. "I didn't come here to cause trouble. I came to apologise for hitting you."

381

Well, here was a surprise. The last thing Ewan had been expecting was an apology. In fact he would have floored any man he saw in a compromising position with his wife and would never have apologised for it. He shrugged his shoulders, neither accepting nor rejecting the apology, waiting for Brendan to continue.

"The point is that I should never have resorted to physical violence when I could hurt you much more without ever raising a fist. How do you think your voters would react to knowing you're a two-timing cheat?"

"People in glass houses, Brendan!" said Paul. "What about you and Yvette Previn?"

Brendan swung around to face Paul. His angry look was replaced by puzzlement as he desperately tried to recall exactly what he had told Paul in Mellow Drama.

Paul gave him a hint. "It must be tough knowing that you could maybe have saved your father-in-law's life had you not been so busy screwing your French mistress while he lay dying in the room next door."

The knuckles on Brendan's right hand began to itch. He waited for the journalist to go on, to accuse him of hitting Frank, of murdering him. There was silence. He rubbed the itchy knuckles with his left hand. Still nobody spoke.

"I could speak to Yvette Previn," said Paul. "Verify some facts. Before going to press."

The knuckles were throbbing now. Brendan longed to relieve the discomfort by slamming his fists into the smug journalist's face. He put his hands into his pockets. He would not give these fuckers the satisfaction of seeing him go to pieces.

"Stalemate," Ewan said. "Go away, mind your own business and we'll forget about assault charges. Deal?"

Brendan laughed into his face. "You have some brass neck, Peters! You're so good at the sincerity thing, aren't you? Fooling the people into voting for you. They should know what you're really like."

"The choice is yours," Paul said calmly.

Choice! When did he last have a choice? Everything he did was dictated by someone else. His wife, his in-laws. Yvette. And he would never be free to choose again as long as Yvette and her RTTI cohorts had the evidence of his row with his father-in-law. Then he remembered. Frank had given him a choice. A severance package. A bribe from beyond the grave. An escape plan. The man whose life he took was giving him the chance to live. No! No, he didn't kill Frank. It was the old man's heart, his clogged arteries, his blood pressure. The tiny room began to close in around him. He loosened his collar.

"Stay away from my wife," he said to Ewan and hoped that his voice was steady.

There was a knock on the door and Eva popped her head in. "Everything all right, Ewan?"

Ewan nodded. "Yes, thank you, Eva. Mr Hearn is just leaving."

Without saying another word, Brendan stood and walked out of the office.

Ewan looked at Paul. "I owe you one."

"You sure do," Paul agreed as he walked to the door. "And be certain I will collect."

Ewan waited a minute or two to make sure he was alone. Then he got out his cell phone and tapped in a message. *Must see you. Call me.* He pressed *Send.*

Then he put on his public face and went to reassure his staff that Brendan Hearn would not be back.

Chapter Twenty

Kevin was working feverishly this morning. Claire smiled, watching his lips move silently as he repeated instructions to himself. Every so often he looked up, waiting for her nod of approval. He would be ready to take over all the routine work as soon as this training was finished. He would be fully trained in everything except the preparation of Serum 6. That should free up some time for her where she could concentrate on bringing the serum forward. Finally, he placed his solutions on the bench beside Claire's demonstration samples.

"How have I done?" he asked.

"Excellently," Claire answered. "You know the next steps. You've done them for me often enough."

"Autoclave. Decant. Refrigerate."

"That's it. Go ahead. I'll be in my office if you want me."

When Claire had signed off the training records she got her mobile phone and read Ewan's message again. *Must see you.*

She unlocked her briefcase and took out the folder he had given her. His plan for Serum 6. Opening the folder, she spread the pages out on her desk and read through them for the umpteenth time. It was a good plan for guiding Serum 6 through the development stages. Or at least, Claire admitted to herself, it would be a good plan if Ewan got elected. If he was in a position of power. If he held significant political clout. That was the problem with his plan. There were too many ifs. And of course, the biggest if of all. Could she rely on her instincts? Should she trust him? Especially now, since Brendan had assaulted him.

Going over to her safe she punched in the code. When the door swung open she picked up the tattered manila folder and brought it back to her desk. The cover had developed a velvety texture from years of handling. Claire stroked the softness now, finding reassurance from the familiar feel of it. She opened it up and let her eyes travel over the columns of figures. Serum 6! Page after page of numbers. Representing year after year of research. Tabulating the progress from theory to the certainty of practical application. From a belief, an act of faith, to an operating system. From the chaos of cancer to the harmonious logic of cancer cure. Poring over the pages of figures, she ticked off sections as she went through them. Then she sat back and smiled. Yes! Yes! Yes! It was all here. Just as she had planned it, had dreamed it, had lived it for what seemed like her whole life.

"Must be funny figures to make you grin like that."

Claire started. Kevin was looking over her shoulder, peering at the columns of numbers. She quickly closed the folder.

"Just some old papers I'm sorting through," she said but even to her own ears she sounded nervous.

How could she have been so careless? She followed Kevin's gaze to the open safe and knew she could no longer store her formula there. It was unlikely that her code could be deciphered but maybe it was not as foolproof as she believed.

"I shouldn't have left the safe open. I'm breaking my own rules now," she said. "Would you lock it for me please, Kevin?"

He puffed up with pride as she called the code out to him. She had not trusted him with the safe combination until now.

"Do you change this combination often, like you do the doors?" he asked.

"I'll let you know if I do," replied Claire, without really answering his question.

She looked at her watch. The time was pushing on. She was due to meet Dorothy in half an hour. More decisions. At least she would not have to make this one on her own.

"Kevin, I've got to go now. I won't be back before you go home. I'm leaving everything in your hands. Understood?"

He understood all right. Understood that she was placing huge trust in him. He would never let her down. He smiled at her. "Don't worry, Mrs Hearn. I'll take care of everything. And I'll guard our lab with my life."

He walked off into the animal room and Claire thought she detected a slight swagger. She smiled, wondering when R&D had become "our lab".

She read Ewan's text again and replied. *Need more time to think. Contact you soon.* As she pressed *Send*, for a moment, for an unguarded instant, she imagined his face as he read her text, a slight smile playing around his mouth.

Shaking her head to clear it, she quickly gathered her things together. Opening her briefcase, she carefully put in Ewan's plan and her manila folder. They would no longer be safe in the lab.

Just to be sure, she called to security at the gate and left instructions that any deliveries for R&D were to be taken at Reception and not be allowed near the lab. Her briefcase containing the Serum 6 formula lay on the passenger seat as she drove. It would always be where she could see it from now on. Even so, she knew in her heart that the time had come when RTTI or their lackeys LabAn were about to breach her defences. They must be desperate by now. And dangerous.

*   *   *

Looking out from the window of Frank Dawson's

office, Yvette saw Claire Dawson's blue BMW drive past. She instructed Trevor Langley to ring R&D. A few well-phrased questions later, Kevin Trill had told her what Yvette needed to know. Dr Hearn would not be in the lab that afternoon. Immediately she dismissed Trevor and then rang her special contact. It was short notice but it was a simple enough plan to organise. Especially since these people had all the equipment needed in stock. Most especially since they were being paid so well. A small price for such a huge reward.

*   *   *

Dorothy arrived at the meeting place just ahead of Claire. They embraced. It was a quick, warm hug, not without embarrassment. Physical affection did not come easy to them but it seemed appropriate to their changed relationship.

"Ready?" Dorothy asked.

Claire nodded and they walked together towards Jeremiah Audley's office. The old man was waiting for them in the reception area. Ever the gentleman, he led them into his office and sat them down.

"Now, ladies. There is something you would like discuss. About Frank's will, is it?"

"Partly," Dorothy answered. "It's about my will too."

"You want to change it?"

"No. I want to enforce it."

Jeremiah looked over his glasses at Dorothy as if not

quite sure how to deal with her. Both she and her daughter were grinning. If he did not know better he would say they were two very silly women. "The prerequisite for that is that you should die first, Dorothy, as you well know. So tell me what is really on your mind?"

Dorothy became very serious. "According to the terms of Frank's will, I am now MD of Dashern."

"That's true. And you have confirmed Trevor Langley as Acting Manager as per Frank's wishes."

"Well, as MD my decision is now to close the factory."

Jeremiah's jaw dropped open and his glasses slipped further down his nose. He made a little sound, which could have been either surprise or shock.

Dorothy ignored his reaction. "Claire is in agreement with my decision, and as MD I have the casting vote. I need to know our situation with regard to RTTI. How committed are we to them?"

Pushing his glasses back up on his nose and taking a deep breath, Jeremiah seemed to take control of himself again.

"Whoa there! Wait! Wait now! This is a huge decision. You couldn't possibly have thought it through. You're still in shock. Understandably so. This is no time to be making such life-changing decisions."

Dorothy leaned forward towards the solicitor and fixed him with the full power of her dark gaze. "Don't you see, Jeremiah, this is exactly the right time for me to make decisions? I'm on my own now. My daughter is perfectly independent and capable of running her own life as she sees fit. I want to emigrate, to turn my face to the sun, to potter around with plants, to go to art classes. I want to breathe. I want to live the time I have left. How could I do that with the shadow of Dashern and RTTI hanging over me?"

Jeremiah stared at her, mesmerised by the unexpected passion in her voice. He had never before seen Dorothy Gore-Croft-Dawson so animated. Observing and supporting had seemed to be her natural role. It was the role she had been born into and had seemed to fulfil so dutifully. She must be distracted by grief. There was no other explanation. He shook his head slowly.

"I can't understand your attitude. Frank has it all set up for you. This Englishman, Langley, will handle the day-to-day running of the plant. RTTI will have their technical staff to oversee the changeover to herbal medicines. You can go to the sun to paint your pictures and grow your flowers. Three, maybe four, meetings in the year is all you will be obliged to attend. Why would you want to throw that away without even considering other options?"

"What options?"

"As you pointed out, you are MD with the casting vote. You could hand over to Claire if you really feel you cannot cope with it. Keep it in the family."

"Not an option," Claire said quickly. "I agree with Mum. Do you realise that our detergent business is on its knees? We have recently lost our biggest contract and our remaining orders are under threat. It is no longer a viable business."

"Yes. Frank told me. Isn't that where RTTI come in? They will provide the expertise and investment necessary to divert manufacture to these herbal cures, or whatever it is they do."

Claire and Dorothy exchanged glances and smiled.

"Maybe that is the point," Dorothy said quietly. "Whatever it is they do. So, Jeremiah, what is your answer? Where do we stand with RTTI? Had Frank signed any binding agreements?"

He sat back in his chair and sighed. It seemed like these women were not going to listen to anything he had to say. The best he could do now was to delay them, give them time to reflect.

"I would have to check that out with my son. The amalgamation is Oliver's brief. He is dealing with the RTTI law team."

"So ask him."

"He's not here today. In fact, he's in the High Court in Dublin all this week. He won't be back until Monday. He's staying over in the city for the weekend."

Dorothy frowned. The old man was stalling. Probably waiting for her to come to her senses. She straightened her shoulders and lifted her chin. She had already arrived at the most sensible decision of her life and she was not going to be sidelined. Fiddlesticks to this old coot!

"This is the situation, Jeremiah," said Dorothy. "I will be seeing our accountant shortly. I know Dashern profit margins have dropped significantly but the company is still just about breaking even. I want to liquidate assets and pay staff what redundancy I can. When I know where we stand financially, I am going to give them one month's notice. And then Dashern will be no more."

"For God's sake, Dorothy! At least consider selling as a going concern. RTTI would probably be quite amenable to that arrangement. They should be glad to buy you out. That would give you some capital to support yourself and keep Frank's workforce in employment."

Dorothy stood up and slipped her handbag onto her arm. She looked regal standing there, so tall, so well groomed. So stubborn.

"I will have more than enough money when Grange House is sold. And by the way, Clive Rigney will not be renewing the lease on the Dashern factory site. As you know it runs out at the end of this month."

Jeremiah stared at the woman he had thought he had known so well. The Commander's daughter. He had not known her at all, had never seen the stubbornness, the headstrong, self-destructive streak. It had taken a strong man like Frank Dawson to keep her in line and now she was asserting herself in the most unsuitable way.

"Why ever did you agree to that, Dorothy? Wasn't renewing the lease for Dashern part of the contract of sale?"

Dorothy gave the old solicitor a smile which could

have been described as coquettish had it not been on her aristocratic features. "Clive and I reached an understanding," she said, as if that enigmatic reply explained everything.

Jeremiah tried another tack. "What about Claire? The research facility is on the Dashern plant."

"You know ClairCo is independent. She can rent or buy any lab facilities anywhere she needs."

"Seems like you two have everything sorted for yourselves."

Claire stood beside her mother. There was very little physical resemblance. Claire was petite, Dorothy statuesque. But the eyes were the same. Dark and alert and challenging. Two headstrong women.

Jeremiah threw up his hands in defeat. "I'll talk to my son on Monday. See how far the amalgamation has progressed. I also handed your patent application over to him, Claire. He has more expertise in that area than I do. I'll see how that is shaping up too. And I would ask you both to please, please, think about this. For Frank's sake."

He saw them to the door. Then he went back to the office and took out the file on the RTTI/Dashern amalgamation.

*   *   *

Yvette looked at Brendan and her nose twitched. "Look at you, Bren. It's the middle of the afternnon and you are drunk. How could you let yourself get into this condition?"

Brendan looked down at his shaking hands and wondered the same thing himself.

"Get yourself cleaned up or dried out or something. You can't go on like this."

He looked up from his hands and saw the disgust in her face. It was such a short length of time ago since she had been winding herself around him, licking and kissing his body. Now she did not even show him pity.

Yvette stood up from behind Frank Dawson's desk and walked to the big window overlooking the plant. She enjoyed the symmetry of the buildings: factory, warehouse and loading bay – and way off in the distance, at the perimeter of the site, Claire Hearn's Research and Development Lab. She was about to turn back when she noticed a van pulling into the parking lot. It was a white van with Calbitron painted in blue letters on the side. Yvette smiled. At last! Eureka!

A young man got out of the van and headed for the reception area. He was dressed in smart trousers and a jacket with Calbitron printed discreetly on the sleeve. Everything about this operation would be discreet, she thought, as a shiver of excitement ran through her. She had to take a deep breath before she turned to face Brendan again.

"You had better go home. I don't want the staff to see you in this condition."

"I'm not drunk! I only had a few glasses of wine. I came to tell you that I did as you asked. I had lunch with Ria Corkery on Monday. She talks a lot. I have plenty of information for you."

"Go home. I don't need your information. It's too little too late. You are not needed here. Trevor Langley is far better at this job than you ever were. Go away."

He continued to sit there, a stubbled puddle of self-pity. He wanted to ask her why she was being such a bitch. So cruel. What had he done? What had he not done? He should tell her everything Ria had poured out to him over lunch. At least what he could remember. He should. But fuck her. Fuck RTTI. Fuck them all! He stood up and walked out of the office.

Yvette waited until he had closed the door behind him. Then she picked up her mobile and pressed a speed dial number.

"Our expert is on site. On his way over to R&D as we speak."

She pressed the *End Call* button, sat back in her chair and closed her eyes. The only variable now was Kevin Trill. In the unlikely event that he would refuse the engineer access to R&D, Yvette was confident she could manage to change his mind. It would be better though if she did not have to show her hand.

RTTI were about to make the biggest discovery in their history. They were about to formulate the cure for cancer. Millions and billions of patients. Millions and billions of dollars. Twenty years manufacturing under patent, twenty long profitable years before other companies could market their generic take on RTTI's development of Claire Hearn's research.

Twenty years where Ms Yvette Previn could build a very nice retirement scheme for when she got tired of boardroom games. She stood and stretched her long, voluptuous body.

*   *   *

Kevin stood back and admired his afternoon's work. The fridge was packed with fresh media, all prepared by him. Now if only Claire Hearn would tell him something about the preparation of Serum 6, he would know as much as her. Well, nearly as much anyway. Little chance of that, he thought as he closed the fridge door. She guarded Serum 6 and everything to do with it as if her life depended on it. It seemed like Serum 6 *was* her life. He wondered again if the pages of numbers in the old folder he had seen her study this morning held the formula for the serum. Claire had seemed very jittery and uncomfortable when he had looked over her shoulder at the pages. The folder wasn't in the safe now. He had checked. She must have taken it with her. He shrugged. Sometimes he thought Ria was right. Claire Hearn was a bit loopy. He was just on his way to the animal room when the phone rang. It was a call from Reception.

"There's a man from an engineering company here. He says he has to service equipment in R&D. Will I send him over?"

"What is the name of the company?"

There was a pause as the girl made enquiries.

"Calbitron."

Kevin hesitated. Claire must have forgotten to tell

him. She was always forgetting to tell him things. What was he supposed to do now? He remembered her saying the calibration company were allowed access, provided they were supervised. Supervised by her? Or by him?

He considered ringing Claire. She had not said where she was going but he had her mobile number anyway. He flicked through the phonebook on his mobile until Dr Hearn came up on his screen.

The girl from Reception spoke up sharply.

"Kevin? Are you there? I'm running out of patience. So is the Calbitron man. Will I send him over to you or what?"

"Yes, do. I'll let him in."

He switched off his phone and put it in his pocket. Her cell number was to be used in emergencies only, she had said. What would she think if he had rung her about a visiting engineer? One of the few people authorised to actually set foot in R&D? When he himself was perfectly capable of supervising the visit? With all the trust she was showing in him, he would expect him to handle something as routine as a visit from Calbitron.

He heard the van approaching the building and went to open the entrance door. A man got out of the van carrying a case of tools.

Kevin looked at him in surprise. "You're not Victor."

The man laughed. "Full marks. I'm Tom. Vic's on holiday. Mrs Hearn wants calibrations done. Something to do with submitting results."

Kevin was relieved. Of course! It was crucial that the equipment be validated if results were to be verified. Everything would have to stand up to scrutiny. Glad that he had made the right decision in allowing the engineer access, Kevin went about his work as the man who called himself Tom placed electronics bugs and miniature spy cameras all over the R&D lab.

* * *

Trish gritted her teeth and smiled at her customer. She wanted so badly to shout and stamp her foot. Ria was driving her crazy. For the last week, she had been mooning over a magazine, staring at her own pictures. And it was all Paul's fault.

When the door opened and another potential client came in, Trish asked Ria to put down the magazine. Instead Ria treated the customer to a page by page review of her photo spread. By closing time, Trish was ready to explode. She put up the closed sign, locked the door from the inside and wearily leaned her back against it.

"You look totally wrecked," Ria announced. "Maybe you should take some time off."

"One of us will have to. We just cannot continue on like this."

"What are you talking about? Chill out, Trish. Why are you so uptight?"

Trish gestured to Ria to follow her. They went into the little back room that served as office and canteen.

Trish sat at her desk and wondered how she was going to get through to the girl sitting opposite her. It was an awkward situation. She had allowed the line between work and friendship to get blurred. She and Paul socialised with Ria and Kevin. But friendship or no friendship, she would have to reprimand Ria now.

"Are you jealous of me?" Ria asked.

Trish laughed at the question. "Why should I be?"

"Well, Paul has spent a lot of time on my portfolio. But no need for you to worry. We have a purely professional relationship. I scratch his back, he scratches mine."

"What do you mean? What's all this scratching about?"

Ria dropped her head and allowed her hair to fall in a blonde sheet across her face.

"Ria! Have you some kind of arrangement with Paul? Just why has he spent so much time and energy in photographing you and promoting you? I know he's called in a lot of favours to get you published. What's going on?"

Ria tossed her hair back. Her pretty face was open and honest without a trace of guile.

"Paul is helping me because he knows I really, really want to be a model. And because he is a nice, kind man. I'm surprised you asked. Don't you know that? Besides, he prefers the more mature woman."

Trish burst out laughing. "Are you calling me old?"

Ria practically jumped out of her chair in an effort to persuade Trish that she had meant no insult.

Trish waved her apologies aside. "Look, Ria, maturity is the issue here. While you are still working for me I want you to concentrate on your job. Which is selling travel, in case you have forgotten. I can't have you ignoring customers or regaling them with your photos when what they really want is to book flights. If you find that too difficult, I'm afraid we'll have to come to a decision."

The huge blue eyes filled instantly with tears. "Are you firing me?"

"Of course not. I'm simply asking you to do your job. Keep your modelling ambitions outside Travelbug."

Ria jumped up and threw her arms around Trish. "I will. I will. I'll be the best. And you'll be the first to know when I get my modelling contract. Promise. I must dash now. I'm meeting Kevin later and I must pluck my eyebrows. Did you notice how out of shape they are?"

Then Ria was gone, leaving a bemused employer in her wake. Trish sat back and sighed. She hadn't got through to the girl about her work rate and she still didn't know why Paul was going out of his way to promote her modelling career.

One thing was sure. Neither Paul nor Ria was telling the truth.

Chapter Twenty-one

Claire had not slept well last night so she should have been exhausted. Instead she felt energy surging through her. She had come into the lab before seven, leaving Brendan on the couch again, sleeping off yet another binge. He seemed to have gone into retirement since Trevor Langley had arrived on site. In fact, since Frank had died. She pushed the worry of Brendan's self-destructive behaviour to the back of her mind. To the part that belonged to broken relationships, partings and feelings of loss she did not want to explore.

When the last of the reports in her office were checked she went into the animal room to monitor the temperature charts. Clarence scurried to the front of his cage when he saw her. He was gleaming with health and vitality. He put his head to one side and chirped and squeaked. She went to the feed area and got some lettuce for him. He nibbled happily on it.

"You're getting spoiled, Clarence," she told him.

He chirped again as if answering and Claire felt guilty. She would have to take another biopsy from the tumour site, or rather the site where the tumour had been, in order to examine the cells. There were no indications of any return of the cancer. She knew there would be none but her testing protocol demanded confirmation. He would not be alone. She had a whole batch of animals that were equally as healthy and as cured as Clarence. It was just that he was the first and the most special.

"It won't hurt much," she promised him as she fed him another leaf of lettuce.

She walked over to her current batch of treatment animals. The ones she had had flown in from England. Not even Kevin knew where she had sourced this batch. He probably assumed they had come from LabAn.

Claire checked the charts. Everything was as she had hoped. Animals on Serum 6 were quickly recovering from their disease, gaining weight and strength on a daily basis. Blood counts and cell cultures were confirming their continued progress towards complete cure of their cancers. She read the charts on the untreated animals. Over half of this group had already died.

She heard Kevin come in and went out to the lab to see him.

"Morning, Mrs Hearn. Looks like you've been here a while."

"I have indeed and I've been going through reports and charts."

Kevin took off his jacket and slipped on his lab coat. He looked very anxious.

"Is there something wrong? Have I made a mistake?"

"Not at all, Kevin. Just the opposite. Let's sit down. I want to have a chat with you."

Her words did not seem to calm him. He sat nervously on the edge of his chair beside her desk.

"I want to thank you, Kevin. I know things have been topsy-turvy since my father died. You kept the trials going smoothly while I was – was otherwise occupied. Thank you."

He slumped down in his chair, visibly relieved. "Not at all. Just doing my job."

"We both know you did more than that. You have spent a lot of extra time here, writing up and doing the work I hadn't time to cover. And you did it very well. There will be a bonus in your next pay packet."

Kevin blushed. "Thank you, Mrs Hearn. There's no need to do that."

Claire looked at him. He seemed so young and innocent. So anxious to please. Maybe that was his vulnerability. He wanted to please everybody.

"I was worried that I had made the wrong decision yesterday," he suddenly blurted out.

Puzzled, Claire asked him what he meant.

"Calbitron. I wasn't sure whether to ring you or not when they called. Then I decided not to disturb you.

You said it was OK to let them in once they were supervised. So I told Tom to go ahead."

"Tom?"

"Yeah. Vic is on holidays."

A cold chill rippled down Claire's spine. It was an instinctive reaction. As if her subconscious knew something horrific that her conscious mind had not yet absorbed.

She took a deep breath and tried to speak calmly. "Exactly what did this Tom do?"

"A complete service," Kevin said airily. "He calibrated everything, even the instruments that Vic had done recently. He was very thorough."

"Were you with him all the time?"

"Most of the time. I had to do the feeds and answer the phone."

"Ria called?"

Kevin began to realise that Claire's earlier good humour had evaporated. He was in trouble now. How many times had he warned Ria not to ring him at work? She had been waffling on about her photoshoot. Shit!

"Yes, Ria rang. So did that new man in the plant, Trevor Langley. He rang twice looking for you. He said something about clearing out your father's desk."

"So you weren't watching Tom all the time?"

Kevin dropped his head and looked down at his shoes. He was blushing in embarrassment. He looked about six.

Claire was beginning to shake. Moving her foot, she pushed it against her briefcase underneath her desk.

She needed the reassurance of knowing that it was there where she had put it this morning. She did not know what to do now, what to say. She needed a breathing space to allow her logic catch up with her fears.

"Excuse me a moment," she said to the now miserable-looking Kevin and made her way into the bathroom.

She closed the door and leaned against it, then tensed as she realised the bathroom might no longer be a sanctuary. She needed to ask Kevin if Tom had used the bathroom but hesitated as she realised how peculiar that would sound. Anyone who heard her ask that question would think it very odd. Unless of course she was studying the toilet habits of calibration engineers. Or fraudulent calibration engineers.

She stepped forward and pretended to adjust her hair in the mirror over the sink. Her reflection paled as progressively more terrifying thoughts began to filter through. Thoughts of being spied on and listened to. This could be the day she had dreaded. The day the security and safety of her lab had been invaded. Violated. She must think logically. Check.

Going back to the lab, she did a tour of the instruments. Each one bore the obligatory tag required when a calibration had been carried out. They appeared to be genuine Calbitron tags and were initialled TF. Tom French? Tom Fuller? Fouhy? What did it matter? It would not be his real name anyway. As that thought settled in her mind, Claire flopped down onto her chair.

She could not think, could not work anything out with Kevin sitting in front of her looking as if he was ready to cry.

"Should I not have allowed him in, Mrs Hearn?"

Claire attempted a smile. She had no proof of her suspicions. Yet. Just the instinct that they were best kept to herself until she had thought everything through. That she should assume the worst and act accordingly.

"Of course you should have, Kevin. Calbitron are authorised. It's just that I prefer anyone, whether Vic or this new man Tom, to be supervised all the time they are in R&D. You'll remember that in future?"

"Yes, I will. And I'm sorry I didn't this time. It won't happen again."

"Fine. There's stocktaking to be done. Would you start that now, please?"

When Kevin had scuttled off to the storeroom, Claire pulled an A4 pad towards her and picked up a pen. She needed to appear to be working in case ... In case what? Did she really believe somebody could be watching? Yes, she did.

Tom's search yesterday would have disappointed him if he was looking for Serum 6. There had been no serum made up that could have been stolen and the formula had been safely with her in her briefcase. But they, most likely RTTI, would not have gone to all the trouble of organising this visit just to have a rummage around. Tom would have used his available time a lot more constructively. The worry was not what he could have taken. It was what he could have left behind him,

Claire reached her hand towards the phone. One call to Calbitron could answer all her questions. Her hand stopped halfway to the phone. If somebody had gone to these lengths, then they would have anticipated her calling Calbitron. Maybe her phone here was bugged; maybe her call would be diverted. Or perhaps somebody in Calbitron was waiting for her call now, a nice RTTI bribe in their pocket. She did not know how these things worked but she did know that she would be told Tom F was a bona fide Calbitron employee. Of course she could go home and ring from there. She could get an electronic company to sweep her lab for spyware.

But maybe she was overreacting. Worse still, being totally paranoid.

Unless … Claire's fledgling thought began to take shape, to fill out, to grow in plausibility. She settled more comfortably in her chair and began to write.

* * *

Washed, smartly dressed, sober for the first time since he had stormed out of the rabbit warren that Ewan Peters grandly called his campaign headquarters, Brendan decided to go to work this morning. His resolve lasted until he reached the approach road to Dashern. He jammed on the brakes and pulled into the side, looking at the plumes of steam from the factory curling into the morning sky. He imagined Frank's office, Yvette usurping his place, Trevor Langley hovering around her. Claire, isolated in her little fortress at the rear of the plant. Pitying glances from the staff as they sneered behind his back. What were they saying? Probably revelling in his humiliation. Fuck them! He threw the car into gear and did a U-turn without checking for oncoming traffic. He drove away at speed, not knowing where he was going, not caring as long as he was putting distance between himself and Dashern.

Every telegraph pole on every by-road in the country was festooned with election posters. It seemed to Brendan that Ewan Peters was following him. Each corner he turned he was faced with the smiling image of the EnVirowatch candidate. The smug, craw-thumping, wife-stealing, would-be public representative and his journo friend. The same hack who had written that smarmy article about Frank in *Newstrack*. Brendan's knuckles itched again as the image of his father-in-law's injured face flashed before him. He swerved and almost hit the ditch. His hands shook and he gripped the steering wheel to steady them. They still shook.

He skidded to a halt. Looking around him, he did not recognise any landmarks. Just fields and more fields. He had headed off in a westerly direction. He remembered passing the airport. After that it had been just election posters and scenery. Sweat dripped off his forehead as the shaking gripped his entire body. His stomach muscles cramped. He looked in the mirror and a sick man looked back at him. He needed Yvette. If only she was here now to put her arms around him, to hold him, to whisper in his ear that everything was going to be all right. If, if, if. Fuck her too. She was playing with him. Using him. And he had been her willing victim. But no more.

He wiped the sweat off his forehead, revved up the engine and drove to the next crossroads. Ewan Peters smiled down at him from a hoarding. Brendan knew where he was now. Familiar territory. The left fork would take him on the road to Dashern. The right fork would lead him home. Back to where he had come from, back to where it had all began. Maybe his subconscious had been leading him in this direction. Back to the place he had consciously left a whole lifetime ago.

The nearer he got to his home place, the more Brendan got sucked into a time warp. Nothing had changed. Not even the trees seemed to have grown. He drove past the collection of houses, a church, a pub and a few shops laughingly called the village and kept going until he came to a row of artisan cottages by the river.

He parked and got out of the car. The river was low, the brackish water moving sluggishly over the stony riverbed. Brendan stood and looked at the cottages. Six terraced two-bedroom little boxes. Small yards, small front gardens. Small lives. He shivered as his eyes were drawn to number four. He had sold it after his parent's deaths and had vowed he would never come back here again. Neither the passage of time nor the addition of a pretentious conservatory had changed the dreariness of the fourth cottage in the row. His home. The little space where he had grown from protected child to dissatisfied youth to ambitious man. The place where his will to succeed had been nurtured by his mother and feared by his father. "The lad has ideas above his station," his father used to say when he thought Brendan was not listening. His mother had never answered. She had always had faith in her only child.

Brendan turned his back to the cottages and walked towards the little stone bridge. That had been his secret place, his escape from the cocoon of depression that had been his home. He leaned over the parapet and allowed the soft sounds of trickling water to soothe his chaotic thoughts. His breathing slowed; the shaking stopped. He stared into the slowly moving stream and saw again the plans and schemes he had imagined in his youth. Graduating from college had been a dream first sketched on the listless waters of this river. Escaping poverty, marrying a woman of breeding and class, holding a management position in a company. He had done it all. He had taken his dreams and made them reality. And then he had fucked up. It was Claire's fault. And Frank's. And Yvette's. They were all to blame.

Brendan felt his temper rise again. Stooping, he picked up a stone and fired it into the water. It landed with a shallow splash. Something about the splashy sound, the physical release in firing the stone, sparked hope in him. He stooped and gathered a heap of pebbles and christened them. One by one he threw

411

stones named after his father-in-law, his wife and his girlfriend over the bridge and into the cold water. He knew now that he could do it. He could salvage some self-respect from this nightmare. When his little stack of pebbles lay on the riverbed he looked into the water again and this time he read his new life-plan, his new dreams and schemes. He got into his car and headed back past the cottages, the village and the unchanging trees. It was time for him to get on with his new life.

*   *   *

The timing of the LabAn delivery could not have been better. Claire was ready for the new batch of animals now.

"Kevin, Reception just rang. LabAn have delivered the new batch of guineas. Would you take my car over to Admin and collect them?"

"OK, Mrs Hearn."

"Everything ready for them?"

"Yes, Mrs Hearn," Kevin said earnestly, taking the car keys she offered him with the same reverence as if she had granted him a knighthood.

When he came back, she helped him unload and settle the animals into their cages. Going through the release certificates, she noticed they were all signed by Ronan Hennessey. Even the controls. He must not yet have replaced Anne Moroney. When all necessary weighing, measuring and monitoring of the animals was done, Claire asked Kevin to follow her into the office.

When they were both seated she looked at him and had a moment's hesitation. He was so young, so trusting, so insecure. Knowing that there was no room for scruples, she forced herself to smile at him.

"You've done so well, I think it's time you ran a trial from beginning to end. Including making up the serum. I want you to take the new batch of animals through the entire process on your own."

He sat up straight. A smile lit up his face and made him look even younger. "Thank you. I appreciate this. I'll do a good job. I promise."

"Of course you will. I wouldn't even think of allowing you to do it if I didn't know that. I'm going to teach you about the serum, about its preparation and application. In fact, I'll be telling you everything I've discovered about this innovative cancer treatment. You have seen for yourself that it cures animal cancers. I am telling you now that it will be as effective against human forms of the disease. But the onus is on us to prove that."

"I know it's going to cure people. I just know it!"

Claire smiled at him. "So do I. But we have tons of paperwork and bureaucracy to plough through before we'll be allowed to run clinical trials on Serum 6 for human cancers. In the meantime we keep working on our animal trials and building up our data. Which is where you come in, Kevin. I will be relying on you to keep the lab in order while I get involved with bringing the human trials forward."

"You can depend on me, Mrs Hearn. You will have no need to worry about the lab."

"Great. Now, something to bring to your attention. I'm sure there's no need to mention it but I am obliged to. You must never, ever, under any circumstances, disclose the information I am going to give you about Serum 6. There are already people who suspect that we have made a very significant advance in cancer treatment. I don't trust them. I want everybody to benefit from Serum 6 so I want to control its progress. I have to ask you, Kevin, for your solemn word that you will never discuss our work with anybody other than me."

Kevin raised his right hand and placed it over his heart. "I swear. On my honour, I will never say one word about Serum 6 outside this lab."

Claire sat back and looked at the young man with his hand on his heart. He was sincere. She knew he was. He meant what he was saying. For now. But he was a vulnerable spot in her defence. If she recognised this, so would the people watching R&D. His girlfriend was a liability. Just how much had he told Ria?

She smiled at him now. "The other thing is that your increased responsibilities will be reflected in your pay. I am raising your salary by twenty per cent."

"Thank you. Thank you very much!"

There was no doubting his sincerity now. He was beaming. Claire stood up and walked over to the bench.

"Right. Better get started on the work. We've got to prepare fresh Serum 6 for your batch. As you may have noticed I do not have a written method. But I realise it's a complex procedure to learn."

She opened an A4 pad on the desk, removed one of the pages and handed it to Kevin. It was covered in her neat handwriting. The method for the preparation of Serum 6. He looked at it in awe. Fifteen steps. Fifteen building blocks to produce the serum that could cure cancer. Serum 6 in fifteen steps. The page shook in Kevin's hand as he absorbed the privilege of the information he held, the enormity of the trust Claire Hearn had placed in him.

Claire's hand shook as she prayed that she had made the right decision. She led Kevin into the lab.

"This is how you prepare Serum 6. Here we go."

Then she ploughed ahead, going slowly so as not to confuse him with too much information too soon.

*   *   *

Ria was agitated. She wasn't used to being kept waiting. She looked around the usual crowd in Mellow Drama and wondered how many of them had seen her photo in the magazine. The women would have anyway. Every girl read that mag. They were probably just being bitchy in ignoring her.

Kevin seemed flustered when he came in the door. She waved at him and he came rushing over to her.

"Sorry I'm late. I was delayed at work. I had to set up some experiments."

"Oh! Very impressive! Does Claire Hearn do any

work these days or is she leaving it all to you?"

Kevin looked at her and thought how beautiful she was. He smiled. "We'll get drinks first and then I have something to tell you. Something very good."

Ria drummed her fingers on the table impatiently as she waited for Kevin to come back with the drinks. She had something to tell him too but it was unlikely he would think it was good news. She felt nervous. How was she going to tell him that she no longer wanted to go out with him? That their relationship was going nowhere. At least nowhere she wanted to go. Her ambitions reached far beyond living in three-bedroom semi-detached bliss as Mrs Kevin Trill. She shivered at the thought.

Drink splashed out of the glasses onto the table as he plonked them down. Ria mopped up the mess with a serviette.

"Slow down, Kevin. Your news must be very exciting. You'd better tell me before you wreck the place."

Kevin leaned towards Ria. "I got a pay rise today."

"Brilliant! Well done. Why? Have you been promoted or something?"

He gave a furtive glance around before continuing. "Sort of. I have a lot more responsibility now. And there's more. I got a bonus too."

"Really? Is she trying to bribe you or something?"

Kevin laughed and took a sip from his pint. "Don't go off on one of your flights of fancy, Ria. I'm not being bribed. Just paid in line with my new status. It reflects the importance of my work."

Ria thought about it. About all the implications of what Kevin had just told her. He might not be the only one who had got a bonus. A very hefty one. She caught his hand. "I'm so proud, Kevin. You're so clever. I could never understand any of the complicated things you do."

"It's complicated all right. But Dr Hearn is a good teacher. I know almost as much as she does now."

Ria moved around the table to sit right beside Kevin. She snuggled up to him and put her head on his shoulder.

"I can't wait," she whispered.

He thought she was talking about their three-bedroom semi-detached.

*   *   *

Claire hid her briefcase at the back of a kitchen cupboard and then put on the kettle. She must move her formula and lab notes into something less obvious than the briefcase – her large leather shoulderbag perhaps.

She was too exhausted after the traumatic day to cook and anyway her knotted stomach would have rejected food. There was no sign of Brendan. Maybe he was dining with Yvette Previn. Maybe not. His interest these days was more in drinking than eating.

The quiet of the kitchen, broken only by the sound of the kettle beginning to boil, compounded her confusion and loneliness. Her fear. Going over to the radio she switched on to Radio One. Ewan's voice filled the kitchen, soothing the terrified space in her soul. He was talking about the environment, his deep and gentle voice washing over her. She grabbed her mobile and texted him, asking him to ring her at home and giving him the number. Begging him to ring her. *Please! Please!*

As soon as the message was sent, Claire regretted it. She sat and listened to the rest of the interview and blushed in shame and embarrassment. What would he think? The woman whose husband had beaten him up, pleading with him to contact her? Angry with herself now, she went and had a shower. She almost missed his call.

"This is my second time ringing," he said. "I was just about to give up. Are you alright?"

Alright? God! Fine! Great! My father's dead, my husband's a drunk, my work is under threat and I'm trembling at the sound of a man I barely know. This is alright? Clare stilled the voice in her head and took a deep breath.

"Yes, thank you. I'm fine. I was just wondering when we could meet?"

"The where is more of a problem, isn't it? I don't want to run into your husband again."

Claire squirmed in embarrassment. God damn Brendan and his filthy mind and temper. She tried to continue on as if he hadn't mentioned the mortifying incident.

"It should be someplace private," she suggested. "It

sounds very dramatic but there may be people watching. Anyway your face is too well known by now."

"I can't complain about publicity. I courted it. Actually I could do with a walk and a breath of fresh air. How about we meet near the Kallen woods? I could be there in an hour's time. Would that suit you?"

That suited Claire very well. It would give her time to get dressed. Casual but smart. Some make-up. Perfume. She was smiling as she put the phone down.

*   *   *

The drive back to Dashern went too quickly for Brendan. There were so many things to organise in his head. His new life-plan buoyed him up until he arrived at the plant. The Administration Building was in darkness. He had not realised it was so late. He must have spent a long time staring into the muddy waters of his past. He rang Yvette's number. Her phone was switched off. The shaking began again. Taking a deep breath, he started the car and switched on the radio. The noise might stop him thinking. Ewan Peters' voice filled the car. He was waffling on about clean air and education and health care.

"Fuck you!" Brendan muttered between clenched teeth as he switched off the radio. He drove home accompanied only by his own thoughts. He arrived there just in time to see Claire leaving. Then he turned around and followed her at a discreet distance.

*   *   *

Kallen woods loomed dark and mysterious silhouetted against the moonlit sky. It was cold. Claire hugged her brown leather shoulderbag to her side, feeling the comforting weight of her research notes inside it, as she and Ewan stood wondering which direction to take. Uphill would lead them into the woods while downhill the roadway led towards the town. Claire felt awkward now. Guilty. Why had they decided to meet here? They had agreed on the need for privacy. Secrecy. But was walking in the darkened woods, as she knew they were going to do, just an excuse for them to be alone? It was as if they were quite deliberately setting the scene for a seduction.

Ewan turned his face into the breeze and took a deep breath. "I'm so exhausted. This breeze should wake me up."

"Let's walk into the wind then," Claire said, glad that she had found yet another justification for heading towards the woods.

She shivered. It was eerie here at this hour of night. Overhead, the treetops swayed and creaked in the wind. Down where they walked, it was quiet and dark and sheltered. Their path was carpeted with pine needles and the compacted decay of past autumns. When Ewan stood on a twig, the snapping noise it made echoed like a revolver shot. Claire grabbed his arm in fright. It seemed natural after that to walk arm in arm as they climbed the path to the summit of the hillside woods.

It was wild and very beautiful at the top. They stood on the plateau, buffeted by the breeze, canopied by the starry evening sky. It was a timeless and very private place. Ewan pointed towards a flat rock. "Looks like a nice seat there. Will we sit while we talk?"

He took off his jacket and spread it on the rock. Claire sat beside him. She moved a little towards the edge. She was too conscious of his warmth, of his strong firm muscles, of his nearness. She had said a private place but could he not have thought of somewhere less remote? Less romantic?

Ewan kept his distance too. He didn't want to brush against her soft body. They had come here to talk about Claire's work and he tried to focus on it now.

"Well, Claire. Have you read my suggestions about how to handle your research? Have you come to any conclusion?" He reached over and, against his better judgement, squeezed her hand. It felt small and warm in his. He held onto it and she did not object.

"I do see potential in your plan," she said. "You advise me to hand over my formula to the state-sponsored R&D company. I know that makes sense. They have the resources to handle patents and clinical trials."

"But?"

"I don't want Serum 6 to become a political football. Manufacture and distribution would still be up for grabs. A prize for the strongest pharmaceutical bidder."

"Can't you see that if the state held the patent, royalties would revert to the government? The money could then be used to subsidise the retail price. That's what you want, isn't it? To make Serum 6 readily affordable to everyone?"

Claire closed her eyes and lifted her face to the wind. What exactly did she want? To be a crusading socialist, the Mother Teresa of Research and Development? To rid the world of cancer by distributing Serum 6 free to all cancer patients? And why not? Because, because, because …!

She turned to face Ewan and, in the moonlight, looked at his solemn, weary face with the blue and yellow stain under his eyes courtesy of Brendan. She really needed him to understand, to know how much Serum 6 meant to her.

"I want to tell you about the Clarence Factor."

He nodded and waited for her to continue. She lowered her eyelids, as if reconsidering confiding in him. The wind swirled and filled the silence with an eerie keening.

"The Clarence Factor?" he prompted.

"Clarence is a guinea pig. One of my trial animals. When I first came into contact with him, he was terminally ill with cancer. And I cured him of his cancer. He was my first true cure. My first real success with Serum 6."

"And you knew then you had hit the jackpot."

Claire pushed closer to him and stared up into his face. "That's not what this is about, Ewan. I always

422

knew I was on the right track with my apoptosis theory. I knew I would get there at some stage. But that is all it meant to me. Just an academic theory. An exercise in pushing the limits of knowledge, in exploring possibilities. Until Clarence. He is not a theory. Not a series of formulae. He is a living, breathing creature and his cancer was real, his pain was real. Seeing him fighting his malignancy, recovering, gaining strength, was a miracle. I had seen Serum 6 as a method of manipulating cancer cells. Clarence taught me what it really means."

"I suppose he told you he is grateful."

Her sharp intake of breath let him know he had hurt her feelings. More than that, he had angered her. Her eyes were blazing in the darkness.

"Laugh if you want to but yes, in his own way, he did."

"So what are you telling me? That you want recognition for Serum 6, that you want cancer patients to be grateful to you? That you need the world to acknowledge you?"

How could she have been so wrong about this man? She had thought he was sensitive and caring. She had bared her soul to him and he had sneered at her. Claire felt tears well hot and salty in her eyes. She stood and began to walk away.

He reached her in two strides and, catching her by the shoulders, turned her to face him. "I'm sorry, Claire. Please don't walk away. I want to hear what you have to say."

She looked up at him and did not know what to

believe. His eyes were pools of darkness. She could not read them.

"I wanted you to understand, Ewan. I thought you would listen."

"I am listening. I just don't understand where you're coming from."

"Serum 6 is the gift of life. That's what the Clarence Factor is. The difference between theory and fact, the difference between a scientific discovery and a life-giving medicine."

Ewan slowly nodded his head. "I think I see what you mean. It must be very humbling to realise that your work can mean the difference between life and death."

"Exactly," Claire agreed. "And that is why it is so important to me that the manufacture of Serum 6 is not treated as a money-making project. I don't want it just to make profits for a pharmaceutical company. And I don't give a damn about recognition or kudos."

"I realise that. I'm sorry if I insulted you, Claire. And I am touched by your story about Clarence . . . but we have to be realistic."

"I am being realistic. It's you who have your head buried in the sand. Serum 6 is going to take massive investment to get it through human trials and licensing and manufacture. There's no other way to get it on the market except through the pharmaceuticals. They are set up to do this. And for all that investment, they deserve some profits. But everyone suffering from cancer is entitled to the drug. Regardless of ability to pay or nationality. It must, just *must* be made available worldwide. But the pharmaceuticals are corporations. Not charities."

She sighed. They were just going around in circles with this argument. This drug had the potential to be one of the most important medications since penicillin. And one of the biggest money-spinners ever. For RTTI or someone like them. She was just a researcher, an academic. It was presumptuous of her to think she could take on the might of the Western economy. The capitalist system that had allowed her to lead a privileged life.

"So what now, Claire? You don't want the state to handle development and you don't want a private pharmaceutical company. Can you do it yourself?"

"I don't even know if I can protect my research any more, never mind develop it."

"What do you mean? Do you think RTTI would actually steal your work?"

It would have been so cathartic to lean her face against Ewan's broad chest and spill out all her fears and suspicions, to tell him about the man named Tom who might or might not be a Calbitron employee, about the risk she had taken with Serum 6 today, about Brendan's drinking, about her loneliness. He would wrap his arms around her and comfort her. Just as he had done in the graveyard. Just like she had imagined in unguarded moments since. Just like she had been planning tonight ...

She took a step back from him, wary now of his closeness. She had lost so much. She did not need to lose her self-respect too. She made an attempt at laughing but the sound that came out was not very happy.

"I suppose I'm a bit paranoid. I see schemes and plots everywhere. Especially where my work is concerned."

"Well, could you develop it yourself? You haven't answered me."

"I have prepared Serum 6 in small batches in my lab. I have no idea how the process would transfer to bulk manufacture. I believe it will be a relatively low-tech, cost-effective process but I don't know. Not my field."

They had not noticed the stars clouding over. There was a soft tapping on the leaves of the trees as rain began to spill.

"Better get back down the hill before this rain gets heavier," he said. He looked at his watch. "Oh! Shit! Look at the time. And I have to be up at cockcrow in the morning."

They started down the narrow path. The woods were darker now. Claire shivered and Ewan put his arm around her. The towering trees and the snapping, crackling sounds of the woods were eerie but they did not scare Claire as much as the warm feeling that was rushing through her body. She had felt like this before, felt the trembles and shivers and quickened heartbeat. It had been when she had first met Brendan. She tried to concentrate on the path ahead, tried to ignore the weight of his arm on her shoulder, the scent of his aftershave.

Ewan's next remark brought her back to reality.

"Your husband came to see me during the week."

Claire put her hand to her mouth and her eyes widened.

Ewan laughed. "Don't worry. He didn't hit me again. Believe it or not, he came to apologise."

Claire walked on in silence. Brendan. Another problem to be sorted. Guilt niggled at her. He had been a bastard. True. But she had not been a good wife to him. She had not been a wife at all. What kind of a wife did Ewan have? Helen, wasn't it? Was she warm and loving and supportive? It would be easy to be loving and supportive to Ewan. The thought almost made her stop in her tracks. What made her think that? And what was she doing here, in the woods, in the middle of the night, arm in arm with a man, a married man, she knew very little about? Carrying her precious formula with her? Telling him about Serum 6. About Clarence, for Christ's sake! She slipped out from under Ewan's arm.

"Are you OK?" he asked.

"I'm fine. Just fine."

She walked quickly on ahead and kept up the pace until they reached the car park. She took out her car keys and turned to face Ewan.

"Good luck with the election. Next Wednesday, isn't it?"

"Yeah. I wish it were tomorrow. I seem to be riding high in the polls now and you know how fickle the public can be. I could be bottom of the list by polling day."

427

"I bet your family will be glad when it's over. They must miss having you around."

Ewan shuffled uncomfortably. He didn't want to be reminded of his family now. Especially by Claire. "If I was elected, I could be a lot more help to you with your serum. I would have more influence with the powers that be."

Claire moved in close to him and looked up into his face. She noticed the little lines at the corners of his eyes, the cleft in his chin, the way his teeth glistened between his slightly parted lips. She stared as if she was trying to memorise every little detail . She was. Storing up his image for the long, lonely time ahead.

"Take care, Ewan. Be happy."

He lifted his hand and touched her hair. "That sounds like goodbye. Does it have to be?"

Claire kissed him softly on the cheek and then turned and walked to her car. Her hand shook as she tried to put the key in the ignition. Her lips stung from the rough bristle of his beard and her eyes stung with unshed tears. As she drove home she remembered the feel of his arm around her, the intensity of his gaze, his smile. His wife. His children.

She did not notice that a car had followed her all the way from the woods or that Brendan arrived home shortly after her. She locked her bedroom door when she heard glasses clinking in the lounge. Brendan frightened her when he was drunk.

Chapter Twenty-two

Claire had to park a distance from the Community Hall. If the traffic outside the voting centre was anything to go by, the poll was going to be very high in this election. A high turnout meant an anti-government vote. A vote for change. That should be to Ewan's advantage. She took her polling card out of the glove compartment where she had put it, thrust her leather bag with its precious contents firmly under her arm and joined the crowd walking in the direction of the hall.

When she got inside, she could sense a buzz of excitement. There was a flash as somebody took a photograph. She looked in the direction of the light and saw Paul Gregan, camera-straps slung over his shoulders. A knot of people was gathered around one of the voting boxes. Ewan's head was visible above the crowd as he posed beside the box, ballot paper poised over the slot. Claire stood on tiptoe and saw Helen by his side, smiling up at him, the proud wife. Ewan saw Claire and for one second the smile faded from his eyes. Claire turned and joined the queue for ballot papers. By the time she had come out of the polling booth Ewan and Helen had left the building. At least she had been able to give him her vote. Cold comfort.

It took ten minutes to inch her way out into the traffic and then she ended up sitting in her lane as chaos built around the polling booth. She got out of her stationary car, glad that her formula was safely locked in the boot, and looked around to see what was causing the hold-up. Up ahead it appeared that the traffic lights were out of order. She sat back into her car and turned on the radio. It was all election news. She switched it off again. Somebody rapped on the window of her driver's door and she jumped with fright. Paul Gregan gestured to her to wind her window down. He was reaching into his jacket pocket for something.

"Here, Claire, have this. I'm sure he would have wanted you to see it." He pushed a piece of paper through the window.

It had obviously been folded and re-folded many times. She opened it and read her father's words, saw his signature. Her eyes were riveted to the end of the page.

"PS. You asked me what I thought was my greatest achievement. It will become very clear that my daughter is. Talk soon. Frank."

She looked from the piece of paper to Paul, a shocked expression on her face.

"I'm sorry," he said. "I should have explained first. He sent me that note from the airport just before he caught the flight to England."

"His last flight."

Paul nodded, regretting his insensitivity. She was obviously very upset at seeing this message from her father. But finding her stuck here in the lane of traffic had been too good an opportunity to miss.

"I've tried contacting you to let you know about the note but you're a difficult woman to get hold of."

Claire smiled at him. "I thought you just wanted a story."

"I do. Mind if I sit in while we are waiting for the traffic to sort itself out?"

Claire nodded and he came around to the passenger side.

"It's like this, Claire. I have a story. It's about bad guys and good guys. The good guys have a magic potion and the bad guys want it for themselves."

"Maybe you should be writing fiction. Are you sure journalism is for you?"

"I am fast discovering that the old cliché about fact being stranger than fiction is true. Who would have thought that a very dominant, multinational pharmaceutical company would be siting themselves here in order to pound the hell out of herbs and mush them up into some kind of a medicine?"

"Put like that, it is very strange indeed!"

"Well, I don't believe it either. But I promised Ewan I would hold off on the story to give you a chance to secure your research. I think you will find it very difficult to keep secret for much longer. When it gets into the public arena, there will be pressure on you to pass your research to whoever can develop it fastest. You can't blame people for that. I'd want it if I were diagnosed with cancer. And guess what? RTTI will be ready and waiting with facilities and expertise. They will take a little break from their herb-bashing and make billions and billions of pounds worth from your – your what? What is it? A tablet, a liquid, what is it?"

Claire would have been shocked at the extent of this journalist's knowledge except that Ewan had warned her. He had said that Paul Gregan was a very sharp journalist. And that he could be trusted. Her father had obviously come to that conclusion too. Frank had allowed Paul Gregan a lot of access to the plant and to his time. Claire clutched Frank's note in her hand. Illogical as it seemed, she believed it was a sign that Frank was still telling her what to do, still looking after her. Advising her to trust Paul Gregan. Advising her to be strong. To be like him. Decisive. In control …

The tattered page fell from Claire's hand onto her lap. She felt at once weak with excitement and very, very strong. She knew now what she must do. She had a plan. A way forward.

Paul was looking askance at her as she stared straight ahead. The note from her father seemed to have shocked her. He asked gently if she felt all right.

She drew her attention back to him and smiled. "I'm fine, Paul, thank you. My research is almost complete. I just need a little time. I must finish what I have started."

The traffic in front of them began to move. Paul jumped out of the car. "I'd better get back into my car. I just abandoned it when I saw you."

He closed the door and Claire put her car in gear. She leaned out the window to him.

"Give me a few days, Paul, and I will fill you in on the bits you haven't guessed. I will give you my story exclusively. Deal?"

He gave her the thumbs-up sign and went back to his car. Claire drove away, her father's note tucked safely in the pocket of her jeans.

* * *

Kevin peered around him furtively before he keyed in the code on the R&D alarm. He was getting almost as paranoid as Claire Hearn. He threw his coat on the bench and headed straight for the animal room. He was worried. The euphoria of being in charge of a whole trial was smothered by the overwhelming responsibility. The big fat guinea pig Claire called Clarence squeaked loudly, begging for food. Ignoring him, Kevin passed by rows of cages and went to where the animals he was treating were kept.

His heart seemed to drop from his chest to the pit of his stomach. This was what he had most feared. No improvement. In fact, the opposite. It was six days since he had injected these animals with the Serum 6 he himself had made up. He closed his eyes tight and counted to ten. Then he looked again. It was still the same. One voice in his head, the more optimistic one, argued that the animals all had cancer anyway. Of course they were sick. That is why they were here. Serum 6 did not cure instantly. It took time to work. The other voice, the one he did not want to hear, said there was no difference in condition between the animals on the Serum 6 he had made and the animals who were untreated. They were all dying. And it was his responsibility.

He walked slowly back to the lab and put on his lab coat. Maybe if he hadn't been thinking so much about Ria he wouldn't be in this mess now. Why had Paul Gregan interfered? If he hadn't done that portfolio for her, Ria would not have got this goddamn modelling contract. On top of all the worry about Serum 6, he had to agonise about Ria going away . And she would go. He knew it. She had already handed in her notice to Travelbug. Claire Hearn was totally focused on her work. She did not allow any interference. He must have got the formula wrong, given the wrong dosage. Wrong, wrong, wrong!

He spent the next hour weighing, measuring, calculating and confirming his worst fears. All the animals, including the ones he had treated with Serum 6, were deteriorating. He went to the safe and took out his notes. Steps 1-15. Where in the fuck had he gone wrong and what was Claire Hearn going to say when she found out? She had been allowing him total control of this batch, keeping out of his way, letting him get on with it.

He froze when he heard the little beeps of the numbers being punched into the door alarm. It had to be Claire. Jesus Christ! He would have to tell her. What was he going to say to her?

"Morning, Kevin. How are you?"

He tried, and failed, to return Claire's smile. He heard himself launching into an explanation, a string of excuses about his failures. Trying to justify himself. Seeing the puzzlement on her face, he wanted to shut up, knowing that he was making an even bigger fool of himself, but he just kept waffling on and on until she finally put up her hand to stop him.

"Kevin. You're getting yourself into a right old state. Calm down. I'll make coffee and we can talk this over."

He followed her into the canteen and sat, head bowed, while she boiled the kettle and spooned coffee into mugs. She placed a mug in front of him and sat down.

"Now tell me, slowly, what is wrong."

"The serum I made isn't working on this batch. I did everything you told me. The correct dilutions, method and dosages. But it's not working. I must have gone wrong somewhere but I don't know where. I'm sorry. I'm very sorry."

Claire was running her finger around the rim of the mug. He watched as her varnished nailed circled round and round. He held his breath as the silence went on. Eventually she looked at him.

"You have to understand, Kevin, that Serum 6 is a very experimental process. Research can be very frustrating. Sometimes things work and other times

435

they don't. The trick is to find out what went wrong and learn from it."

"But the cancers responded when you made Serum 6. You cured it. Why couldn't I do the same?"

"See. There you go again! Blaming yourself. I'm sure you did nothing wrong, Kevin. Anyway, you've given up way too soon. Your results may pick up yet."

He smiled but there was no conviction in it. Claire lowered her head and closed her eyes, giving herself time to think. This was so unfair on Kevin. But what else could she do?

He looked at her bowed head and waited for her to say the words that would ruin him. She was going to fire him. Ria was going to leave him. The animals were all going to die. He was fucked.

She raised her head. "C'mon, Kevin. You have work to do."

"You mean I still have a job?"

"Of course. We'll sort through the data, maybe tomorrow. Then we'll see what's gone wrong. If anything."

"Thank you, Mrs. Hearn. Thank you."

Immediately Claire left, Kevin gave Clarence a feed to stop his infernal squeaking. Then, chastened and humbled and less sure of himself than ever, he settled back into his lab routine.

Claire went straight home. It was urgent now that she finish her work as soon as possible.

*   *   *

Over in the Admin Building Yvette was frowning. The last thing she had anticipated was Serum 6 not working. She took out her earpiece and dialled Jacques Rondel's number. Better that he hear the news from her. His mobile was switched off. It was not until she contacted his office that she remembered Jacques was attending a family funeral. Marriages and funerals were sacrosanct in the Rondel clan. He had left strict instructions that he was not to be disturbed. Under any circumstances. What to do now? Tell Vincento McIntyre?

Yvette sat back in Frank Dawson's chair and tapped his desk with her long nails. She thought back over the conversation she had overheard between Claire and that dimwit Kevin. Why had Claire not fired her incompetent assistant? Maybe she felt it was just that the boy was too anxious to prove himself, too impatient? She certainly did not seem very upset by his hysteria. Moreover, she had just gone away again and left him on his own. Of course it could be exactly as Claire had said. Serum 6 was experimental and prone to glitches. Besides, a whole army of RTTI staff was constantly monitoring the relays from Dashern Research and Development Laboratory. The professionals amongst them would soon have the situation under control.

No. There was no need to disturb Jacques. No need at all.

*   *   *

The meeting with the accountant was much as Dorothy had expected. Dashern was now operating on a drastically reduced profit margin and projections all indicated a downward trend.

"I did advise Frank to consider winding up the company," the accountant said. "But as you know his preferred option was to diversify. Risky in my opinion. I told him it would take a long time for the new operation to become profitable."

"And he said: 'John, do your sums. That is what I pay you for. I'll make the decisions.'"

He looked up in surprise. "He told you?"

Dorothy smiled at the dour man sitting across from her. "He didn't have to. I knew him too well. All bark and a bit of bite thrown in for good measure."

The accountant was not sure how to respond to that so he got back to the balance sheets where he felt comfortable and in control.

"Audits are in hand. In fact, I can let you know now precisely what your liabilities are and exactly how much you could hope to realise from disposing of assets."

Dorothy flicked through the pages he passed across to her until she came to the last page. The balance. She smiled. "Enough then to pay Frank's staff a decent redundancy. He cared very much about them. Saw them almost as family."

"Are you sure you won't sell out to RTTI? I would definitely recommend that as the best option for you."

Dorothy stared back at him. He looked away. She

was as stubborn and strong-willed as her late husband and a lot more intimidating.

"I want absolutely nothing to do with RTTI. If Dashern cannot continue on as an independent company, which as we see it cannot, then it is my wish that it ceases to exist."

He was going to point out to her that the decision was not hers alone to make but his courage failed him. Instead he handed her a sheaf of documents which she folded and put into her handbag. She stood and shook his hand then sailed out of his office, armed, willing and able for the battle.

*   *   *

Claire was surprised to see Brendan's car in the driveway when she arrived home. She hesitated before putting the key in the door. Suppose he was drunk again? Of course he was drunk. What other condition was he in these days? He would either be drunk morose or drunk aggressive. She shivered. She put the key in the door and turned it.

The house was quiet. She was relieved. He was probably gone to bed to sleep off his latest binge. She put on the kettle and made a cup of instant coffee. Her mind was buzzing with her plan. Now that she knew exactly what she wanted to do, she could not wait to get started. Mug of coffee in one hand and her leather bag in the other, she walked into the study. She almost let her coffee fall with fright when she saw Brendan sitting in front of the computer.

"What are you doing here?"

"I live here."

"No. I mean what are you doing at the computer?"

Brendan swivelled the chair around to face her. She stared. He was pale and gaunt. The dark stubble on his face made him seem even paler. His shoulders were hunched and his hands were shaking.

"Come over here," he said. "I want you to see. I want you to understand."

She walked slowly towards him, drawn by the intensity of his stare. She put her mug of coffee on the desk and her bag at her feet. She looked at the screen. A Word document was open. He had put the date on top and then started what was obviously meant to be a letter to her. It had got no further than *Dear Claire*. She stared at her husband, wondering if he was losing his mind as well as his dignity.

"That's it? 'Dear Claire'?"

She had been wrong. This man was not drunk. He seemed to be in the grip of a force far more devastating than alcohol. The depth of sadness in his eyes made Claire want to hold him, to kiss away his pain. She had to put her hands behind her back to stop herself reaching out for him.

"I know I have made a mess," he said softly. "Such a stupid mess and I am really, really sorry that I dragged you into it."

"So is that what you were going to write? An apology?"

He gave a wry grin. "That would be typical of me, wouldn't it? 'Dear Claire, our marriage was a mistake and I seem to have lost my way in life. Sorry. Love, Brendan.'"

"And is that what our marriage was to you? A mistake? Didn't my father keep his end of the bargain? You got your company shares. That was what you wanted, wasn't it?"

Brendan bowed his head and she noticed a few grey hairs. He gave a very deep sigh.

"I suppose we have reached the stage, Claire, where all we can give each other is the truth. Yes. I did marry you so that I could have a one-third share in Dawson Chemicals, as it was then. I thought you were very pretty and very intelligent but I did not love you."

"You loved the lifestyle you thought I could bring you."

"Something like that. But I had every intention of making a go of our marriage. I wanted children, Claire. I wanted to provide them with the type of upbringing that only money could bring. I wanted them to have music and tennis and riding lessons, the best schools, skiing holidays, posh accents and parents they could be proud of."

Claire reached over and touched his hand. His skin felt clammy. "I never realised you had wanted so much to have a family. And I didn't realise until very recently why I did not."

"You had your work. Your precious research. That was your baby."

441

She shook her head. "That is what I used to think too. But that's an excuse. Work was my shield. My escape. I was just hiding in the lab, afraid to go out. I couldn't have children because I was still a child myself. I had never grown up."

"And you have now?"

Claire looked at their entwined hands, hers small with French-polished nails, his large hand bony and sweating and shaky. Even their hands were a mismatch. Dorothy had been right from the beginning. She looked into his eyes and slowly nodded her head.

"Yes, Brendan. I am starting to grow up now. To make my own decisions and to take responsibility for them. And my first and most important decision is to end our marriage."

They were both silent. Remembering. Regretting. Maybe it could have been different. If only …

"Do you love Yvette Previn?"

A look of intense pain flashed across Brendan's face. "Love has to be a two-way street. We learned that. I have finally realised she feels nothing for me. I think she used my infatuation for her to try to get your research."

"I'm sorry," Claire said and was surprised to find that she meant it. She would genuinely like her husband to find the happiness with someone else that she had never been able to give him.

"I think you should be warned, Claire, that RTTI will stop at nothing to get hold of whatever it is you are working on."

She nodded acknowledgement but said nothing about her work. Maybe it was caution or maybe it was because this conversation was just about the two of them and their failed relationship.

"Ewan Peters?" he asked.

"No. Ewan is a lovely man but there is no romance between us. We really were just talking that day you hit him. Anyway, he's married."

"I saw you in the woods with him. I followed you."

Claire blushed. Had Brendan seen her arm in arm with Ewan? Pretending to need the privacy of the woods for their discussion but each of them secretly planning to seduce the other? Not that they admitted that, even to themselves. She could not admit it to Brendan now either. Nor would she admit to the times she thought about Ewan. The dreams she had. How jealous she had felt today when she saw Helen by his side …

"We genuinely were just discussing Dashern," she assured him. "The truth is we were hiding from RTTI."

Brendan nodded, deciding to accept her explanation. The final proof, if she needed it, that he did not love her, that he would not have fought to keep her anyway. He smiled at her, a sad, empty smile.

"So where does all this truth leave us, Claire? How are we going to handle this? I suppose I'll have to leave Dashern. I don't want to work under Trevor Langley anyway."

Claire hesitated. How much should she tell him? Should she warn him? He seemed to be sincere. Hurt and vulnerable. Then she remembered some of the times she had been duped by his apparent innocence only to discover that underneath Brendan was incapable of being honest, even with himself. "You could always ask Jeremiah Audley about the provision my father made for you in his will. We are still married so your rights will not be affected. All the divorce legalities will take time. I think Dad anticipated our splitting up."

The muscles in Brendan's stomach knotted so tightly that he bent over. How far was this truth session going to take them? Claire, I killed your father! I hit the old man and caused his fatal heart attack! Ask Yvette Previn if you don't believe me. She has proof. You can watch me split his face open. See how I murdered him!

Claire put her arms around him. "Are you all right, Brendan? Is there something I could get you? Paracetamol? A glass of water?"

"A glass of brandy, Claire. A double. Jesus, I need a drink!"

She held onto him, not knowing what to do. His face had a grey tinge and sweat beaded his forehead.

"Will I call a doctor?"

He leaned his head into her and she could feel his hot tears drench her blouse, craving acceptance and forgiveness in equal measure. "I'm sorry," he sobbed over and over until Claire, finally, was crying too. She tried to comfort him and to take comfort herself from soothing him, but they were both caught in a vortex of guilt, unable to reveal their deepest secrets on this, their day of honesty. He could not tell her about the wound on her father's face, the one so easily explained away by his fall against the vanity unit. She could not tell him that he would not have to make a decision to leave Dashern, that Dashern would be no more. Trust was as absent in their parting as love had been in their marriage.

He pulled away from her and wiped his eyes. "I'll sleep for a while. We can sort out the details later. Tomorrow maybe. About the house and that sort of thing."

She nodded. "You do need to see a doctor, Brendan. You've lost a lot of weight. Promise you'll make an appointment?"

"I'll deal with my own problems, Claire. I know I've been hitting the bottle. I just have to stop. I don't need a doctor. I don't need anybody."

"You could get help, you know. You don't have to fight this on your own."

"I'm best on my own. Relationships don't work for me. At least Dorothy will be pleased. This is the outcome she always wanted for us."

Claire was about to contradict him, to tell him that he did not understand Dorothy, just as she herself had misjudged her mother for so long. Then she realised he was probably right. He smiled at her, a wan, pathetic, tear-stained smile. She kissed him on the cheek and he walked slowly out of the study and up the stairs.

Claire sat there and tried to fill the empty space inside her with self-congratulation. She had done it! She had dragged her hurt and humiliation from its hiding place and confronted it. But she had not reckoned on dealing with his hurt too. She felt no triumph. His contrite vulnerability had denied her the satisfaction of victory. There was no victory. Just the sad emptiness of shared defeat. It had been such a quiet conclusion. No raised voices, no anger. No passion.

She deleted his letter and closed the Word application. Then she opened PowerPoint and started her work. Her plan. She typed late into the night.

Chapter Twenty-three

The new baby was going to be a boy. Helen was throwing up, just as she had for five months before their son had been born. She had carried their daughter without suffering even one day of nausea.

Ewan threw back the quilt and put on his dressing-gown. He went to the kitchen, plugged in the kettle, got out the packet of cream crackers and put some on a plate. Tea and cream crackers. He had not forgotten her cure for morning sickness. When the kettle was boiled he filled up her cup, then switched on the radio to get the early headlines. They led with Election news. It had been a very high turnout. Seventy-two per cent. He fished the teabag out of the cup and dumped it in the bin. Just as he was leaving the kitchen with the tray, he heard his name being beautifully pronounced by the newsreader. He put the tray down and turned up the volume. "*. . . Exit polls indicate he may top the poll in his* *constituency. If these predictions firm up into votes this will prove to be one of the surprise results of the election."*

When he got upstairs Helen was back in bed. Her face had a greenish pallor. He placed the tray on the bedside table and put pillows behind her back. She smiled at him.

"Thanks, love. I don't deserve you."

Ewan put the tray on the bed and started to prepare for his shower.

"Your navy suit is ready. And a blue shirt. They're the best colours for television. I'm going to wear my Armani suit."

Which is not actually paid for, Ewan thought bitterly.

Then he felt guilty. He felt guilty for resenting her pregnancy and the debt she had drawn on them but most of all he felt guilty about the fact that she was not the woman he wanted by his side today.

The phone started ringing as he was dressing. It was as if his phone number had been announced on the news bulletin. So many people wishing him luck in today's count, so many people with trust and faith in him. Eva, almost hysterical with excitement, arranging to meet him at the count centre. Paul, reassuring him that things were looking very positive. People he knew well and people he was barely acquainted with. He was just about to knot his tie when the phone rang yet again.

"Leave it" Helen advised. "You could spend the day here answering the calls. I'll do it when my tummy settles down. You get off to the count centre. All your team will be waiting for you."

"Just this one," he said as he straightened his tie and picked up the phone.

"Clive Rigney here."

Ewan's knuckles whitened as he gripped the phone tight. The euphoria of all the good wishes suddenly disappeared to be replaced by a gut-wrenching anger. The scrawny little prick with the big bank balance was going to name his price. Now. Today. Before the votes were even counted. It was payback time.

"Yes, Clive. What can I do for you?"

"That's the attitude I like from my public representative. For now, I just want to wish you luck."

"Thank you for your good wishes, Clive."

"But?"

"Oh, come on, Clive! We both know there is a hidden agenda here. Isn't it about time all the cards were on the table?"

There was a crash as Helen swept the tray aside in her dash to the bathroom.

"Everything all right?" Clive asked.

"Helen is sick. I'll have to go but we must meet soon and talk things over."

"I'd like to be at the count. Do you think you could get a pass for me?"

"Of course. I'll leave it at the door for you," Ewan said and put the phone down.

Helen was kneeling over the toilet bowl. Ewan wished he could do the same. How cleansing it would be to vomit the bile of Clive Rigney into the sewer system.

*   *   *

If Ria had not already handed in her notice, Trish would fire her now. The sooner she took up the offer from the model agency the better. Luckily enough the shop had not been overly busy.

"You may as well go, Ria. There's only an hour left and I don't think you're going to do any more work anyway."

Ria did not respond. Trish sighed. God! This girl! She had spent her time here on overdrive. Talk, talk, talk non-stop. Now, all of a sudden she had gone silent.

"Ria! Are you all right? Are you worried about going to Dublin? What's wrong?"

Ria finally answered and it was obvious that she was bringing her attention back from a long way off. "Of course I'm worried about going to Dublin. This modelling contract is my big chance. My opportunity to make something of myself, to do what I really want. Do you realise there has never been a time in my life when I have not dreamt of being on the catwalk?"

"Everyone who knows you, even vaguely, knows that! So why the worry now? You're guaranteed success after the contract you've landed. They wouldn't take you on if you didn't have the potential. Is it Kevin? Are you having second thoughts about being so far away from him?"

Ria bowed her head and hid her face with her hair in that very affected way that was now getting on Trish's nerves. Then she suddenly lifted her head and flicked back her hair in her well-practised, dramatic manner. "Yeah. That's it. I'll miss him."

Ria picked up her newspaper, tucked it under her arm and glided out the door.

Trish sat down and gave a big sigh of relief. She had lots to do, including contacting the employment agency to find a replacement for when Ria left next week, but for a few minutes she would just enjoy the Ria-free atmosphere. And next time she would make it a condition that Paul would not photograph her staff or promote their ambitions to move on and up from Travelbug.

*   *   *

Ria looked around her before she slipped into the phone box. Checking to make sure nobody was watching. Just like she had seen in films. She opened her newspaper to the page with the advertisement she had circled in red biro. *"We pay you for your stories."* The number to contact was in small print. Ria's movements were decisive. She had spent long enough debating with herself whether she should do this or not. She put coins into the slot and dialled. Her call was answered immediately.

"Newsdesk, please."

"Hold the line. I'll put you through."

She read through the ad again as she waited. *"Any interesting news in your local area? We pay you to tell us."* Ria smiled. She had the scoop of a lifetime!

"Newsdesk. How may I help?"

Eyes closed, Ria rattled off the speech she had

rehearsed. There was silence on the other end of the line while the listener seemed to be taking notes.

"Right. Is that it?"

"Sort of," Ria agreed. "The nature of the research is very sensitive. I will have to be paid a lot of money for this information."

"Could you meet our reporter tomorrow? We have someone in your area reporting on elections anyway."

"You know where I am?"

"Caller, of course I know where you are. Tomorrow evening then. Seven o'clock. The foyer of the Elmside Hotel. And it would help our reporter if we had your name and a description."

Anxious to help, Ria forgot her obsession with cloak and dagger and gave her name and a detailed and only slightly exaggerated description of her appearance. She put down the phone and folded the paper into her bag. The guilt she had struggled with all day was gone. She no longer cared that Kevin would be in trouble and maybe lose his job or that she was under an obligation to Paul Gregan. *Newstrack* was a rubbish little paper anyway and could not handle a national – an *international* – story like this. Bottom line, *Newstrack* could not pay her price. She thought about the money she was going to get. This publication had a reputation for paying big money for stories. Maybe they would pay her even more for this world exclusive. Her nest egg to get her started on her new career! She was smiling as she walked out of the kiosk.

*   *   *

Pile after pile of first-preference votes were stacked on the table assigned to EnVirowatch. Ewan kept glancing at them, afraid to hope, reluctant to believe the evidence of his own eyes. The feedback had been positive, the polls promising but this was beyond all expectations. His hand was sore from people shaking it, even though the result had not yet been announced. Eva and all the team were ecstatic. Just one remaining box left to open and sort and then the returning officer would be declaring the results of the first count.

Helen tugged at his sleeve. She was radiant, all the paleness of her morning sickness long gone.

"It's getting very late for the children. I'll drop them home to the baby-sitter and I'll be back in time for the count. They reckon it's going to be another hour before results."

Ewan stooped and kissed his overtired and overexcited children. They put their arms around his neck and hugged him. He held them close to him, realising that if he did get this job as TD, it would take him even further away from them. He watched his family as they made their way through the crowds towards the exit of the count centre.

"She does look the part, doesn't she? A good woman by his side is the best asset any man can have."

He turned around to face Clive Rigney. He had not seen him come in. The little man offered his hand to

Ewan. He took it reluctantly.

"Congratulations, Ewan. Great showing at the polls. Maybe even enough to get in on the first count, I hear."

"Could be. Not long to wait now anyway."

"You wanted to have a chat with me?"

Ewan looked around the crowded, noisy hall. Even as he was standing with Clive Rigney, people were patting him on the back and shaking his hand. It seemed like everybody wanted to touch the poll-topper. He called Eva.

"I'm just going out for a breath of air. Won't be long."

He indicated to Clive to follow him. They made their way slowly through the crowd. By the time they got outside the front door, Ewan's shoulders were as sore from being patted as his hand was from being shaken. He took a deep breath of the cool night air.

"Bet you're glad the Taoiseach's brother-in-law got caught with his hand in the till," Clive remarked as yet another person clapped Ewan on the back.

"It's not all an anti-government vote," Ewan said defensively. "EnVirowatch policies have stood the test. People back our aims and principals. They want change, yes. But not just for the sake of change. They want –"

Clive put up his hand and laughed. "Enough! I voted for you, man. You're preaching to the converted."

"That's what I wanted to talk to you about. Your sudden conversion. And the other matter."

People were still pouring into the hall. Word had got out that the first count was expected soon. Ewan nodded to a pathway leading to the car park. They could talk there without being overheard. They made an odd-looking pair as they strolled along the narrow path, the tiny businessman and the very tall election candidate.

When the noise from the count centre had faded to a distant buzz, Ewan felt it was safe to say what was on his mind. He turned to face Clive.

"Right. Here is what I want to say. I have already told you how grateful I am to you for your contribution to EnVirowatch. Not alone the money but the refreshments you provided free of charge for our team. I appreciate all that and you were no small help in getting us to the position we are in tonight."

Clive folded his arms across his chest and looked up at Ewan. "When are you going to get to the point? You didn't bring me out here to thank me."

"What in the fuck do you want? Why did you decide to back EnVirowatch? Why did your wife encourage Helen to get into debt? Was it to have some kind of hold over me? Because I want to make it clear to you here and now that I will not be coerced or bribed. I would resign the seat rather than take it under those circumstances."

Gravel crunched as Clive shuffled his feet in agitation. He puffed out his chest and Ewan could see that he was very angry.

"What makes you think you, Ewan Peters, have the monopoly on principle? You have insulted me. I happen to believe that what our country needs is careful management and protection of our resources. I also believe that EnVirowatch has come of age. I watched it develop beyond its eco-warrior phase and I think it is ready to take a place in mainstream politics now. That is why I backed you financially. I think our constituency needs a representative who cares about our local environment and what happens to it."

"So you will never ask me for any political favours, never ask me to influence policies or decisions?"

"Don't be so fucking stupid! Of course I'll ask you. Isn't that the way our system works? And I hope you will use the influence, which I helped you to gain, in my favour. But I will never, never force or bribe you. And I'm furious that you should think like that."

Ewan looked down at the little man and searched for any sign of pretence. There was none. From the flushed cheeks to the flecks of spittle at the corners of his mouth, Clive was the epitome of genuine anger and indignation.

"So what about Helen then? Julie must have known we couldn't pay back the kind of money she was encouraging her to spend."

"You poor gullible man! Helen didn't need any encouragement to splash out. She has expensive taste, that wife of yours. Julie held her back, tried to talk sense to her. Otherwise, believe me, your wife's debt would be much bigger than what it is now. I believe the girls have come to some arrangement about repaying. I'd say forget about it except that you'd probably accuse me of bribery again."

"I wouldn't have that. You will get your money back but it may take some time."

"That's fine."

Ewan waited for Clive to go on, to add some conditions, some veiled threats. Instead the little man was silent, looking back towards the count centre and then checking his watch.

"Shouldn't we be getting back?" Clive asked. "They'll be noticing that the star of the show is missing."

Ewan put a hand on the smaller man's arm to stop him moving away. "One more thing. This is none of my business but I believe you're going to buy Grange House from Dorothy Dawson."

"No secrets around here, are there? Yes. I'm in the process of buying the house and the whole estate. And I'm going to build the biggest, the best, the classiest eighteen-hole golf course in the country on Grange Estate to rival the K Club. Grange House will become a five-star hotel. We're going to host top class tournaments and events. Every celebrity in the world will want to stay in Grange House. I'm going to put our part of the country on the map, not as a centre of industry, but as the home of Grange House Golf Course."

Ewan laughed out loud. The cute little bollocks! "Now I get it! Now I see why you're against RTTI! How could you promote your Grange House development if a chemical plant with a sinister environmental record was one of your neighbours? One of your tenants once you become owner! Yes. RTTI would be a drawback to your plans. It makes sense now."

"I hope you understand as well that I'm going to ask

for your support when I apply for planning and grants and anything else it will take to get this project underway. I'm putting everything I have into the Grange House project. It must work."

Ewan put his hand on the small man's shoulder. "Clive, you have my backing on that. Your development might be a golf green but at least it is green! I can support that wholeheartedly. But I'm afraid RTTI is a different matter. There are some developments that I can't discuss with you. All I can say now is that they have a very good reason for staying here."

"We'll wait and see. RTTI could be getting some surprises soon. It may not be too easy for them to stay. Not on my property anyway." Clive's mouth tightened and his eyes narrowed. Despite his size he looked intimidating. Not a man to have as an enemy.

"I'm sorry," Ewan said. "I jumped to some very wrong conclusions."

"You did. And not just with me. I sent my wife out to make contacts in the right circles. You know, the type of people who would stay in Grange House Hotel. That's what her socialising in Dublin was about. She did not set out to drag Helen off on a spending spree. Helen did that all by herself. There never was a grand plot to entrap you."

Ewan looked at the man he had regarded with such suspicion and regretted how distrustful he had been. He meant it when he said that he would back the Grange House development but if RTTI got hold of Claire Hearn's formula there would be little he could do to help. They would most certainly manufacture here to benefit from the tax concessions. Right in the backyard of Grange House. It was up to Claire now. To the brilliant dark-eyed woman who was haunting his dreams. He turned to Clive and smiled at him. Together they walked slowly back towards the count centre.

Fifty minutes later the presiding officer declared Ewan Christopher Peters of EnVirowatch as the first candidate to be elected in his electoral area.

*   *   *

Claire had the packages in her hand when she opened the front door. She smiled at the uniformed man.

"Thank God for your twenty-four-hour service. These are very urgent. You guarantee me that they'll be delivered as soon as possible?"

"Immediate delivery for the local one and the other four will be on their way as soon as their flights take off."

"No! No, no, I want them all delivered at exactly the same time."

"Of course. I'm sorry. My instructions are concurrent delivery."

Claire still held the packages in her hand. Now, at the last minute, she was reluctant to let them go.

The man put his hand out. "Ma'am?"

"You will be careful with them? Can I be sure they will be handed directly to the persons to whom they are addressed? Nobody else?"

"We run a very efficient service. Guaranteed person-to-person delivery worldwide in the quickest time possible. You can check if you like."

"I have."

Reluctantly Claire handed over her five packages. He put them into a canvas mailbag.

"Careful now. Remember they are very urgent. And important."

He practically ran to his van. She stood at the door until the van drove out the gate. Closing the door she stood in the hallway, wondering what to do next. Now that the packages were on their way, she was feeling totally drained.

She saw Brendan in the lounge, sprawled in front of the television, remote control in one hand, glass in the other. Had last night's conversation meant anything to him? It suddenly struck her that maybe he did not remember now. All the soul-searching lost in a fog of alcohol. Or was that what he wanted her to think? She was too exhausted to sort it out. She would just remind him about the meeting.

"The AGM in the morning, Brendan. You got notification. Do you remember?"

"Yeah, yeah."

He had found a channel with motor-bike racing. Claire gave up trying to talk to him. She closed the door behind her as she left to block out the sound of the screaming engines. He may as well enjoy his drink and his sport channel tonight because tomorrow he would have to face reality.

Chapter Twenty-four

When Dorothy Dawson opened the door to her husband's office, Yvette Previn was sitting at Frank's desk and Trevor Langley was seated across from the French usurper. As soon as Dorothy said good morning to Trevor, he jumped to his feet and went out the door.

Dorothy smiled at Yvette. "I usually have that effect on men. Now if you don't mind, I'll take my place please."

From the expression on Yvette's face it was obvious that she did mind. She stood up from Frank's chair and strolled over to the big window. Sitting on the window-ledge, she crossed her long legs and stared at Dorothy.

"You look busy," she remarked as Dorothy put her briefcase on the desk and opened it up. She continued to stare as the older woman sorted out papers on the desk. There seemed to be a method to whatever madness had possessed the widow.

"May I be of help?" asked Yvette.

"Yes, indeed. Come and sit down here, please."

Yvette unwound her legs and walked slowly over to the chair just vacated by Trevor Langley. She was beginning to feel just a little uncomfortable. Not as in charge as she should be.

Dorothy looked at her and smiled. "Now, would you please explain to me why you are here?"

"Pardon?"

"Let me put it more clearly. What are you doing in my office? Who gave you permission to be here?"

"I don't need your permission! Look, Dorothy, what's going on? What's the matter?"

"The matter is that you and your company have taken a lot for granted. We are still in the process of negotiating an amalgamation. Note, negotiating. Dashern and RTTI are still two separate companies. In fact, technically, you are trespassing on these premises."

Yvette was no longer lolling in her chair. She was alert and sitting forward, trying to work out just what had got into the older woman. "I'm here, Dorothy, as you well know, because I am representing the interests of my company."

"Stop there. Don't try to talk down to me, young woman. You do not have a legal or technical function with RTTI. You are their PR representative, their window dressing, their mouthpiece when they need to deliver a message to the public wrapped in nylon stockings and designer gowns. So I will ask you again. Why are you here?"

Yvette lowered her head and looked up at Dorothy

through her long, dark eyelashes.

"What if I told you Frank invited me? Promised me a role in the new company."

"I would know you were lying. Now leave my office, please. If I want to deal with RTTI, I will ring Jacques Rondel. The monkey and the organ-grinder. All that business. You understand?"

Yvette stood up. Clearly she was not going to either charm or intimidate Dorothy Dawson. Why had the doddering old Lady of the Manor suddenly cast off her gardening gloves and become a boardroom diva? Yvette shrugged. She was under instruction from Jacques to keep a low profile until the scientific team had gleaned all the information they needed from the R&D surveillance. Just what were they doing? The data had been transmitting from Claire Hearn's lab for over a week now. She had warned Jacques that they should be out of there as quickly as possible. Claire was a very intelligent woman. Her father's death seemed to have slowed down her punishing work schedule. She was spending less time in the lab since Frank had died but her period of mourning would not last forever. She could very well uncover their covert operation if they did not get a move on.

She glanced at Dorothy, sitting tall and proud at her late husband's desk. Yvette turned her back and walked out. The sooner all this Dashern business was finished the better. These Hearns and Dawsons were all insane!

*   *   *

Claire reached her lab later than she had intended. It had taken some time to wake Brendan this morning. She could not leave home until she had been sure that he was in a fit state to attend the AGM. That meant pouring black coffee into him and steering him in the direction of the shower. It was up to him now. She could not very well drag him there.

Kevin Trill seemed even more depressed today. It was obvious by now that his batch of Serum 6 was not going to cure the sick guinea pigs.

"Where did I go wrong?" he asked, handing her his work logbook. She glanced through it. Serum 6 in fifteen steps. Perfect. Just as she had instructed. How was she to convince him not to worry?

"You've done nothing wrong. You followed the procedure exactly. I told you these things happen."

Kevin gave a wry smile. "It seems that is what everyone is saying to me these days."

Claire raised an eyebrow.

"Ria. She's going to Dublin and she doesn't want to see me again. She's signed up for a modelling contract. Guess what she said?"

"These things happen?"

Kevin nodded miserably. Claire looked again at the notes Kevin had made and wondered what to do. She could not bear to look at him. He would get over all this but he was suffering now. Shit!

The phone rang and she grabbed it, glad of the break from the intense feelings in the lab. It was Dorothy.

"Are you ready, Claire? Time to get the AGM show

on the road. Boardroom in five minutes."

"Be with you now." Claire put her hand on Kevin's arm. "Look, Kevin, I can't do anything to make you feel better about Ria but I do not want you worrying about your work. You are an excellent technician. You have done nothing wrong. Serum 6 is complex. We'll talk about it later. Promise you're not going to brood on it any more?"

He nodded but there was not very much enthusiasm in the gesture. Claire picked up her bag and dashed to the door. Dorothy was not in the mood to be kept waiting.

*   *   *

Dorothy looked up from her documents and called, "Come in!"

Brendan stood just inside the boardroom door and stared at his mother-in-law.

"I suppose she told you," he said sullenly.

"If you mean did Claire tell me she is going to apply for divorce, then yes. She did."

"You must be glad. You've been wanting this ever since your daughter married me."

"Sit down, Brendan, and stop being so melodramatic. Of course I'm not glad that Claire is getting divorced. What kind of mother do you think I am?"

There was another tap on the door and Claire came in.

"Ah! The divorcée!" Brendan said.

Dorothy stood. She was an imposing figure at the head of the table.

"Right, you two. This is a business meeting and will

be conducted as such. I will not tolerate any more personal comments like that, Brendan. If you would both sit now, I would like to declare the meeting open."

Before long, Brendan was glad that he was seated. He would have fallen when Dorothy invoked a special resolution under section 251 of the 1963 Companies Act. He shouted at her, "Are you mad? You can't wind up the company! Close it down completely? You're insane!"

Dorothy went on to explain patiently to him why she could, and would, close down Dashern Chemicals.

"What about RTTI? What about the investment they've made here? The amalgamation? What about the plans for herbal medicines? For increased employment?"

"You, of course, would know far more about the implications for RTTI than we do," Claire said.

"I might have guessed you would be backing your mother. Very cosy. Your two votes against my one."

"You're lucky to still have a vote."

"Is that what you call it, lucky? If your father –"

Dorothy put up her hand. That was enough to silence both Claire and Brendan. Then she went on to organise the vote on the winding up of Dashern Chemicals. The minutes would reflect the fact that all the statutory requirements had been fulfilled.

Brendan pushed back his chair and stood up after he had cast his vote.

"I can't do any more than register my complete and utter disagreement with your decision. I hope neither of you expects me to help with the wind-up. And what about you, Claire? What about ClairCo and your precious research? Are you winding that up too?"

Claire smiled at him. "I'm tying up all the loose ends. You should know that."

He banged the door on his way out. Both women were quiet for a minute, each of them thinking about Frank Dawson as they presided over the demise of his company.

* * *

Yvette's heels clicked on the parquet floor as she strode along. She was angry. Dorothy Dawson had dismissed her as if she were a naughty three-year-old. Nobody did that to Yvette Previn and got away with it. She was not sure where to go now. She needed a place to cool down, to think. She must find a space where her temper could simmer and cool and then – then Dorothy Dawson, beware!

She noticed that the door to Brendan's office was open. Brendan was not there. Probably in a pub somewhere. Yvette went in and sat at his desk. She took out a cigarette and lit it. After puffing on it she began to feel better. How could she have allowed a half-senile old woman who knew everything about begonias and nothing about business to upset her?

Yvette's temper waned and indignation began to take its proper place. First things first. The recently deceased member of the Rondel family must be well and truly buried by now. Jacques never stayed away from work for long anyway. She got out her mobile phone and tapped in his number. He answered immediately.

"Coincidence, Yvette. I was just about to ring you. Where are you?"

"I'm at Dashern, of course. Just wait until you hear –"

"No. No. You listen to me. We've done it, Yvette! We have Claire Hearn's research. Our own scientific team are working on their first batch of serum as we speak and our lawyers are right onto the task of patent. We've done it!"

Yvette stood in stunned silence. What was she going to do now? She had never heard Jacques so excited. He would not thank her for spoiling his party but yet …

"What is it, Yvette? Why don't I hear celebrations from your end of the line?"

Yvette superstitiously crossed her fingers before answering. "I know you were away on family business for the past few days, Jacques. You may not be aware of all events in Claire Hearn's R&D. The latest batch –"

"You mean the Serum 6 the lab assistant produced? He fouled it up, didn't he? So have you, Yvette. Whatever made you think that Jacques Rondel would not be in possession of all the facts?"

She had started to apologise, to grovel, when Jacques laughed.

"Let's not spoil this auspicious day," he said. "We must look forward now, not back. And RTTI have so much to look forward to, thanks to Mrs Brendan Hearn."

Yvette breathed a huge sigh of relief. None of it

mattered any more. Even if Claire Hearn found out now there was nothing she could do. RTTI researchers, the best that money could buy, would soon be curing cancer. Dorothy Dawson's days of swanning around this plant were numbered.

Yvette laughed. "I can't wait to see the look on Claire Hearn's face when she realises we have beaten her!"

"True, Yvette. You can't wait. That was one of my main reasons for ringing you. I want you out of there now."

"Why?"

"We need you back at headquarters. We hope to go straight to human trials. And then very quickly to manufacture. Public demand would move the bureaucracy along very nicely. Do you know what I mean?"

"I understand, Jacques. A leaked report here, a hint there. Information from inside RTTI research about the secret wonder drug. The miracle cancer cure. That kind of thing."

"Your kind of thing, Yvette. Come home."

"Gladly. Do I leave Trevor Langley in charge of our end of the merger here?"

"What merger? There will be no RTTI-Dashern. We don't need to waste resources on that herbal nonsense any more. I've just instructed our lawyers to withdraw."

Yvette's face was very beautiful as her smile lit her amber eyes and added a golden glow to her skin. This was so good! Both Dawson women humiliated in one blow. Dorothy Dawson could park her big derrière on Frank's chair and preside over the slow and painful wasting away of Dashern, while her pasty little daughter would fall into a black depression at the loss of her exclusive hold on Serum 6. Pity she could not be here to see them squirm but when Jacques said now, he meant it.

"One more thing, Yvette. I want Brendan Hearn on board."

Yvette gripped the phone tightly. Had Jacques Rondel gone mad? Brendan Hearn was a liability. A fool.

"What possible use could he be?" she asked as calmly as possible.

As soon as she had asked the question she realised it had been a mistake. Nobody questioned Jacques' decisions. At least nobody who wanted to survive in RTTI. And Yvette was a survivor.

"I'm disappointed in you, Yvette. You of all people. You should not have to ask me. Brendan Hearn has given us a lever, a great big stick to wave over his head. Does he still believe that we have evidence against him?"

"Yes. I made sure of that," she said in an effort to redeem herself. "He thinks we have a video of the assault he perpetrated on Frank Dawson."

"Well, there you go. Brendan Hearn will be the perfect RTTI employee. Co-operative and willing to obey any order. Even the less comfortable assignments. *N'est pas*?"

"Yes, of course, Jacques. I understand your reasoning. He will have to toe the line, as they say. Do what he's told."

"Indeed. He will regret that punch to his father-in-law's face all his life. Even more so, he will regret telling you about it. Make sure he understands what is expected for our silence. Do whatever you have to to bring him along. And organise for the surveillance to be removed from Claire Hearn's lab. Best not to leave any traces. What was it you wanted to tell me?"

She smiled and shrugged her shoulders. "Nothing important."

When Jacques had said goodbye she immediately rang her special contact number. The bugs would be removed from R&D. She left no specific instructions. They were being paid enough to figure it out for themselves. Then she switched off her phone and went in search of Brendan.

* * *

Ria was finding it impossible to concentrate. She had only a few more days' notice left to work in Travelbug but she wished with all her heart that she could pick up her bag and walk out the door now. Trish's sulky face and the demanding, finicky customers were driving her mad. She needed time to think about important things. Things like modelling contracts and her meeting with the reporter.

But then, just as she had decided she had had enough, her day brightened considerably. A very attractive, very loving couple had just come into Travelbug. Yvette Previn and Brendan Hearn seemed barely able to keep their hands off each other. They smiled and looked into each other's eyes as they asked Ria to book flights for them to Zurich. As soon as possible. Ria searched for the flights and, tearing off a printout from the computer, went to the counter.

"I'm sorry, Miss Previn. The best I can do at such short notice is to book you on the late-night flight to London. Then you could get a connecting flight to Zurich from Heathrow in the morning."

"*Bien*," Yvette said. "We'll take that. What about accommodation for tonight? Could you book a London hotel for us? Near Heathrow."

"Of course. What type of accommodation would you like?"

"A suite," Brendan Hearn said.

Ria tried not to show her surprise. She went back to her computer but could not help glancing at the Frenchwoman and Claire Hearn's husband as they held hands. Suppose Claire Hearn happened to walk into Travelbug. Boy! Would she have a story then! Research scientist, famous for the discovery of cancer cure, attacks husband's mistress in travel agency. Tragedy was prevented when the beautiful model Ria Corkery threw herself between the rivals. Ria tossed her hair back and refocused on her job. She went to the counter with the flight tickets and booking forms.

"Flights out tonight at ten minutes past midnight. Then you catch the eight thirty to Zurich in the morning. And your suite in London has also been booked."

Yvette Previn handed Ria her credit card. Ria swiped it and handed it back. It was a company card. RTTI were paying for the little tryst. Why would they be doing that? Ria shrugged as she watched her satisfied customers going out the door. Whatever they were up to, the reporter would figure it out. She looked at her watch. Not much longer to wait now until she came face to face with the person who was going to write her story and secure her future.

*   *   *

It had never happened before. This was the first time ever Claire had stood outside her laboratory and decided she just could not go in. Images floated before her eyes. Brendan storming out of the boardroom, Dorothy pinning a meeting notice to the board in the canteen, Kevin's puzzled and worried face. She lifted her hands and rubbed her temples. Still the tight band of stress cut into her head. She turned back to her car. There was only one place she could go for peace.

She drove too quickly and reached the graveyard in twenty minutes. She locked her bag into the boot of the car but took her phone with her.

"Nice evening," an elderly woman said as Claire passed her on the way into the cemetery. The woman had a bunch of flowers in her hand. Claire stood still. She hadn't even thought of bringing flowers to her father. She had come here, needing him to help her, but she had not thought of doing anything for him.

The grave had sunk quite a lot in the month since Frank had made it his new home. Weeds had begun to grow, a thistle, a clump of grass, some dandelions. A pot of violas had been placed beside the headstone. Dorothy.

Claire knelt on the kerb. She looked up at the Gore-Croft angel and looked away again as the sightless eyes stared back at her. "Dad," she whispered, but she heard nothing except the crunch of the old lady's feet on the gravel path. What had she been expecting? Her father to jump up and say: "Well done, Claire. I'm glad you and Dorothy are selling out. Glad you are getting rid of the factory I spent my life building." She began to tug at the weeds. They were tough. The leaves broke away in her hand and she nearly fell back. It was almost as if her father was saying to her that she would fall on her bottom. Claire smiled. Frank would never say that. He would say, "Mark my words, girlie. You'll fall on your arse." She threw the leaves back on top of the grave. They belonged there with the dead.

She stood and rubbed her knees where the stone kerb had bitten into her flesh. This had been a silly idea. A sop to her guilty conscience. Frank would not have travelled down the road she and Dorothy had taken. He would have done anything to keep the factory open, his staff in employment.

"Sorry, Dad," she whispered as she looked down on the pile of crusted earth that was her father's resting place.

"Frank Dawson was your dad then?"

Claire jumped with fright. She had not heard the old lady come up behind her. She nodded.

"I read that lovely article about him in *Newstrack*," the woman said. "He was a great businessman. You must be very proud of him."

"I am. He was a great father too."

"I'm sorry for your loss. May he rest in peace. He has earned it. He had no more to give."

Claire looked at the little old woman with the wrinkled skin and faded eyes. She looked so tired, so worn out. Yet so wise. She was telling Claire something she should have worked out for herself. Her father's obsession had used him up. His obsession with Dashern, his pride in his achievement. Farm boy to factory owner. The story of his life. His whole life. Had he known that it was all crumbling around him? That there was no place in today's economy for a small, privately owned firm? That they could never have independently developed Serum 6? That bringing in RTTI had been an admission of failure? Had Frank's heart been broken, not diseased? Yes, indeed. He had earned his rest.

"Take this," the old lady said, handing Claire a rose.

Claire smiled at her and gently laid the white rose on top of the dandelion leaves on Frank's grave.

"Rest in peace," the woman muttered and with a gentle pat to Claire's arm she shuffled down the path towards the gate.

Claire strolled over to the ruins of the church. She stood in the roofless building and looked up at the evening sky. The sun was setting on another day. The loneliness of endings brought hot tears to her eyes. The ending of a day, a life, a marriage. Tears spilled over and every fibre of her being longed for the comfort of Ewan Peters' strong and gentle arms. The ending of love before it had even begun. But not the ending of hope.

She clutched her phone tightly, willing it to ring. If that call came. No. When that call came, she would know she had done the right thing. Her phone was silent on the drive home, silent as she bathed, silent as she cooked dinner. But still she hoped.

*   *   *

Ria felt very nervous as she stood outside Elmside Hotel. This city was too close to home. It was possible that she might meet someone she knew. What would she say then? "I'm just waiting for a reporter? I want to sell him the story of Claire Hearn's research?" She could say she was waiting for her agent. Yes. To sign her new contract. To audition for a film part.

Happy now with her cover story she went into the foyer, found a seat and watched people coming and going. How would she know the reporter? He'd be more sophisticated than Paul Gregan certainly. A real reporter. With a tape recorder and notebook. Thirtyish. Tall, dark. Brown eyes.

The person approaching her was about thirty. But that was where the fantasy ended. The woman put out her hand.

"Ria Corkery? Debbie Goggin. *Daily News.*"

Ria just nodded. She needed a minute to readjust.

She had not been expecting to be met by a smartly dressed woman. What the hell! Money had no gender. She smiled at the reporter.

"It's a long story. Would you like something to drink at the bar while we talk?"

The woman looked at her watch. "I have a deadline to meet for tomorrow's issue. I'm sorry. I'm a bit tight on time. Could we just get down to business?"

Stung by the curtness, Ria began to feel less sure of herself. Just as well she knew her speech by heart. It flowed now, word perfect. The reporter was still, listening. Not reacting. Not writing. Ria finished and sat back.

The reporter picked up her bag and stood. "Thank you, Ms Corkery, and goodbye."

"Where are you going?" asked Ria in sudden panic. "What about my deal? My money? I've given you the story!"

"You have given me a story. I have *the* story."

Ria's heart began to thump. She was being cheated. They were taking her story and not going to pay her. "I know this is a huge story. For Christ's sake! It's the cure for cancer and I can tell you where and when and how it –"

"Ria, if that is your real name, stop wasting my time please. I already know that RTTI have developed the cure in their R&D in Zurich. Their PR department have just given me an exclusive. Your story about an obscure scientist operating from a detergent factory is ridiculous."

"But it wasn't developed in Zurich. Can't you see?

They must have come here to steal it. That's why they're setting up this herbal cure thing. Was it Yvette Previn? Was she the one you were talking to?"

Debbie Goggin put the strap of her bag over her shoulder and took a step away from Ria. "I'll give you the benefit of the doubt and say that you've been completely misled. If you really want to know about RTTI's intentions, read tomorrow's *Daily News*. You might find it interesting.".

And then she was gone, leaving Ria sitting alone in the foyer of the Elmside Hotel. Ria's phone rang. She looked at the caller ID. It was Kevin. She switched it off. To hell with him. To hell with Trish and her crappy little travel shop and Paul Gregan with his rag of a news sheet. Fuck *Daily News* too. She would sell her story to someone else. She just had to get out of here. Tomorrow. In the morning. She could not stand it any more. She went home to pack.

*　　*　　*

Claire drizzled cream into the sauce and stirred. She sniffed. The aroma was appetising. She went to the end of the stairs and listened. Brendan was still walking around the bedroom. Over and back, bang, clatter, over, back. What was he up to? He had been there for more than an hour. She called up the stairs.

"Dinner is ready. And we need to talk."

She returned to the kitchen and set the table. On impulse, she went into the garden and cut some carnations. A proper setting for the Last Supper. She was at the counter dishing up when he came in. She continued working as she spoke to him.

"We can't pussyfoot around for ever, Brendan. We must talk about, you know, arrangements."

When he didn't answer, she turned around to look at him. He was standing by the door, two suitcases on the floor beside him. Claire looked from the cases to her husband. Her face crumpled as reality hit her. Her marriage packed in leather luggage.

He walked over to her and put his arms around her. He stroked her hair as she cried. When she reached to get a piece of kitchen towel to dry her eyes, she looked at him. He was beautifully groomed. Shaven, clean, his eyes brighter than she had seen them for some time. She dabbed at the wet patch her tears had left on his shirt.

"I'm sorry. I've ruined your shirt."

"I'm sorry too, Claire. About everything. So sorry."

"It's for the best. Maybe we will both have a chance at finding happiness now. Where are you going?"

He shuffled his feet and lowered his eyelids.

Claire knew then that wherever he was going, it would be with Yvette. She thought for a moment about warning him. Did he know about Yvette's lesbian ruse? What a cynical and very effective trick that had been. Or maybe she was indeed lesbian and her affair with Bendan was the ruse. She was a dangerous woman. But then, Brendan himself was not above using deceit to get what he wanted. Maybe he had at last met his match. In any case, she wished him well.

"I hope it works out for you and Yvette. I mean that, Brendan. I know you love her. Paris, is it?"

When he looked up there was a smile in his eyes. A glow. "We're flying to London tonight. Zurich tomorrow. I have a meeting with Jacques Rondel. RTTI have offered me a position."

Claire frowned. Brendan thought he was sophisticated and smart. RTTI would chew him up. He was not in their league. He was not even smart enough to realise that. Why should they want him at all? They must be pretty certain by now that he had outlived his usefulness in their hunt for Serum 6. What game were they playing?

"Be careful, Brendan. Don't trust them. They'll only be on your side as long as you are of use."

It was as if her words had unplugged the dam of his anger. His face paled and a vein began to throb in his temple. She took a step back from him.

Flecks of his spittle sprayed as he shouted at her. "Always the same, aren't you? You don't trust anyone! You are fucking paranoid! You poison everything you touch! It's all your fault! If you hadn't been so bloody selfish – wanting to keep all your research to yourself, for your own glory! What kind of a twisted human being would find the cure for cancer and then not want to share it?"

Claire leaned on the counter behind her for support. Her legs were shaking. The man standing in front of her was out of control. "Just calm down, Brendan. Can't we at least be civil to each other now?"

He snorted in reply. Her eyes were drawn to the white lines around his mouth and nostrils. His entire body was a seething mass of anger.

"Civil, is it? The Dawsons are very civilised, are they? Grow up! Your father was an ignorant bully. Your mother is a domineering snob. And you, my wife, my ex-wife, you are a conniving, spoiled, selfish little bitch! You and your family cut me out of your inner circle. Never let me into your tight-knit little club. The only thing I could get into was your knickers. And that was certainly not worth the trouble."

He took a step towards her. She could feel his breath on her face. The counter top bit into her as she leaned back. She had nowhere to go. He had his right hand bunched in a fist, rubbing the knuckles with his left hand. She could not move, could do nothing to protect herself. Claire closed her eyes and waited for his fist to slam into her face. There was a loud bang as he thumped the counter behind her.

Brendan stood looking at his knuckles. They were bleeding. The red drops oozing over the skin and bone seemed to hypnotise him. She slipped out from in front of him and dashed over to where her phone was. She picked it up and held it shield-like to her body.

"Brendan, would you leave now, please? If you don't I'll have to ring the police."

He turned around to face her, still holding his injured hand. He was smiling. "No, you won't. Your mother would hate the scandal. And you are her puppet."

Claire hesitated. He was right about the scandal.

Both she and Dorothy would hate it. But this man was dangerous. He was calmly washing off the blood under the tap now as if nothing had happened.

"You need help, Brendan."

A car horn hooted outside. He walked over to the door and picked up his cases.

"Yvette is outside waiting for me. That is all the help I need. I'll be in touch with Audley's. I'm assuming you'll apply for your divorce through them. Split everything down the middle and if you want to stay in this house, you are welcome to buy my half. Add it onto whatever is due to me from Frank's will. Bye. Good luck."

He turned on his heel and walked out as if he had not had a psychotic episode, as if he had not intended murdering her. As if their marriage had never meant anything to him. Claire sank onto a chair. Her legs still felt weak. She prayed that Yvette Previn could save him from disaster. He was not capable of saving himself.

* * *

Dorothy kept going over her speech, trying to memorise it. Frank would not have read an address to his staff. He would have looked them in the eye and spoken from his heart. Hell! Frank would never have made this speech anyway. He would not have allowed Dashern to close. Dorothy glanced up at Frank's sherry-stained portrait and then looked quickly away. Niggles of guilt and doubt crept uncomfortably around her mind, disturbing her concentration. When the phone rang, she grabbed it, glad of the distraction.

A smile slowly lit up her face as she listened to Jeremiah Audley's news. The RTTI legal team had informed him that they were withdrawing from the amalgamation with Dashern. No herbal medicines, no investment, no RTTI-Dashern. When she put the phone down she breathed a sigh of relief. Jeremiah Audley's news made everything easier. Took away the onus of responsibility. When she stood in front of Frank's workforce tomorrow she could honestly tell them that all options for keeping Dashern open had been exhausted. RTTI's withdrawal was the death-knell. They would understand that. And they would blame RTTI. No need for them to know that Dorothy had beaten RTTI to the closure.

Then she remembered. The speech she was to make to the staff. The one she and Claire had spent so long composing and she had spent so long trying to memorise. It was all wrong now. It would have to be rewritten to incorporate the RTTI situation. Drat! Thinking no time like the present, she packed the speech into her bag and drove over to Claire's house.

*   *   *

Both cars were in the driveway. Dorothy hoped that Brendan had gone to bed or was too drunk to talk. She could not face him now. She rang at the door and waited. No reply. She rang again, more insistently this time. She was beginning to think she would have to use her key to let herself in when Claire finally came to the door and opened it just a crack. She was pale and shaking. She looked terrified.

"My goodness, Claire! Whatever is the matter with you?"

Claire fell into her mother's arms and sobbed out the whole story about Brendan.

"They're well suited, you know. Yvette and Brendan."

"No, Mum. You've got it wrong. He is not that bad really. He's sick. I think he may be having a nervous breakdown. It's all been too much for him. The amalgamation and Dad's death and now our marriage breakdown."

"Hmm."

They both laughed.

Dorothy sniffed. "What is that lovely smell? I'm starving. Can't be bothered cooking for myself."

Claire realised with surprise that she was hungry too. Maybe it was time for some comfort-eating. She heated up the chicken and poured the sauce over. Then both of them sat at the table and enjoyed the meal Claire had prepared for Brendan. Dorothy pointed to the phone sitting in the middle of the table beside the vase of flowers.

"You must be expecting an important call."

Claire looked at the phone and her stomach curled into a knot. She pushed her plate away. "Yes. Very important."

"I have some important news myself," Dorothy said. "The reason why I'm here at this hour of night. I got a phone call. A very interesting one. From Jeremiah Audley. And guess what?"

"He wants to marry you. He is admitting his passion after all these years!"

"Better than that. He told me RTTI are withdrawing from the merger. He said he has been trying all day to dissuade them to no avail. They are insistent. No amalgamation. No phyto-whatever plant. No RTTI."

Claire smiled. Alleluia! Part one of her plan was in place. They had taken the bait. Her instinct had been right. Now all she needed was for the phone to ring.

"Leaves us in a pickle with our little speech, doesn't it?" said Dorothy.

"Easily sorted."

She led the way into the study and switched on the computer.

"It is a relief, isn't it?" said her mother. "I honestly believed that we were doing the right thing. And I really doubted RTTI commitment to Dashern. Still, it is good that the staff will know it wasn't just we who decided to pull the plug on them. Isn't it? Claire, are you listening to me?"

Claire had her head cocked to one side. Suddenly she jumped up and ran to the kitchen. She knocked over the vase of carnations as she grabbed the phone.

"Yes. Yes. This is Claire Hearn."

She nodded several times and then thanked the caller. She put the phone down and stood still, staring at the puddle of water and tumbled flowers on the table. Part two of the plan had just fallen nicely into place. .

Chapter Twenty-five

Paul Gregan loved the cold freshness of new mornings, the quietness before the noise of living crowded the day. The night security man was still on duty in the *Newstrack* building.

"Well! Good morning Paul. Must be something big on to drag you in at this hour on a Saturday morning."

"There's been a lot of excitement around with the election."

Paul was just about to go to the newsroom when the security man handed him an envelope.

"This was dropped in for you," he said. "At two o'clock this morning. By a tasty little thing, I might add. You're a dark horse, Gregan."

Paul took the envelope and went to his desk. When he was sitting, he tore the envelope open. It was from Claire Hearn. A handwritten note. Note-writing seemed to be quite a little habit of the Dawson family.

Paul read it over and put it down. Now he would be able to either confirm or deny Ria's version of ClairCo's research. It had better be a good story. Ria's model portfolio nonsense had certainly caused problems with Trish. Kevin was none too happy with him either. He picked up the note and read it again.

Paul, I appreciate you holding off on publication until I was ready. It is time to tell the full story now. Could you meet me at Reception in Dashern at nine o'clock? If you can't make it, I will try to get to you. Please ring me at the number below and let me know.

Claire

A glance at his watch told him he had plenty of time before going to Dashern. He started into his work. His feature article on Ewan Peters TD. Ewan had given him an exclusive. A little nugget of information. Helen was expecting another baby. Not earth-shattering stuff but everything about Ewan Peters was news. His popularity was a phenomenon. He had attained the cult status that Paul had anticipated, clearly vindicated by his election result. Paul sifted through the photos until he found a shot of Helen gazing, Nancy Reagan-like, at her husband as his election count was declared. If he went with that shot and a new-job, new-life type text, he would have an article he could syndicate.

When he was finished, he went to the dispenser and filled a large carton with the dark brown liquid that masqueraded as "fresh roast coffee". He swallowed it as he would any foul-tasting medicine. Then he went to find the early morning papers. Keeping tabs on the opposition publications was a task he enjoyed. Or at least, he had enjoyed until today.

The *Daily News* headlines left a more bitter taste in his mouth than the synthetic coffee. Fuck! Fuck! Fuck! Pipped at the post. He should never have agreed to Claire Hearn's timeline. When he calmed down, he read the *Daily News* report again. This time he read between the lines. Then he picked up his phone and dialled Claire Hearn's number.

* * *

Yvette was ahead of Brendan in the queue at the check-in. He liked being behind her, watching the way her waist narrowed in and then curved so gently out to her hips. When she moved her bottom swayed. He wanted to put his hands on her now, to run them the full length of her body, to glide them over her golden skin. His breathing got quicker. She turned around to him and smiled.

"You being a naughty boy? What are you thinking about?"

He just raised an eyebrow in reply but that was answer enough for her.

They collected their boarding passes. It was an hour yet to boarding. Time to take a stroll around Heathrow and to go to the newsagent's. While Yvette was buying *Le Figaro*, Brendan went to the section with the Irish papers. It did not take him long to decide which paper he wanted. He grabbed his copy of *Daily News* and paid for it.

The article was not very well written. It was full of repetition and cliché but it got the message across anyway. RTTI were aborting their tentative investment in Ireland. No phyto plant. No herbal cures. And why? Because *"they must concentrate all their resources on developing some very significant research being carried out by their R&D in Zurich"*. Words like groundbreaking, miraculous, lifesaving, earth-shattering sprinkled the page. *"A reliable source revealed that an announcement about the development would be issued shortly by RTTI."*

Brendan looked at the beautiful woman beside him and knew that she was *"the reliable source"*. What a misnomer! He had no illusions about the woman he loved. Yvette was unreliable, greedy, ruthless.

"So you finally got Claire's research. Why didn't you tell me, Yvette?"

She smiled at him and lifted her hand to stroke his face. "Slipped my mind. I must have been thinking of something else."

"Does this mean you can give me the video you have? The evidence about – about you know what?"

"About how your father-in-law died?"

Brendan nodded and as she looked at his devastated face she almost felt sorry for him. She brushed her lips against his.

Brendan understood. She would hold that evidence, or the threat of it, over his head for as long as they were together. However long that would be. He closed his eyes and allowed the feel of her, the scent of her to invade him. Still the dark, sad image of Claire kept appearing. How had RTTI done it? How had they succeeded where he had failed? What would Claire be now without her research? Yvette darted her tongue into his mouth. Here in the crowded lounge of Heathrow Airport! The image of Claire faded into the private place in his mind where Frank Dawson and his injured face lived on.

Brendan had a drink on the plane. Just a little one. A toast to new beginnings.

*   *   *

The layout of the Dashern plant was pretty familiar to Paul Gregan by now. He glanced up at the big window of the old man's office on the first floor and felt sad. He had liked Frank Dawson, liked his honesty and earthiness.

When he walked into Reception, Claire Hearn was waiting for him. She seemed bright and wide awake.

"You don't look like someone who was delivering notes at two o'clock in the morning."

"Actually the secret is, I didn't sleep at all. When I finally get to put my head down, I will probably sleep for a week."

Paul followed her up the stairs and into Frank's office. When she sat at her father's desk, Paul thought he could see a resemblance between father and daughter. Not in the features – they were fine, like her mother's. But she had a certain way of holding her chin up, a direct gaze, which was pure Frank Dawson. He would not have been surprised if she had taken out a cigar and lit up.

"Are we a bit late with this interview, Claire? According to *Daily News*, RTTI have made some astounding developments in research. So astounding that they have to abandon their investment here. Would this be the very same research I was going to talk to you about? Is it Serum 6?"

Claire smiled. "That's what they think. They're staking everything on what they have stolen from me."

"They stole it? That's a big accusation!"

She stood up and walked over to the window. She looked out over the plant. Just like her father used to do. She turned back to face Paul.

"You were kind to my father. He liked you. He trusted you. And I am going to have to do the same, Paul. I trust you not to publish everything I'm going to tell you. Some of it must never be made public."

"How about I give you the same deal as I had with your father? Nothing goes to press without your permission. You edit. You have the veto."

She smiled and the sparkle was back in her eyes again. She sat directly across from Paul and started her story from the beginning. Back at her thesis for her master's degree. Then she brought him through the different stages of research right up to animal trials.

"I had to submit an outline of what I was doing for my animal trial licence. That put some information out there in the research community. I had suspicions about the animal supply company. Ewan Peters confirmed them for me. How is Ewan by the way? He had a great victory, hadn't he?"

"Helen, his wife, is pregnant. Anyway, on with your story. You believed it was working. You were curing the animals' cancers. And then?"

Claire felt like she had been kicked in the stomach. Jesus! Pregnant! She knew he was married. Had she wanted to believe he never had sex with his wife?

"When is the baby due?"

Paul looked at the dark eyes with the pain in them and he realised that here was another story he would never publish. So there had been something between Ewan and Claire! Something deep and sad. He shrugged as casually as he could.

"Don't know. Next July, I think. So what about Serum 6?"

She took a deep breath and refocused, tried to recapture the feeling of triumph. "Well, I thought I should patent. I had started to look into it and found out that it's a long and expensive process. I put the wheels in motion but it is still at the initial stage. Anyway, the more I investigated, the more I realised that developing Serum 6, manufacturing, marketing, distributing, was a job for a big company. Not Dashern. Or ClairCo. Then my father died and that decided me. I couldn't even think of going ahead without him. But where to place my research? Not with RTTI for sure."

"Did they ask you for it?"

"They knew that would have been pointless. They came up with a plan luring Dashern into amalgamation. The whole herbal medicine scenario. "

"I see. You knew Serum 6 was successful. You didn't think you could develop it yourself but you didn't want RTTI to have it. So what happened next?"

"I knew the calibre of RTTI. They would stop at nothing to get what they wanted. I tried to keep everything in my lab as secure as possible but I realised it was just a matter of time before they breached my security. So when my calibration company called unexpectedly to the lab with a new engineer my suspicions were roused. I didn't know for sure of course."

"Did you check with your calibration company?"

"I couldn't, could I? If they really had the lab bugged, they would know I was suspicious. I didn't want that. I wanted them to believe I felt secure enough to give Kevin the formula for Serum 6 and to allow him carry out all the procedure himself."

Paul frowned. None of this made sense. If Claire suspected the lab was being monitored why had she gone ahead as if it wasn't? Unless . . .

"Did you use Kevin as bait?"

Claire nodded, not proud of admitting that she used Kevin like that.

"I gave Kevin the formula for Serum 6 and let him make a complete batch himself from scratch."

Paul whistled. "So are you saying *Daily News* is accurate for once? RTTI have your formula. They stole it. They can now make Serum 6."

"No. No. I didn't say that at all. Think of it like this. Making Serum 6 is a twenty-step process. I gave Kevin fifteen steps. I was stuck at that stage for a long time."

Paul thought for a moment and then he smiled. "You vixen, Claire Hearn! You gave Kevin his fifteen-step procedure and let him off. RTTI monitored him in action. Mixing and measuring. Whatever. You led them to believe it was the complete formula. Right? "

"Right. And they may never develop it any further. I was lucky to stumble on the answer."

"Did Kevin know?"

"He does now."

Claire lowered her eyelids so that Paul could not see the guilt in her eyes. Would she ever be able to make all this up to Kevin? She looked up again when Paul spoke.

"Did you not trust him?"

"Ria."

Paul allowed himself a hearty laugh. Claire's one word reply said it all. Of course Kevin would not deliberately pass any confidential information to Ria but it was certain she would somehow manage to tease it from him. He knew from personal experience what a tough bargain she could drive.

"What about Serum 6?" he asked. "What about the cure for cancer? What is going to happen to it now?"

Claire sat up very straight and proud when she answered him. "There are five companies worldwide, five established, well-respected pharmaceutical companies, one of them in this area, who can develop Serum 6."

"So you want to sell it to one of them?"

She shook her head. "Not sell it. And not to just one of them."

Paul shook his head in disbelief. "Are you telling me you want to give your research away? To five other companies?"

"Yes. I always had my formula encrypted in a secret number code. Only I knew the key. I decrypted the formula and printed it out. Sent it by courier all over the world. Anonymously. These people will race each other to get Serum 6 on the market. It won't be long before each one becomes aware that the information gifted to their research lab landed in four others as well. They will all try to claim the honours and the profits."

What a story! What a fucking story! Paul stood up and began to pace. "So what you'll have is five companies, all making the same drug. Pointless patenting. Copyright their brand name, maybe. Huge market. Huge demand. Price competition. End result: cancer patients everywhere have access to a cheap cancer treatment drug! Am I right, Claire?"

Claire watched him as he paced about, trying to contain his excitement at having stumbled across the biggest scoop of his career. This could mean so much to his future. She took a deep breath.

"Paul. Now for the part I do not want made public. I do not want my name mentioned in connection with Serum 6. Some people will guess. The local company will probably work it out. But it is in their interests to say nothing. Just go ahead and develop the information they have been given. Put their own stamp on it."

He had stopped pacing and was staring at Claire. What was her motivation? Why did she not want the honour and glory, the acclaim and rewards? What was wrong with this woman? She had walked over to him and was standing in front of him now, looking up at him.

"I will give you the names of the companies. You can chase up that story. I have sent a report to Jacques Rondel of RTTI, warning him about his incomplete research. I have filed a copy of that report with my solicitor as an assurance against them marketing that research as a cure. But I would ask you to please, please, leave me out of it. I want to change direction now. Leave all this behind. I'm not proud of it. I hated using Kevin. He did not deserve that. I have arranged a job for him with the college when we close here. I hope that makes it up to him in some way."

"What do you mean? Is Dashern closing?"

Claire looked at her watch. "We have called a special staff meeting. In just over two hours my mother and I will tell the staff that Dashern will have to close its gates. An RTTI amalgamation is no longer on the agenda – if it ever was. You know, I'm sure, about the detergent contracts we have lost. It's better to go now, while we can still afford to pay some redundancy. So, another story, Paul. Why not come to that meeting?"

"And to think that I was considering moving on because there wasn't enough news here!"

Claire walked to the window again and looked out at her father's domain. His kingdom. She saw nothing but an under-utilised production area and an overstocked warehouse. No longer a kingdom. Frank's domain now measured three by eight and had dandelion leaves and a white rose withering on its roof. She turned her back on the ghosts and looked at Paul.

"How about a tour of the plant before the meeting? There is somebody special I want you to meet. Somebody who has had a big influence on my decisions. His name is Clarence."

If Paul Gregan thought Claire was totally lunatic when she introduced him to a guinea pig, he did not say so. Maybe it was because his respect for this delicate, dark-haired, self-contained woman was growing by the minute. Yet he still could not quite understand why she had willingly sacrificed her personal honour and glory for the benefit of people who would never even know her name.

He understood a little better when two hours later Dorothy Dawson stood in front of the assembled staff of Dashern Chemicals and delivered the news about the closure. The aristocratic lady was proud and dignified. And very brave. Claire Hearn had inherited her father's strength and her mother's dignity. But these characteristics in Claire were tempered by a vulnerability, a softness not apparent in either her mother or father.

Claire walked back to his car with him after the meeting.

"What are you going to do now?" he asked. "What's next?"

She stood still and regarded him with her huge dark eyes. "Remember I told you I've organised a job in the college for Kevin? They've offered me a research post there too. I think I'll probably accept it."

Paul nodded. It made sense. "So you and Kevin will still be working together?"

"Kevin and I and a lot of other people. That's the point, Paul. I'm starting over again. But this time, I won't have to work alone."

Claire looked around her at her father's legacy. As lifeless now as Frank Dawson. The next month would be all about wind-up and shut-down. Dorothy would pack her bags to go find her own self-contained, sun-splashed, flower-filled space. Clive Rigney would banish the Gore-Croft ghosts from Grange House. Brendan would continue chasing his dream but some day, some horrible tear-filled day, he would realise that he was running away from his nightmare. And Ewan, handsome, principled Ewan, would learn compromise in the uncompromising world of public life.

Claire smiled at the earnest young man by her side. The man she trusted with her secrets because her father had trusted him.

"This is a new beginning for me, Paul. But this time I'm going to have it all. The parties, the friends, the sharing, the laughter. The fun. Even the glittery make-up." She leaned towards him and kissed him on the cheek. "Remember. I have the veto before you go to print."

Paul nodded solemnly, aware that Claire was one of the greatest people he would ever have the privilege of meeting. A child-woman who had changed the world. He said a fervent prayer that the child would find peace and the woman happiness.

Epilogue

2 years later

Claire did not think of her invitation until she was stopped at the gate by a burly security man. How ironic. A pass to drive up the avenue of what used to be her home. Feeling like an impostor, she rummaged in her bag until eventually she found the card which invited her to the official opening of Grange House Hotel and Golf Club. The security man waved her on.

The orchard was a parking lot now. So much had changed, been ploughed under, cemented over, reshaped and renewed. Only the façade of Grange House remained the same, stolid and stone-faced.

Clive and Julie Rigney, both groomed to perfection, stood in the hall welcoming their guests. She wished them well and continued on into the reception room. A quartet played near the Adams fireplace and societies finest, richest and most glamorous preened and pried in the room where generations of Gore-Crofts had elegantly entertained.

Looking around for a familiar face, Claire spotted Paul Gregan, his partner Trish and Kevin Trill. As she approached them, she saw that Betty, Kevin's new girlfriend, was there too.

"I can't believe you grew up in this house!" Kevin said by way of greeting.

Claire just smiled, knowing that none of her growing up had been done in Grange House. That had happened slowly, joyfully and sometimes painfully over the past two years.

"You look very preoccupied," she remarked as she noticed how fidgety Paul seemed. "Are you covering this event for *Newstrack*?"

"I'm just waiting for someone to arrive," he said vaguely, looking in the direction of the hall.

"Someone important! As Ria would say!" Kevin laughed and then blushed.

They all looked uncomfortable, no one wanting to meet Betty's puzzled eyes.

Paul frowned, his expression telling Kevin for the umpteenth time to forget Ria. She was gone and she wouldn't be back. The only place any of them would ever see her again was in magazines or the social pages of the press.

"I like your hair that way, Betty," Trish, ever the diplomat, said.

Paul suddenly began waving in the direction of the doorway. "He's here! Now I can make my announcement."

A tall man waved back and began to walk towards them.

Claire felt her breath catch in her throat. He had aged in the years since last she had seen him face to face. More lines, more grey hairs, more pain in his eyes. More attractive.

He greeted everyone in turn and then looked down at her and smiled.

"How are you, Claire?"

She was well. Contented, busy. Grown up. "Fine. And you?"

"Still fighting the good fight."

Paul tapped the glass he was holding and called for attention.

"Right. Listen up, gang. I have very important news. I have asked Trish to marry me and, thank God, she said yes. So raise your glasses to the future Mrs Gregan!"

There was a flurry of handshaking, kissing and back-slapping.

Trish was radiant, her happiness reflected on Paul's face.

"When is the wedding?" Betty asked.

"Three months' time. You are all invited, even the politician. *Especially* the politician!"

Ewan laughed. "I'll be there. I wouldn't miss it for anything. Where are you going to hold your wedding reception?"

Paul and Trish looked at each other and, at exactly the same instant, said: "Here!"

"I think we should go find Clive Rigney. Make arrangements," Paul said, dragging Trish off across the room. Kevin promptly ushered Betty off in their wake, as if the move had been rehearsed.

Which it probably was, thought Claire, hiding a little smile from the man beside her.

Ewan and Claire stood together, just absorbing the music, the buzz of conversation, the closeness of each other.

"Do you hear from Brendan?" he asked.

"He's with Yvette Previn somewhere in South America. And Helen?"

"You probably heard that she left me for someone else. She and the children are living in Galway now."

A passing waiter offered them drinks from a tray.

Ewan took two glasses of champagne and handed one to her. Raising his glass, he smiled.

"To Paul and Trish!" he said.

"Paul and Trish!" Claire responded as she raised her glass.

"I need a walk," he said, putting his glass down on a nearby table. "Some fresh air."

She shivered as she remembered the last time he had said that to her. Kallen woods with all its shadows.

He led her out through the French windows and into the garden. Dorothy's garden. They strolled through the grounds where she should have played when she was a child.

Claire felt safe, protected by his side. The noise of the party faded as they left Grange House behind and climbed to where they could stand and see the golf course laid out beneath them. The ninth hole was where Dashern used to be.

"It's all changed," Claire said, remembering her father's pride in his factory, his life's work.

Ewan caught her by the arms and turned her to face him. Lifting his hand, he touched her hair, her cheek, with his stong but gentle fingers.

"Do you regret it, Claire? Giving away your research, other people claiming the honour and glory of discovery?"

"So Paul told you."

"Not until you gave him permission. I was going to contact you then but ..."

They were silent as they thought of the intervening years so full of "buts". So full of partings and new beginnings for both of them.

His fingers lifted her chin and she smiled up at him.

"Serum 6 is curing cancer all over the world," she said. "That's my reward. The only one I need."

The sun was low on the horizon by now. It was getting cooler. Ewan took off his jacket and placed it around Claire's shoulders. She snuggled into it, breathing in the scent of him from the fine wool fabric.

Then they turned their backs on the place where Dashern used to be and began the trek back towards Grange House Hotel.

Towards their future.

The End.